Praise for Mark Powell and

SMALL
TREASONS

"An excellent, suspenseful ride . . . Powell digs deeply into some heavy themes, exploring pervasive violence and the startling path to radicalization that disaffected teens can find themselves on . . . Readers will be eager to find out how these lyrical and tense stories entwine, and they eventually do, with surprising but inevitable results."

—Publishers Weekly

"Part family drama, part psychological exploration of the confusion of modern life, and part thriller, Powell skillfully intertwines the plot with the human, political, and religious subtexts."

—The National

"Crack open the spine of a novel that examines a marriage coming ever closer to splintering. Tess Maynard and her husband, John, are both immersed in the atrocities of terrorism, but from different perspectives. While living in John's Georgia hometown, things begin to unravel as tensions and complications mount."

—Southern Living

"[Mark Powell] brings his diverse education to bear, both in his convincing descriptions of drone piloting and intelligence gathering and even more in his depiction of the corrosive effects of sin and guilt on the human psyche."

—Tuscaloosa News

SMALL
TREASONS

A Novel

Mark Powell

GALLERY BOOKS
New York London Toronto Sydney New Delhi

Gallery Books
An Imprint of Simon & Schuster, Inc.
1230 Avenue of the Americas
New York, NY 10020

First Gallery Books trade paperback edition January 2018

GALLERY BOOKS and colophon are registered trademarks of Simon and Schuster, Inc.

For information about special discounts for bulk purchases, please contact Simon & Schuster Special Sales at 1-866-506-1949 or business@simonandschuster.com.

The Simon & Schuster Speakers Bureau can bring authors to your live event. For more information or to book an event contact the Simon & Schuster Speakers Bureau at 1-866-248-3049 or visit our website at www.simonspeakers.com.

Interior design by Colleen Cunningham

Manufactured in the United States of America

10 9 8 7 6 5 4 3 2 1

Library of Congress Cataloging-in-Publication Data is available.

ISBN 978-1-5072-0338-5
ISBN 978-1-5072-0337-8 (pbk)
ISBN 978-1-5072-0339-2 (ebook)

for my daughter Merritt
and
in memory of
Pat Conroy, old courage teacher
1945–2016

This is a lesson in the intimacy of distance.

—DON DeLILLO, *Players*

. . . when Americans pray, they pray first that history will step aside and leave them alone, they pray for the deafness that comes with a comfortable life. They pray for the soothing blindness of happiness, and why not?

—BOB SHACOCHIS, *The Woman Who Lost Her Soul*

Prologue

They watch it in Washington, in London, Berlin. Al Jazeera runs it on a loop, and down in a subbasement at Langley analysts play with its pixels, enlarging this, erasing that. There's a team at one of the strip-mall spy shops along the Dulles Toll Road that does nothing but contrast. You heat the color, you cool it. Another shop does sound, sonic mapping, a processor advancing the volume forward at the rate of picoseconds.

They watch it at home, too, American homes living their American lives. At least until it disappears from first the networks and then the Internet. It will reappear, of course, in a few days' time, pirated on a thousand servers, but for the moment those who know better than you have seen to its erasure. But before it vanishes she will find it.

She will watch on her wafer-thin tablet, sitting on the far corner of the made bed, barefoot and cross-legged and huddled over the screen as if to keep all the changing light for herself. She is scared, of course, but she is also ashamed. Her husband, John, is at work—John is always at work. Her children in the living room in front of PBS Kids. But there's still the fear, irrational as it may be, that someone will walk in and then it's all *hey, babe, what are you*—or *Mommy, I need*—and how could you ever explain it? The how-to-explain-it part which, beyond the shame, is its own form of grief. Because grief is there, make no mistake about that.

There is grief.

But why can't she get past it?

Shouldn't she be able to get past it?

Tess considers this more often than she should. She's unloading the dishwasher or changing a pull-up—step out, baby, step out for mommy—or watching *Daniel Tiger's Neighborhood* and it comes to her that perhaps it isn't her fault, that perhaps it seeks a certain viewer and then adheres? Like the way the street people always seem to single her out, not deep calling to deep—ha! what a joke, Tess, so funny, you—but crazy seeking crazy. Husband and children around her and somehow they come straight for her. Homeless and bad-eyed. Dreadlocked and dirty. And here's Tess with her pockets stuffed with tissues and small bills. Green Chiclets like you don't even know they make anymore. *They just see something in you, honey.* Her husband explaining. *They've got a radar for it.* It's true. She knows it's true. There's a gawkiness about her and some days she expects to be led away in restraints. Other days she feels a hand-clap from sanity. But not this week, not today.

Today, she watches in the bedroom.

She watches the black flag with its swirl of white letters, elegant in everything except intent, and then the flag is gone and what she is looking at is a man in all black: pants, shirt, boots. His face hooded. Only his hands show and in one is the long blade of what she has read is a ceremonial dagger, a *khanjar*. At his feet kneels a man in an orange jumpsuit—orange for noncompliant in Guantanamo protocol, she has read this, too. They are alone in a desert: colorless sand, a wash of pale blue sky. The horizon bisects the standing man just above his waist. He shows the dagger, raises it. The kneeling man—Western, exhausted—makes no move, not for several seconds. And then he cants his head. She watches for it, studies the time markers for twitches, anticipates the slightest of gestures. When he begins to speak—the man in black, she means, this in the thirty-ninth second—words begin to block across the bottom of the screen, that otherwise lovely Arabic script.

But he is speaking English.

He is speaking perfect English in what strikes her as a rather refined British accent. She only half hears. Over multiple viewings she has absorbed it, and the more she absorbs it the less sense it makes. Or not *sense* exactly—*sense* isn't the right word. It's all *Allahu akbar* and infidel this and infidel that. America, Obama, Israel, the Jews. It's interchangeable and not relevant to what it is she's trying to get to the bottom of. She wants an answer to the gut-level panic she feels every time she watches the video; she wants to know why it's so satisfying. She wants an answer as to why she can't stop watching. It's evil, yes, but don't give her *evil* for an answer. Somehow that feels too easy. That there's something coming off the screen—yes. Just sitting there with the tablet in her lap she feels it. A radiation of sorts, a presence. Something dangerous she has invited in.

A demon, her husband would say, were her husband ever to know.

But don't give her *demon* either. Too obvious, too easy—no matter how true it is.

Don't give her *blood* or *terror* or *horror*. Don't talk to her about the train wreck of decapitation or the lure of suffering. Some bottled-up Christian thing. So long as there was a living memory of actual crucifixion the cross was not an icon. No pendants, no bracelets or T-shirts. No elaborate HIS PAIN, OUR GAIN tattoos. She heard someone say once that it would have been like walking around with a picture of the electric chair on your back. She doesn't know the answer except to say that isn't it.

All she knows is that she can't stop watching.

All she knows is that it has begun to permeate things: her hair, her clothes, her room, her life.

Outside is an entire world of sunlight and bees and the way her children run through the dewy grass imagining they're animals, jaguars and pumas, but none of it is half as—she wants to say *real*, but the word feels so heavy, so freighted with the kind of significance that generally speaking embarrasses her. So she doesn't want to say anything. She only wants to see it. She only wants to feel it because feeling it is so much—Christ forgive me—feeling it is so much like prayer that it frightens her.

She puts the tablet on the floor, checks the kids, checks the driveway, and then eases back to the bedroom. Shuts the door halfway. Mutes the volume for the tenth time. She has a website listing the kidnapped bookmarked; you have to refresh the page to make sure there hasn't been another. Next will be the man in the basement, the American with his flaking scalp, completely alone but for a handmade chessboard.

Tess knows things about him.

He has skin problems and a graduate degree in philosophy. Right out of undergrad he spent two years teaching elementary school in the Mississippi Delta with a service organization. These things are known. What else? The chess pieces are little cardboard squares, the images scratched in ballpoint pen. One of the released prisoners smuggled out a pawn. She's seen a photograph of it online.

She knows the story, too.

How he was driving in northern Iraq, west toward the Turkish border when he and his translator—a Shia who had fled Tikrit— stopped at an Internet café to e-mail the pictures the journalist had taken. He was meticulous about this, always a little paranoid. He'd seen other journalists lose their entire cameras, taken from them by local police, government officials, anyone with a pistol and the ability to point. It was so deeply ingrained, this fear, that he could barely photograph a few kids playing soccer in the sun before he was plugging his memory card into an Internet connection and e-mailing them to New York.

They were less than forty kilometers from the border, could be there in a half-hour, but it was the border he feared. They stopped.

Dusty, dark, cool. Men drinking arak. A few computers against the far wall. Two thousand dinars for a half-hour. No one meeting anyone's eye until a large bearded man with a knife on his belt—there was a name for it, too, this knife—a scimitar! A bearded man with a scimitar in his belt stood up, barked something drunkenly at the journalist and his translator, and staggered out.

Ten minutes later they were on the road. Five minutes after that they saw the roadblock. Hooded men. Kalashnikovs. A Hilux across the asphalt. They pulled over. What else could they do? It was surprise as much as fear. The roadblock wasn't supposed to be there. But then again the man with the scimitar wasn't supposed to be there either. Other prisoners, those who had been released—Turks and Italians, a trauma surgeon with the Red Crescent—spoke of how out of place he seemed, shackled in the basement with his handmade chessboard and psoriasis. They talked about how he didn't seem to belong, and this is the part that scares her most, the lure of randomness, the gravity of chance.

She opens a second tab to check CNN. U.S. and French jets are bombing targets on the outskirts of Kobane. Turkey has closed the border. It's possible the man in the basement is somewhere in the city. It's possible the man in the basement can hear the bombs falling.

What she can hear are the boys in the living room, arguing.

And what she wants to know is what difference does it make if she watches or not? She believes it matters, the this or that of her choosing, only she can't say how. For the moment she puts the questions aside, closes the CNN tab so that in the center of the screen beats a great arrow, right-facing and almost heart-like in its insistence, and she touches it so he can begin to die again, and so that she can watch again.

And so that she can think again: amen.

Part One

The Man in the Basement

1.

John Maynard took his Prilosec, hugged his kids, and headed out
the door to work. This, he believed, was as it should be. There
were limits to what could be known—he knew that now—the
unknowable was vast. So instead of the unknowable, he had a house
in a nice neighborhood on the edge of town, and in the evenings
he and his family would walk through the pine- and diesel-scented
humidity, north Georgia simmering in the unblinking summer heat.
Everywhere sculpted lawns and chirping sprinklers, expensive cars
gliding over the cobblestones—a universe of cut grass and chlorine.
He walked to work and never minded it. The walk meant he was
alone, at least for the mile past the community gates to the college
on Highway 76, where, from the edge of campus, you could see the
gentrified downtown with its coffee shops and CrossFit. Beyond
that stood a line of gas stations and souvenir stores, the handmade
Cherokee moccasins machine-made in China, the idling caravans of
RVs. Beyond that there were only trees, mountains and trees.

Those trees, those mountains—the absence of the larger
world—was, perhaps, the point.

John was in his fourth year as director of the Garrison College
counseling center and had spent much of the first three holed up in
his office with forms and online learning modules and every other
administrative duty the college threw at him. In between videos
on workplace behavior and sexual harassment he visited various

campus groups, cultivating a deep and enviable list of followers on Twitter through which he disseminated the occasional inspiring/ spiritual/multicultural quote. It was a way to appear busy, as much to himself as anyone else, and there were days he told himself he looked forward to the moment when he could spend more time outside his office. But just as often—more often lately—he admitted to himself he was hiding. To come out would be to risk exposure, the chance for them to know what he had done. Which would tell them not who he had been, but who he was still.

His office was the perfect place to disappear.

The Sojourner Truth Center was spare and modern and buried in a dense forest on the back side of campus. Thirty offices housing a collection of academic and professional odds and ends, all the entities too small to command their own space: Gender Studies, career counseling, the Office of Social Justice. Despite the façade it had an antique feel: beautiful conifer trees around a finger of lake. Peeling blue paint and carpenter ants—someone from maintenance was always spraying—shelves of books read and forgotten.

It was only in the last spring he had started to make trips out to the college quad, the stone fountain and fir trees. The cobbled walks that spoked from the center. He would walk out and try to take the measure of the place. The lawn care was world-class and he had come to appreciate it, the flowers, the predawn gauze of sprinklers. The students complained. A group of them had come to him wanting to organize a protest. How much of their precious tuition was going to irrigation, to mulch beds, to ground cover?

Too much, John was certain, but equally certain it didn't matter. Later, when he told the story at dinner parties, people laughed. But he had approached the matter seriously. He asked the students if they thought it a sin, this constant attention to appearances, and they had looked at him with equal parts sympathy and dismissal.

Maybe not a sin, professor, so much as a misappropriation of funds.

They were right, of course, yet the moment you stopped believing in sin something settled. It was what happened to them at Site Nine, this forgetfulness, this failure to believe, and the moment you stopped believing you started talking about tactical mistakes, policy errors instead of distance from God. But God, John knew, is alive, and so is the Devil.

He thought often of the Devil.

At night, sitting with the lights off, drinking his gentlemanly bourbon, he could see the students who would slip through the trees down to the banks of the lake and there, on blankets, or beneath blankets, make love. Unseen. Or so they imagined themselves. It held no real interest for him, no prurient fascination, though he always watched. The methodical rippling of old quilts or, on the rare occasion, and only among the fearless, the bodies atop the quilts, the panels of flesh, the sounds which from behind a pane of glass he could only imagine.

So yes, he watched. The way they touched, the way their bodies met and parted and met again, seemingly without the slightest consideration of God or the Devil—he envied that. Sometimes, having friended nearly half the student body on Facebook, he tried to put faces—or legs or stomachs or backs—together with names, amazed that anyone anywhere had enough energy to do anything, let alone make love beneath the late-summer stars. John Maynard was very tired. But if his wife, Tess, wasn't happy—and on this he was agnostic—he could at least counter that he was exhausted.

But exhaustion was a small price to pay if it meant the past was lost, blessedly lost.

Then one day the past reappeared in the shape of James Stone.

John saw him from a distance, leaned against the smoked-glass exterior of the Truth Center, one foot hitched against the wall, hands laced over his stomach as if in anticipation of pain. He stood, John thought on seeing him, almost as if he knew John was waiting for him, which John both was and wasn't. This was on a Saturday in late August, Move-In Day, and the smile on Stone's face seemed to imply he was about to rewrite the day. Another thing that both was and wasn't the case.

"Jimmy," John said.

"So now it's Jimmy, is it?"

"What are you doing here?"

"I scare you?"

"Surprised me."

"Surprised you. Seems like a fair response. Not exactly generous, but fair."

"What do you want?"

"Delighted to see you, too, John." Stone pushed off the wall and stretched his arms as if waking. "You know you never used to call me Jimmy. It was always, 'Stone this,' 'Stone that.'"

"We haven't said a word to each other in what?"

"As if that's my fault."

"Six years it must be."

"Six years." He waved them away with a brush of his hand. "You know you never even said goodbye the day you left. Just headed up the road to Kraków and caught the evening Lufthansa to JFK. Gone before I knew it."

"I had to see someone."

"That sort of hurt my feelings, leaving like that."

"I had to see Peter."

"Peter? Fuck Peter. You left us. It was just Ray Bageant and me, alone with all those goddamn Polish commandos. The slivovitz and prison tats. And not so much as a goodbye from you."

"That was sort of the point, the not saying goodbye."

"The one guy with the rhinestone sheath for his mobile phone. You remember this? All the little charms of Site Nine."

"I work here now."

"Of course you do. Why else would I be here?" Stone stepped from the pine bark and pointed at the building's rear doors, one of which was propped open. "Did you see them inside there? Those guys are GBI."

"What guys?"

"Georgia Bureau of Investigation. See the plates?"

He was talking about the license plates on the two SUVs that John now noticed parked sideways across a line of handicap spaces. State of Georgia. Fulton County. Fulton being Atlanta.

"Oh," John said finally. "What are—"

"Don't worry," Stone said, "they aren't here for you. Not yet. But 'oh' is certainly right, my friend. They're taking his hard drives, his phone records. Got his filing cabinet on hand trucks. Every last bit of his stuff."

"Whose stuff?"

"Professor Hadawi, of course. Aren't you two tight?"

"Edward Hadawi you're talking about?"

"I think I heard that somewhere."

"What do you mean 'not yet'?"

But Stone only smiled, shook his head, and walked away. Crossed the campus grass and headed around the building toward the quad. No hesitation, no explanation.

Six years.

Six years and just like that John was thrown back into the mistake of that other life. Working for Peter Keyes. Sitting in the control room, staring at the monitor, watching. Ray Bageant in the other room. Jimmy Stone with the camera. One of the Poles really did have a rhinestone sheath for his phone. It had been a running joke, the thing the three of them talked about so that they could avoid the primary fact of their existence. That being the extent to which they'd been wrong.

But Stone was right about Professor Hadawi. John stood outside and watched as Hadawi's things were loaded in the backs of the two SUVs and disappeared with an efficiency John could only envy.

2.

It was possible to see without seeing.

For instance: her husband and sons were in the kitchen. Her daughter Laurie was just across the pillow beyond her, fingers curled, translucent eyelids veined and drawn. Sun fell across their bodies, separating them into parts, these tines of light, warm and swirling with dust. Tess was in bed with her eyes shut and it wasn't so much that she knew these things as she saw them. She saw one other thing too: she saw the man in the basement.

Tess would have considered him—she would have considered many things—had she not heard John downstairs, singing. She had absolutely no problem with this. Her only complaint was the noise. She could hear the traffic headed north to Chattanooga or Gatlinburg. Nearer, the mowers running. Without opening her eyes, she saw big pickups pulled flush to the curb, trailers bristling with rakes and clippers. Hispanic boys carrying weed-eaters and drinking water from gallon jugs. And beneath it all, her full-throated husband, singing.

Likely he'd been up for hours. If he was off work today—she couldn't make sense of his schedule—but should he be off, he would take Daniel and Wally to his parents' where his mother would have a giant breakfast waiting on them. Biscuits and gravy, eggs, bacon. *Y'all boys eat now. Don't be shy.* This was supposed to give Tess the morning to gather herself, but if that was John's intention wouldn't he take Laurie too?

Tess came into the kitchen in her housecoat, her daughter in her arms. John was packing his messenger bag. He would leave through the side gate, cross the yard, and go to work as head of the campus counseling center at Garrison College.

"I was hoping you'd get up," he said, and kissed her cheek, kissed their daughter's head.

"You're leaving?"

"It's after eight. What's the plan for the day?"

"No plan. Are you coming home for lunch?"

"Maybe. But it's the first day of classes. Could be crazy."

"Okay."

"I'll call you. Love you."

Only when the door was shut, only when he was through the side gate and moving out over the yard did she call the boys.

*

Her six-year-old was out in the backyard attempting to echolocate, her three-year-old a half-step behind him. This was the nature of being six, the possibility of it. She had shown Wally several documentaries on the Discovery Channel and then last winter, seven months pregnant with Laurie and barely able to move, she and John had driven the eight hours from north Georgia and taken the boys out on a harbor cruise down in Tampa where they had spotted a pod of migrating sperm whales. It was like a blessing, the sudden spurting eruption, the shape of their giant drowsy heads. People hung off the railings to snap photographs and point.

It hadn't been until the next day they realized they had witnessed something as rare as it was tragic. The whales were disoriented and lost, wandering inside the vast sameness of the bay, unable to find their way back to open sea. What they were doing in there—what they were doing in this part of the world—no one could say, except

22

that it was bad. The Coast Guard shadowed them. NOAA had a boat in the water. Marine biologists from SeaWorld tried to lure them with a bucket trail of dead squid. They called it a pod in the news, but it seemed more like a family to her: the bull male, the female mother, the calf. Three whales, stateless—could you say such a thing? Or was it simply that they were lost, they were in the wrong place?

She could hear her oldest, clicking.

He popped his tongue against the roof of his mouth, moved over the grass with his eyes shut. Now and then his hands flew up for balance or safety. Was he in his socks? She couldn't quite see from where she sat in the rocking chair on the screened porch, holding Laurie and her book. If he was in his socks they would be ruined. She thought of calling, but didn't want to wake the baby. It didn't matter anyway. One thing she had learned was that once you reached a certain point there was no sense in complaining—complaining was an indulgence, a selfish act.

She watched him out beyond the azaleas, pipe-cleaner arms and giant sunflower head. He was squeezing shut his eyes, not enough to merely close them. Daniel followed him, mimicking every move with the reverence reserved only for older siblings, the kind of veneration she could sense herself already beginning to mourn: it was a love incapable of surviving the glare of childhood. Daniel was three years old and the look in his eyes, the way he studied his brother, the delicacy of his arms swimming up and back—it would be gone in five years' time. You couldn't live like that, that was another of her reluctant conclusions. You had to moderate your feelings. It was too easy to scare people.

"Wally," she whispered, looked at sleeping Laurie, undisturbed. "Wally? Daniel?"

The whales had eventually found their way out, a baffling occurrence. For three days they crossed and recrossed the bay, seemingly panic-stricken, and then one night they disappeared. By that point the plight of the whales was on the front page of the paper, leading the nightly local news, getting picked up by CNN where a professor at the Scripps Institute spoke of creaks and slow clicks and codas. There was a certain amount of guilt involved: they had the largest brain on earth, but had been hunted to near extinction. It was possible they used actual *names*. The shore was lined with volunteers ready to push them back into the sea should they beach. But for two days—nothing. And then on the third day they were sighted by a passing trawler, forty miles out to sea and headed south. That was what echolocation could do for you. You could see without seeing. You could get out.

Laurie stirred, began to cry. Tess tried to soothe her, but it was too late, and she took advantage of the opportunity to rise briefly out of the chair and look over the azaleas for the boys. She could just see them in the far corner past the swing set.

"Wally? Daniel? Baby, come down where I can see you, okay?"

"What, Mom?"

"Play where I can see you, all right?"

She watched them wander closer, onto the sliding board, attempting to walk up it. They were good boys. They listened. She shifted her hips beneath her and gave Laurie her left breast. The clicking was inaudible.

*

"Are you all right?" It was Tess's little sister, Liz, calling from Savannah. "Mom called asking."

"About me?"

"Worried."

They were still in the yard, the boys on the swing set, Laurie asleep in the Pack 'n Play. Tess was reading Proust on the screened porch, a giant pillow across her lap. It was her summer project but now summer was gone and still she was little more than halfway through the first volume. She felt fat-footed and dumb. She was sweating, eternally nursing, and when not nursing, rocking or cooing or bouncing. Making grilled cheese or playing Legos on the floor. There were blots of sweat all over the pages of her book. Crusted milk in the cups of her unwashed bra. These were her parents' complaints, she reminded herself. But the word wasn't *complaints* because they never actually voiced them, and she couldn't hate them for thinking them.

"I think she's planning on sending you money," her sister said. "She was feeling me out."

"That's ridiculous."

"That's what I told her. It was this general sort of exploratory vibe and I was like, Mom, seriously?"

"That's just ridiculous."

"That's what I told her, but, Tess? You are all right, aren't you?"

"Am I all right?"

"That's what I'm asking."

She almost laughed, almost felt it take flight. "I don't know how to answer that. What sort of question is that?"

"Mom used the word *depressed*."

"Depressed? I don't know what to say to you. I'm fine."

"I'm not trying to trick you."

"Completely and totally fine."

"I'm asking because I love you."

"I don't even know what to say."

"You've been like this since summer and that's totally normal. After Laurie was born—"

"This has nothing to do with Laurie."

"Then what is it?"

"It isn't anything."

"This is what I think."

"Liz . . ."

"I think you're home by yourself. I think John isn't around like he should be."

"I don't even . . ."

"It's normal to feel a little crazy is all I'm saying. You start to feel trapped. Then you look out at the world and what do you see? I know you, Tess. I know how you think. You look out at the world and you see people dying. You fix on all the suffering and then you start to absorb it."

"That's . . ."

"I know you, Tess. You absorb it."

"I don't even know what to say."

"You've been like this since summer and that's totally normal. After Laurie was born—"

"This has nothing to do with Laurie."

"Then what is it?"

"It isn't anything. I don't even know what to say."

She didn't know what to pray either. But then what was the point in praying? In college, people were always saying how the Lord never gave you more than you could handle, and yes, she felt guilty thinking such, but she had come to the conclusion that that was complete and utter bullshit. The world was made out of what you couldn't handle. The world *was* what you couldn't handle. What you couldn't handle, she thought, was actually a pretty good working definition of life.

✳

She brought the boys in for lunch. PBJs and little corn puffs in the shape of baseball players. A green apple cut into eighths, the core delicately removed because if they saw any brownness, if they saw the scooped bell of the seeds they wouldn't touch it. Laurie was back asleep in her crib. Wally's socks were ruined.

While they ate, she took a moment to go to the computer. U.S. and French jets were still bombing targets around Kobane. ISIL—today they were calling them ISIL—was advancing block by block. It had been going on for days now and she had watched, surreptitiously, because she wasn't yet sure how she felt.

It was when she went back into the kitchen that she saw the man coming up the sidewalk, a dirty man in work boots, some sort of headscarf tied around his neck. An Arab man, a Persian man—how was she supposed to know these things? She didn't know anything. But she felt the pull of it, the catch like a hangnail run through a sleeve. Some dull pain, as sudden as it was satisfying.

When she realized it was a Hispanic man on one of the yard crews she felt it release. He was pushing a wheelbarrow of mulch she had somehow completely missed, and for a moment she imagined the sweet pine smell—*Jesus, Tess*—and for a moment more she hated herself.

✳

They walked to the campus library, Laurie and Daniel in the double stroller, Wally beside her, holding onto the handlebar and helping her push. He wanted to know things. How old was the road? How did the universe get made? Why did people have to die? She started with the age of the road. It was a complex issue, she explained, because was he referring to how long it had last been since the road was repaved or paved initially or was this a question of how long people had traveled this actual path?

"Just how old is it?"

"Fifty-seven years," she said.

"You're sure?"

"Let's get another book on whales."

"But, Mom, the road?"

"Fifty-seven years, almost to the day."

"And you're positive?"

"Absolutely."

She wanted him to get another book on whales because she needed to know about these things, the creaks, the slow clicks, the codas. It was possible the click of the bull sperm whale was capable of stunning a squid into a temporary stupor. She'd seen this—embarrassing, but true—on a cartoon. When she tried to confirm it online she encountered sharp divides. Apparently, the notion of the click as a weapon was highly controversial. It might not be real, but you could detect the need of many to cling to it. Many others badly needed for it not to be so. But thank God its ability to echolocate was unquestioned. There were reams of data, YouTube videos, links on the National Geographic page.

She wanted, maybe, something on the Middle East, too. She could read at night between feedings. Sunni versus Shia. The Alawite minority. She didn't know the geopolitics of the region. She didn't claim she did. But she wasn't stupid, either.

✳

They looked at their new books while she stood in the kitchen and debated supper, Laurie in her carrier. There were canned vegetables and soups and shrink-wrapped chicken and heads of lettuce and also leftovers she could simply heat up. Since Laurie was born someone was always bringing them a meal, just dropping something by. Had extra and thought I'd just drop this by, know your hands are full.

Her sister was wrong. It wasn't postpartum, whatever it was she felt. It had nothing to do with Laurie. It was John.

What did he do all day?

She thought of this more than she liked. There were occasional appointments, but she knew his counselors handled most of these. He filed reports with academic affairs, but what beyond this? That was an afternoon of work, she thought. A day at most.

Maybe he prayed. It was possible he was locked in his office, down on his knees in prayer. She'd gotten saved at twelve at a youth rally in Tampa. A mass altar call and she'd gone because all around her everyone was going and then she'd looked up and seen the youth pastor and the way he looked at her, that expectancy, the sense that he was doing everything short of holding his breath. She had gotten up, she had gone. How could she not have? And she loved the Lord, she loved the Gospels. She did. It was only the Crucifixion that bothered her. The Crucifixion was ghastly.

She put them, her hands, into the cabinet.

He was a good man, but what did he do?

*

John called to say he would be late. The Ward girl, did she remember Julie?

Of course she did. Julie with the red hair. Lives in Conrad Hall. She wore the gray boots with the buckles like so.

"Something's happened to her," John said. "I'm not sure what, but apparently she's locked herself in the bathroom and won't come out. Her RA thinks it's about a boy."

"On the first day?"

"Apparently she spent the summer saving up all her drama. It could be a while."

"When should I look for you?"

"I don't know," he said. "It could be late."

The boys were in bed, Laurie in her crib, and Tess was on the screened porch, the white noise of the baby monitor fizzing by her feet. The single green light like a fallen star. She watched the bats swooping down from the bat houses to feed on mosquitoes. They reminded her of the jets on television, the wobbly dive just before the bombs fell, and this bothered her more than she thought it should. Not their violence, but her insistence on similarity. That everything reminded her of something else, that nothing simply *was*.

In World Religions, they'd spent a week on Buddhism, a barely glancing pass that had revealed itself in a single line she carried with her still: the bedrock experience of human life is disappointment. What a joke that would have been, how silly and hopeless it would have seemed, had anyone bothered to notice. But there were trips to Busch Gardens and Young Life conventions and some friend's band was playing praise sound Friday nights at the coffee shop. They flew past the sand mandalas and chanting, past the saffron robes. But sitting in the gathering darkness it seemed less silly, less hopeless, too.

But she wasn't complaining about that, certainly not. Her only complaint was the noise. How down beneath the hum of the monitor she could hear the park traffic. She could hear horns and voices and the sound of a giant motorhome braking on the asphalt. She wasn't crazy. She wasn't depressed. It was just that she could hear too much was maybe the problem, that she could hear everything. Down beneath the hum of the monitor she could even hear the man in the basement.

She could hear him clicking.

3.

Sunday they went to church. The five of them across the pew like one of those stick-figure families on the rear glass of minivans, a little ridiculous but not exactly something to apologize for either. John Maynard by the aisle, the boys between him and Tess. Laurie in Tess's arms. Wally and Daniel had toys, misshapen monsters that might have been human, or near human. Bulky superheroes carrying two-inch assault rifles. Not the sort of thing encouraged here.

The spire of the church marked the center of campus, and like the rest of Garrison College it was expensive, ambitious, and astoundingly white. The college had been founded in 1867 on the grounds of an old mountain resort of fir and pine and breezy summer days, a mosquito-free idyll for the antebellum rich. During the Civil War it had been a hospital for the Army of Tennessee and after, as if to banish the bone-sawed ghosts, was transformed to a college charged with educating freedmen alongside the children of defeated Confederates—a noble history prominently displayed on every piece of official literature. Progressive. *Socially minded* they called it when the faculty senate nearly voted to divest from Israel or did vote to support gay marriage or wage equality.

John scanned the faces.

To the extent that the faculty attended church, they attended here, avoiding the Baptist and Pentecostal congregations that began just past the college gates. Those places were for the anthropologists recording traditions in messianic faith, the sociologists studying movements in the rural mountain South. The ones taking careful note of the world John had grown up in. The vinyl tablecloths and pedal pushers the women had lately taken to calling capri pants. The Friday ballgame and Sunday sermon. The do-gooder women with their arthritis and prayers. The stoic men with their cans of Bud. John had gone off to get what they called book-learning. But he hadn't learned a thing, hadn't gained a thing, except perhaps a thorough schooling in his own capacity to hate. He regretted it. Not exactly the loss of innocence so much as the casting away of beauty.

He looked at his children and their toys, the angular eyes and puffed muscles. All the beauty was there, whatever rightness existed in his life embodied by his two sons and infant daughter. But something had changed, some brute force seemed to have entered their world. Button-eyed toys, little rabbits or bears stitched back from blindness. Nobody had those anymore, a tiny four-hole button sewn to the face. Where had those gone?

He looked around as if he might find them in the crowd, looked around at the faculty, the parents. The service was meant to mark the beginning of the new academic year and all the usual folks were here, the president of the college, the dean. He didn't see Professor Hadawi and that seemed significant. Hadawi had spent the last year teaching on a fellowship in his native Yemen and there was a rumor that he had decided not to return. People were talking about it. There was another rumor—this one only whispered—that he was under investigation by the FBI. Whether it was public knowledge that Hadawi's office had been emptied, or whether John alone had witnessed it, he couldn't say.

He knew Hadawi only in passing. He was—or had been—a full professor in Global Studies, a hybrid of political science, modern languages, and theory. He was outspoken, said to be angry, said to be the hardest grader on campus. Had almost come to blows—so went the story—with a former marine taking Hadawi's required first-year course in political identity.

John had met him on the college Values Council, a mix of faculty and students who came together to plan the twice-a-year Values Day wherein classes were canceled and students were urged—begged, bribed—not to sleep in, but to attend forums on diversity and citizenship. LGBTQ rights. Sustainability. Islamophobia—that had been Hadawi's, and the last Values Day had been given over to a visit by an Atlanta-based organization that worked to foster a better understanding of Islam. That day Hadawi hadn't seemed angry or impassioned. He had seemed grateful, shaking John's hand, introducing him to the visiting imam. John surprised and a little flattered Hadawi knew his name.

Behind the administrators and faculty sat the students.

John had spent the last few days walking among them as they moved in and attended various workshops. Campus engagement. Fostering cultural diversity. Combating sexual assault. Here in his fourth year he had become numb to a certain type, the wealthy kids, the sons of privilege straight out of prep schools in Nashville and Asheville, walking campus with their lacrosse sticks and well-groomed entitlement. The daughters of the rich, mamma the social butterfly with an addiction to sleeping pills. Daddy a Pioneer for the last Bush campaign, writing a tuition check and grumbling that his daughter went to school with a bunch of trust-fund socialists.

John preferred the ones on scholarship, the poor kids winged up from Southern ghettos, the projects of New Orleans, the trailer parks of South Carolina. That they had walked out of one world and into another never failed to register on their faces. Natural Light and beauty pageants for the white kids. Hennessy and smoothbore .38s for the occasional blacks. Their hand-me-down Jordans years past expiration. But all scrubbed now, gleaming, these brilliant bookish anomalies that never quite fit in at home.

He touched the Orthodox prayer rope that hung around one wrist and stared up at the stained glass behind the pulpit.

With Jesus and John the Baptist were Lincoln and King and John Brown.

Harriet Tubman.

Dorothy Day.

And, of course, the benefactor, William Lloyd.

There was a certain blinding quality to so much moral light, and John had made it through his first winter at Garrison hunkered in his office listening to Levon Helm, still to some degree in the shadow of his and Tess's time on St. Simons Island and all that had entailed—his breakdown, his failure to confess. The looming specter of Hassan Natashe and what John had done to him. As if his past were this living thing never quite on the verge of dying, as if John dragged its damaged form behind him.

Which, of course, he did.

Just that morning he had woken to the fingers of his once four-year-old daughter tracing figures on his back. His first wife, Karla, had died in a wreck that left a filament of scar tracing his daughter Kayla's nine-year-old face. Kayla was grown now, twenty-one and living in east Tennessee. She wrote letters, actual paper-and-ink letters to which John failed to respond because—in his defense—what could he possibly say?

There was a way in which you could squander things, toss them aside in the most careless of manners. But careless or not, the manner was irrelevant. When something was gone, it was gone. That, perhaps, was the lesson of Site Nine, and Site Nine, both what had happened there and what had not, had become the central tenet of John's being. That it was nearly a decade behind him was meaningless. That until yesterday when Stone reappeared he hadn't seen any of them in years—not Jimmy, not Ray Bageant—mattered not at all. That Peter Keyes was dead meant nothing.

It was different with Karla, and he often wondered what had happened to his wife. Besides the actual dying—he understood the dying.

The dying wasn't what he meant.

What he meant was that the first thing you noticed about her was how contingent she was, how it would all end in flames, or tears, or simply how it would all—probably sooner rather than later—just end. But this was hindsight; these were the conclusions of the man *after*. For eleven years John considered little more than the light slap of their stomachs as they made love. Standing in the bathroom after, both naked, and she names something.

"I hadn't thought of that in—"

"I know, right?"

Except he could no longer remember what she named.

They stood for the Benediction, and from the distance of years he thought he would trade everything to know what she was thinking in that moment. Or any moment.

4.

He had lost the kid.

Sunday morning Jimmy Stone sat outside a shitty duplex in the even shittier Kirkwood neighborhood of Atlanta and admitted as much. The kid wasn't here. The kid was gone. The kid being a twenty-two-year-old dumbass named Reed Sharma, son of the CEO of the Reliance Corporation, yet another Keyes Group subsidiary and of late a major player in that great American game of domestic whack-a-mole. A game also sometimes known as let's entrap some sad-sack kid and call it justice.

Which was fine—it was a game Jimmy played even if he didn't particularly like it—but he'd come to think of Reed Sharma as particularly ill-suited and the operation as particularly predatory, even by the standards of the bureau. There were kids who it was just a matter of time before they got violent and they were fair game. You go after those kids, charge them with material support, lock 'em up. But then there were kids who would never get violent were they not groomed for it, kids like Reed you had to coax and coach, stoking their isolation and boredom until it grew into something like hatred. Technically speaking, it was called entrapment, it was called ruining a life, and Jimmy had a problem with this, even if it was Jimmy who had belt-fed him all the Goya and Dostoyevsky. Even if it was Jimmy who had handed him *Demons*, for God's sake.

Shall we discuss the moral possibilities of violence, Reed?

What say we sit around and debate the godlike power of suicide, you wanna?

He sat in his car stewing in sweat and regret.

Not that it was completely Jimmy's fault. True, the kid had been in his little black book for years, but turns out he was in Professor Hadawi's book, too, and this was a serious problem, getting himself on too many bucket lists. Stone had tried to intervene. He had met with Reed just over a week ago at a McDonald's off I-75, given him a phone to keep in touch.

There was a camp—this was the kid talking. It was up in the mountains somewhere.

"Where?"

"I don't know. North."

"North," Jimmy reminded him, "north is a cardinal direction, Reed. Would you care to narrow it down for me?"

"Shit, I told you. I don't know."

All Reed knew was that Professor Hadawi had taken him there and was planning to take him back. He was joining the struggle. He would kill for the caliphate, the umma. Strap on some lovely hip-hugger of a suicide vest and turn himself into hate and light. After his time in New York, *after the way you mocked me, Jimmy,* now it was happening, finally it was happening. Poor Reed. When Jimmy had known him in New York he had been straight bridge and tunnel. Yet smart enough to know another life was out there. Jimmy thought of him alone in Queens hearing rumors of guys with waxed mustaches getting laid in Park Slope, the bumps of coke taken on old Motown album sleeves salvaged from this cousin or that uncle, the morning-after CoQ10. The families with golf carts and people employed for the express purpose of driving those carts. But poor little Reed was stuck at home with his IKEA furniture, a universe of pressboard and bullshit wooden dowels, cracking the Fabergé egg of his head against the block walls. Poor little Reed alone with his

Internet conspiracy theories about the Federal Reserve Bank and his used copy of *The Autobiography of Malcolm X.*

But lately he seemed changed, and Jimmy thought it had something to do with being in Atlanta, and something to do with Hadawi's attention. Reed talked liked he'd never heard mention of the Patriot Act. As if the war on terror was a video game and Bin Laden a mechanical engineer in Riyadh. The kid had every reason to lie, but Jimmy didn't think he was, at least not on this. The professor had spent the last three years at Garrison College and if there was a camp it would be there, tucked into some forgotten corner of the forest, back where only the meth chefs and the Christian Identity folks roamed. Deep in some pine forest where the sun don't shine. The problem was, Jimmy had lost track of the professor, which had sent him running to his old pal John Maynard. Which, Jimmy thought, talk about your desperate moves. John sitting around with a regret that bordered despair, how useful is somebody like that?

Now he had lost track of Reed, too. Nothing coming through the telescope app on the phone since Jimmy had been treated to a close-up of a Chick-fil-A milkshake. Peach it might have been.

This was Jimmy's third day staking out the place and not even Reed's scrawny pal Nawaf was to be seen.

He sat another ten minutes, window down because though it was only morning it was morning in Georgia which meant it was hot. A big, steady heat, a genuine end-times heat—eight A.M. and blazing, light jumping off the metal of a shopping cart pushed into the kudzu and trash. Skullcapped winos on the busted stoops of Section 8 housing. There were birds in the median along the sidewalk, egrets, eating garbage from the uncut grass. They'd be gone by nine. It would be suffocating by ten, past time to swallow a Xanax and slip into the morning siesta which—explain this to me—how is that a bad idea?

Jimmy had always had a thing with heat, and there were moments when he could almost believe in his own self-immolation. That God would take him up in a column of fire, Jimmy reconstituted as a pillar of ash and smoke and deposited at the right hand of the Father. They had talked about it in New York. Prague in '68. The Arab Spring. The end to the Vietnam War. They all started with it, Reed. The burning, the body as a pyre. You soak the flesh with accelerant, transform anger into political will, and voilà: you're lifted out of the mortal realm. Think of Yahweh taking Elijah in a whirlwind. Think of Enoch, Reed. Or maybe my theology's off here, my history. Jimmy had made a study of it, self-immolation, and even if his facts were not exactly facts there were still laws of attraction involved. That if you thought about something long enough it began to gravitate toward you. That sitting in the warm car was just an early tempering for what was to come.

He was dozing off when the door of the duplex opened. Except it was the left door of the duplex, not the right, and it was the woman who was calling herself Aida, and not Reed, coming down the stoop and up the street toward him. She came around the car in what seemed an impossibly slow transit and then flattened her badge against the windshield, eye level before she let it slide and scrape a bit toward the wiper.

"I don't even know what I'm supposed to call you," Jimmy said. "It's Aida, right?"

She was in her headscarf, but only just. It appeared more piled on her head than tied around it. A paisley thing. A white girl, very plainly a white girl, in a paisley headscarf.

"You need to stay off this street, Jimmy."

"Like you wouldn't miss me if I was gone?"

"People are starting to think this is your show," she said. "And you know good and well it is most definitely not."

The badge had the brass eagle with its brass wings, the raised letters cut deep enough for even the blind to read. Kind of a ballsy thing, really. Whipping it out right there in naked view.

"You're out of the game," she said. "So time to pack up your shit and leave."

Jimmy tapped one knuckle against the inside of the glass. "Maybe so. But you shouldn't have cleared his office. That was a stupid move."

"That wasn't my decision."

"You want unnecessary scrutiny, sure, go clear out his office. You only get two thousand students talking, then their parents, then the State Board of Regents."

"I told you that wasn't my call."

"Whose was it then?"

"It was his."

"Christ. Are you serious?"

"Clear the fuck out, Jimmy. And yes, I'm completely serious."

"Are you, now?"

"I will fucking—I give you my word—I will put a hole in your ass."

"A hole in my ass? This flair you have."

"You think I'm joking."

"You know I'm really into the badass vibe."

Her lips spread, but not into anything approaching a smile.

"I thought you were only into the boys," she said.

"Who, me?"

"Even the dead ones."

"I'm ecumenical in my way, but dead"—he put his knuckle back up to the inside of the glass and tapped at her badge—"I draw the line at dead."

"Really? 'Cause I heard otherwise."

"All right, my dear. Time to get your tin off my windshield."

"I heard you get all hard for this guy Hassan Natashe, bring in your best people. Rolodexed some psychologist out of retirement. But then—whoops—you got a dead motherfucker on your hands, right, Jimmy? Time to start forging signatures, time to start shredding reports 'cause here comes the inspector general. Here comes the Obama administration and turns out we aren't quite as thrilled about enhanced interrogation as we used to be. What a surprise, right?"

"Get your shit off my windshield, Aida."

"Don't come back, Jimmy."

"Get your shit," he said, and started the car.

"Don't come back here."

He dropped the car into drive.

"Don't worry about it."

"This isn't your show," she called.

"Never you fucking mind," he said, and drove off with her standing there, pressing the badge flat to her body with one hand, waving goodbye with the other.

5.

They had Sunday dinner with John's parents. This was Tess's thing, Tess's insistence. Her own parents so far away, but John's parents so close. Why would we not go see them, honey? It's like a half-hour and it means so much to them? Part of it was that they were old, not merely aging like Tess's parents. John's father sat in a lift chair paid for by Medicare. The right side of his mother's face betrayed the slightest of heaves, that pinch of grief that was the remembered slide of Bell's palsy, barely perceptible beyond the nagging sense that something in her jaw that was once very vital had died. But when they saw their grandchildren something came alive in them.

It's good for them, John. It's good for us.

It was also a way to get John to spend time with Wally and Daniel, something he didn't do so much anymore. At least not to the extent that he once had. That he'd had an entire life before her she understood, she accepted. She knew that there would always be a part of him closed as much to the world as it was to Tess. She had made peace with this. But in exchange she asked for his presence. Not just his physical presence, but his emotional presence, his attentiveness. She asked for him to hold his daughter, to play with his sons. His singing in the morning—was it wrong to say she detected something false in it? The holdover of what had been happiness having evolved into habit.

Visiting was also a way to get Tess out of the house, out of her own head, which God knew she needed. She kept seeing these Middle Eastern men who both were and weren't there. The Syrian family that ran the Quik Stop on the farm-to-market. The guy in the Microtel off I-75—he was Iranian, or maybe Indian? One day she saw a man of indeterminate origin sitting behind the counter of the 7-Eleven past the beef jerky and capsules of XXX Herbal Enhancer playing chess with what appeared to be his grandson. She bought a bottle of water in order to get a closer look and turned out they were playing with actual pieces, not the handmade scraps of rooks and knights she'd half-expected. Then she walked out the door and ran into another. They were everywhere, these men. She was even seeing women, women in hijabs shopping at Lenox Square mall in Atlanta, women wearing headscarves and surgical masks on the MARTA as if they were in Beijing and not Georgia. She'd be out shopping and see them, the children bored, Laurie hungry, and would you like to donate a dollar to the Boys and Girls Clubs, ma'am? The St. Jude Children's Hospital? The Make-A-Wish Foundation?

Debit or credit?

I'll take next available.

These voices around her, these people.

Just go ahead and sign with your finger, honey, that's right.

Go ahead and swipe your card, ma'am.

They were everywhere. But the question was: where had they been? If they were real—if they weren't figments of Tess's imagination—why was she only now noticing them?

Shouldn't life hold itself together?

That seemed the essential problem: none of it held.

Eating the big Sunday dinner. John taking the boys on a walk through the woods while John's mother was in the yard and his father dozed in his recliner, a bag of microwave popcorn on his lap, ESPN Classic on the TV. That 1990 Portland team, you remember them, John? And her husband reeling off the lineup: Drexler and Terry Porter in the back court, Jerome Kersey at small forward...

None of it quite held, these things collected into life.

Or they both did and didn't. Either way, it was too late to turn back.

6.

John couldn't turn back either, or wouldn't, at least. It was raining now, not hard but hard enough, and he crouched in a thicket of mountain laurel, sheltering over Wally and Daniel. The boys didn't care, the boys wanted loose. They had crossed the ridge that marked the back edge of his parents' property and were on Forest Service land, green and dense but for the graveled fire roads and hinged gates. John watched the sky. Cloud traces visible through the canopy. Beyond it a blue openness that would arrive without warning, the day becalmed, almost apologetic in its clarity.

In a few minutes it would be gorgeous.

There was no reason to turn back. The day was warm, the boys loved the rain. *Can we run around, Dad? It's not cold or anything.* Fine, that was fine, and they did, they ran. *We're like wolves, Dad.* This was Wally. *Woofs*, Daniel called them. The boys raced barechested through the newly dark trees, hair matted, palms upright as they spun in circles. It was a slight miracle the way they turned, the way the water beaded and ran. They were honey colored from summer and in their loping strides there really was something wolflike about them. It was one of those small gifts that reminded him that even if he had given up his hold on the earth, the earth had not necessarily relinquished its hold on him.

He looked back in the direction they had come.

He had no intention of going back, at least not until he had to.

Because honestly, what was waiting for him back at his parents' house? Not Karla and Kayla but reminders thereof. The sense of loss he felt everywhere there, their consistent and eternal failure to appear—it had gone on so long it seemed less like death and estrangement than something willful, something spiteful.

He watched the boys spin, and began to pick at the beggar lice that had adhered to his pants and shoes, everything below the knee. These green triangles the size of an infant's fingernail. Their legs were flecked with mud. They were here and that was real—he understood that, he knew it. But there is a tension in absence that is almost equally present, an area of damage spread over the skin like scar tissue, a mapped silver so bright it almost shimmered.

He saw it everywhere he looked.

7.

Tess walked around the house.

Laurie was asleep in her Pack 'n Play, so she had a few minutes alone and this was what she wanted, the chance to explore. The farmhouse had been built in the 1940s. The original home place was somewhere deep in the woods, hand-built in the 1830s and passed down through his father's side of the family. But this wasn't the house John had grown up in and because of that, or maybe despite that, he seemed to have no desire to visit. John had grown up south of here in Peach Creek, halfway between Atlanta and Garrison, where his father worked on the assembly line until a faulty drill press collapsed on his right hand. His parents had used the settlement to pay off their house and moved here—moved home—after John graduated high school. He had spent only a few college summers here and seemed to care nothing for it.

Tess, on the other hand, was fascinated by every nook and corner. It seemed to come from another world, or not just *come* from another world, but hold open a window on a little outpost of the past. A thousand square feet of shuttered life, of ceramic figurines and a clock that chimed bird song. A northern cardinal at noon. At three a tufted titmouse. There was a linen closet full of their canning, Mason jars of chow-chow and tomatoes and peppers and okra stacked along the contact paper. Louis L'Amour Westerns. An actual family Bible.

In the refrigerator was a cellophane-covered pitcher of sweet tea and a few biscuits packaged individually in Ziploc bags. But there was also a spareness. The walls were wood pasteboard and largely unadorned. The big oaks and tulip poplars buried the house beneath permanent shade. It was the kind of place that would soon be gone. You'd walk up to find it deserted, to find it had become the kind of place where you might scrounge for relics. You'd sit on the ruins beside the chimney and reconstruct the lived lives, knowing all along you were insufficient to the task.

She walked into John's old room—to the extent that it ever was—and sat on his bed. More recently it had been John's daughter Kayla's room. Technically it still was, even if she lived in Sevierville now. She worked at the desk of a fitness club and attended a community college where she studied something practical Tess couldn't quite remember, dental hygiene, maybe. Radiology tech. It had been her room, Tess knew, from the time she was eleven and John went to work in California until she graduated high school and moved two hours north. How much her husband saw of Kayla Tess didn't know. Very little, she suspected. Tess had met her only once, purely by chance when Tess brought the children here and Kayla was visiting. Her sense was that was once more than John intended.

She did know John sent her money now and then. And Kayla wrote to him. There were occasional letters that came in the mail from her, addressed to John. Bright, cheery stamps, glowing hearts, waving flags. She hoped to God John responded. Kayla was quiet and sweet, content, it seemed, to disappear into whatever landscape she occupied. A pretty girl who always seemed to have one hand in front of her mouth, half-obscuring the thin filament of scar tracing the lower half of her face. Tess had looked her up on Facebook and gleaned the contours of her life: education, employment, a few pictures.

A bird tattoo on her thigh, planets and stars on her shoulders.

The hair pink-streaked and ponytailed.

The snaggled bottom teeth.

She was a fitness competitor of some sort and there were pictures of Kayla at the gym, Kayla working out. Kayla in Lycra, laughing in front of a rack of dumbbells.

But her privacy settings didn't allow Tess to look any deeper, and Tess wouldn't dare send her a friend request. So to Tess, she wasn't a person so much as an idea, sentimental and a little uncomfortable, but never real. Which meant there were times Tess had to remind herself that John hadn't lost his daughter in the wreck that took his wife. Even though in certain ways, he had.

So it was John's room to Tess, and always would be.

John's room, John's life.

Not Kayla's, and surely not Tess's.

They had been raised in different worlds, John's childhood cemented in the working-class South of the '80s, the Budweiser and Bocephus. A world of revivals and potlucks and a day of summer vacation at Six Flags Over Georgia. They ate Jell-O salad and feared the Soviets with their parades and tactical nukes because at that point it wasn't a joke, it was their lives. His mamma cleaning houses and selling Amway to schoolteachers in teal wind suits. His daddy paying off the mortgage by losing three fingers at the tool-and-die plant, a year before they shipped the whole operation to the maquiladora belt. It would have been a sad country song punched into the jukebox—B3, E6, F5—if it hadn't been true.

Tess's childhood had been privileged and coastal, a world of citrus and light and a Chopin nocturne playing softly in another room. Walking the acres of orange grove her father kept as a hobby. She was in her early teens on September 11 and the only world she had ever known was one of war and surveillance, a planet of muted fear animated by that gnawing sense that somewhere out there was someone who wanted very much to kill you. Not that we would ever deign to talk about it. Not when there were vacation pics from the Caymans to upload to Facebook or turn into a calendar on Shutterfly.

Some of John's things were still in the closet. Beneath Kayla's plastic-bagged winter coats and zippered prom dresses were John's basketball trophies. His medals from high-school track and cross-country. There were a few books, running shoes, old L.A. Gear high-tops. Bottle rockets. Slim red-sticked fireworks, banned now even in Georgia. It was one of the first things he'd ever told her about his life, these giant bottle-rocket fights they would wage in pastures. Tossing them. Firing them out of PVC pipes. A vanload of his college buddies in their army surplus camo, a few in pool goggles because that shit can blind you. Hammering a bottle of Mad Dog while one gets out to open the gate and then close it behind them, drunk and giggling.

You put the sticks in your teeth—she remembered him telling her that. You carried the bottle rockets in your mouth so your hands were free and when it was over you had this clown's smile of red dye. Nose full of cordite. Thumb raw from the wheel of the lighter.

But had Karla ever been there? Tess knew they had met in Peach Creek, gone to high school and college together, started dating after Christmas break freshman year. So had she been there, out in those fields with the boys? Nineteen and laughing in her cutoffs, white pockets against tan thighs? Mouth breathy with Boone's Farm?

Karla had surely sat on this bed, lay on it, made love and then napped on it. There was no doubting that, no reason to ask. Karla had been here with John, and not some rumored pre-John but John himself, John as he was.

Something within Tess didn't like it, the memory, the room. This sense that her own life was the by-product of tragedy, that had Karla Maynard not lost control on a stretch of wet interstate Tess

Maynard would not exist. And neither would Wally or Daniel or Laurie.

She found a cardboard box and carried it onto the screened porch.

A light rain was starting to fall. She heard it first in the trees, ticking the leaves so that their glossy bellies showed, and then she heard it thumping into the soft ground, the moss and pine needles. The trees were streaked silver, brighter despite the clouds. The air cooled. Everyone would be coming in soon, but she didn't feel rushed. She simply opened the box.

Immediately, she could tell it was newer, more recent than the trophies and old shoes. It had about it the John she knew. The flesh-and-blood John she passed as they trafficked in and out of the shower. Everything else was the John of hearsay, everything, perhaps, but this.

She didn't like it.

She could tell that right away too, but she dug in anyway. The first thing she came across was a box of chocolates, the sort of commemorative thing not meant for actual consumption. It read CARLY SLOVENSKO in slanting script. Twenty individual chocolates, each bearing the image of a different landscape. Mountains, barns, rivers, churches. It was Czech or Polish. Maybe Hungarian. Then she found the label, a single word buried in the vowel-less print: it was Slovak.

Below that she found the axe, or hatchet, maybe. Wood handled with a brass blade. Not a real weapon or tool but the sort of thing you bought at an airport gift shop, an afterthought, a way to blow through those last few euros.

The postcard was below that, a crowded beach, behind it mountains.

GREETINGS FROM SUNNY YALTA in three languages and two alphabets.

She stopped when she came to the photograph. It was John's daughter, it was Kayla, four or five years old in a pink leotard. Kayla before she became fixed in the universe by memory and a collapsing guardrail. Kayla before she became defined by the idea of *too fast for conditions* and a wiggle of scar tissue.

Looking at her, Tess thought of that verse from the Bible, not even the verse but the line. But it wasn't the Bible. It was William Blake. Something about "thy fearful symmetry." For that was exactly what she was in the photograph, this fantastically made child who soon enough would be unmade, who would be lost. Then she remembered—my God! What a fool I am—that Kayla was alive and so far as Tess knew, happy.

She put the photograph back, intentionally burying it in the bottom.

Which was how she found the USB drive. A Memorex thumb drive meant to be attached to a key chain. But it was attached to nothing beyond her hand. It was, it occurred to her, hers.

If she wanted it.

But she didn't, and she dropped it back in the box.

It was only when they had strapped the children into the van for the ride home, folded the Pack 'n Play and given hugs that she changed her mind. A second before she knew they would drive away, she suddenly needed to pee—so sorry, gimme like sixty seconds—and ran back inside not to the bathroom but to the closet where she hid the USB drive in her bag.

It was hers. She just hadn't wanted to admit it.

8.

Monday morning a university-wide faculty meeting was called at which the provost explained that Professor Hadawi had tendered his resignation and would not be returning to campus. That was all. It hardly seemed worthy of announcement. Professor Hadawi had spent the last year on sabbatical, teaching courses on social justice in his native Yemen on a fellowship from the Soros Foundation. He had decided, so said the provost, to accept a permanent administrative position there. There was no mention of the clearing of his office.

The provost dismissed the gathering without opening the floor to questions.

Some hands went up and hung there, ignored. There was a general grumbling, but eventually they all got up and returned to their lives. John went back to his office and sent friend requests to thirty students.

The next day Stone called and asked him to meet him at a club in Atlanta.

"I'm hearing rumblings," Stone said. "Lots of information and disinformation. Puts me in mind of the good old days. I want you to meet me Saturday evening."

"This is about Hadawi?"

"Come Saturday and find out."

"Sorry, can't do it."

"You know the Show Pony in Little Five Points? We'll have a little powwow."

"Can't do it, James."

"Ask the wife for a ride. Take the family car, I don't care," Stone said. "Just don't stand me up."

"Jimmy—"

"We have history, John. Don't sit there and act like we don't."

✳

Or if not history, John thought, at least a shared past.

After his wife—his *first* wife, he reminded himself—died in a car wreck on I-75, after the funeral, after the surgeries to repair the arm, shoulder, and face of his daughter who didn't die—his *first* daughter—after the drinking necessitated by watching his daughter endure her surgeries, after the temporary leave of absence from his teaching position that was immediately understood as permanent, which is to say, simply, *after*, John Maynard accepted a position at a conservative think tank situated on the campus of a small Jesuit college north of St. Cloud, Minnesota. The think tank was ill-defined yet well-endowed, and he spent ten hours a day reading and sipping the bourbon that had replaced his wife.

Kayla was ten by then and almost whole, enrolled in the college's school for faculty children. She was quiet and attentive in a way John was not. Almost as if it were her father and not her who'd been catapulted into the windshield, her father and not her with the silver thread of scar that unspooled across the bottom of her face. Besides heightening her already shy nature, it didn't seem to affect her.

John was different, lonelier, less able. His single friend was a fellow drunk named James Stone, a documentarian with a muddled past and connections to right-wing causes. A man, it was said, who had access. How he had landed at the think tank no one seemed certain and John never asked. Stone hinted at some spiritual crisis he intended to drown, something too painful to address directly. There was a rumor he made high-end porn in Miami.

A few nights a week they drank, together but alone, Stone sitting behind John's desk, downing J&B from a paper cone and holding forth.

"My past." Stone saying this. "Let us dignify it henceforth by referring to it as my *private history*. I didn't go through life with this jammed in me. This is what I'm saying. This is not my area of operations, squalling and bitching."

It appeared to be the same paper cone, night after night, beginning to fray, going transparent.

"I got a brother. Guy's got three daughters and a lovely wife. A house in Sleepy Hollow with like five bedrooms, and you think those girls aren't gorgeous? Christ. Left and right you get the boys coming around. My own brother, younger brother, just for the sake of the record, and here's this free-range grassfed American dream. How do you think that makes me feel?"

John tried to imagine. That was, in fact, what he did during that period of his life: he tried to imagine the way others lived. His daughter, alone in their campus apartment. James Stone, alone in his brother's kitchen at night. Stone would go to give the milk carton a little shake before pouring it on his cereal—you wanted to do that, that little shake—and the cap would fly off, milk all over the goddamn counter because someone had failed to secure it. His brother, his brother's wife. Those three gorgeous daughters. He should have known. Still, you see a closed cap and you assume security. Was he wrong in this?

"You think I don't consider these things? Look at me, John. This is a question I'm asking."

His brother's wife had a running joke that the loudest sound in the world was James Stone taking the plastic cereal bag from the box. Not ha-ha funny, but you get it. But that wasn't the real issue. The real issue was why you needed a cellophane bag *inside* a cardboard box. Milled corn. Sugar. That's what we're protecting?

One night they watched an episode of *Frontline* about Bin Laden.

"Fuck Bin Laden," Stone said. "He didn't jar us out of our American mythos. If anything he allowed us to sink deeper into it. War belongs on TV, not in the streets. We know this in our heart of hearts. Dead brown people. That's become our normative state. We grow up with it, always far away and always dead."

Same paper cup, same wandering hand.

"We need them—the Japs, the gooks, the hajis. They hate us and we need that. We need their hate to assuage that deep Puritan guilt nobody talks about anymore. Our world had been flipped and we had to right it. We kill brown people on TV. It's what the people expect and for seventy years it's what we've given them. The Japanese. The Koreans. The Vietnamese."

He numbered them on his fingers.

"The Iraqis, the Afghans. The Iraqis once more for good measure. We kill them and they hate us—it's symbiosis. And don't give me that look, all right? I didn't make up the rules. I'm just telling you."

And then Stone wasn't telling John anything. Stone's appointment expired and just like that he disappeared from John's life, or so John thought at time. A few months later Ray Bageant walked in. Ray Bageant was the link between them.

In between, John had published a thin book called *Regarding What Is Lost*, a treatise addressing absence and regret, theorizing the way in which the gravitational pull of suffering binds the world, and in turn makes plain the world. But the book was so abstract— he never even mentioned Karla—what started as a memoir about the death of his wife gradually came to seem a work of prophesy. Suffering and loss were revelatory and what they revealed were the hidden workings of life. There was a secret wound through the universe yet buried beneath the accumulation of living. But to burn through this, to lose, to suffer, was to gain access. There was a pattern, and if you could stand in the presence of suffering, if you could stand on the edge of death, you could know it. And you could live.

It was a blur of Catholic theology and featherweight Zen packaged with tables and flow charts regarding gross domestic product and projections of glacial melt, all of it just banal enough to be a great, if brief, success, read in the halls of power in Washington and New York and London, discussed on news shows before being exposed—rightly—as the ravings of a damaged mind. That several opportunities were offered, positions in government, or with NGOs—let it be said that he drank away those opportunities.

The point being he was alone in his office—both physically and metaphysically—the day he learned of Peter Keyes's interest through his assistant, Ray Bageant, a thin, angular man with the gray skin of a porpoise. John was staring out at the lake, his back to the door, when Bageant cleared his throat and John found him standing on the threshold, hands spread apologetically.

"I hope you don't mind," he said. "There was no one out front."

"Catherine," John said, for some reason calling the name of the office manager. "She's at lunch."

"I supposed as much. You're Professor Maynard, I presume. I've come quite a distance to see you, Professor."

They talked in the office and later in the rented Prius Bageant had driven north from the Minneapolis airport, following the narrow lanes that spread out from the college toward dairy farms and wide expanses of wetland. Peter, Bageant referred to him only as "Peter," was interested in meeting him. He had read John's book and felt John could offer some insight that might help drive his thinking.

"We are poised," Bageant told him, wheeling past barns red and collapsing, "on the verge of a great shift. The way we live, the way we conceptualize our very lives is about to change, abruptly and profoundly. The wars are pushing us, technological advances are pushing us. Peter is a great believer in this push and wants to position himself to fully embrace what is next. How to think around issues," he said, "certain theoretical blocks to which we are acculturated, Peter wants to bend beyond those. To shatter old ways of conceiving life—this is Peter's purpose."

The zeal of an evangelist. Some small-town Mormon selling whole-life policies. Except there was always the hint of mockery, the closet apostate who, for nothing more than shits and giggles, lays it on extra thick. Or maybe he believed, maybe he truly believed. Peter Keyes certainly did. Keyes was a self-made billionaire with a cultist following in futurist and libertarian circles. A visionary of sorts: half the social networks, half the companies fabulously wealthy but pragmatically useless, had been founded by Peter or one of his acolytes. He was one of the fathers—grandfathers, by that point—of Silicon Valley. A newly uncloseted homosexual. A former Republican money-man disenchanted with party politics and now pouring his wealth into obscure start-ups and causes that might have been championed by Milton Friedman.

"Are you familiar with the Keyes Group?"

"Afraid not."

"Good," Bageant had said. "That's a good thing. We would prefer that, actually."

The Keyes Group had long been doing work for the government, electronic surveillance, data-mining. But just after the September 11 attacks their contract had expanded broadly when they acquired Global Solutions, a very discreet, very influential consulting firm based out of DC but operating all over the Middle East and Africa. Global Solutions' area of expertise was the gathering of human intelligence. The then-current administration in Washington was functioning in legally nebulous areas and they knew it. They needed to ensure their activities could withstand the scrutiny and restrictions of some future administration. By 2004 it was already clear there would be inquiries and commissions, clandestine officers taking public oaths swearing to tell *nothing but the truth*. There would be talk of overreach.

"Understand our objective after nine-eleven wasn't to necessarily strike the right people," Bageant said. "Our objective was to strike, to act. It's what great powers do, Professor. It's the very definition of a great power."

It was important for John to remember that people really did say these things. They talked about *great powers* and the precariousness of our position as the world's policeman. Every conversation was framed by the governing presence of *the post-9/11 world*. There was so much money suddenly pouring out of Washington and into private companies that talking that way wasn't so much lavish as necessary, linguistic justification for the fact that the Pentagon had just increased your operating capital by a factor of 300. John could say that he never heard the expression "Great Game" uttered by anyone within Global Solutions. It was the sort of meta-comment they were all supposed to be past. Irony and cynicism were for the people on the ground, the trauma surgeons with Médecins Sans Frontières, the boys in the Third Special Forces Group.

They rode all day through the winding hills of central Minnesota, past the greening fields, past the barns with stars and horseshoes tacked above the doors. Bageant quoted Einstein: no problem can be solved from the same consciousness that created it. He invoked German loanwords, things Goethe might have uttered in his sleep. By evening they were somewhere outside Duluth, wending through a morass of empty suburbs, lost, had either of them given any thought to it.

"So what does he want from me?" John finally managed to ask.

"He wants you to do your thinking in-house," Bageant said. "There would be no formal expectations, only that you apply your cognitive powers to the service of Peter's agenda. Think of it," he told him, "as an advisory position."

The pay was ten times what John made as a fellow at the institute, a position that would anyway expire in a few weeks' time. He suspected he would have to complete his appointment but that was not the case: they were happy to see him go. So he packed all that he owned in an overnight bag and unplugged his laptop. Kayla flew to Atlanta where his parents picked her up. He would send for her when he was settled, but it turned out he was never settled. He was in and out of California and then he was at Site Nine, regretting everything, if only he'd had the courage to.

I still think of it like the Blitz, Ray said after. *A few RAF pilots holding the line against the barbarians.* And there were barbarians, this was true. But there were also men like Hassan Natashe.

And then there was the man behind it all—and this was John— John was the man watching.

9.

Tess's father called. He wanted to know if she was happy.

She was at the playground with the children, Laurie strapped to her chest while Tess moved between Daniel on the baby swing and Wally on the big-kid swing because if either went more than a single freaking second without a push they would start to melt down.

Whales—

She was telling them about whales and dolphins—listen to me, honey. They can hear at 160 kHz. That's like eight times higher than we can hear which is pretty amazing if you think about it—talking and talking when her cell went off and there was her father, sitting in his orange grove and humming Shostakovich. Her mother was a former pianist, not a concert pianist, but talented, adept. Her older brother was at Wells Fargo in Charlotte. Her little sister was in a Savannah loft, busy selling purses on Etsy and cultivating her gut flora. But it seemed all anyone could think about was Tess. Was Tess—this seemed to be everyone's question—was Tess happy?

"What is this sudden concern with my happiness?"

"Honey, I'm always concerned with your happiness, always have been. You and your sister and brother. All of you."

"I know, I just mean—Liz called. Apparently Mom thinks I'm depressed."

"Your mother worries."

"Apparently she wants to send me money."

"Honey, do you need money?"

"No, Dad. I'm fine. Please. If she wants to send me something tell her to send her prayers. Tell her to pray for me. Tell her to pray for the world."

"Don't be like that, darling."

"I'm not being like anything. I'm being serious. Tell her to pray for the world."

Did Tess pray?

She thought she did, but to some extent she was no longer sure. There was a thing Wally did, though. He must have been about three when he developed the habit of "washing" his washcloths in the sink. He would soak them, wring them, and then spread them in the porcelain basin. It broke Tess's heart, her son's focus, the delicacy of the act. He called his shadow his "statue." He kissed her hands. It broke her heart. Everything broke her heart. She had those things now, but she also wanted those things back. Except she couldn't exactly name the things. She wanted everything back but couldn't name a damn thing.

Was this wanting a form of prayer?

A few days ago she had stood with her eyes shut a few feet from the bedroom wall and clicked her tongue until it wasn't a sloppy wet click but an elastic pop. And was she imagining it when she felt the sound wave go out from her? Was she imagining it when she felt it return? Was that prayer?

She went back to pushing, back to whales and dolphins.

"Listen to this," she told Wally. "If something's that high frequency it can materialize and dematerialize matter. Some people think it's connected to levitation, to healing. Sometimes sick children swim with dolphins or pilot whales. Are you listening, baby?"

But she was hardly listening to herself.

10.

A few nights after Stone's reappearance, John and Tess had the Glenns over for dinner.

"You know how hard it is being the oppressor, Professor?" This was Pat Glenn, a member of the local college-and-business alliance on which John sat. He was in his early forties and had inherited three dozen pest-control trucks and two fiberglass bass boats he kept at a lake house, also inherited. He was paranoid and angry, his life a nest of pistols and pills.

"Stop it," his wife said.

They were on the couch, Tess in the kitchen preparing an enchilada casserole.

"Keeping the colored man down. The ragheads. The—the what? Wetbacks, for lack of a better word."

"He has this shtick he does."

"Wetbacks encompassing everyone south of the Oklahoma State line, all right?"

"It's also vaguely anti-Texas which actually, if you think about it, makes like no sense."

"The capitalist system," he said. "All the structural injustice."

"Stop it, Pat." His wife had a boob job and foil-tipped highlights.

"'I can't breathe, I can't breathe.'"

"You're terrible."

"'Can't we all just get along?'"

"Honestly, stop it."

At the table Glenn started talking about Hadawi. What's the story they're telling? No, no, no, didn't take no admin job. Nobody voluntarily takes no freaking job in Yemen, I don't care where you're from. That SOB is on the run. Had John not heard this? *Stop it, Pat. You're making things up.* The hell I am. There's a mosque in Atlanta. We used to do the pest control until guess what—the feds raided the place and shut it down. *Pat, stop!* How did y'all not hear this? The place was a front for jihadis. All these charities supposedly pumping money to poor little starving Arab kids were really buying 'em suicide vests. And your buddy—pointing his fork across the table now, jabbing it at John—your *colleague* was their main man.

＊

Tess cleared the table and stayed in the kitchen until they were gone.

"I can't stand him," she said.

"I know."

"His just general awfulness. He's evil."

"He's not evil. He's just conservative."

"My father's conservative. *You're* conservative. That's not conservative. That's being a bad human being."

"Maybe so."

"Maybe or not, I hope we never see him again."

"I know," John said, but found his mind wandering not to dinner but to Stone, to the way Stone had stood outside his office. Not the way he'd looked or the way he'd dressed—jeans and blazer, more or less standard campus attire. But the way he had pushed himself off the wall and stepped toward John. Almost as if he'd intended him some harm, if only as a reminder of their past.

＊

The next day John avoided his office and walked the campus, something he didn't do as often as he should. Just speaking to people. Hey. Good morning. Nice to see y'all. A circle of tables was spread out over the grassy quad and arranged around the fountain, each covered with literature and posters and sign-up sheets. The Org Fair it was called. The day every campus organization came out to attract new students.

Oxfam and the Spirit Club.

The ACLU and Students for Disability Access.

Clubs against cyberbullying, sexual assault, child soldiers in Africa. In keeping with the school's ethos they were all socially minded and mind-numbingly elitist. A pack of private-school biology majors from Buckhead paying $21,000 a semester to conduct field research in Ghana. Not Ebola, mind you—that was real. But there would be some scary, if actually harmless, strain of infection, frighteningly complex when named in Latin, that would look lovely on med school applications.

Another group painted murals around town. Another tutored the poor Appalachian kids, the sons and daughters of the folks cleaning their bathrooms or mowing their grass. There was a de-stress station with massage chairs and squeeze balls and actual golden retriever puppies. A few dozen barefoot twenty-year-olds played red rover. Posters read BE RESILIENT! It was all high-minded and well-intentioned, all heart-breakingly naive. *You think any society that sells life insurance could be anything other than damned?* Another of Stone's drunken rants. Not that it mattered. If they wanted to play white savior let them play white savior. What John had discovered when he lost his wife—and he hated himself for it—but what he had discovered was that there were ways of dealing with everything, even the end of everything. Maybe that most of all.

He smiled and waved, asked about their classes, their families. Everyone looking up now and then from their phones to say how fine everything was. Classes were fine. Parents were fine. Me? Yeah, I'm fine I guess.

What he wanted to ask about, but wouldn't, was what was being said about Hadawi. There had to be rumors. A campus rally had fizzled. The article in the student newspaper mentioned only his resignation. The silence was so deafening it seemed contrived. Where was the student outrage? Cops on *our* campus? Hadawi was hated by many, but he was also loved by a small but vocal minority.

John walked out to the edge of campus on through the arboretum and past the athletic fields to stand on the edge of Highway 76. A long line of RVs stood at the traffic light by the college entrance. Winnebagos and Colemans and Starcrafts. A few cars between them. Garrison sat on the edge of the Chattahoochee National Forest in the lower reaches of the Southern Appalachian Mountains and this was the last of the late-summer vacation traffic. In a few weeks they would give way to the leaf peepers. He'd never heard the term growing up, but figured the simple act of watching a tree change color had become exotic enough to require its own name.

He watched the light change, called Tess on his cell.

"Out visiting," he said. "How 'bout y'all?"

"Laurie cried all morning but she's finally asleep. I'm about to fix the boys lunch."

"It's like—it's like ten A.M., Tess."

"Well, it's that or three breakfasts."

"I understand."

"I'm getting sick of the second and third breakfasts."

"I understand," he said, and said goodbye before she could say more.

He knew he was killing time, delaying what it was on his mind to do which was call James Stone. Finally, he gave up and dialed.

"Got curious, did you?"

"Shouldn't you know this already?"

"Somewhere there's a big computer that runs the world, John. But so far nobody's handed me the password."

"We were on a committee together. That's all. I barely knew the man."

"Yet here you are ringing me up."

"I can meet you Saturday."

"It'll be precious, John. I want to hear all about the new wife and kids. I want a little coffee klatch, just the two of us. We'll knit a tea cozy and talk about our hopes and dreams."

"I'll be there Saturday. That's all I'm calling to say."

"That you'll be there? Oh, Professor," Stone said, laughing now, "I never doubted it for a second."

11.

It was September when Tess started running again. At first it was a neighborhood thing—she would push the double stroller while Wally rattled beside her on his training-wheeled bike—but after a week she felt things returning, her legs, her lungs. The way she could swallow air in giant gulps and then live off it for what seemed hours. It had started one day when she was hurrying across the parking lot to the walk-up ATM, John and Laurie and the boys sitting in the Chick-fil-A parking lot. Without thinking, she had broken into a jog, a trot, really, the simplest of things. The knee flexing—ball-of-the-foot, ball-of-the-foot—and it occurred to her that she hadn't run in better than four years. Not a single step. All those years, all those miles, and to have it go out of her like breath. To exhale something that had been so much a part of you, and so easily. She slowed to a walk, almost a crawl. They could wait. Even if John and the children were in the car they could wait.

The next day she made her initial foray around the neighborhood with the children. This wasn't necessarily easy. You had to get Wally interested in his bike—he wasn't really. You had to get Laurie asleep or at least sleepy. You had to get Daniel interested enough in a book that he wouldn't wake Laurie once she did finally fall asleep. And of course he would eventually wake her no matter what. When the crying set in—first Laurie, then Daniel—the run was over, but by that point Wally was actually interested in his bike—*finally!*—and was mad and himself on the verge of tears that his ride had been ruined. The ride being, as he explained it, the only thing he'd been looking forward to all day.

"Please," she would say.

It was a general appeal, intended for whatever audience would listen.

But after a week she was waking up to run alone. It didn't matter how early—she could feel the addiction spilling back into her body. Running as a suitable response to what was in the fridge. Running as answer to a world of V-neck T-shirts and sex in the missionary position, a world like the inside of chain hotels. Desk, chair, bed. Some vaguely impressionist print hung on the drywall. She needed to be out running because otherwise she'd go full-blown crazy.

She was still hearing things, and it wasn't just the man in the basement, it wasn't just his clicking. At night, she could almost hear the USB drive, this thing that seemed to have acquired a heartbeat, the faint pulse she sensed from the nightstand where it had slept buried beneath old greeting cards and the boys' art projects and an album of wedding photos. It was almost sentient, the way that as she thought about it, she felt it thinking about her, conspiring against her. Stupid, she knew. It wasn't alive. How could it be alive?

She was seeing things, too.

She was room mother for Wally's kindergarten class. Paper hearts, shamrocks, granola. They preferred the cupcakes bran, these matronly childless devotees of Maria Montessori. They were learning to write code. Scratch 1.4. They did holidays, class performances—you couldn't exactly call them plays. Field trips to the dairy, the fire station. The second-graders got to go to the Nickelodeon in Atlanta and how's that for something to look forward to, Wally, how about that? Nights were electric toothbrushes—not the spicy toothpaste, Mom!—prayers, books—Huckle, Critter, Arthur. Nights were soft and sweet, but days—days she saw them everywhere, these Middle Eastern men. Women in headscarves, hijabs, whatever they were.

Twice she went secretly to a Christian therapist, told John she was doing a Zumba class at the gym, not that he asked. Tess—stupidly, it turned out—told the therapist about the man in the basement, about watching the videos. But she—Tess had specifically sought a *she*—didn't get it. Why this, Tess? Why this fixation on suffering? And Tess wanted to scream, Tess wanted to tear things off the walls, pictures, diplomas, because *why?* Seriously? How about because people are dying? Because they are cutting off heads. Because bombs are falling while we sit here with your brochures on "Biblical Truths" and "Clinical Skills." *If I'm fixated on suffering maybe it's because no one else is,* she wanted to scream. But she didn't scream it. She didn't even say it. She just sat there while the therapist talked about the pointing finger versus the moon, the idea of reflected light.

Luna, Tess, from the Latin.

The Old French was *lunaire*.

Had she considered this idea that she was orbiting her husband's and children's lives?

And Tess admitting no, she hadn't, and then wondering later how she had ever considered her life as anything else.

A week after graduation she had moved to St. Pete with Emma, her best friend and teammate, who, like Tess, was a middle-distance specialist and as wiry as the rigging of a ship. They rented an apartment a block off the beach and got jobs waitressing at a raw bar in Pass-a-Grille, a weightless time, basically living the young adulthood they never experienced at Florida Wesleyan. Running but not logging the miles. Drinking Michelob Ultras after her shift ended. Failing to record her hours slept or resting heart rate. It was irresponsible when she held it against those regimented college years, and it felt wonderful. She felt an airiness gather beneath her, as if the breeze moving over the sand and families camped beneath beach umbrellas past the cabana shade might be enough to lift her.

Often it was.

For weeks she ran when she wanted, drank when she wanted, stayed up late, slept through church. She didn't want a husband or a career, at least not yet. She wanted to have fun.

In July she entered a road race—an Autism Awareness 5K—and the night before they got tipsy at the pre-race party, Tess and Emma in skirts and heels and lipstick, and the men, everywhere the men were noticing them in a way they never had, introducing themselves, bringing over fresh cups of the cheap keg beer. It was harmless fun—the men were runners after all, how dangerous could they be?—and they went home to sleep alone in their separate bedrooms. But Tess hadn't really slept. Rather she had simply lain there, feeling her body hum.

The next day she arrived at the starting line still jangly with the night, the energy, the fun, the spell she seemed to have cast not only over every man in sight but over herself as well. Possibly, she was still drunk. But it was equally possible she was simply awake, *aware*, in a way she had never been.

When the gun fired she reeled off three 5:35 miles, hardly conscious of what was happening. She had never run like this. There was no strategy, no pacing. There was no *thinking* and that had never happened. She had simply run, her mind captive to her legs and heart.

In the final stretch she felt the road narrow to a sort of tunnel (it wasn't), a shaded arbor that folded over her (it didn't), and she sprinted the length of it, barely out-kicked by the lone male runner who finished just seconds ahead of her. My God! And you want to talk about reflected light! She felt more like a star newly made. She had never run like that. She had never *lived* like that, and ran past the finish line onto the beach where she slipped off her Nikes with the timing chip wound in the laces and ran straight into the Gulf, not stopping until her race bib was plastered against her still-heaving chest.

And that was where she heard him.

The man called to her when she was coming out of the water, mid-thirties and already tipsy on the post-race beer. Cock-eyed and smiling. Too old for such, but then again, Tess, twenty-two-year-old Tess, was probably too old for running a sanctioned 5K semi-crocked. Even if it was the best race of her life.

She talked to John Maynard out of amusement, or maybe curiosity, or maybe a chemical overload of endorphins. Whatever the reason, they spent that day and the next together. Two weeks later he invited her to his friend's place on St. Simons Island and out of some otherwise dormant sense of propriety she insisted on driving her own car.

She was both relieved and disappointed to find they were sharing the house with a few others, but it had turned out to be an amazing day. Swimming off the dock, cooking on the charcoal grill, all of it in a lazy haze of vodka lemonade. She and John had been a couple then, but not really. A sort of couple, but she was hoping. Then that evening they went swimming alone and she came out of the water with her T-shirt matted over her top and John said: that shirt you have on makes me think of you with no shirt on at all. It was the dumbest line she'd ever heard, but then again she wound up with her shirt off, all her clothes off, so how dumb had it really been?

He proposed a week later.

Crazy, no other word for it. But maybe it was the crazy that had so enticed her. Since returning to St. Pete they had made love at least daily, usually twice, once three times, the final act coming against a wall of sacked Old Bay seafood seasoning after she let him in through the rear service door of Salty Mike's during her ten-minute break. It was a sort of delirium and in the context of the sex and drinking and the long morning runs along the beach—hung-over, but the hangover unable to touch her—a marriage proposal seemed not only sane but logical, the only possible culmination of so much wild excess. That she didn't know exactly what he did for a living or where he was from or how he'd spent the last decade only made it seem crazier, which, naturally, made it seem more right.

They were married on the beach on a Sunday in early November, her parents and brother and sister in reluctant attendance. They were happy for her in that way in which *happy* signals a million things, none of which exactly equate to gladness, but don't preclude it either. In a family of risk-taking achievers, it had always been Tess they had chided, Tess the dutiful, Tess the chaste. Now that Tess had gone and done the most reckless thing any of their well-bred imaginations could conjure, could they really be anything other than supportive, even if their support was as lukewarm as the water they stood beside?

Their indifference only made her love him more.

Barefoot on the sand in strapless white. Body brown and lean. Her sister and Emma as her maids of honor. Her brother David as John's best man. At her insistence they went back to the borrowed house on St. Simons Island for their honeymoon. He wanted to take her far away, but she wanted what she realized she had wanted that first day driving up: she wanted the two of them together and no one else, the two of them swimming and drinking wine and making love in the third-floor bed with the windows open and the curtains billowing. Brown pelicans diving into the surf, wings tucked like the coat of arms of some ancient central European family. She wanted shortening days and cooling nights. She wanted vanilla candles and sand bedded in her scalp, and she got that, she got everything she wanted.

For a while, at least.

They wound up staying almost three weeks. She lost her job, but who cares, right? She was inside this giant house she was pretending was hers, inside this giant life that maybe was hers, her only link to the greater world her morning runs and the occasional phone call to Emma who couldn't believe how unbelievably lucky she was and what else could Tess do but agree?

Some days they snorkeled, the water not exactly clear, not green like the Caribbean, or even aquamarine like the Gulf, but what mattered was that here they were, man and wife, swimming together 100 meters off the stony point where the beach made its turn.

They might have stayed forever had the friend—whoever he was, wherever he was—not needed the place back. They returned to St. Pete and she hauled what little she had to John's condo on Redington Shores. She was happy there, if a little isolated. John, she discovered, was a psychologist who worked as a professor when he wasn't working as a consultant to the government. He'd also written a seriously misunderstood book on understanding grief (she had sat up one night and drunkenly read every single one-star Amazon review). But he didn't seem to be working much at the moment. He had saved money he said, he was between things.

Christmas was at her parents' on Sanibel—there was still no mention of John's parents, or of anyone else; she as yet knew nothing of his first wife and daughter and none of it seemed terribly relevant at the moment. She was happy, she was running, halfheartedly looking for a job until he asked one day why she didn't just focus on her training. If she could completely devote herself to running couldn't she be like an Olympian or something?

The thought both flattered and scared her. In truth, she knew she no longer had either the fire or the discipline to train and race at that level, and it was because of him. Because of what he had awoken within her. She had fallen in love with a certain amount of ease, the world's lovely *give* that can surely be found if only you go looking for it. And she had. It was out there, and she had found it. Only once she found it, once she experienced the idea of self-indulgence, she knew she could never go back to self-denial.

And why should she?

She'd lived her life according to training plans and schedules and everything else that denied everything that was normal, that was comfortable, that was American, and now she had gone and fallen in love with the everyday.

So why suffer? Running was akin to going to war with yourself. The 800 comparable to an attempt on your own life, immediate and irrevocable. The 1,500 was slower, there was thinking involved, positioning. But the pain was also less theoretical. The slowness of seventy-two-second quarters had a way of revealing layers previously unimaginable. Self-immolation. Hurt tucked within hurt, and all of it arranged in the heart. As if it had been sleeping there all her life, waiting for the opportunity to flood outward into muscle and lung. She didn't want that anymore.

So when he asked if she wanted to devote herself to her running she knew it was impossible.

Still, she said yes, she said thank you, she said of course, and some days she ran furious 400-meter repeats on the Eckerd College track or eighteen-mile distance runs across the causeway or down to the Sunshine Skyway Bridge, ran with the sort of clear-eyed focus reserved for the God-sent, the ones who define life in terms of some staggering mission. But some days, many days, she did nothing more than put on her sweats and spend hours at a coffee shop refreshing her Facebook page.

She won every local road race she entered, but made sure to stay local. The training was enough to make her the fastest woman in greater Tampa, but not enough to push her beyond. She did regret it, her lack of conviction. She did feel the requisite amount of grief: she had been given a great opportunity for which she cared not at all. Which was another way of saying she wasn't ungrateful, but wasn't exactly grateful either. What she was, was satisfied.

It showed. In so many ways it showed, this sudden smugness.

She lost touch with Emma, lost touch with old friends. Lost touch with everyone except John.

Reflected light?

She could have told the therapist that the idea that John's life illuminated her own was actually a rather generous assessment. More than his light, she felt his gravitational pull, the way he seemed to sling her through the greater universe. She loved to run, to cook, to while away the days on their balcony watching the kite-surfers skim the sliding surf. But she was also coming to terms with her boredom.

It was around the time she started thinking of a baby that John began to unravel. It started with his inability to sleep which led to all those foggy predawn conversations which led to his eventual revelation of a prior life, one that had ended, of course, with the death of his wife and eventual estrangement (if that was what you wanted to call it) from his daughter. That he had hid this from her—that it had been too painful too share, but now he was sharing it—only made her love him more. It was not unlike her parents' poorly masked disapproval: it wound them tighter. At least that was how she chose to interpret events.

So his revelation of tragedy: it started with that.

It started with his taking some undefined government job that took him away for months.

It started there. It ended back in the house on St. Simons Island, almost two years after their first visit. John bedridden for weeks, depressed and scared though of what he never said. It ended when she told him she was pregnant. It ended, to the extent that it ended, only with the birth of Wally and their move to north Georgia. The logic something like: John needs a fresh start, John needs to be working.

The logic must have been something like that, but it was impossible to say since one day he simply came home to announce he had accepted a position at Garrison College and that they would be moving. At the time, she was sitting in the living room, nursing Wally and suddenly calling to John who had already disappeared up the stairs to the bedroom because I'm sorry, what? What position? What college?

And he hung his shirtless self over the rail to say Garrison College in Garrison, Georgia.

A joint appointment in counseling and psychology.

Which answered her question but told her absolutely nothing she actually needed to know.

From the distance of years, she saw the extent to which it stunned her.

It took her away from her parents.

It took her away from her life.

Reflected light?

She never went back to the Christian therapist. She didn't need therapy.

She needed to know those things that lay just beyond her. She could tell you her husband was in his office or meeting some administrator or conducting a counseling session, but she couldn't tell you what he thought about at night when he lay beside her and pretended to sleep. She could tell you the migratory patterns of sperm whales—she'd read up—but not the extent to which they loved their young. She could give an exhaustive biography of the man in the basement, complete with schools attended and jobs held, but she knew nothing about what hope might harbor in his heart.

It was possible, she thought, that the answer was contained in the hard plastic of the USB drive, still sleeping in her nightstand. She felt it was there, this knowledge. But she sensed there might also be things she didn't need to know, things she wouldn't be able to unknow, things it would be impossible to forget.

＊

"A man came to see me recently." John talking from one end of the couch, Tess on the other. Between them slept the boys, Laurie already in the crib. He muted the volume on whatever it was they were watching and in the darkness there was only the soft snoring of their sons. "James Stone. I don't know if I ever mentioned him."

"I don't remember."

"'Jimmy' I might have called him. Haven't seen him in years and there he was outside my office."

"Was something wrong?"

"Since oh-eight, it's been. Which is what, six years?"

"A figure from your dark past. So spooky."

They made love with the bedroom door open, the boys still asleep on the couch. It lent something of the exotic to the act, the slightest whiff of danger. Total darkness so that other senses became acute, touch, taste, hearing. The smell of each other. Skin and milk—that was hers. His was a feral scent that bordered on rankness, the smell of unwashed business socks, the metallic taste of cologne.

It was only the second time they had made love since Laurie was born and they both felt it, the pent-up energy. He bit her shoulder, put her legs in the air, pulled them so that they bent around his waist where he stood by the bed. It was more aggressive than she was used to, a calling back to those Florida days, those few months before his St. Simons breakdown, that period when she felt herself to be wholly body. Not living in a body, but body alone.

She felt his hips shudder and they washed into each other, panting, a little raw, a little angry. He let go of her ankles, her legs, released her in stages so that she felt the lingering imprint of his fingers running her length. Something desperate about it, the last grip of used-up power.

She lay there letting the tingle circulate a moment longer while he showered and came out in a towel to tell her he had to be in Atlanta all weekend.

12.

The Show Pony occupied the top two floors of what appeared from the street to be office space. John took the elevator five floors to the glassed roof where a bouncer in bib overalls found his name on a clipboard. The room was steamy. Water streaked the glass and bright aqueous light waved from the surface of the pool where boys in tiny trunks splashed and laughed. The air was eucalyptus. The vibe was exclusionary. But it wasn't the first place John knew he didn't belong.

He spotted Stone at a small table near the diving board, alone with a bottle of champagne, a glass of pomegranate juice, and a bowl of mixed nuts. Barefoot in a sports coat and hemp pants, the trace of yesterday's eyeliner visible against his brown skin. His face hung over his phone, big finger swiping the screen.

John watched him, and in watching discovered that he was no longer afraid of Stone. It was particularly strange because it had never occurred to him that he was afraid in the first place. Stone's eyes were glossy and appeared to have sunk deeper into his head, his hands were swollen. His skin had once been a sort of walnut—he had some native blood, Comanche maybe—but now appeared sallow, more yellow than brown. He wasn't the same man John had worked with at Site Nine, no longer the auteur with his godlike omniscience, no longer the man with the camera, John's eyes, the lens through which John suffered the world.

"I'm making a Spanish-language version of *Anna Karenina*," he said. "Today we shot the scene where Anna and Vronsky have sex for the first time." He dug out a macadamia. "I've got a Cameron Diaz look-alike in jodhpurs and a dog collar. It's bonkers. Absolutely out of this world."

A second bottle of champagne came out, along with a salad. Stone stood up a stalk of romaine and began to shave green fiber. "You've been avoiding me. All these years. But honestly, I get it."

"You weren't exactly looking for me."

"I get it, I do. The point is I suddenly have folks whispering in my ear."

"Who's whispering?"

"You bailed on us, okay, fine. I can live with it."

"I never bailed on anyone."

"You walked away, John. You walked away from me and you walked away from Ray. The work wasn't complete and you knew it."

"What happened with you and Peter?"

"I honest to God wanted to spit on you. You were needed, but where were you? Crying your eyes out in my—goddamn it, John—*my* house on St. Simons. That's where."

"Tell me about Peter."

Stone shook his head.

"You know he's dead," John said.

"The whole world knows. The great Internet billionaire prophet gone to that glorious URL in the sky. I assure you they were wailing and gnashing teeth outside every Apple store in Southeast Asia, these slick little two-point-oh humanoids. But honestly, fuck Peter."

"The thing is, I never understood what it was you were doing in California. No one ever said exactly."

"Because they were required to do that, right? Explain it to you, clear it with you. I was doing the groundwork for a biopic if it's any of your business." He gulped his champagne. "Have you even considered what the last few years have done to my heart? I pine for the days of nitroglycerin. Little brown tablets dissolving under the tongue."

"A biopic as in a film?"

"It was going to be high art. Think Leni Riefenstahl on mood enhancers."

"I never heard anything about a film."

"A side project until finally I got tired of his shit. Watching him run around the world like Obi-Wan off his Abilify. Now I've got three hundred hours of footage locked in a bank vault."

"This is from Site Nine?"

"There's no Site Nine footage. Not anymore. The day I heard rumor of a subpoena was the day I set fire to our life's work." He took a bite and swallowed. "Ray Bageant sends his greetings, by the way. He said last he saw you, you were passed out on a couch in some Gulf Coast village of the damned."

"That would have been Ray, not me."

"You do look like you've been living clean. The young father vibe."

John lifted Stone's glass of champagne. "I'm not that young anymore."

One of the honey-colored pool boys cannonballed into the water.

"You work in a building called the Truth Center," Stone said. "That occurred to me the other day. You and Professor Hadawi."

"I hardly knew the man."

"Yet you're here."

"I have no idea why I'm here."

Stone shook his head. "This isn't the John I know. You remember those nights in Minnesota? The pure unadulterated consumption of booze. You remember these?"

Stone appeared about to say more but instead pointed with his fork, flexed his jaw, and shifted it from side to side as if testing its utility. "You know the way Tolstoy writes it, Anna, she's a corpse, and our man Vronsky has murdered her. Goddamn Tolstoy. The man thinks he invented love."

"Is this just a reunion, Jimmy?"

"Versus what's the alternative?"

"The alternative would be—I don't know—that you're messing with me."

He put down his fork and leaned close enough for John to see the sparkles in his eyeliner. "You think I would hop a plane for the sake of a joke?" he said. "I completely reject that line of inquiry." He threw a cashew at him. "We have history, John. We have water under the bridge. And don't stare at me like that. So I drink pomegranate. Sixteen ounces a day. Big fucking deal. It explains my healthy glow."

"Jimmy."

"You want something to eat?"

"I want to go home."

"Home? Christ. Home he tells me. Where is home? Kindly provide me with some GPS coordinates and I'll cue the violins."

Around them daylight was fading into a band of salmon. John streaked one finger down the glass and watched the water run. Go home. Forget. It was Peter who said this. There is another life—it was Paul Éluard who said that. There is another life, but it is within this one.

"Look," Stone said, "I'm here because I need a favor. Your famed Professor Hadawi who decides to just go strolling off into the sunset."

"He was on a Soros Fellowship."

"In goddamn Yemen. I'm fully aware."

"Who are you working for, Jimmy? This film—"

"I already told you: Peter wouldn't commit."

"There was never any film."

"Fuck you, you don't know. And that has nothing to do with the reason we're both sitting here, now does it?"

"So why are we sitting here?"

"We're sitting here because I need a favor."

"Are you still one of the good guys?"

Stone fished out an almond and held it before him as if for inspection. "I need access to Hadawi's shared drive."

"They took his computer."

"They took the computer from his office. But there's more than that."

"The Georgia Bureau. You were standing there."

"There's a shared drive and I happen to know for a fact your very privileged, very progressive employers have conveniently failed to mention it. Hadawi could have used it, right? Did committee work on it? And if he did, no one would ever think to look there."

"Then get a court order."

"All that information buried in some obscure server. But you were on that committee, weren't you, John? You'd have access."

"You think any court in the state of Georgia is going to deny your request?"

"You know it doesn't work like that. Besides," Stone said, "I'm not asking the court. I'm asking you."

Night had fallen, darkness beyond the dewy glass. The bartender was a blonde girl with an ear full of loops and a sleeve of intersecting tattoos. She caught John looking at her, smirked, and for a moment he felt a slippery hit of misguided lust. The pouting mouth, her complete disregard.

"There's a mosque in Atlanta," Stone said finally. "The Masjid of Al-Islam. They've been on and off your campus."

"There was never any biopic, was there, Jimmy. But there was going to be a film."

Stone balanced his hands, palms up like scales. "Peter wanted things documented, this is true. What we were doing over there—it was necessary, John. I don't question its necessity. What if we'd achieved some psychic breakthrough, right? But Peter also knew the day might come when they would turn on us, try to bury us for doing exactly what we were told."

"We deserve to be buried."

Stone waved him off. "You don't know shit about it. You forget I was there. South of Canal. I saw the second goddamn plane and never, not a single fucking time since then have I questioned the necessity of what we did."

"Yet you still have the dreams."

"We all have the dreams. Fuck the dreams. It's the waking life I'm worried about. The walking around part."

"Ray Bageant said a long time ago someone would come looking for us."

"Well, they found me, John, and now they've found you."

"So I help out," John said. "I cooperate, and they forgive and forget?"

"That seems to be the crux of it."

"Who are we talking about here, the Justice Department?"

"Would it make a difference?"

"Did you really burn all the footage?"

"You're luring me toward a speech."

"Everything we did—Site Nine, everything we did for Peter—it was all perfectly legal. Every bit of it. I've read the opinions, the rulings. I know this for a fact."

"It's really more of a story than a speech."

"I need to go."

Stone put his hand on John's wrist to keep him from rising. "See I tried to join the army once, way back in the day I'm talking about. Wouldn't let me in, though. True story and here's the true part: my dick's too big. You understand the moral here?"

"I need to get back."

"The moral is this: you needed a dick back then and I had it. Jesus, I had it. But no one wants to be reminded of his own insufficiency, his paltriness when everyone starts whipping it out. No one wants the zealous hanging around queering the brew."

"I appreciate the drink."

"Hassan Natashe, John."

"I don't need to be reminded."

"Yeah, well, neither do the feds."

"Are you really working for them again? I don't see it."

"I had aspirations to be a folk singer. Somewhere things went a bit askew. I admit this."

"I need you to level with me."

"Level with you? We're all going to spend our golden years in some low-security prison, John. How's that for leveling with you? Basic cable and a starchy diet. We'll wear those denim slippers and complain about our bowels." He shook his head with what might have been disgust. "I make high-end porn in a Liberty City warehouse and you want me to level with you? I come home from work with pubic hairs on my goddamn sleeves. How's that for leveling with you?"

13.

Sunday morning Tess drove the children the half-hour to John's parents. The college sat at the first rise of the Blue Ridge, the gentle up-sweep of the mountains beginning at the edge of campus, scrub pine giving way to white pine, to the tall conifers and the bare skeletons of elms blighted a generation ago. Garrison was a college town, one of those pricey mountain enclaves featured in *Garden & Gun* and marketed as quaint. Which meant everything was overpriced and artisanal. But there was a good Thai place and a theater that ran Terrence Malick marathons. A used bookshop and a Lord & Taylor. You could get Rolfed, you could get trigger-point therapy, you could get organic hair-seeding.

And then you couldn't. A mile outside town there was a granite quarry and after that it was all gas stations and spills of kudzu, rebel flags and NO TRESPASSING signs that ran north until you hit the national park. The highway switching back on itself as it followed the course of a nearly dry river, a slim ribbon of water eddied and stagnant and attended by a flock of Canada geese.

She didn't mind the drive.

The boys were watching a *Wild Kratts* DVD in the back. Laurie was asleep.

Tess was in her running tights and Nikes, the idea being drop the kids off and go for a run while John's parents took them to church. Come back and shower—she had a change of clothes—and spend the afternoon together. She liked the visits. It had been months into their relationship before John had even mentioned them, and had he never endured whatever it was he had endured—and what about what *she* had endured?—they might never have come up at all.

She turned on the radio, kept it low so as not wake Laurie, then turned it right off when she realized it had disrupted the cartoon the boys were watching.

"Mah-om," that two syllable whine that had replaced her name.

"I know. I'm sorry."

"We're watching this," Wally said.

"I know. I just forgot."

"How far now?"

"Don't wake your sister, honey."

"How far is it?"

"Just a few minutes. Don't wake your sister, all right?"

He had left yesterday while Tess was still in bed, John she meant, dressing while she pretended to sleep. Which seemed to be a new activity between them—one pretending to sleep so as to avoid talking to the other. The single thing they shared. He was in Atlanta for a conference on something and she mostly believed him. She believed he had a reason to be in Atlanta, at least, conference or not. Beyond that, she didn't really care. He didn't sing in the morning anymore, and she didn't care about that either. It was strange to realize as much.

She turned the Odyssey off the highway onto a track of gravel road and thought of her grievances against Karla and Kayla.

Stupid, that alliteration of names. Sometimes she thought it stupid and she hated herself for that. The pettiness of resenting the dead. Like the wound of finding out there was someone—two someones—before you was simultaneously scabbed over and raw, because it can be that way.

But she didn't care about that either. What she cared about—what she told herself she cared about—was on the thumb drive, and along with her laptop, the thumb drive was in her bag, waiting on her.

✳

She sat on the screened porch and nursed Laurie from her right breast while she pumped her left. The verb was *express*. She expressed four ounces, she expressed five ounces. The boys were inside, bouncing around the kitchen, waiting for the moment they were released into the world. When Laurie was finished and the bottle full Tess would pass both over to John's mother and the five of them would leave for New Canaan Baptist Church and Tess would be alone in the house.

She listened to the children, the sound of their high voices going up like kites, that little clutched fear that came to her now and then that they would keep lifting, keep going higher, and she would be left alone, earthbound. Yet another stupid thought. If she wanted to worry about something real wouldn't it be handing her sons and seven-month-old daughter over to her aging mother-in-law for the next three hours?

Maybe, probably. There was a part of her that knew it wasn't the safest thing to do, but there was another, larger, part of her that saw both how much the woman needed it, and how much she, Tess, needed it, too. You want that balance, that place, she was always telling herself, where your self is both a part of and separate from your children. You want—

Laurie came off her nipple.

The bottle was full.

She fixed her too-tight jog-bra and shirt and went into the kitchen where Daniel and Wally sat in her father-in-law's lap, *The*

Tom and Jerry Show on the TV. Her mother-in-law took Laurie. Are we all ready now? Yes, I think we are. Turn that off, Thomas. Let's load up, boys. Turn that off, please. Come on, boys.

And they were all out the door and yes, I love you, and yes, I'll be here, and yes, have fun and listen to Nana and Papa, all right, boys? Kiss me one more time. And they did, and then they were gone, Tess alone on the front step waving goodbye as the car pulled away.

When they were out of sight she stood on the front steps, stretching her hamstrings and debating going back to John's old bedroom and plugging the USB drive into her laptop.

She tightened her laces.

What else might she find?

She was on the verge of finding out, and knowing as much, she sprang into the yard and onto the gravel of the road, running.

14.

James Stone's heart hurt. Not a metaphor in this case but some actual myocardial throb. Radial pain like a constellation of falling stars, as if he were finger-tipping his way around some distant nebula. It was a bad sign. He was probably dying—he granted the point—but dying would have to wait. He intended to find Reed Sharma first.

Thus the van.

Thus the fact Jimmy was driving the streets of midtown Atlanta looking for him.

The kid had gone too far, obviously, and Jimmy felt some responsibility—how could he not? Jimmy had encouraged him, teased him. Pushed him toward the sort of radical act Jimmy needed in order to make a move. Now he'd lost him. Not so much as a puff of smoke since he'd run into Reed's pseudo-girlfriend outside the duplex in Kirkwood. Which had been stupid. He realized now he never should have allowed himself to be seen. But that wasn't his worst mistake.

Jimmy's worst mistake, his *first* mistake, was failing to realize the kid was serious. His mistake was failing to realize all of it was serious, or if not serious, inevitable. That once you waded in hip-deep you couldn't exactly hop right out. It had its own engine, self-aware, self-propelled. But *serious* wasn't exactly the word. The kid was *malleable*. He wasn't a criminal but could easily enough be made into one. That was the game a lot of folks played, call it the conversion game. Take the lonely but harmless kid and make him harmful. Hand him a shoebox full of fake explosives and when he goes to plant them descend like an avenging angel. It was how it was done. Run a successful sting and next thing you knew you've climbed another pay grade.

But that wasn't Jimmy's game.

It was the reason he'd made a call in New York, couple of years ago this was, and had some fun at the kid's expense. The Voice of Goddamn Reason—Jimmy had made it up on the spot, convincing an actor buddy and his wife to help him out with a harmless little joke, and what a joke it had been. But all for the greater good of shaking the kid out of his wobbly passion.

But let's confess, Jimmy, to the fact that your little plan failed miserably.

Let's confess to the fact that the kid was now hanging around the wrong crowd at the wrong mosque and for it had acquired an FBI tail in the shape of a shapely pretend Emory coed calling herself Aida. Living in some sleazy Kirkwood duplex with torn window screens and an air conditioner made during the Nixon administration. Hosting gatherings of ShariaNow! and such bullshit.

Let's confess to the fact that this was Jimmy's fault.

Now Reed Sharma was undeniably missing. Jimmy had kept tabs on him for months but suddenly the kid was gone. The rumor was Reed had become Professor Hadawi's bitch and if that was the case that was a big-league problem. Hadawi was running his own shop and if the kid was involved he was playing a very serious game. More serious than the kid could handle, which he would realize sooner or later, and when he did . . .

Jimmy had this fear the kid was going to kill himself. A recurring nightmare replete with all the moving parts. The self-inflicted gunshot wound to the head. The suicide note of full-throated earnestness. Jimmy his reluctant confessor. Sometimes he composed the kid's mea culpa in his head, imagined him bleeding ink in some cheap motel by the interstate. An ice machine in the breezeway. The indoor-outdoor carpet soggy with rain. The kind of place that attached the room key to a giant spoon. The paper itself would be crumpled and then smoothed, as if he couldn't decide whether or not to pull the trigger, debating the *this* versus the *that* right up until the moment he removed the rear wall of his cranium.

Dear Jimmy,
I am sitting here.
I am sitting in a motel not far.
I am writing you because I don't know how else to explain things.

The rest would be boilerplate regret. A confession of getting involved with some nasty people.

Unconvincing bullshit. Bottom line: he got inside a Hefty bag with a pistol and blasted his way out.

At least that was how the nightmare played.

Fuck it, though. Jimmy wasn't worried at this point. If his heart exploded in the next twenty-four hours—and he thought it just might—it was all irrelevant. The professor could make his move, the kid could make his, and the world would know or it wouldn't. Either way, it was just another something floating in the cloud of unknowing. Mind traffic for the conspiracy theorists.

Some goddamn hipster honked at him.

He was on Peachtree, wheeling past a farmers' market and trying not to spill a pomegranate-and-prune concoction all over the Econoline van he'd rented from the fifth floor of a strip mall. Walked in to find the girl asleep on the couch with a ratty terrier in a rhinestone collar. It was no way to run a country, and the moment filled him with doubt, every second of their exchange draining his hope just a little. She had no idea who he was and when he handed her the reservation form she seemed to resent him for it. Puffy-eyed. Acid-washed jeans. Cute girl if she would just get off her ass and wash the sleep from her eyes.

But he had the van.

What he needed was the kid. He kept telling himself it was a moral obligation, kept running through the possible versus the merely probable. Possibly the professor had the kid squirreled away somewhere, a gear in some greater machine. Possibly they were at the mosque, prostrating themselves and trying on the fall line of suicide vests, the new cutesy things with Velcro straps like so, the pastel colors suitable for Easter Sunday. Then there was the possibility of a training camp somewhere in the mountains to the north. Jimmy was hearing rumors—it wasn't just Reed's bullshit bragging. It was possible the kid was there.

But it was equally possible he was off drunk with his buddies, haranguing high-school girls on the Internet and generally wasting his parents' money. Doing, you might say, what drifting twenty-somethings do.

But Jimmy was hearing otherwise.

Jimmy was hearing doom and gloom of the *Do not doubt this book* variety.

He was hearing monkey bars and bombs, and this was not a good thing to hear.

Whatever was going to blow up would blow very soon. The kid, the situation, Jimmy's actual physical heart—

He had his left arm out the open window, fingers tingling.

Somebody tell me please I'm not dying here, somebody convince me.

And if his heart didn't get him his bowels would. But he didn't want to think about that. He was trying hard not to consider the fact that he was badly constipated, trying hard not to allow it to affect his worldview.

Another horn.

The intersection full of assholes.

Women in knee boots carrying their heirloom squash and what the fuck is artisanal okra anyway, can someone tell me, please, I'm asking here?

At this point he didn't even know where his hotel was, but that was beside the point. The point was to drive around, to get a feel for things. The point was that the kid was going to just saunter by, all innocent-like, and Jimmy would be on the evening flight to Miami, conscience assuaged. He'd get back to work, throw himself into it. All that footage of Keyes. He was serious about a film, sort of serious. The Gatsby of Silicon Valley. An Internet robber baron in skinny jeans and ironic tie. Let's not hide it under a bushel—that was his worldview. He had Keyes on film and now that he was dead the footage had that ghost story appeal. He could make the movie, sure, but then what?

Then nothing.

Retire to Sedona. Get his Obamacare and watch the sunset. He could sell the place on St. Simons for three times what he paid for it, drop the money in the bank and live off the 6 percent interest. Unlike John he wasn't haunted by what they'd done at Site Nine. What they'd done was exactly what had to be done and if mistakes were made, well, fuck it. Land of the free and home of the brave, right?

Another horn.

Did they understand the cosmological implications of the finger over here?

They honked again.

It was so freaking common in cities, these constant horns. He liked the countryside. He liked rural places where the honking of a horn was justification for the employment of small arms.

He palmed the Glock that rested inside his jacket, pulled to another stoplight, waited.

The kid was out there. The kid was going to walk right by.

Except when he looked up it wasn't the kid walking by, but my God—

Crossing the intersection without a care in the world was Professor Edward Hadawi.

And damn if he didn't appear to be in quite the hurry.

15.

The trail started a half mile back toward the highway, an overgrown footpath that angled off the gravel, the ivy and sumac only beginning to thin in the gathering cool of fall. The trailhead had a laminated topographical map, a swirl of yellow and red and green paths that paralleled the dark ovals that marked elevation. Tess ran the yellow, a meandering loop of nine miles, but so long as she went right at every junction it eventually took her back to here.

It was National Forest and she saw no one. She liked that, liked the way she could pass through stands of black walnut and dogwood, thickets of mountain laurel and flame azalea. There was an aloneness to it, but she wouldn't exactly call it loneliness. The loneliness was for John. Also the distrust.

He had about him some hint of evasion, an air of offensive friendliness, a sort of preemptive concern. The questions he was always asking—they were practical questions, the right questions: feedings, naps. But Tess wasn't buying it. There was something withholding about him, the way he eased around the corners of things unsaid.

She stopped at the top of a ridge, the mountains spread before her. Stopped her watch and ate one of the two vanilla GU packets she kept zipped in the waistband of her running tights, drank half of the eight-ounce water bladder. Zipped everything back up and started along the ridge before she could get stiff from standing.

Let the downgrade of the slope carry her, dew flicking onto her shoes and calves.

Fog over the trees.

At night she felt his toes moving. Or maybe this was the running. The running brought with it a frightening lucidity, it always had. But there were days now it crossed some invisible bridge and carried her into a land of paranoia. Imagined grievances that would become real if only she could figure out what the hell they were. If that even made sense. Which she knew it didn't.

Neither did going left when the trail forked at the bottom of the ridge.

To stay right was to get back, to know her way. To go left, to step off the yellow trail onto the red or green was to acknowledge some form of disorder. It was to make a mistake. But she did it anyway.

The path re-entered the trees, the bristling white pines, the soft-needled path. Darker here, cooler. When it leveled off she picked up her pace and it felt a little as if someone was behind her, as if she were being chased. Not by the men she kept seeing, but by something less—*corporeal* was the word, ridiculous as it sounded. She ran hard through a field of wildflowers and black flies, crossed a footbridge, the creek a hush of fast-moving water, started up another rise.

John—

Sometimes she saw in him a man engaged in exotic danger, some cutting-edge project meant to propel humankind. Other days he seemed like a man consciously broken, but working hard to hide it. A man who counseled girls with eating disorders or handed out pamphlets explaining the legal intricacies of date rape. A man working to counteract an entire planet's worth of unhealthy body images.

There were nights he stroked her nipple for what seemed hours, just one nipple. The motion was circular and singular. Never the prelude to sex. Just this meditative act that seemed to ground him physically: John in this bed, in this life.

She turned around at the top of the next rise, a little confused or maybe—

Not lost, the word wasn't lost. Though turning around she knew she'd have difficulty finding her way back to anything recognizable. For the last forty minutes she had made lefts and rights, no pattern to it, no deliberation beyond the vague idea that she wanted to disappear for a while. She thought of the whales in the bay, that missing day—what had happened, besides the obvious, of course? Besides the fact they had somehow found their way home. She'd been running for ninety-three minutes now. Even on the rugged trail time enough to have completed her run.

She ran another half-hour and ate the other GU packet, left maybe an ounce of water in the plastic bladder if only for motivational purposes. Started jogging again, a little slower now, observant. She wanted that hit of panic, the blood spiked with adrenalin. But it never came. In its place was a detached coolness that carried her down into another clearing, one she hadn't seen before because there on the edge of a creek—the creek she'd crossed earlier, or a different creek?—stood what appeared to be a wooden outhouse.

Maybe slightly larger, she thought as she grew closer. Maybe a cabin of some sort, the plank siding a deep shade of moisture and age and lichen and moss. She stopped her watch and stood on the clearing's edge. The outhouse, the cabin, the whatever it was sat preposterously close to the creek, the denuded bank nearly undercutting one of the cinder-block supports, and though the land must have once been cleared it had grown back unchecked. A roadbed had sprouted saplings, wisps of pine that rose to her waist and waved like hands when the breeze moved across the field. Then she realized she was looking at the old home place, the original cabin.

Inside was a shrine of some sort, the walls tacked with crucifixes and loops of beaded jewelry hung from roofing nails. Photos too warped to make sense of. There was a bench and a bowl of what she thought might be holy water, or maybe water from the creek, whatever difference it made. There was a kneeling cushion, and to kneel there was to stare up at the largest crucifix, the one mounted on the wall. Or to not look, to kneel and not look, though eventually she came to look. Eventually, she came to make the sign of the cross against her body, though she thought it more out of superstition than belief.

The tightening in her legs brought her back.

She crawled out into a brilliant day, no idea how long she had been inside. Maybe two minutes, maybe two hours. But the day was alive, resurrected in a cloud of butterflies. The fog gone and the sun blinding, white and nearly directly overhead. Birds sang. The creek ran.

She felt her skin prickle. That feeling of someone near her, of someone watching her.

The weight of some bodiless threat.

She made no move. It seemed important to remain calm, still, one of those decisions you'd look back on and thank God you didn't panic. She drank the last swallow of her water, and ridiculous as it was she felt a thousand eyes watching her, or one eye, and then she felt it so near it seemed to scrape against her arm and then crawl over her, and for a moment she saw not the sliver of creek she could see before her but the sliver of road she had glided right off. Karla, she meant. John's wife. The sliding a long ache, something more than mere psychics, what she felt. What Tess felt was the presence that had sat with them, mother and daughter, the presence that had held them, and, even as they took flight, refused to let go.

✳

It took another hour to get back to the main road and another fifteen minutes beyond that to get back to John's parents. Whatever bliss she had experienced, whatever moment she might have had, was gone now. Spiraled down the drain of hunger and fatigue. Her throat was dry and her feet hurt—there would be blood in her pinked socks. She felt her blood sugar scrape bottom. She'd run for almost four hours but walked the last 200 meters, too exhausted to register anything more than a faint relief at the sight of the house, her van and her father-in-law's car parked before it.

John's father was in the kitchen and he jumped up as she entered.

"There you are. We were just about to get worried."

"I'm sorry."

"You're okay? Sit down, Tess."

"I'm fine. I'm sorry about this."

"Sit down, honey. Let me tell Glenda. She had me driving up and down the road looking for you."

"Are the children okay?"

"The children are fine. Let me tell Glenda."

The children were in the backyard making pinecone bird feeders. You spread the peanut butter, sprinkle on the birdseed. Out the window Tess could see her mother-in-law wore Laurie in the BabyBjörn, the straps splayed to accommodate her wide frame.

Her father-in-law walked out, spoke to his wife, and a moment later returned.

"I didn't mean to be gone so long."

"I'm just glad you're okay," he said. "You got lost?"

"Yes. No." She shook her head. "I don't know. I guess I did."

"Not much up there but trees and wild hog. Deer."

"I'm really sorry."

"I drove up and down the road honking the horn."

"It's okay. What's this?"

"I didn't know where else to go."

"It's okay. What is this you're watching?" she said, because she had just noticed it. CNN playing on the small screen where a few hours before it had been Tom and Jerry. "Is this?"

"Yeah."

"Oh, my God." The TV was muted but it was plain enough. Another video from Syria, another video from ISIS. The hooded jihadi, a man in an orange jumpsuit. Middle-aged, down on his knees. He showed the knife, the standing man, the swift parabola of blade, and then it cut back to the studio, it cut to commercial. She collapsed into the wicker chair, let herself sink into the patterned cushion, salt lines describing her mouth, legs mud-flecked, chiggers and thorns caught in the fabric of her tights.

"They killed him?" she asked.

Her father-in-law pressed the power button. Out the window the children and Glenda were crossing the yard, coming to her, coming to Tess.

"Cut his head off," he said.

"Is this the American?"

"British guy. An aid worker. A real humanitarian it sounded like."

"But it's not the American?"

"The bastards," he said. "Killing a man over there trying to save their starving children."

16.

Sunday morning John drove to the cemetery. He'd known ever since he agreed to meet Stone this would happen, the proximity, the gravitational pull. He wasn't thinking about what Stone had said, his offer or his threat or whatever it was. John had spent the evening at a Red Roof Inn off 285 considering nothing else. But when he woke it seemed not so much silly as settled, decided so that it became the least of his concerns. Beside the prospect of visiting Karla's grave it appeared paltry, and it was. He knew what he was doing with Stone. It was everything else that was confusion.

He drove north on I-75 toward Peach Creek, felt the tug of the exit before he saw it.

Despite living an hour away it had been years since his last visit. There was no reason to come, besides the greatest possible reason. But reason in the shadow of grief always appears small, to the extent it appears at all.

He drove Main Street and it was *tienda*, pizza joint, Vape Shoppe, E-CIGS HERE, Western Wear, boarded window, Thrifty's Discount Drugs, boarded window, LEASE THIS SPACE CHEAP . . . FOR RENT . . . FOR SALE. Folks inside with their SNAP cards and reruns of Barney Fife. The Kuntry Kupboard in the fellowship hall of what had been the First Baptist before they rebuilt near the interstate. The brick chimney of the old Turner's mill. The old rail freight lines, four tracks narrowing to two and leading to the high loading bays, dockless and opening onto cracked asphalt, weeds, trash. The cover of a softball split like a hickory shell. The All-America City sign no one even bothered to shoot.

It shouldn't have surprised him. Peach Creek had never been one of the hip left-leaning suburbs that ring Atlanta with their coffee shops and baby strollers and MARTA stop. This was red clay Georgia, a part of the state too distant to even attempt to crawl toward the city. But it had tried just the same, and crippled itself in the process.

The city had declared bankruptcy and there were no municipal services—no fire or police, no garbage pickup. The local elementary school had been taken over by the state. The roads potholed and the traffic lights dark or blinkered, forever flashing.

A few gas stations were still open.

A 7-Eleven. A Scotchman.

Yellow and red condom wrappers tangled and blossoming in the limbs of a dead shrub.

It was like a natural disaster except it wasn't natural, and anyone with the means to leave had left. The people with pensions or savings had gone to Chattanooga or Atlanta proper. The rest, the elderly, the poor, the folks who would rather die clinging to what they had earned—they stayed.

His parents had left, of course. That continued to amaze him.

Packed the house, held a big yard sale, and drove to the old home place as if they'd never lived anywhere else. Out of the world of fast-food heat lamps and the power line cancer clusters on to what? Back to the world they thought they knew, he supposed. The world they had both been raised in and by. Never thinking that the last thirty years had changed them, never thinking the selves they carried home were no longer the selves they'd carried out.

The last time John had visited alone had been months ago. Tess thought he took the boys there for breakfast but he didn't, couldn't, if you got down to it. He took them to the pancake place in town and then to his office where they played games on his computer. Once, he'd driven them all the way to Sevierville where he sat outside the 24 Hour Fitness where his daughter worked the desk. Wally wanting to know what they were doing here and weren't they getting out and John just shushing his son, barely hearing him because through the angle of glass he could see Kayla, ponytailed and smiling. He sat there until she stepped out of sight and then dropped the car into reverse, drove back in a glaze of uncried tears, downshifting through the rust of memory. Got the boys Frosties at a Wendy's in Dalton to buy their silence.

But his parents . . .

His father watched old NBA games on ESPN Classic. The Celtics—Bird, McHale, Danny Ainge—versus the Lakers, versus Magic and Kareem. *He's a Muslim, ain't he, son? I never much liked Kareem.* It wasn't racism, not exactly. They were his parents and what they were witness to was the falling away of everything they had ever known: observers trying to keep track of a universe that wouldn't quit undoing itself, wouldn't quit tearing apart the only world they had known. And they weren't bitter. This amazed John, this cool acceptance, and only with time did he come to see it for what it was: a shedding, a last (necessary?) step before one is given over fully to death.

They watched the Jazz versus the Bulls, the Sixers, the fuzzy images of a floating Julius Erving. When his father's diverticulitis calmed they watched the vaunted Knicks, Bill Bradley and crew decades before they leveled the old Garden. The brilliant blue and orange. Clyde Frazier postgame in an aquamarine suit.

His father had exchanged three fingers for the mortgage on the Peach Creek house and the bulk of John's college tuition, and the idea, John's idea, had always been law, something useful. *I'll come back. I'll take care of both of you* and he carried that line in his head long after he knew it wasn't true. He wasn't coming back. He wasn't going to take care of anyone beyond himself.

It was Christmas senior year when he told them he planned to go to divinity school. He talked for a while about his interest in Christology and Rahner's conception of the Trinity. He mentioned Bonhoeffer and Óscar Romero, Gustavo Gutiérrez and liberation theology. Thomas Merton and Dorothy Day. As if he might name-drop his way to their blessing.

But there was never any doubt of their blessing. They listened. They didn't interrupt. They were believers. But more than that, they were his parents.

"And you want to study theology?" his father asked.

"I do."

"But not be a preacher?"

"No, sir."

His father's lined face appeared soft, his fingers—the fingers left to him—knotted in his lap.

"Well, if it's important to you," he said, "I think you should do it. Glenda?"

"Of course he should. Of course you should, John."

That was who they were, it was who they remained. They were his mamma and daddy. He was their boy. They'd sacrificed everything for him and seemed grateful for having had the opportunity.

It was at divinity school that he became interested in trauma theory—Judith Herman and Cathy Caruth, a natural progression because what was the Crucifixion but a great trauma? What was Christianity but collective PTSD?—and when he finished his MA he decided against a doctorate in theology and instead went into psychology. After that it was teaching and writing and somehow it all had led to watching. Working for Peter Keyes. Sitting alone in that tiny control room at Site Nine.

Yet another reason he couldn't go back.

Yet another reason he was unable to sit there while his mother wore her housecoat and made grilled cheese or slapped out salmon patties.

The game on the TV until the game went off.

Ulcers, his father said, a glass of Pepsi balanced on his thigh.

The game and then the wars.

They sat with the TV on and watched the wars.

Another violent day in Iraq . . . a bloody day for coalition forces in Afghanistan . . .

John and his father and his mother, and all around them were ghosts.

But no one said Karla. No one said Kayla.

✳

He drove around town, past the propane tanks and mobile homes, past the Big Lots. He saw the large in their support hose and muumuus, the ones riding electric scooters. But there were also people made lean with need: the garbage pickers, folks stripping the copper from abandoned buildings, stealing the air handlers right out from under the window. The streets felt burned with their hunger, deserted. What was left were Pentecostal churches and health clinics addressing diabetes and Lyme disease. Dairy Queen and Dollar General. The plastic cutlery and wire-caged lights. The miles of chainlink. He passed a Bob Evans marooned in the cattails along the highway shoulder. He passed his old high school, abandoned now, though he heard things still. The sound of the lanyard ringing against the metal flagpole. A wet towel dragged across the locker room tiles. There was graffiti. There was gang violence. Los Zetas wannabes selling pot and OxyContin. White kids hooked on meth and Aryan bullshit.

He drove by their old church. A vast circular structure with an arched roof, a sort of coliseum that had once housed a congregation of several hundred singing evangelicals. Much of his childhood had been spent in a smaller sanctuary, bulldozed years prior to make way for this prefab temple.

The Sunday service was going on as he passed, but he'd seen enough. Eventually, he had. Eventually, he made it to the cemetery.

How could he not?

And what more need be said?

That he sat in the car for a half-hour, Bojangles coffee going cold in his hands? It was a small green rise, a knoll just off a two-lane road, no more than a hundred graves. The grass needed cutting. She was in the back corner, in the shade of the pines. There were birds in the low boughs of the trees and she would have liked that, the little house sparrows and towhees, but they meant nothing to him. None of it did.

The grave was marked with surveyor's line for the track-hoe operator.

He had no use for this information.

The casket was lowered on belts.

What was he supposed to do with such knowledge?

Sometimes he imagined his daughter beside his wife, how close it had been. Imagined the dimensions of her foreshortened grave, the abbreviated length—just imagining it kept him away. As if he might top the rise to find the past had up and changed, that Kayla had somehow slipped in beside her mother, obedient to the end.

As for Karla, men would see her and wonder, they would hope. Her jewelry opalescent. Her fingers long. She was serious and focused and abundant in her care which seemed to spill into love with everyone she met. Little things. She loved birds. She loved owls and swallow-tailed kites. She loved large dogs. She knew everyone's name. She would say your name, repeat it. You came to dinner and it would be John this or John that, and it was more than seductive— though it was certainly that. It was kind. It was the simplest of kindness, her knowing, her awareness, and what was left of it was now locked inside an aluminum casket.

He thought of the time when she kept dropping things, this time when things seemed to scatter from her hands. Glasses, keys, books. What was this a sign of, this inattention, this failure—as he had sometimes imagined it—of reflex? This misrouting somewhere between fingers and brain.

The night at dinner she twice spilled her water or the way her purse would skate out onto the kitchen counters. *Dear Lord, again! Why am I so clumsy?* John had imagined it something physical but it seemed now something more essential. It was like part of her was losing another, smaller, part. She was shedding that physicality, maybe, that part that would keep her soul from lifting while her body flung itself over the guardrail and into the winter trees. He hoped that was true, though much of him suspected it wasn't.

He stood on the cemetery's edge, and then went back to his car, back to his cold coffee.

What made him go back to the church he didn't know. Maybe it was just seeing it, the driving past and all that it conjured. He'd been married there, in the old sanctuary before it was plowed and realizing such made him consider the idea of breakage. That he'd lost his wife when a guardrail failed, lost his daughter in the boozy grief of after when his nerves failed. His father had lost most of his left hand when the shield on a drill press came loose.

All this failure, as if it could be an accident.

As if they could be anything but a people around whom things fell apart.

✳

The service was over by the time he got there, the building empty and locked. He stood at the front doors with his hands cupped to his face, but could see nothing beyond the dim foyer. It was time to go home, time to do what it was he'd promised Stone he would do. But he wasn't ready yet. The marquee promised a service at six—JOIN US FOR AN EVENING OF PRAISE!—and he decided he would get some food and come back for it.

He found a sports bar on Lee Street and settled in. Two-for-one drafts while the Falcons made a mess of things against the Saints, an interception, a fumbled punt. Seven-dollar burgers but he wasn't hungry. He drank his lunch and arrived back at the church leaning into himself, consciously overcorrecting against a world that lurched off plumb.

Welcome, welcome.

One usher shook his hand, double-clasp, firm.

Another gave him a bulletin.

He was welcome here, they all wanted him to know that. How welcome he was.

But more than welcome, he felt sad. He had been in New Life's current, and surely last, incarnation only twice before, many years ago, but even with such scant familiarity he knew the place had fallen into a sort of fatal decline. The fraying seat cushions. The faded carpet and shuttered coffee kiosk.

And of course the people, less than he'd ever seen. At the height of its dizzying power the church had shepherded a flock of 700 or 800 white folk. The working class like his parents with their family reunions and college-savings plans. The management class with their weekend barbecues and trips to Six Flags or Stone Mountain. All of it for Jesus. All of it in His Name. All of it to the glory of God and Reagan and Lee Greenwood singing "God Bless the USA" while the Blue Angels came screaming low and tight over the lights of Fulton County Stadium, Dale Murphy with his hand over his heart. Paul Harvey on the radio—his father always listened—and *that's the rest of the story.*

But that night the cavern of the sanctuary held no more than 200 people, most of them brown. The scattered white people, the few, like his parents, who might remember New Life in all its moderate Republican glory were old, or older, at least, than the families of immigrants from Mexico and El Salvador, the Philippines or Thailand.

He sat exactly where they had always sat, and how strange, that sense of orientation. Right aisle, a quarter of the way down to the altar. John recognized it from the church he knew as a child. Or sensed it at least, this spatial recognition passing as some kind of holy spirit. A few of his parents' friends came by to ask about his mom and dad and then to brag on him, John the Professor, John the Author. Better, he supposed, than the other things he'd been called: the Absent Father, the Drunk.

When the service started he spotted Erin Porter almost immediately. She was on stage singing, a lone adult face in a sea of children, a choir of some sort. Some after-school social club for inner-city youth. Fifty or so ten-year-olds singing "Hallelujah, Christ is King!" and there, at the back, stood Erin, urging them on.

They'd had how many classes together? All of them, really.

She was the smart girl with the curled arm, her left arm, slim and short, the fingers tucked as if gripping something only she could see. It wasn't the arm of a baby. It was the arm of a child—it belonged to something that might yet be. It was the slightest of birth defects, mostly hidden by her clothes, but it made every encounter charged and John remembered an awkward moment in ninth grade when she'd turned to him in sixth-period English to ask if you capitalized spring. As in the season. But he'd heard something else, some reference to the braces he wore, the coils that hinged his jaw, and in a strange pantomime had pointed to his own mouth, meaningfully, he'd thought, but more like a captive ape trying to communicate, and she had sat there confused, shaking her head slowly, not daring to speak.

That was as close to friendship as they'd ever come, which was to say not at all. She'd been closer to Karla. Though they'd eventually drifted apart, they were nearly inseparable their last two years of high school. He kept looking at her, barely aware of it, and eventually she caught him staring at her, and she mouthed a single word: *you!* Half-recognition, half-accusatory, so that after the service when she rushed up to him he had no idea what to expect.

"You," she said again, "I had a dream about you."

*

They drove to the Mexican place off General Johnston Boulevard, scene of the crime for how many Friday nights John couldn't say. But the place was nearly empty. Just John and Erin and a few scattered families.

"I work for a services agency," she said. "Children mostly, but sometimes the parents, too. More and more the parents."

She operated out of a strip mall, the dress shops and noodle restaurants and nail salons mostly gone. They were privately funded by a foundation in the northeast. Reading programs. Nutrition. Midnight basketball leagues and bags of fruit to take home over the weekends. Lots of talk with the children about the four food groups. But now the parents were coming in as well. Asking questions. Trying to be—but mostly incapable of being—parents. So she was running classes on that too. Changing diapers, cooking, serving meals that didn't come in paper bags. Money management. Time management.

Pain management, she said, that's what it comes down to in the end.

"I feel sometimes like I'm alone here." She was on her second margarita, arms on the table, earnest. "You read about sociological trends. How everyone is fleeing to the coasts and it's true. Except what they mean by *everyone* is *everyone with money*. The rest are stuck here. Most of them are grateful, let me point out, to have what they have. Really, it's only the white people who are gone." She looked at him. "Did I hear you were out in California at one point?"

"San Francisco, but not anymore."

"See," she said, "see."

She was joking. It wasn't accusatory; mostly it wasn't accusatory.

The food came out and the place started to fill and soon enough all around them were people laughing and eating and John thought how strange was his sense of things. Or perhaps how wrong. Since he'd arrived he'd registered only great sorrow, the gray film of his former life. The sidewalk litter of meth baggies, the no-knock raids by the county SWAT. Men with face tattoos and forearms that read INFIDEL. But here everyone appeared happy.

"I know, right?" Erin said catching his eye. She leaned closer, a little drunk. "You know why, don't you? It's because all the white people are gone. They're happy because all the white people have left. It's just you, John."

"What about you?"

"Me? No," she said, "not me. I have this"—she eased forward the twist of her left arm—"which means people stare at me. Which means I'm just like them." She smiled. "Sorry. It's just you, and you're on your way out the door."

"Am I?"

"Where are you now? Someone said you were teaching up at Garrison."

"Counseling mostly. A little teaching."

Erin started telling him about old friends. About her parents, both of whom had passed in the last two years. When your parents are gone, she said, it isn't so much that you lose the sense that that one sure love has gone out of your life, though that's certainly true. What you're forced to part with is the myth that you can go home, that you have a home, beyond, I mean, that small—and suddenly you realize just how small it is—that small place you've scratched out for yourself.

"But you are home," he said.

"Not really," she said. "Or maybe when I'm working with the kids, maybe that's home. These transient lives. Maybe when I'm with them, yes, maybe."

She was near tears, yet still managed to laugh.

"Oh God, John. You're back."

"Briefly."

"Too good for us, I know."

"That's it exactly."

"You know I downloaded your book."

"You didn't."

"I did. I'm serious. I liked the chapter titles."

"You're making fun of me."

"Isn't there one called like 'Blood & Treasure?'"

"Chapter Five."

"Wow. Okay, so yes, now I am making fun of you. But just a little."

John was sipping his beer, already thinking ahead to the drive home and what waited there. But Erin was on her third fishbowl margarita, bright-eyed and swaying, her mouth a wet flower. Little crystals of sea salt between their hands, which were almost touching. She was still talking about her work, talking about old school friends, talking about everything else except Karla. Which was clearly what she was talking about. And then it came out of her, memories, stories, things John had never known. The day Erin and Karla went to the Sam's Club and bought a pallet of SunnyD, the logic being endless screwdrivers, right? Or the trips to Lake Lanier, swimming off the dock where the lifeguard with the Clash tattoo was stationed. They both loved Depeche Mode. Why was there not a greater appreciation for Depeche Mode? Karla always wanting to know this. And let's not even talk about the Cure.

"I loved the Cure," John said.

"I still do. I have them in my car right now, and—oh, God, I'm sorry."

"It's okay."

"No, really, I didn't mean to just start in."

"It's all right."

"I still think of Karla. Probably more than I should."

"Me, too."

She squeezed one of his hands. "Of course you do, honey. Of course you do. How is Kayla these days?"

"Fine. Up in Sevierville."

"How old is she now, twenty?"

"Twenty-one."

"Legal. Wow. We're getting old."

"We are old."

"I guess we sort of are maybe. I don't know." She touched her drink, but didn't raise it. Just touched the stem, gently, and then let it go. "I still think of Karla," she said again.

✳

The old ways. They drove around the neighborhood listening to *Disintegration* and drinking red wine some well-intentioned 7-Eleven clerk had bothered to chill. Erin mildly drunk but refusing to give up the wheel. Like there was anyone out there on the road to even hit. At best—at worst—she would wind up ramming a telephone pole and killing them both. He thought it might happen. He felt like Karla, beside her old friend, windows down as the night cooled. A part of him wanted to never leave, to sit there somewhere in the late '80s, waiting for Roxette to start singing because "it must have been love," right? What else could it have been?

"Let's drive somewhere. It's Friday, John."

"It's not Friday."

"It's Friday," she said. "I'm in love."

But there was nowhere to go and eventually they gave up.

She dropped him back at his car in the church parking lot, gave him a hug and her number. Call me when you come back, *if* you come back. Sure, right, of course.

Was he sober enough to drive home?

Was she?

She waved him off.

"Hug that girl of yours for me," she said.

He waited until she pulled onto the road before he started north, John having said not a word about Tess or the children. Erin having said not a word about her dream.

An hour later he parked outside the Truth Center and let himself into his office. There were nineteen e-mails between Professor Hadawi and the Masjid of Al-Islam mosque in Atlanta, each written through the shared drive used by the Values Council on which John had sat. He didn't bother reading them, just copied them into a single file addressed to James Stone.

He didn't much care about Stone's threats of the Justice Department.

He didn't much care about the idea of redemption either.

Still, he sent the file.

17.

Jimmy Stone gave the professor a three-block head start before he pulled onto the road and followed. Hadawi was headed for a parking garage and when he came out Jimmy tucked a few cars behind him and followed him to the on-ramp. As soon as he headed north on I-75 Jimmy knew what was up.

Those rumors of a camp in the mountains.

The monkey bars and bombs.

He took a sip of his pomegranate—three parts pomegranate to one part prune on account of his constipation—screwed on the cap and merged into traffic.

All right, boss. Take me to Reed.

He stayed close, but not too close. It felt like some big-game expedition: the lion in its natural habitat. He'd only met the professor a few times. All in passing, but even in passing you sensed the way his presence shaded reality, pushed larger, otherwise independent causal chains in Lord only knew which direction. You could never say how, of course. But to meet him was to know the ellipse of your own orbit had somehow been altered. It went a little this way, a little that. You didn't know if it was good or bad until later, and maybe you never did, and it didn't much matter anyway.

The man was a legend and the truth was, Jimmy admired him. He was one of those people born to run the world because what it needed most was running.

This world. Right here, Jimbo. The one you're sitting in, you bottled-up bastard.

They kept going north, the professor leading, Jimmy following. He wanted to stop, needed to stop, but it wasn't going to happen.

Still, his stomach—

This was fast becoming a greater concern than his explosive heart. The bottom line was, he needed to shit more than he needed to not die. Six days. Going on a week despite the laxatives and juice. Not that he was completely closed up. He couldn't sneeze without needing a change of underwear. But that sort of leakage didn't cut it. It failed to *satisfy*, to summon the simple poetry of defecation. He felt cosmically stuck and how could it not reflect the state of his soul? This withholding of contaminants.

But the thing was about to play out and that would be it.

The moment he found Reed he was on the first flight back to Miami. He knew a guy in Coral Gables that did the best colonics outside of greater Los Angeles. No more fooling around. Twice today he'd pulled into service stations and begged the bathroom key, all for the privilege of sitting fruitlessly on the bowl, forehead moist, almost heaving, almost in tears for the never-ending, ever-loving terror of it all.

But he knew the kid was up there and that the thing would play out if only he could hang in a few more days. He chugged his juice, tongue purple, teeth as stained as his spiraling heart.

Take me to him, Boss.

18.

It was only when they were home from John's parents, only when Tess had bathed the boys and nursed Laurie, everyone in bed except John who was still not back, only when she put on her nightgown and took up the book she'd gotten from the library, another book on whales, it was only then that Tess sat up in bed, panicked at the thought she'd forgotten something, only then that she remembered the USB drive.

But it was still in her bag.

It was still waiting for her.

Part Two

Hands of God

19.

Tess kept not plugging it in, the thumb drive.

Not plugging it in, but constantly aware of it.

Somewhere in her mind an hourglass was sifting down toward zero, toward the empty globe that would contain nothing beyond her knowing, the moment she would give up on the life around her and look. But she refused to give up, and because of that she refused to look.

Meanwhile, the leaves fell and the days shortened and mostly life was unchanged. The wooly lamplight of dusk, yellowing evening as if scratching the edge of some greater night, and then the day was gone and it was truly night. Mornings she took the boys on long walks, the grass full of spiderwebs, silvered and wildly complex. The webs changed as they moved, revealed themselves. She named things: ivy, caterpillars, leaves holed with potato bugs.

A new county detention center was going up and she took the boys to see it. A modular construction of steel girders and prebuilt cells. They'd wrap the thing in aluminum siding and plant crepe myrtles and if this wasn't exactly life, it wasn't necessarily death either. Which, okay, think of it like that, Tess.

"Mom, is it true when I sneeze the dust goes into space and forms a star?"

"What, baby?"

"A star." This was Wally calling from the back seat on the way back from Whole Foods, Tess trying to merge with the video player on and Laurie crying. "Dad said."

She was crying a lot. They watched a video of a blue whale and its calf, but then a pod of orca attacked the baby and she had to cut it off, both boys crying and then Laurie crying too. She cut out Halloween decorations for Wally's class with tears in her eyes, pumpkins and friendly ghosts. The same when she made cupcakes. She watched *Cosmos* on Fox with Wally and after he fell asleep cried through the last half-hour and it wasn't just how small we are—if you mapped all 13.8 billion years on a twelve-month calendar all of recorded human history was the last fourteen seconds—that was part of it, but that wasn't all. It was how everything looked like something else. The universe a honeycomb. The Milky Way a nautilus shell.

In the one-year-calendar-thing Jesus was born five seconds ago but God was eternal. So how could you know a God of something so big and so old? But also—given the resemblance, the overwhelming sense that in the structure of things was some base truth—how could you not?

She was whimpering into her pillow when Dr. Neil deGrasse Tyson signed off and Wally woke to ask *what's wrong, Mommy?*

Great question.

It was possible that she was developing—maybe had already developed—some chemical dependence on the man in the basement. Checking his status online, watching and rewatching the black flag ISIS murder porn, and each time her brain delivering a hit of serotonin or dopamine or whatever substance was necessary for the continuation of Tess's harmonious existence.

She did the laundry, folded clothes, put away the clothes, and then checked the computer.

Took another HoneyBaked Ham from its crinkle of gold foil (*just thought I'd drop something by*), and then checked the computer.

Made lunch, brushed teeth, said prayers. Then checked the computer. Sometimes she checked it in between each act, always guiltily, always secretly so that it was:

Life.

Computer.

Life.

Computer.

Except you couldn't say they were separate. The organic white-cheddar cheese puffs and cartoons meant to convey fluid gender roles. The blonde Elsa hair extension Daniel had taken to wearing everywhere. The trip to the butterfly garden off New Canaan Road with its greenhouse of black-eyed Susans and snowball bushes and she can't name a single butterfly except monarch and that's just a guess. Was it not all a product of the man in the basement's tenuous hold on life?

One day she made another appointment with the Christian therapist and then canceled it at the last minute because reflected light—seriously?

The next Sunday she took the children back to John's parents. Driving home past the trampolines and paintball fields, wire spools tipped on their sides for cover, she stopped to get gas, and when she walked inside the convenience store where the Pakistani clerk sat bored and waiting she heard a faint click within her skull, as if a lock had turned, but only barely. Instead of screaming, she turned and walked out, straight into the awful Pat Glenn.

"Easy, girl."

"Sorry, I just—"

He looked at her shoes and running tights.

"You got to quit running in them woods," he said. "Bow season."

*

It was a Saturday in early November when her sister called.

"Are you ducking mom's calls?"

Tess was on the glassed sun porch, the children playing Legos in the living room.

"What? Did she say that?"

"Basically, yeah. So are you?"

"Maybe," Tess said. "But she only called like twice."

"You're not contributing to her sound mental health, Tess."

"I know."

"I'm quoting here."

"I know, I'm sorry."

"It's fine. I know how she is. But listen," her sister said. "What she's wanting to know about is Thanksgiving. She hasn't heard from you."

"Yeah."

"I think she just wants confirmation you'll all be there like usual."

"Are you going?"

Her sister laughed. "Seriously? Is there a way out?"

"Because I'm thinking we're not this year."

"Okay."

"John's parents."

"Okay."

"Just that they're pretty frail."

"You totally don't have to justify to me, Tess. But you might want to call mom."

It had just come to her, this possibility of not going to Florida for Thanksgiving. All afternoon she went about her day suddenly aware that one of the clouds weighed above her was the idea of going to Sanibel for the holidays. She couldn't escape Christmas, but Thanksgiving. A day in the van for two or three days of stiff meals and parades on TV. Another day riding back. And then right back down in a few weeks for Christmas.

She waited till she knew her mom was out and called not her cell but the house phone, left her a reluctant, apologetic message, then hung up and accidentally on purpose left her phone in the bedroom where she wouldn't hear it when her mom called back. John was in Atlanta again for God only knew what, but she was too happy to care. She'd tell him when he got home and he would be thrilled even if he refused to admit it.

The thought of it made her so happy she didn't even watch the video. Seven or eight times she'd seen it and every time it was the same, that rush of weightless adrenalin that was eventually replaced with the sagging heft of guilt and sadness. Because the thing was, nothing changed. Every time he died, every time his head came off.

Yet, she needed it. The rush of emotions felt like something that demanded cultivation, some cruel project of self-actualization, something that made her more *her*. Which was endlessly stupid, she knew, and that too was part of the guilt.

But she felt so buoyant she didn't watch.

Instead of watching she found Kayla on Facebook. The pink hair and bird tattoo, the gym photos, the stars and planets. She'd done it before, but this time, almost drunk with happiness, Tess sent her a friend request. There was a moment of regret, enough to consider taking it back, but she didn't. She let it go. She let it happen.

When John came in late that night she made love to him a little more recklessly, a little more aggressively than he might have been expecting so that after, in the glow of the bathroom nightlight, her hair appeared wild and blown out as if by a storm. She was happy and went to sleep happy, the doors locked, her children safe, her husband beside her. Yet, she woke in the morning tired and vaguely angry and couldn't for the longest time figure out why.

Then she remembered she had dreamed of St. Simons.

Not their honeymoon, but the time after.

20.

The first time John lied to Tess was a Saturday in October.

(He didn't count the years of evasions and omissions. He meant *lie* lie. As in to her face.)

It seemed endlessly complex, but the short version was this: John wanted to see his daughter and he didn't want Tess to know. So he told her he had to be back in Atlanta—he didn't count the lie about meeting Stone either—the conference he was attending was a multiday event that dealt with relicensure. But instead of heading south he took 74 North until he hit the Great Smoky Mountains National Park where he fell into the long queue of RVs and motorcycles. He didn't mind the slow crawl around the overlooks and switchbacks or down through the ribbed tunnels where everyone laid on the horn. There were things in life to be gotten through and this seemed just another of many. The larger question surrounded what the hell he was doing.

It had something to do with Peach Creek. That much he knew. Seeing Erin Porter, hearing about Karla—all these unseen angles, the stories he'd never known—had excavated something he'd spent years imagining buried. So he had to see Kayla. And here was part of why he had lied to Tess: it was embarrassing, the lengths to which he had gone.

First—

He stopped at Newfound Gap. It was cold and overcast and there were starlings in the trees and on the ground. He made himself slow down, made himself notice. The iridescent plumage, the infant squeaking they made. He intentionally made himself walk down to the restrooms off the parking lot, intentionally made himself read the historic marker mounted on the stone wall, the talk of Roosevelt and the CCC, because what was he doing here?

What had he done?

Well, first, he had found the website of the gym where she worked. Then, he found the community college where she studied, looked up the course schedule, and found the name of the instructor who would likely be teaching radiology tech. Then he called the gym and identified himself as Kayla's teacher. She was missing an assignment and he had missed her on her cell. He didn't want to give her a zero because he was sure it was just a mix-up.

Was she in?

And this was the part where he felt his heart ratchet up, because if she was in he wasn't sure what he would do. Hang up, most likely. But he also felt something heedless in him, some germ of self-destruction that would just as quickly run to self-abasement, and—

She was off today. But would be in tomorrow from eight to four. Did he want to leave a message?

He did not.

Instead, he got up early, lied to his wife, and started north. If it was stupid, it was also harmless. He suspected he would do no more than he had the time he drove up with the boys: sit in the car and watch.

And that was exactly what he did.

Several times he started to get out, once going so far as to actually open the door and put both feet on the asphalt, knowing all the while it was impossible. But he forgave himself. It was like a mole, burrowing out of the ground to stare at the sun. It was too much.

He forgave himself and was back on 441 before it occurred to him what he should have done in the first place. He had to pull over to find Erin Porter's number, but he did find it, and he did dial it.

"I mean, if you're free," he said.

"So you're back in town?"

"Heading that way."

"Well, how about lunch?"

"If it's a late lunch."

"That's fine," she said. "Do you know the Grotto, over on Elm?"

"No."

"How about the Abbey? It's out behind the old high school? You know it?"

"I pretty much don't know anything anymore."

"Yes, I see that," she said. "Well, how about this, John? How about you just come by and pick me up, all right? You got something to write on?"

21.

Tess woke alone in the predawn blue of the streetlight. She thought she heard Laurie but it wasn't Laurie that had woken her. It was the bed's emptiness and the almost real feeling that its emptiness held or maybe hid the presence of something larger. Was someone in the room with her? It was 3:52 on the bedside clock, but there was no John. She climbed from bed, disoriented, almost staggered to the living room where out the window she saw the car in the driveway: he was home. But where was he?

Should she call to him?

Was that ridiculous?

She stood in the living room uncertain what to do, on the verge of turning back to bed, on the verge of something, though she had no idea what. There was the glimmer of possibility that she might watch the video, the slow decapitation by starlight, and considering it she felt her nipples tighten. Her breasts were rivered with blue veins that roped their way down to the enormous pale pink of her nipples and all of her, the entire construction, drew itself closer. Laurie was going five hours between feedings now—the sleep really was getting better—but what gripped her was something else entirely.

She should go back to bed.

She should sleep.

Yet she didn't move.

She stood there slatted by the porch light that fell through the blinds and clicked her tongue against the roof of her mouth. It was a perfect click, the sudden popping of a vacuum and she felt it travel out over the furniture and scattered toys and then she felt it return to her, warped.

Warped, she thought, by the presence of what she had allowed into their house. It was in her hair and her clothes and on her skin—this thing that established itself a little more firmly every time she watched the man die—but it was also in the air. It was in front of her and behind her, and feeling it she sensed herself pulling tighter still.

She remembered then the photograph she had found of four-year-old Kayla.

Thy fearful symmetry—and then she remembered the rest of it, or at least another line. It was addressed, maybe, to the presence she felt around her. It was addressed to what she had let into her house and her life:

Did he who made the Lamb make thee?

She kept her eyes shut and waited for an answer.

When no answer came she sent out another click, and followed it.

She found John in the upstairs guest bedroom, dressed and sleeping atop the comforter. Tess locked the door behind her, and no more than slid into bed before she was pushing her hips against him, kissing him, fingers in his hair. In apology. All of it, it should be said, in apology, though who could say for what. But she wasn't thinking about that. She was moving, simply moving, reaching through the fly of his boxer shorts.

"Tess?"

"Don't talk."

"What—"

"Don't say anything."

And John seemed to get this, to sense that so long as they were silent in the dark there were ways to make what was imagined real, and what was real no more than imagination, a fantasy, a guilty dream signifying both what was and what never would be again. She felt herself pulling down his shorts, felt herself hooking her thumbs in the waistband of her own underwear. She did it quickly because if she stopped to think about the fastness holding her it would explode into words and tears and all the other things she wanted none of.

What she wanted was this.

Stomach to stomach. Tucking her knees up beneath her while he held her hips, her breasts gorgeously giant. Her breath catching in her throat while below her, her husband chanted to God. Quicker, more desperate, until he curled into her like a burned leaf, something that would destroy itself in fire, but be more alive for it, if only briefly.

She tensed her thighs, the pleasure barely measurable against the grief, for that is what she felt rising: some inarticulate grief, a great swell of sadness, ebbing and flowing so that she confused it with the rhythm of the swaying bed. She shut her eyes. His hard hands gliding the surface of her stomach and out to the tips of breasts, his touch almost painful, but she liked it, wouldn't dare push his hands away because touching her, she realized she was finding her way into him, his mind.

And—

She thought he was finished and then he flipped her onto her back.

It was sudden, almost violently so, and she found her face in the crook of his neck, his lips somewhere in her hair, panting so that she felt strands go in and out of his mouth. He was moving against her like he hated her and she thought this was a good thing: were there not reasons he should hate her? Were there not reasons she should hate him back?

After, she found herself pinned beneath the weight of this known man who said nothing.

He only breathed, that was all, the very human shuddering of his chest as it pressed to her own, and slowly she was aware of her body again. Slowly, she felt it around her like driftwood beached well past the tide, the presence against her, the brush of the prayer rope he wore on one wrist.

He rolled off her and she waited until she heard him snoring before she clicked once up at the ceiling, and that click was enough to carry her back to bed where she lay on her back, covered by the sheet, and waited for her daughter to wake.

He was a good man, but what did he do all day?

22.

He decided to take the boys out to breakfast. It was a Tuesday, and he didn't have any appointments until ten. He was up before six, showered and dressed and feeling better than he'd felt in days. Tess was already in the kitchen, drinking coffee in an oval of lamplight. The day otherwise dark, the day otherwise unformed.

"Hey," she said. "You're up early."

"You, too. Sleep all right?"

"I guess. There's coffee."

He poured a cup and went to the sink, stared at the ghost of himself in the window there, the yard beyond, the trees and bird feeders, the pinecones stripped clean of peanut butter and seed.

"I was thinking of taking the boys out," he said.

"This morning?"

"I don't have anything until ten."

"To your parents?"

"Maybe just the pancake place here. We could go early."

"I'm sure they'd like that." She put her finger in her book. "They'll be up soon."

"It's no rush. What are you reading?"

"Oh, this." As if she'd only then noticed it, this massive doorstop in her lap. "*The Great War for Civilisation.* Robert Fisk."

"No more Proust?"

"I gave up on Proust."

"Poor Marcel. What's this about?"

"The Middle East."

"Heavy stuff."

She shrugged.

He finished his coffee and refilled it. She was reading, or pretending to read.

"Maybe I'll wait," he said. "Do it another day."

"I can get them up."

"No."

"They're probably awake anyway."

"Are you going to run?"

"I already did."

"What time did you get up?"

He saw now that beneath her loose housecoat she wore running tights and a T-shirt, her hair pulled back in a ponytail.

"Like three?" he asked.

That shrug again. He hated that shrug. He went back to the window where the day gathered in cold yellow spots, spans of light that slowly crept over the yard. There was something abhorrent to the way it spread, the insistence of it all, the way it wouldn't be still. It had a neediness that signaled some ill-defined menace.

"We need to take those pinecones down," he said.

"That the children made?"

"Squirrels."

"The bird feeders? They made those with your mom."

He pointed, knowing she wasn't looking. "They're just gnawing them. There's not even any seed left they're just . . ."

She wasn't listening. He wasn't listening, either, and went back to his coffee. He'd make the boys pancakes and go in early. The idea of breakfast out no longer seemed viable. It seemed, in fact, ridiculous. Yesterday, Jimmy Stone had called. John hadn't answered and Stone hadn't left a message, but it seemed to require some response, if only internal. He needed to sit with it. He needed to go in and be alone with whatever it implied, even if that were nothing.

"You know he's learning to write code," Tess said.

"What?"

"Wally, I'm talking about, at school."

"I thought it was a Montessori school?"

"They play *Minecraft*."

"On the computer?"

"It's supposed to help with problem solving is sort of the nature of it."

"Blocks. I thought that was sort of the nature of it, beads on an abacus."

"I can wake them," Tess said.

"Forget it."

"Okay, sure, let's forget it," she said, a little brighter than he thought necessary. "Hey, I had a thought. Thanksgiving."

"What about it?"

"I thought what if we didn't go to Florida this year. Just stuck around here. I mean we're right back down there for Christmas."

"What about your parents?"

"What about them?"

He turned back to the window.

This is my life, he thought.

Right now.

In front of me.

23.

It was late October when Jimmy Stone attached himself to a yard crew contracted to nip and tuck the lawn of Dr. Soren Sharma, chief executive officer for the Reliance Corporation and father to the newly disappeared Reed Sharma. The idea was to act like he belonged and then get close, to listen and learn. Cross fingers and toes that maybe some little goodie of information would fall into his lap.

It was a two-day job, and the first day was nothing but Jiffy Pop bullshit, Stone the only outlier on a team of Salvadorans who seemed to work at light-speed while he stood by the truck drinking coffee. He thought the possibility to get into the house and Reed's room might present itself, but instead he wound up doing a half-assed job weeding the flower beds and edging along the walk. Thankless stoop work while the economist's wife eyed him from behind the blinds. Half suspicion, half sexual boredom, and Stone spent the afternoon entertaining thoughts of the lady of the house on the upstairs bed, her legs up around his neck, her hands wringing sheets of a ridiculous thread count. She'd be breathless and flushed and grateful in the way that well-kept fifty-something women always were. She had a loopy deviant grin, or maybe she was just crazy, unhinged by the vanishing act her boy had pulled. He wasn't really interested—it was like cross-dressing back on the rez—just another way to pass the day.

He came back the second morning, stiff and running on two Aleves and a Rockstar, and she watched him that day too, a little too closely, he thought. When she went inside in the afternoon he worried maybe she had sussed out his intentions and his tenure at the residence was over. Instead she came out looking for him. *Hello, sir!* she kept calling. *Excuse me, please.* He was bored and might have gone to her, but he was wary too, and slipped around the edge of the house. He was outside the kitchen when Dr. Sharma stepped out and waved him over.

"I sent my wife after you," the man said. He stood on the top step, smiling with a glass of orange juice in one hand. Behind him ran one of the zero-turn mowers. "I know you understand me."

Stone was silent.

"Look," he said, "you're obviously not one of them, so let's just drop the act, okay? In fact, I know exactly who you are. Would you come inside. Come inside, please." The smile was gone. "You needn't worry about that," he said, gesturing perhaps toward his wife's distant voice, perhaps toward the ongoing lawn work. "But we do need to talk about a few things."

Stone stepped into the kitchen. The good doctor was shoeless, socked feet and a dark suit, tie loose. There was a noticeable bulge beneath one lapel.

"I'll be brief," he said. "But I do have some questions."

"All right."

"First, I'm not going to ask who you're with. Federal, state, some sort of contractor—that's irrelevant so far as I'm concerned. I would, however, like confirmation you know my son."

Stone said nothing.

"Look," Sharma said, "I don't care if all you can do is nod your head, but I would like some confirmation."

"Let's say we're acquainted."

"Professionally, so to speak. At least that was how it was explained to me."

"I guess you could say that."

Sharma sipped his juice and gestured at the door. "You know you could almost pass for one of them with that skin. More brownish than brown."

"That how you recognized me?"

"I made some calls. Global Solutions had quite the reputation."

"So they read you in."

Dr. Sharma stepped past him and shut the door. "Only to the point where you and your buddies went all Josef Mengele and murdered an innocent man. Is *murdered* how you put it?"

"It's not exactly the company line," Stone said, "but why not."

"Don't get me wrong. I'm not casting aspersions."

"They declined to prosecute."

"I want you to know I'm sympathetic."

Stone shrugged. "It was bullshit anyway."

"It usually is." Sharma put his glass in the sink. "I'd offer you something to drink, but we're both in a bit of a hurry here. Is my wife still out there?"

"Are we on the same team, Dr. Sharma?"

"I believe she's about so let me be quick. I don't expect you to tell me anything. But I want some assurance you all know what you're doing. Can you give me that?"

"Your son's not exactly incapable. I mean he is, but he isn't."

"I heard he's a rattlesnake."

Stone offered his open palms. "They aren't necessarily inconsistent."

"Well, whatever he is," Sharma said, "he's my son. I have a wife to think about. His mother—"

"I understand."

"I don't care if he returns here. That may not even be possible. His mother cares, but she isn't in her right mind at the moment. But I do need some assurances that whatever happens, wherever he winds up, that he's all right. Can you give me that?"

"I'll do my best."

"You know you could have just approached me directly."

"I'm not so sure."

"The FBI was here, the Georgia Bureau. You aren't part of that world, are you?"

"Not officially. Not anymore."

"You were with Global Solutions and now that Global Solutions doesn't exist you're just another bug in counter-terror. Conjectures of another guilty bystander, busy regretting the past and wondering what the hell happened to his security clearance. That sound about right?"

Stone did his shrug thing again. He was starting to miss the yard work, the clarity of pulling and tossing. Then Sharma reached inside his jacket and took out a brick of cash. He placed it on the bar.

"I would like," he said, "something slightly better than your best."

But Stone wasn't listening. He was looking at the money, looking at it with as much repulsion as fascination. It looked like an infectious thing, but of the sort you couldn't help but touch. "You offer me this because of the fact of my brown skin," he said. "You think I'll take it because I'm an Indian."

"On the contrary. I offer it to you in spite of the fact of your brown skin." He pushed the brick toward him. "I think you'll take it because you're an American."

Stone looked at the money for some time before taking it, but he did take it, and when he did he liked the heft of it.

"Consider that a retainer," Sharma said. "There might always be more."

"Might?"

"So long as you take care of him."

Stone nodded. "So I guess you're the big chief now."

Sharma was already on his way out of the room. "You're goddamn right I am," he called. "Now get the fuck out of my kitchen and go find my boy."

And that was exactly what Stone did.

24.

One day in early November Tess ran into the awful Pat Glenn in the grocery store. She had seen him only once since that night they'd been over for dinner and Glenn did his racist shtick about wetbacks and ragheads and Professor Hadawi while his wife listened adoringly or dismissively—it was hard to tell which. Since the day at the convenience store, Tess and John had turned down a few invitations and not asked the Glenns back. Pat seemed a little pissed about it. He also seemed a little drunk. It was four o'clock on a Wednesday, but that sort of logic didn't seem to hold.

"Where's this husband of yours been?"

"At work, at home. The usual. How's Martha?"

"How do you mean 'the usual'?"

They were in the cereal aisle with the Fruity Pebbles and Cheerios, the bags of granola and sleeves of oatmeal. It was too bright and too crowded and on the speakers they were playing Christmas music just a bit too loud.

"What's he doing down in Peach Creek?" Glenn asked.

"I'm sorry?"

"Heard he's been running around Peach Creek."

"He's at some conference every Saturday," she said. "Relicensure. But that's in Atlanta."

"Atlanta? That's what he told you?"

She was in her black running tights with the reflective stripe, a black windbreaker pulled over a white tank top and she wasn't flattering herself in thinking his eyes kept sliding down to her legs and then back up to the hollow between her breasts. She wasn't flattering herself. She felt ashamed of herself.

"Where are the kids?" he asked.

His cart was nearly empty, ground beef and mayonnaise, skim milk and a suitcase of Natural Light. She thought of his wife at home, or maybe not at home, with her saline breasts and spray-on tan.

"With John, actually."

"So you're all alone, are you?"

"Not really."

"Sounds like you are," he said. "Kids with their daddy." And here he looked openly at her breasts and then up at her. "You still nursing that girl?"

"I need to go."

"Seen your husband," he called as she wheeled away. "Might want to check with your husband on that whole relicensure thing, honey."

*

She went home and stood alone in the kitchen and it was like being in the condo of St. Simons all over again. There were days she felt she had never left. Days she tried to fix her mind on the now, the present. But what fixed was that winter. What fixed were the long walks, the shower with no curtain, the way someone else's mail kept gathering in the slot. The waiting. She remembered the waiting. John in bed for days so that for company she had not her new husband but the seabirds and migrating waterfowl.

In the spring of their second year of marriage John was called away on business. What exactly that business entailed she didn't know, only that he would be gone for several weeks, and communication would be limited. He did contract work for the government. That was all he could tell her. He was going somewhere and asked that she not ask where or why. He would be safe, he promised her as much. He wasn't a spy or a soldier. He was a psychologist. But beyond that he offered no explanation, and Tess never asked because that was what she did back then and did still: she didn't ask.

John didn't want to go, that much was clear. In the week leading up to his flight he became depressed, moody in a way she had never seen. The day before he left he told her about Karla, about Kayla and the wreck. It was stunning in a way, but also not. There was always the sense that he wasn't telling her everything, or anything, really. So when it came out, sad as it was, it was a relief for Tess. It made them closer, she thought. It definitely made her love him more, and when she took him to the airport she kissed him goodbye feeling she knew him better and deeper than she ever had. She didn't know where he was going or why. But he would be back soon. Everything would be fine.

She stayed in St. Pete, alone through the spring and into the summer. Her mother called. Her father wanted her to come home to Sanibel. The news was all bad. There were dirty bombs and suicide bombs and every night more dead in Iraq. A car bomb here, a drone strike there. The airports were patrolled by police in riot gear carrying the sort of assault rifles that had become familiar on the news. Still, it was better here than elsewhere. Better here than wherever John was.

Not that she knew, but she had a sense of things. He promised to e-mail and did for a while. But the intervals grew longer, and by late June she'd heard nothing from him in weeks.

Then one night she watched a journalist being waterboarded in the interest of something she was made to understand was noble. While he retched and gasped the process was explained in bullet points:

- The individual is bound securely to an inclined bench.
- The individual's feet are elevated.
- A cloth is placed over the forehead and eyes.
- Water is applied to the cloth in a controlled manner.
- As this is done, the cloth is lowered until it covers both the nose and mouth.
- Once the cloth is saturated and completely covers the mouth and nose, airflow is slightly restricted for twenty to forty seconds due to the presence of the cloth.

She had the volume off. The man appeared to be vomiting. Then she realized he was crying.

- During those twenty to forty seconds, water is continuously applied from a height of twelve to twenty-four inches.

Then she realized she was crying, too, and not because of the violence, at least not exactly. It was more the realization that this was the world, and *had always been* the world. She was just too busy running and laughing to bother noticing it.

The next day, on the TV in a bar on Treasure Island, she watched two men fighting in a cage, and the next day she watched again, this time online. She was amazed by the absolute brutality, the relentless head strikes that registered as damage, damage, damage. But it was also comforting in that it was just two men. What you had to face literally stood before you. Unlike the small-boat sense she carried, the small boat on the wide unsettling seas. The whole adrift thing she was letting fester into high art.

She watched and watched, and by July—with no word from John in several weeks—she had come to feel violence as a natural state, no different from sleeping or eating. She watched the men fight and walked through her day thinking constantly of pressure points and submission holds. She would look at someone and discover she was actually considering the vulnerability of the temple and eyes, gauging the softness of the throat. What she was learning was that the human body was frighteningly fragile and transient, a construct to be dismantled by the patient practitioner. At night, she would wake and think her way through the breaking of someone's instep or the tearing of one's ears, the mere availability of pain enough to see her through until morning.

And where was John?

Where was John so she could tell him this?

Every day she expected an e-mail and every day it failed to arrive.

She started Googling his old life. A Facebook memorial page for his wife. Newspaper accounts of the wreck. His daughter was online in all the usual places and Tess lurked to the extent she could. Then one day she made herself stop. She wasn't sure why exactly. Only that if she kept on searching she would find something, and whatever she found she would regret. It was a world about which she knew nothing and if she persisted it would swallow her.

So instead of searching she went back to the one thing she knew: her body, particularly her body under physical duress.

Every day she ran or lifted weights, usually both, and one afternoon caught her reflection in the far mirror past the Cybex machines, back arched, hands on her hips and mouth gasping for air. It took a moment to know it was her. She looked elastic and powerful, wiry and—she liked to think—more than a little dangerous. Beneath the halogen lights she appeared jagged and warlike, not unlike the fighters she watched.

After that, she stopped expecting to hear from John.

It seemed almost as if she'd forfeited him.

Then, with no warning, he returned. It was October and the world was just beginning to shed itself. The sky rift by weather, sun and then rain, one coming as certain as the other, and with it came her husband, shoaled back into the world of the living. He had been gone almost six months, long enough to have become a ghost, but now he was waiting for her on the street when she came out of the condo as if no more than an afternoon had passed. They walked to a Pakistani place in Bayside. His hands shook and his once-tan skin was pale and dry. He appeared sick.

"I am," he told her. "I'm dying."

"You're dying?"

"Of boredom, exhaustion."

She told him about watching the online fights, about the desire to hurt someone, and when he laughed at her she realized there was something cruel in him she had never detected.

After lunch they walked toward the Dalí, past the cafés with their rattan furniture and carafes of kombucha, past the buskers strumming *this land is your land*, past the boutiques and food carts and the marina with its clutter of boats. He'd been back since September. He told her this near the museum steps. He'd seen her twice, had spent an entire day just following her.

Why had he done this?

He didn't know.

Why was he telling her this?

He didn't know that either.

"Something's happened to you." It was less accusation than objective observation for at that moment she felt outside herself, suspended above where they stood by the museum steps, stones in the current of human traffic. "You've changed," she said.

"Everybody changes."

"You've turned cruel."

"That was inevitable."

She found herself pleading with him. "Oh no, John, it doesn't have to be."

"Everyone turns cruel. Given enough time."

"No."

"Given enough time," he told her, "everyone does."

But it wasn't cruelty exactly. It was something else. It was frailty, the fragility of his pieces—for that is what she discovered over the months that followed: that he was no longer the sum of his parts. Rather he was simply his parts, separate if intact. A collection of neuroses and fears and shakes and habits (all bad) to which they referred to as John.

Where were you?

He wouldn't say.

What were you doing?

I can't tell you.

What happened to you over there?

Nothing, nothing.

What he said was nothing.

There was a flurry of lovemaking and then, as if exhausted by it, he barricaded himself into the condo. She begged him to come out, to come back into the world, desperate enough to take him to parties with women she'd known in prep school, to a reunion of high-school assholes grown taller and richer. These wealthy strivers back in town to network. Their world was Daddy's getaway on Captiva or Mom's loft in the East Village. Sunset cruises when they were on the Gulf. Christmas envelopes for the doorman when they were in Brooklyn. Everywhere hired help, everywhere someone to sweep the snow or cut the grass while you studied for the bar exam on an heirloom Biedermeier desk. Saturday nights they clustered around banquettes and drank signature cocktails.

And John, John laughed at them, mocked them. How failed they were as human beings. Trading junk bonds and buying bread machines. Papa flying to Savile Row for his bespoke shirts. *Lord, preserve me from the bread makers.* They are decent people, John. Laughing again: *Lord, preserve me from the decent people.* She begged to know where he had been, what he had done.

Instead of speaking, John stayed home. For seven days he stayed in bed and said nothing. Tess would start to the Publix for groceries and then turn back, panicked that he was—what?

Not dead. She knew instead of dead he would be awake when she got home, online, and hounding out suffering. Surfing through the archived photos. Auschwitz and Bergen-Belsen. The gulags. The dead in the Congo. The dead in Rwanda and Darfur and Bosnia and Iraq. He spent hours staring at images from Abu Ghraib.

Will you stop?

Please, John, can't you stop?

But he gave no answer.

Did she resent this?

And if I don't now, how long until I do?

Those were the questions she asked herself, city bus lurching, folks leaned against the windows, ears plugged with headphones. Do I resent John? Do I hate him because I'm afraid? That's not a reason to hate him. But Tess couldn't definitively say that she didn't.

At the end of the week, they left the city. Her idea, and it wasn't a bad idea. But where to? What about the place on St. Simons? A place to rest, a place to recover. John gave her a number. Call him. You can trust this guy, he said. He's one of us. But who are *we*? she wanted to know. Ask for Ray, he said. Ray can help. Which was no answer at all. Still, she called. The man—Ray, she supposed—said they could stay, but it would take a few days to arrange. Be patient. Let me make a call to Jimmy, okay?

"But who are you?" Tess asked. "You keep saying *we* this, and *we* that."

"We," he said, as if he finally understood her. "We are America. We are your invention, my dear."

The next day everything was arranged. Ray had called Jimmy and Jimmy wasn't happy about it, but whatever, right? Here's where you find the key.

"Take care of him, all right? He's fucked up right now, but he's a good man."

By noon they were settled. Her winter retreat, as she gradually came to think of it, her tower, her redoubt, if that was even the word. Four narrow stories facing the finger curl of bay.

It wasn't at all like she remembered it from their honeymoon. Physically, of course, it was no different. But everything felt a half-tick off. Just little things, but she noticed. For instance, on the top floor was the master bath, the tub centered in the room. Except there was no curtain, only the mosaic tile that beaded wetly. Showering was like a performance. Except there was no one to watch.

There was a commercial icemaker, but no water line.

There was a spyglass, but it faced inland.

She walked and considered these things, and at some point, while she walked and John slept, winter came. She walked the footpaths and she walked the boardwalks and all around her were birds she could not name. Plovers. Sandpipers. They came wheeling from the beach, bedded in the soft banks, their tracks checked in the mud like runes. They hopped, she would watch them hop and then walk home to find the mail. The mail kept arriving—addressed to a Mr. James Stone, *let me make a call to Jimmy, okay?*—piling in the iron slot, the bills and fliers and pleas for donations. She stacked it in a wire basket, made the daily gathering of the mail a sort of practice. It was like watching the birds. It was like tending to John, except John was the one need that didn't actually need tending. John did nothing.

Still, she counseled herself to pay attention. Change the sheets. Bring him soup. Take away the soup. Let nothing pass you by.

And it worked, to some degree it worked.

She started noticing things.

The empty house.

The empty bay with its brittle grasses.

The sky was gray with snow, downy and ill-lit, so thick it began to tear and fall. But what was it but water and air and light? What was anything but water and air and light and, perhaps, thickening dust?

The reducibility of things was astounding.

To fall in love with spareness—there were entire days it felt like a blessing.

Nights she would cut off her laptop, cross the cold floorboards, barefoot with a blanket slung over her shoulders. It would be two, maybe three in the morning, the glass door open a few necessary inches so that she could hear wind in the street, the barred owls that flew at dawn.

She wasn't running anymore.

She wasn't calling her parents or her brother or sister or Emma.

She was standing in the center of her life like a fool.

John asleep in the bedroom, or pretending to sleep, a foot protruding from beneath the heavy comforter.

"What are you doing?" he asked.

"Standing here."

"Go to bed," he told her.

Go, she thought, not *come.*

She stretched her walks, one hour, two hours, sometimes three. Houses everywhere but mostly empty. It felt more than seasonal: it felt permanent, the island abandoned. The beach shacks, the starfish painted on plaster, the stucco, the bead board, the three-story Victorians, fish-scaled and leaning back from the sea.

She started a list of questions she might ask John and then abandoned it, because honestly, why? The walk to the grocery store was over a mile along the cobblestones, half the length of the island, and instead of questions she listed items to be purchased. Soap, coffee, creamer—creamer was an indulgence. Shower curtain—she wrote the words *shower curtain* on her list.

It seemed significant, but what came to her was the sheer abundance of trivia, the sludge of mindlessness, and how this is life. Even when someone is in the next room, dying—or not dying, as it may be—what actually mattered was the accrual of everything else. The clipped nails, the taste in the corners of your mouth.

"All I want to do is see death," he told her. It was when? It was November. One of those terrifyingly lucid states he would sometimes enter. "Something is happening."

She moved around the room tentatively never taking her eyes off him, because the scary truth was, he seemed predatory. Tess felt like something hunted, like something being lured in.

"Like what is happening?" she asked.

"I don't know. I've been thinking a lot."

She waited for more, but he waved her off.

"Yahweh," he told her, "is just the sound of the breath, the in and out of being."

She didn't recognize his voice. Not just the words but the actual sound of his voice.

She had no friends. In place of friends there were those long walks across the cold sand, through the streets where everything looked unfinished, constructed from mail-order parts that never quite arrived. She found a church on Demere Road. A conch shell of holy water. An ivory Christ on his whalebone cross.

Come down, she whispered. It was her first prayer in months.

Because she was desperate.

Because she was tired.

Had she gotten old? She was twenty-four and looked mostly the same, though she knew she wasn't. Her urine smelled. One day she just noticed it. Old, medicinal.

She could no longer think of a child. In place of a child she had the fawn-colored water. The ocean-like grasses and the wish to swim it. The wish to be carried out to sea. She knew now her mistake was too quickly abandoning her new life, rushing into marriage, giving herself away before there was a self to give. She'd fallen through it like water. It was traceless. But you have to scar the body to remember. There has to be a mark.

She kept walking to the church, along the beach, past the houses with the outdoor showers for washing the sand from your feet, the lattice of grille to stand on, the joinery of metal pipework above.

One night they managed to make love for the first time in weeks, but it was with such robotic movements it felt like shapes moving behind a curtain. When he came inside her he turned his head and exhaled. It felt like grief, a hiss of steam, like less than nothing. But a part of her floated away with the vapor.

Still, she went on doing everything for him, she cleaned him, fed him, cared for him. She did everything except listen to him. She did watch him. And watching him she came to understand that it was completely possible to believe every word in the Gospels and not believe it at all.

"If I can just tell you this—"

"Oh, John."

"If I can just tell you this I can walk out of here. We can walk out of here."

But they were past the telling of anything. There was no hiding from as much. To look at him lurching to the bathroom in his gray sweatsuit, blanket shrouded over his shoulders, unshaven, unwashed. To see him was to know there was nothing left to explain. If they came out of this, *when* they came out of this, the approach would be simple: forget it ever happened. Don't speak of it. Don't acknowledge it. Don't even think about it. Go on with your life together, go forward, the two of you.

But that was the thinking on one of her strong days.

The day she realized she was pregnant was one of her weak days, and that day she decided to go home to her parents, to leave him.

"I have to go out for a little. Get some things."

He was beneath the covers, Tess beside him.

"I'll die here alone," he said.

"Groceries. One hour. You won't die. Please, John."

It wasn't for an hour—she had known that from the start, but only admitted it to herself when she was driving. She cried while heading south on I-95 but was dry-eyed by the time she made the Georgia-Florida line. Late morning and nerves seared with coffee and anticipation, but dry-eyed. Absolutely cried out and fine with that, happy, actually, that there was nothing more to cry about. Because it wasn't fear that made her decide to go to her parents, it was exhaustion.

What made her decide to turn around she didn't know, only that she did.

When she told him about the baby he got up.

As simple as that. Got up as if he'd lain there for months simply because he had no reason not to, and now she had given him one. She didn't know whether to weep or laugh or to hit him as hard and as many times as possible. In the absence of clarity, she spent the day packing and cleaning and the next morning they pulled on their coats and headed out the door.

They were back in St. Pete by that night, and here were crowds coming out of restaurants, Christmas lights hung along Fourth Street. Here was the world just as she had left it. He bought her a new pair of running shoes and an expensive jogging stroller and a GPS wristwatch, and it was as if nothing had happened—John was John—but also everything had happened so how could that be?

She had no answer, only that it was. John became the same solicitous, doting husband he had been before. He didn't talk about death or suffering or God. He talked about baby names, a list for girls, a list for boys. They moved into a sublet while they looked for a new condo, something bigger. They looked at cradles and baby clothes and at night he rubbed her feet. In the mornings he sang. The rest he left out. He never mentioned Ray, the man she had called. He never mentioned James Stone, the man whose mail kept arriving. He never mentioned any of it. Life went on as before, better than before.

Wally was born.

They moved to Georgia.

Daniel was born and then Laurie. They were happy and John seemed to have no memory of those months so why should she?

It was years ago. It was over.

She needed to let it be over.

25.

Jimmy Stone sat in his van, flush against the loading dock at the rear of the Food City which appeared to be a shitty grocery store if ever there was one. It was dark, close to midnight, but he could see enough from the lights of the parking lot to watch Ahmad and four boys pile out of a hooptie, climb into the two dumpsters, and then climb out with bread and fruit and a freaking sheet cake of all things, smiling like kids. Which was exactly what they were.

A lesson in urban survival, Jimmy thought. A bit theatrical, if necessary.

Ahmad gathered the haul and sent them back in. Not like they needed encouraging. Probably the best food they'd had since arriving. The shit they were serving at camp. A breakfast of oatmeal and amphetamines. A little chemically induced brain light with your steel-cut oats. But how else could you survive?

Jimmy had followed Professor Hadawi north, and what he had discovered was that he had been right about everything, right about the professor, right about Reed. Right—as if such needed confirmation—about the generally toxic state of this fallen world.

Right about the camp, too.

It was on the back side of a ski resort. The place was closed for the season, but even had the snow been falling and the lifts running no one would have spotted them. They were in an abandoned section that had once been a gem mine for tourists, a place to pan for gold except there was no gold. Serious backcountry with no decent access besides an overgrown fire road. There was a converted barracks with a half-assed kitchen, a fire pit for gatherings, a few storage sheds, and the remnants of mining troughs and conveyor belts.

Jimmy had watched the place for weeks, making certain the professor was nowhere to be found before venturing up. That Ahmad was the instructor was a nice surprise. He knew Ahmad from back inside the high blast walls of the Green Zone. The months of poolside barbecues and Filipino maids and the occasional senator doing a windshield tour of the New Iraq. It wasn't exactly what you would call a war, at least back then. The insurgency was still in its infancy so besides the occasional mortar attack it was like being at camp: sleeping in a dorm, eating in the KBR cafeteria. You had Bible studies. You had twenty-something Ivy League staffers running entire departments because Daddy gave big to Bush-Cheney.

Occasionally rocket fire hit the Al Rasheed and almost daily the burned-out shells of Humvees were towed, very quietly, to the Vehicle Sanitation Point, but it wasn't exactly real. He saw Ahmad again, years later in Afghanistan, and it was different then. A time of HESCO barriers and fentanyl lollipops, the moon reefed in silver clouds. Jimmy and Ahmad stuffed into MOPP suits and waiting for the All Clear. That was the time when he began to think about the body as a candle, the body as this lit thing, flame devouring hair and skin and adipose tissue so that it became pure. Because at times it seemed preferable to the waiting. Not that he told anyone. Not that he told Ahmad, though Jimmy suspected deep down they all felt it. They all shared that same desire that it be done with. So it was convenient, discovering his old pal. Still, Jimmy didn't rush right in. He watched them run in the woods, took a few photos for the sake of posterity, and didn't approach until that night.

In the meantime, he got glamor shots of every kid on campus. These beardless wonders, almost interchangeable with the sunken eyes and glazed faces. But he knew Reed right off. He was skinnier than the night Jimmy had met him at a McDonald's near I-75 but little else had changed. Jimmy recognized the walk, that sort of apologetic creep, but arrogant, too. Like he knew he was better than you, even if no one else was in possession of such information. They had something like a bond, maybe. He'd told Jimmy once about the girl in New York—pale legs, the elevator girl—and Jimmy could tell the kid had immediately resented Jimmy for having heard. You don't want to spill things, but then sometimes you go and do it anyway. Jimmy had told the kid some things he regretted, too, but it had been that sort of time in his life. Panicked. Frayed.

New York in a particular moment. Rebar and yellow construction cranes down at Ground Zero. Disease everywhere. Not just anthrax, but methicillin-resistant *Staphylococcus aureus*. You heard rumors about the prostitutes in Brownsville and East Harlem and then it crept south to Midtown. MRSA. SARS. Rhinovirus. Cops having to Lysol their cars. Cops refusing to haul hookers at all. Call the fucking paddy wagon, call HAZMAT. You could buy Zithromax on the street because Zithromax don't do shit. He rode out to Borough Park for latkes. You couldn't tell the police from the army, all masked, all armed, everywhere in their MRAPs and helicopters. There was talk of the National Defense Authorization Act. People referenced the Posse Comitatus Act. Dirty bombs—someone was caught planting one in a Times Square mailbox. Cesium-137 wrapped in plastique. Or maybe the bomb wasn't actually planted, maybe it was still in the planning stage. Or maybe someone had just *talked* about a dirty bomb. Maybe someone had just thought it.

He was a different kid now, but Jimmy recognized him, spotted him hauling himself in and out of the trash.

Jimmy had his camera with him, but didn't bother with it.

Tonight was for watching.

He'd already relayed an update to Dr. Sharma and for it had acquired a second brick of cash. Like the first, it was tucked above a ceiling tile in the kitchen of a lake house Stone kept deep in the mountains.

Things were coming together. He had the e-mails John had sent. Pair it with the photographs and it was the start of something. But put the e-mails with the pics with the confession of the kid and you're talking federal probe, you're talking somebody call the inspector general. Forget *material support*. It was straight-up entrapment and Jimmy wondered how the federal district court might fancy such. Then again maybe he would just let the kid walk. If possible, Jimmy felt certain he would. Use some of Daddy's money to facilitate a permanent vacation.

He'd wait a few days, let the kid hit the breaking point, and then go up and get him out. Get him papers and drive him to the lake house for a bit. Get John on the phone, get him to come over and it would be just like the old days which, no, not really. But they'd be after the same thing. Only this time instead of trying to get some kid to spill his secrets they'd convince him to keep them. To shut up and disappear, to start a new life somewhere else.

John would say no at first, but he'd relent. You pressure a guy like John, you get his moral dander up and it was too easy, really. A guy like that couldn't say no.

He watched the kids load their food into Ahmad's car. One of the boys had a bag of grapes it looked like, and it was just a crazy thought, but Jimmy was still thinking it, thinking: here he is, old Reed, so what if I just called his name? Could we sort this whole thing out, just the two of us?

He imagined Reed striding over, spotting the van past the angle of the loading dock, spotting Jimmy who had his hands on the wheel in a sort of shy shrug as if to say, *Hey, hi, howdy there, remember all those mornings I would call early and wake your sleepy ass up?*

Would it be a mistake or not?

But he knew better than to call to him.

Instead, he watched the boys load up and drive away, drive back to the hell of the professor's camp. When they were gone Jimmy took out his cell and dialed John's number.

26.

Stone dialed again the next day but John let it go to voicemail too.

When he called a third time later that week John intentionally walked out of the room. It wasn't like you could hear Stone's voice, but John didn't like the thought of it. Besides, it was Saturday and he was on his way out the door.

He wanted to be in Peach Creek with Erin.

He didn't want to be in San Francisco with Peter Keyes. But talking to Stone would carry him there.

John had been in the Bay Area two weeks before he actually met Keyes. Peter's office occupied the upper floors of the California Center on Sansome Street. But John worked out of an office park just beyond the gates of Stanford called the HIVE. Downtown Palo Alto with its boutiques and food co-ops. Parking lots thick with Lexus SUVs. John was given an apartment in Southgate and made the commute on foot.

The HIVE was an area of desks expanding radially from an open center lined with couches and video game consoles. He was the oldest man—there were only two women—a dinosaur among three dozen twenty-something dropouts from graduate programs in physics and engineering, newly minted PhDs in the philosophy of mind or nanotechnology. What was happening in the world—what was about to happen—was happening already, only oil wasn't yet completely exhausted, the regional wars were still just that. They weren't yet beheading journalists in the Levant. Most still opened the tap to find cool and drinkable water with just the correct dose of fluoride. But that was not the sense within the HIVE. The sense was of limitless possibility, of detecting ways in which crises might be exploited. The room was loud. They wrote algorithms and ate lunches of red chard.

John drank Budweiser at a frat bar, pitchers of it, weaning himself off the hard stuff, and then walking home through the California sun, past the iron-grilled bodegas and dim sum shops, the apartment complex swimming pools where the Stanford girls tanned. His was a sloppy existence, made sloppier still against the measured lives of his younger colleagues. Where he slumped through the drunken days and blacked-out nights, they weighed everything: calories, drinks, bonuses, neurons. Somewhere there was a ladder and they intended to climb it. Or were climbing it already. It would be revealed in time, its largeness, its largess. All were seeking the authenticity that works as cover for what is at base the selfishness that allows a CEO to be a Buddhist, or an upper-middle-class white woman in Greenwich to speak of her self-actualization at an upstate yoga retreat. They wanted the money, of course, but they wanted to feel good about the money; that was their right. If they knew anything, they knew that to which they had a right.

John knew this path.

Even if he was no longer traveling it.

Then one day Peter sent for him. It was a common thing for a new hire to be taken for an afternoon to Sansome Street to meet the principal. Still, there was an air of jealously the day a car was sent to pick him up. They were like a harem of lovers, some favored, some forgotten, and there was always some wrangling for Peter's attention.

And here was further justification for John's sense of superiority: Peter Keyes looked a great deal like him. They were both tall and thin, both late thirties, a couple of sad-eyed waifs in cable-knit sweaters and worn shoes. Of course, Keyes was a successful billionaire, a feverish ascetic who refused carbohydrates and sex with boys over nineteen. While John was no more than an overeducated good ol' boy, a Bible Belt scripture whiz gone rogue.

The room overlooked the bay, the Golden Gate. Federalist chairs and a collection of Francis Bacon triptychs. Bowls of floating edible flowers. Keyes was a man who ate kale and slept in a hyperbaric chamber. A man with no intentions of dying. It was silly, really, and John kept waiting for someone to bring out a carafe of beet juice.

The next day he was back at the HIVE, unchanged. Someone had left a note on his desk, Arial, 12-point font: *Before enlightenment you chop wood and carry water. After enlightenment you chop wood and carry water.* Still, he detected glances, the muffled insinuations. Until his visit no one had left the HIVE in months and there were rumors that the principal had lost interest, that the operation would be shuttered by the end of the year. This proved to be only partially the case.

In the meantime, John went back to work, sat with his books while the young talked of seasteading or angel investors. They were vegan or paleo or on caloric-restriction life-extending diets, and everyone ate mixed greens and drank espresso from little postconsumer waste cups. You would look up and see someone flossing free strings of cabbage, oblivious.

Then one night, for the first time in years, he went for a run.

Later, months later when running the inner perimeter of an abandoned airbase somewhere in Poland had again become the central tenet of his being, he realized that surely he had given up the act because it brought on such clarity, such gorgeous lucidity. Running, he couldn't escape the self-examination that ultimately folded into self-recrimination.

Did he know then what he would be doing a few months later?

Things were coming. The bursting bubbles—tech sector, bond market, housing—the ubiquitous surveillance. Soaking the face of a college student with pepper spray while our sensitive president read poetry and signed off on drone strikes—it hadn't happened yet, but it would. The crowds would go needy and then scary and then the police would roll in riding their armored personal carriers. It was years away but it was already in the air.

The following week he was summoned back to Sansome. Only this time the car picked him up outside his apartment complex and Keyes was in the back with a proposition of sorts: that John come work for him.

He told Keyes that he already worked for him and Keyes shook his sad head.

For me, he said. Me as in personally. There was a sub-group beneath the Keyes umbrella called Global Solutions, a consulting firm acquired in the near past, and he wanted John to join it, to be his personal liaison. The men were older—they were all men. They were grimmer. They were working under contract for the U.S. government, carrying out the gathering of human intelligence. They were scattered throughout the world, the Mideast, Asia Minor, Eastern Europe. John would be *tasked*—Keyes's word—with running an office in Poland.

"I read your book. Grief," Keyes said. "Suffering, but to a particular end. Suffering as a means of revelation. There's a secret, John. You said so yourself. It's locked inside all of us and it takes trauma to bring it out. Wasn't that what your book was about? The necessity of suffering, the revelatory nature of it. We're going to open up souls. But it isn't going to be random. We'll open souls in a *controlled* manner. There is no other laboratory on earth that can offer what I'm offering. I ask only that you be ready for as much."

He was, or wasn't, but didn't care, and for the second time in as many weeks he said yes.

A week later, at a decommissioned air base in Poland, John watched a man on a high-definition screen have his arms placed in restraints and twisted behind him so that his orange jumpsuit pulled tight across his chest. And then they raised him as if he were being crucified. That was John's work, that was why he was there.

He was there to watch.

27.

She had to chase Wally off the computer, flapping her arms the way you might scare vultures from a carcass. But he wouldn't quite scatter.

"Where are you learning this?" she wanted to know. "At school?"

"Watch this, Mom."

"This is *Minecraft*? These little blocks?"

They were in the living room, Tess's laptop across the slim expanse of Wally's lap. She'd left it just a moment before and here he was, having swept in without a sound.

"Where did you get this?" she asked.

"I downloaded it."

"The game?"

"I've got whales, all this marine life. There's this mod you can get for large-brained cetaceans."

"Whales?"

"They're all down on the bottom just sort of like hanging out." The little block figure that was, she supposed, her son, floated over the block sea and it was true: there was something down there, something beneath the surface but just above the tabs he had minimized: Facebook, CNN, a recipe site with a vegetarian shepherd's pie that called for Greek yogurt which she didn't have so forget it.

"Where are they?" she asked, closer now, her mouth by the swirled crown of his head.

"You have to go deeper, really deep," he said, and his little figure did exactly that. "You have to be willing to wait."

Then there was something, the block rippling out of which emerged the block shape: the head, the pectoral fins like great flat paddles. It was a whale! It was down there. A bell chimed.

"You made this?"

"It's a mod you get."

"I don't know what that means."

"It's just something, I don't know."

"What's that sound?"

"I think you got a message."

"Hop up," she said.

"Wait."

"Hop up, honey. Come on."

She lifted the computer from him and he allowed it to be taken, his body suddenly limp so that he lurched into the couch like some protester given over to authority. She opened the Facebook tab and there it was:

I can't tell you how excited I was to get your friend request
and also so so sorry for my slow response. I'm not on
here as much as I should be I guess. But so excited.
Obviously, I don't hear much from my dad but I'm cool
with that. Truly. But would luv to get together sometime
if that's not too much. Please message me. ☺

It had been long enough for Tess to stare at the screen for a moment in confusion.

"Who's that?" Wally asked and she turned to block the screen with her body, folding the screen forward.

"Go check on your brother for me, honey."

"Who's that message from?"

"Go check real quick, okay?"

She waited until he slouched out of the room before raising the screen. A message from Kayla Maynard? Then the memory of the friend request Tess had sent arrived with a hit of euphoric panic. They were *friends* now. She spent naptime scrolling through Kayla's pictures and posts. She seemed so happy, her scar barely visible. What did Tess have to fear?

She wrote back: I would luv, luv, luv to get together sometime. Let me know when works.

Then it came to her: Thanksgiving up in the mountains. A condo with a kitchen, maybe a hot tub for her and John because the children were out at like seven, seven thirty at the latest. It was just a thought. None of it having anything to do, of course, with proximity to John's daughter.

She sat for a moment in front of the screen and then found a condo by the Pigeon River. Indoor heated pool. Jacuzzi tub. She got out her credit card and booked it.

Why not? she thought.

They could always cancel.

28.

When John finally checked his voicemail it was Stone, of course, which wasn't surprising. That Stone mentioned Ray Bageant was. *Talked to Ray, John. He sends his hugs and kisses, you heartless bastard.* But by then John was headed south on I-75 and couldn't be bothered by Stone's pleading.

Why the fuck are you ducking me, man? I just want to talk.

That was Stone's question.

"What the fuck are you watching this for?"

That had been Ray Bageant's, asked the night he staggered into John's Tampa condo, a six-pack in each hand, plastic rings hooked on his index fingers. He stood with one foot out and his toes turned, as if it was Ray on the verge of walking away when they both knew it had been John who'd left. But instead of leaving Bageant gestured at the television where a thousand miles away Senator Obama stood in Grant Park.

Election Day 2008. Or maybe by that point it was the day after Election Day.

Either way, Bageant was making progress on drinking one administration into the next.

"Be the change, John."

"Ray. What are you doing here?"

"I am the change you've been waiting for," he said, and dropped the cans onto the carpet. "And I come bearing bad tidings."

It had been over a year since John had left his position with Global Solutions. He had left Site Nine and all that it involved the previous summer, and in the intervening months he'd had no contact with anyone from that life, save the deposit that appeared every month in his bank account. This was the remnant of John's own walking away: the remainder of the contract he had refused to complete. The only thing that linked to him to those days. Besides, of course, the dreams. Besides, of course, the damage done.

Bageant slumped into the couch and cracked a beer.

"Where's the wife?"

"She took our son to spend a few days with her parents."

"A son. I hadn't heard."

"Wallace."

"Wallace. Hey, congrats."

Despite everything Bageant looked no worse for the wear than the day John had met him so many years before in Minnesota. In fact, he looked better. He had gained weight, but it appeared more as solidity than anything else. The sort of mass that signaled his presence.

"What is this we're watching, John?"

"His acceptance speech."

"My God, what a stupid America we live in. How about try again."

John said nothing.

"You don't know?" Bageant asked.

"Why don't you just tell me."

"What we're watching is our death warrant, all right? What we're watching is the official issuance of our demise."

John shook his head.

"Don't do that," Bageant said. "You're shaking your head because it's still buried in the sand of the Bush administration."

"I don't know."

"You don't know? Look at Biden up there. You see him. The second they close Guantanamo you know what his job is? His job is to start an investigation into enhanced interrogation. His job is to start rolling heads."

"I'm not so sure. The past is past." John pointed with the remote. "That's what he's saying."

"The past is past?"

"That seems to be the message."

"It's morning in goddamn America? This is what you're saying."

"I'm saying: change. It's what he's saying."

"Change? How about change as a probe by the U.S. Justice Department?"

"Come on, Ray."

"How about change as a congressional inquiry with subpoena power? Truth commissions, all right? You honestly need convincing?"

He didn't. You listened to a man like Ray Bageant because Bageant, in his circumspect way, was an adept of the twenty-first century. A dialectician of the working groups and video chats, the occasional pithy, well-timed tweet. It wasn't hard to imagine him striding through the world of global finance, quoting interagency position papers and checking his phone from one of the lie-flat beds on the overnight to Berlin or Myanmar. Yet here he was, slouched on the couch, popping the ring-tops off can after can while people clung to streetlights to get a better cell phone shot of the president-elect.

"Peter can't protect us," Bageant said finally. "Peter," he said, "is dead."

"As in truly and officially?"

"As in he has ceased to exist."

"And this is a permanent state, his death?"

Bageant smiled with what might have been exasperation, but John knew wasn't. Peter Keyes had been a sort of god to John, burnished and almost bright with wisdom. He'd given John a chance to do something that mattered. But he knew it had been different for Ray. "It's death, John. What can I say beyond that? He was wrong about a lot of things. He was right about a lot of things too, but on the question of death, well."

"I understand."

"It doesn't give me any pleasure, if that's what you're thinking."

Like the rest of the world, John had seen it on TV and read about it online. But half of him had believed it was another rumor, another legend. Another lie. But it was true. When last he'd seen Peter he was wasting away with an autoimmune disorder. Then there was word of his recovery. And then word of his violent expiration. Not that his death was surprising. After a report surfaced identifying the Keyes Group as the parent corporation of Global Solutions, named as one of the accused in the case of Hassan Natashe, there were plenty of people who wanted to take a shot at Keyes. So it wasn't his actual death.

It was the manner that unsettled John. All the talk of immortality, the antioxidants and hyperbaric chamber, the grooming of telomeres—only to be shot by some third-rate jihadist. A California-born convert who walked out of Friday prayers with his balled hatred and an antique machine-pistol. Peter must have walked into the bullets like rain, never believing in his own death, never having time to. Twenty years old, was the rumor online. A white kid, a college dropout singing *Allahu akbar* in the shower. It hurt to think it hadn't even been a proper assassin, though John supposed it was fast becoming a traditional form of death: the disappointing killer with the failure-prone gun that, just this once, doesn't fail.

"When you came to Yalta."

"I remember."

"I didn't want him to meet with you, but he insisted." Bageant let his hands float up as if disavowing what he had just said. "Make of that what you will."

When the beer was gone they decided to get dressed and walk to the corner bodega. Bageant needed alcohol. John needed air.

They came home with a box of Franzia and drank wordlessly until the sun came up.

"I still think of it like the Blitz," Bageant said. "A few RAF pilots holding the line against the barbarians."

"We few."

"We happy few." He held the box of wine as if it were a child, one finger curled around the spout. "I'm not trying to sound all high and mighty. Mistakes were made. We know this. Some very regrettable decisions in the heat of the moment. There was confusion on the ground."

"Fog of war."

"Fog of war. We know this. We also know we did exactly what we were supposed to do and that's why they'll come after us."

It was hours later that Bageant shook John awake.

"You need to shut up," he said.

John's eyes opened slowly. Outside it was day, another day.

"What's wrong?"

"You were saying his name in your sleep."

"Whose name?"

"Whose do you think, asshole? Hassan Natashe."

✳

Erin lived in a neighborhood of shabby-chic bungalows and old trees, a world of silver propane tanks and underpinned mobile homes stuffed in the margins. But of all the places John had seen in his hometown, it seemed to have best survived what seemed a plague of collective indifference. Not that he didn't question how he defined the world. For years he had railed against the bourgeois norms of trim lawns, the policy holders, the ones with whole life and major medical. The comfort that encapsulates. The luxury that cushions. The heart's carapace, he would say.

Or some such shit.

The day he drove to Peach Creek from his failed non-visit to his daughter, they had sat on Erin's porch drinking wine and talking, and the talk had carried them through the afternoon into the evening where at some point they realized they were both hungry and drunk. They had wound up with takeout egg rolls and hibachi, John passed out on the couch and then up and on the road before Erin ever woke.

Since then they had been talking online, always at John's initiating, never really intending to, but doing it anyway because when he talked to her there was the possibility he was talking to a past that wasn't so much gone as misplaced. When they talked he could almost believe in the only resurrection he cared about: the resurrection of his wife. Going to see Kayla had been an honest mistake. But he saw now how foolish it had been, the nuclear option, the sort of all-out engagement he could never survive. It was different with Erin. At times she seemed as lonely and sleepless as John.

John: You awake?
EP: You 2 huh.
John: Roger that.

He had said nothing about his wife and children and wondered sometimes if Erin knew. It would be hard not to: if she had looked him up on the Garrison website or almost anywhere online she would have found mention of family. But maybe she chose not to look. Maybe she chose to allow John to reveal what he wanted to reveal. Or maybe she simply didn't care.

John: I miss talking to you.
EP: Then come back.
John: I will.
EP: When?????
John: Soon. I promise.

That first day at her house she had given him this drunken half-cocked look, a little incredulous, a little mocking. So here's John. Back again. Slumming.

She was on the porch again when he next came, same rocking chair, same look, and it was at this moment he would later realize that things began to gather speed. The quickening started with her standing and smiling. That they wound up first in the shower together and then her bed, tangled and panting, seemed more an accident of acceleration than anything else. He didn't really begin to think about what he had done until after when he sat naked on her mattress while she pulled on a T-shirt and went to bring something back in from the porch: a small jewelry box that held a baggie and lighter and several sealed hypodermics. He realized then what it was he had interrupted: sitting on the porch, she'd been on the verge of shooting up.

"My God."

"Honey," she said.

"That's crack."

"Crank, actually."

A leather belt from her closet, the way she popped at the crook of her bent arm, slapping it as if trying to wake a small child. She shot up and her entire face went slack. Later, they made love a second time, slower, and afterward held each other lightly.

That was it. He thought that was it, a single Saturday fallen into his life like a stone.

But then it was every Saturday. Relicensure, he told Tess, who always seemed to be putting on her running shoes or taking them off. Relicensure, reaccreditation—he could hardly keep track of what he said, but knew, too, she wasn't listening. She was running, she was trying to wean Laurie, she was trying to sleep through the night. He was attentive. In so many ways he was a good father. He did prayers and bedtime stories and breakfasts, but every Saturday, he was gone. Because he had to. Because to some extent he felt himself squaring those days drinking wine with Erin against his past, against his time in Minnesota with Stone and in California with Peter Keyes. That lost world of disaster and haute vegan cuisine. The women who appeared to be in constant pursuit of rare hand lotions. The men tapping on the screens of tablets, such an unnatural sound, like a deaf child imagining rain.

He squared it against the love they made, so tentative, as if giving birth to some frightened needful thing. Coaxing out their truer selves, what they might yet be if only they could sit still long enough to realize it.

He squared it against his time at Site Nine, too, his time of watching.

But then he squared the entire universe against that, every good thing he'd ever been or done against those months. The goodness of his children, the strength of both his wives, the purity his parents had maintained. He put it all on one side of the ledger, put Site Nine on the other, and prayed—to the extent he prayed, which was not at all really—that it balanced, knowing all along it did not.

He didn't see her shoot up again, but recognized when she had: that glass-eyed splendor, that brittle-boned brightness he remembered from the Mexican restaurant their first night. She'd wind her heart like a clock and go out and spend the next twenty-four hours doing good.

Teaching children to read and parents not to beat those children.

How it was better to repair than wreck.

When he asked about the drugs she only smiled, a little sadly.

Oh, honey, did you think for one teeny second you were entitled to an opinion on it?

Some nights she would light a joss stick. For atmosphere, she said, but he knew it was to make him uncomfortable.

"Are you high right now?"

"My god, you're living in a state of constant fear."

"High or stoned or whatever you call it."

"It's going to keep you from being alive."

"That's possible."

"But not from dying."

"Probably not."

"Definitely," she would say, crawling across the bed toward him, "not."

It was dizzying, with Erin one moment, with his family the next. He took the boys to see his parents and his mother suddenly burst into tears and begged him to have bloodwork done, full panels, cholesterol, kidney function, and he decided he couldn't go back, at least not for a while.

Where he could go was to Erin.

"I think you've been sent to me," she told him. "I am a messenger and the message is that it's time for you to put everything behind you and live."

He believed her.

The problem was, he believed Stone, too. There was another message, and then another, and finally John decided to call him back late one Saturday night as he drove north.

"One other thing I need, John."

And he waited for it because what was the point in not waiting, what was the point in trying to dodge it? He had called Stone after all.

"One other thing I need because to be totally honest, the first thing, Hadawi's e-mails—which I do appreciate," Stone said, "but the first thing was mostly for my personal edification. This is more official. I need you to meet someone."

"Who?"

"He's just a kid, but I've taken a shine to him."

"Honestly, Jimmy, I don't much give a fuck."

"You don't give a fuck? All right, I get that, I do. But before you hang up, listen to me, all right? This isn't simply something involving your ever-evolving legal status. This is beyond that. This is beyond some legal whatever."

"What is it then?"

"It's redemption, John. Do you believe me?"

"Who is he?"

"I'm about to call Lazarus out of the grave. I'm about to resurrect your life. Do you believe what I'm saying? Do you?"

And across the distance of miles and drinks, he did.

It was mindless and pointless and he knew he'd regret it, but John believed him.

29.

She had waited for this without realizing it.

In bed, everyone in bed. The children tucked in, John asleep beside her. Outside the moon lodged in the high dark of winter.

In two days they were driving to Pigeon Forge for Thanksgiving, their first family trip since Laurie had been born. And on Friday—Black Friday—Tess was going Christmas shopping at the outlets. But that was only a small part of it. The larger was that she was going to meet Kayla. John would keep Laurie and the boys—he knew nothing about Tess's plans—which meant Tess would have the entire day.

So maybe it was the fact that her meeting John's daughter was settled.

Maybe it was the fact that everyone was home and safe and sleeping, and *that* was settled.

But whatever it was, she realized a certain moment had arrived.

She folded the page of the book she was reading and dimmed the bedside light. The USB drive was buried in the nightstand but it took only a moment to find it. In the kitchen, she turned the laptop so that the screen faced only her. She inserted the drive and opened the file to a gallery of thumbnail photographs.

They appeared to be vacation photographs from somewhere cold and distant. Rainy landscapes, gray castles, city streets. Gingerbread men and mulled wine. The occasional sign appeared vowel-deprived and she thought of the box at John's parents', the Slovak chocolate, the postcard from Ukraine. An apron of beach below the orange rooftops below the blue mountains.

Concrete dust on a monument.

A poorly lighted park and a blur of traffic.

She kept clicking until she came to a face.

Not John. It was a man she didn't know. Except she did. The face belonged to one of the men she had met at St. Simons so many years ago. That first weekend she had insisted on driving up, she and John only barely dating, a maybe couple still in the process of becoming what it was they eventually became.

The man looked older in this picture, he looked tired. But Tess felt certain it was him. Then she thought of something else, she thought of the mail that had accrued during that winter retreat, and she remembered the name: James Stone.

Hadn't John mentioned it recently, some old friend?

Jimmy I might have called him. Haven't seen him in years and there he was outside my office.

She was staring at the face of James Stone.

The next image was of a man, seen from behind. He was kneeling on the floor so that she saw the dark soles of his slippers against the orange of his jumpsuit. Not his face, not his hands. He was without any identifying markers.

He was, she thought, the man in the basement.

Or some man in some basement.

Something told her to stop.

Something told her to slowly pull her hand back from the touchscreen. When she trusted herself to move, she closed the window and removed the USB drive. But she couldn't get up, at least not yet. That same something told her to look, but not at the thumb drive, and she brought up the CNN website and there, bannered across the page in large font was news that the man in the basement, the American, was dead, beheaded online for all to see.

She made no move.

There would be a new video now, there would be a record of it.

Still, she made no move. Someone was very near. Someone stood directly behind her, close enough to touch, if only Tess would turn. Yet she made no move. She made no sound. Then, moving very calmly and very deliberately, she put the laptop to sleep and went back to bed, put the USB drive back in her nightstand, and took up her book. John was still asleep. He hadn't stirred.

She flipped to a chapter on nineteenth-century whaling.

The tails of sperm whales, she read, were a constant danger to whalers chasing them in small boats. They could smash timber, they could break necks. They were so dangerous that whalers had once referred to them as the Hands of God. Which spoke not only to the sudden violence, but to the unpredictability of their movement.

30.

Jimmy Stone's place was in the mountains off I-40 and just south of the North Carolina–Tennessee line, the forest dense and steep, the road a constant switchback. The last half mile was a gravel road overhung with fir and then the sky opened and there in the clearing was the house to which Stone had given John directions.

It was a 1950s lake house—the gray-green water began just down the slope—refurbished, but not recently. A big screened deck with a canoe tucked beneath. Asbestos siding painted a dark red. A rotten-looking hammock. There was an Econoline van and beneath a shed what appeared to be an old Camry. John parked and stood in the yard. The only sound the wind in the trees and the slow rotation of a weather vane.

Stone waited on the porch, smiling, a drink in one hand. He had acquired a cut down the left side of his face, closed, scabbed over, but puffy and still unhealed. The kind of wound that stays with you.

"You found us."

"Yeah."

"Not that I had any doubt. What are you drinking?"

"What happened to your face?"

"A misunderstanding is all. What are you drinking, John?"

John didn't answer, just followed Stone inside where he stood beneath a trophy buck and poured something brown into a glass.

The room was long and narrow, low-ceilinged and decorated with down-home kitsch. The needlepoint cushions. The prints of mallards. All of a piece except for the painting thumbtacked to the wall. John stepped closer. It was a page torn from a book, glossy and creased where it had been folded, a horrific image that registered only vaguely.

"Goya," Stone said.

"Torn out of a book?"

"He brought it with him." Stone motioned across the room. Through the sliding glass door John could see someone sitting on the back porch, staring out at the lake. "Reed Sharma, not that it matters."

"What am I supposed to say to him?"

"You said to me something once about understanding regret, about having to live with it."

"I said that?"

"Jesus. You wrote an entire book about it. About wanting to undo what can't be undone. I want you to tell that to him."

"Tell him what?"

"Your past," Stone said.

"Which part?"

"That boy—he's on the verge of doing something beyond stupid. He's on the verge of becoming us. You get what I mean when I say that?"

"Which part?"

"All of it," Stone said. "Except one thing. Tell him about your wife. Tell him about your daughter. But no Peter Keyes and no Site Nine."

"That boy?"

"Correct. That boy right there. The only other human being in plain sight."

"You said Lazarus on the phone."

Stone motioned with his drink. "That's Lazarus right out there watching the bass jump."

"I thought I was Lazarus."

Stone shook his head in disappointment. "You want to try to make some amends. You want to try to undo some of the damage you did—"

"Don't you?"

"I stand by what I did. I did what was necessary. But I know you don't necessarily share the sentiment."

"I don't know what to say."

"You don't know what to say? You're a counselor, aren't you?" Stone said. "So go counsel him. Go out there and tell him what you did, and then tell him how you live with it every day. Tell him how you're living with it still. Or maybe tell him how you're not living with it if that sounds more like it. Tell him how you're failing to live with it."

"All right," John said. Because that did sound more like it. The not living, the failing.

"All right," he said. Because that sounded exactly like it.

The failing was his past. The failing was where he would start.

Part Three

AltKombat

31.

As for Reed Sharma's failing—which was just another way of saying his past—you might start after his graduation from an expensive Swiss boarding school, that lolling period that was more like twenty-odd months but his mother chose to call his *gap year*. Endless drift—that was more the truth of it. Nineteen and hungry but who could say for what? Working as a runner at a brokerage house, a job reluctantly secured for him by his disbelieving father. But Reed had taken it because it put him inside the machine, and even then he knew all about the machine.

You might start there.

Or you might start with his father, chief economist for an influential consulting firm, and well placed in the lucrative intersection of government and private sector cooperation. Or go back further still: Reed's grandfather had emigrated after the partition of India, a secular thoracic surgeon who knew better than to walk to Pakistan with nothing more than his new bride and an antique British service revolver.

Reed's own father was born three years later in the Baltimore hospital where his immigrant father—Reed's grandfather—would soon be chief of staff. It was in Baltimore where Reed's father went on to meet Reed's mother, a snow-white society girl studying literature at Johns Hopkins. The result being money on both sides, influence compounded quarterly, and a scrawny kid—Reed—who appeared more Italian than anything else. Nobody went to the mosque, nobody got on their knees. His mother was Catholic, but only at Christmas and at Easter, because their religion was the self-actualization of wealth. Which is another way of saying they were Americans.

So maybe start there, start with the money Reed didn't want.

Start with the privilege he couldn't stand.

Start with nineteen-year-old Reed, pissy and depressive and stuttering.

Start, perhaps, with Reed in New York.

He had come for the movement, the revolution, it didn't matter what exactly so long as the underlying principle was disruption, so long as the order of the day was the destruction of his father's world, the stomping of money's clogged heart. This was just after Occupy had been flushed from American parks, their Gore-Tex tents and vegan meals hosed out of city squares from New York to Oakland. But he knew the energy had not dissipated so much as been sublimated, gone underground where now and then it would rear up, not uncommonly in the tags and murals that began to appear on the façades and glass fronts of banks.

It was why he had come. Word would go out that a graffiti artist had hit the HSBC on Fifth Avenue or Goldman down in the Financial District and Reed would rush out to see it before it was pressure-washed into oblivion. It felt like the beginning of something rather than the end. These wannabe Banksy boys with theirs spray acrylics and paperbacks of Chomsky—who could possibly stop them? That they were tagging everything, reaching impossible locations, first the walls of some corporate building and then the lobby itself, the expensive bas reliefs, the fountains carved with dates and names—it spoke to their omnipotence. That they were inside the Bank of America Tower was proof, Reed thought, of the helpless decadence of his father's world.

Then it went online. First Anonymous, and then its children, these cyber-anarchists who called themselves the Jackals, the Aliens, the Werner Herzog Metaphysical Collective Devoted to Cosmic Indifference. They were shutting down banks and government websites, redirecting traffic from Wells Fargo to a dummy site promising to redistribute stolen wealth. An ATM in Columbus Circle was spitting out receipts printed MOLOCH IS GOD AND JANET YELLEN HIS PROPHET.

Yellen? For realz? Janet-fucking-Yellen you're saying?

No kidding?

Reed loved it and was determined to make contact because it's not a cliché if you actually do something, right? He was what they needed after all: a believer, but a believer on the inside. He had access to whatever it was he had access to. A laminated swipe badge he wore on a lanyard around his neck, keypad entry to the seventh floor.

Everyone at the firm knew of his father.

Everyone smiled and nodded.

Business had been grim once but not now, now there was money to be made. Meanwhile, Reed bided his time, made coffee and lunch runs. Espresso. Sushi like maki rolls and ika nigiri and never did he forget the extra wasabi because you have to *attend* to things, you have to pay attention.

Meanwhile—within that previous meanwhile—he was putting out feelers, asking questions, letting it be known that he was willing to act, poised, perched. Prepared for something beyond riding the A train to a delicatessen near Fort Tryon Park. The special pastries from Park Slope. The cupcakes and craft beer. These refined palates that reminded him of his father's students back in Palo Alto, econ majors concerned with junk bonds and flavored popcorn. People getting obsessive over shade-grown roasts, debating coffee blends as runic as apocryphal gospels.

And still the feelers were out there, Reed's antennae up. Reed attuned, awaiting. Anxiously awaiting, yes, admittedly, but knowing too it was a time for clarity, for thinking things through. Like what he was against: things like corporate capital, bullies, the repeal of the Glass-Steagall Act. His father. Also the shits on the seventh-floor equities desk who so obviously knew all that there was to know in the entire fucking universe even though they were barely older than him. Fuck those guys.

Now a list of what he was for, but admittedly it was a vague list: whatever the man in the street is screaming about, the old guy with the sandwich boards and the lazy eye, the dreadlocked white girl wrestled to the ground by riot police, the kid shot dead in the face with pepper spray: Reed was for whatever it was they were about, no hesitation, no questions asked.

Meanwhile—because this was a period of *meanwhiles*, each stacked one inside the next like nesting dolls—meanwhile, he got a room in a railroad apartment in Flatbush and spread his arms so that his fingertips grazed the walls so narrow was his single room, and he loved that, the constriction of physical space mirroring his narrowing focus. This was *clarity* speaking its truth-to-power as clear as the ring of an old rotary-dial phone. He loved the rotting window casement. Loved the radiator beneath it and how sometimes he forgot and left the dial set at five so that he woke on his synthetic foam mattress in a funk of sweat and body odor.

He had rashes.

He talked to the cab drivers. Sikhs in turbans. Smoke-eyed Nigerians. The average cab driver had a PhD in systems theory and a familiarity with the use of thumbscrews. Before the coup they were cabinet secretaries and legal advisors to the now-deposed junta.

But how to let them know he was *simpatico*?

He tried to talk to the black guys on the subway, giant earphones wrapping their heads.

Fuck you looking at, nigga?

Cornrows. Winter coats like spacesuits, like they were packed inside, bundled for some Mars mission. He walked up to them, looked at the mud-spilled eyes, the jaundiced skin, the uncut nails. Watch caps. Dreds tucked under a do-rag.

You need to shimmy the fuck on, cornbread.

He didn't care. Coat-hanger tattoos of puffed brilliance. Wounds slathered with antiseptic cream and wrapped in panty liners. Acne. Shave bumps. Not just blacks, but Mexicans, Salvadorans, Hondurans, Chinese, Indonesians. These were his people. He wanted to make contact, to know them, to share the struggle if only they would realize he was one of them, inside he was one of them.

He kept going, walking, doing.

The war was on TV, but not so much anymore. People were sick of the war.

Sand and palms. An artillery shell stuffed into a camel's ass.

I ain't saying it again, cornbread.

He began to suspect skin mites, but the point was academic: given the right mindset you could cup suffering in the bowl of your joined feet.

Girls took interest, or maybe one girl, a passing interest that manifested itself as a shy wave or—on two, arguably three occasions—holding the elevator door for him. But Reed had no time for this. Shrugged her off because there came a time when a man had to think, goddamnit. He hid behind his stutter, the way his tongue couldn't seem to stay off the back of his teeth, the way it failed to climb. The aggression he was holding in check. The way he stood there in front of God and his fallen world with his finger in the dike, waiting.

He was called upon by a documentary filmmaker named James Stone who took Reed's deference for latent homosexuality. Reed wasn't gay, but he was lonely, and allowed Stone to take him to the occasional meal, another time to an indoor firing range in New Jersey where Stone held forth with his ear protectors up on his head like plastic growths. *Let me tell you what fear will do for you.* Stone saying this. *Fear will wipe you clean. You can depend on its redemptive powers, Reed, on its potential to re-create. It's why guys like me go to firing ranges, yeah? A handgun is pure potential. The only genuine re-creation any of us will ever get. A gun, a bomb, a* weapon, *young master Reed, is the simplest and surest way to reshape the world.* He slid down the ear protectors in a much too studied manner. He was faintly brown skinned, darker than Reed. He was making a film about a collective of anarchists. He was possibly in love with a Jesuit priest. Possibly, also, it was a nun and Reed was imagining the whole gay thing. *You aim with your dominant eye, but* do not *shut the other. That's the trick.*

Another day they shot pumpkins with an Adaptive Combat Rifle at a range out near the Newark Airport. Stone's face was just starting to give, the first expression of sag and paunch. He kept one finger near the rim of his nose but never quite in it. He believed he was having a spiritual crisis. These goddamn anarchists had him confused and he was not a man conversant in muddle. *I'm seeing things. Fairy-tale ghosts. Sometimes these white clouds follow me like smoke rings.* He called early, day after day. Referred to them as Reed's wake-up calls, a public service available for a limited time because shortly he was off to finish his documentary. These American anarchists working for peace in Baghdad or maybe it was Damascus or also, possibly, Mali.

Half-asleep, body chewed by bedbugs, it was difficult for Reed to keep such details straight.

"It's endlessly childish and mean but don't think violence doesn't happen. These people stand in the way, Reed. Human shields. Half-crazy, half-brave."

"Let me sleep."

"It doesn't actually *accomplish*. This is what I've discovered. Violence, I'm talking about. It doesn't accomplish. Yet it still beckons."

"What time is it?"

"You don't sound tired. You slept well, didn't you? Clear conscience. Or maybe you mean physically, eight solid hours."

"I want to sleep to quarter to six, that's my dream."

"That's your fantasy, taking place in said fantasy world where the bad guys don't go blowing the good guys up."

"You're the one who said it beckons."

Jimmy, then, with his big *Ha!* "Like you have no idea."

Stone had a one-bedroom in Nolita, barren but for the pasteboard furnishings it came with, the spare dresser and bed, the mini-fridge, the floor lamp with its shrink-wrapped cord. Reed visited once and found Stone blaring Leonard Cohen. A neighbor knocked against the wall with what sounded like a broomstick.

"All I wanted to be growing up was a folk singer," Stone said. "John Prine or Joan Baez, I didn't care. Then my mother went and convinced me what a mistake that was."

Then James Stone disappeared, off to finish his film in Baghdad, to screen a film in Telluride, to do something somewhere that wasn't here. Reed half-remembered talk of a fellowship from a think tank in maybe Missouri or maybe Minnesota because, again, at times it was difficult to keep things straight.

One day at work he got into the office personnel file and double-clicked his name and then double-clicked on the PDF of a reference letter from a former teacher and when he read "You wouldn't think boys like this still exist" he stopped right there because the sentence was pure possibility. It could fall either way but as it stood—as Reed let it stand—it was like that moment in a car, rolling backward but already you've shifted from reverse into drive and at any moment that sudden catch will wake you.

His mother called.

The girl held the elevator a third time—possibly a fourth time, given your point of view.

One day, Stone called wanting to talk about self-immolation, a sacrificial act, Reed. They're doing it right now in Tibet, in China. They did it in Tunisia. This isn't just an inventory. There's an ecology here, a web on which you might plot desire and anger and the endless bullshit called life on planet earth.

"Jimmy—"

"Don't think this isn't timed to climate change, to glacial melt. All these burning bodies heating up the atmosphere. You need to know this, Reed, but I'm warning you: don't speak of it. You speak of it and you silence a room. Mothers will hush you, come and put a hand on your arm, comfort you. But rest assured that someone somewhere, some young man, eager but sad, he's going to set himself on fire. Moscow, let's say. Red Square. And that'll be the last you hear of Putin."

He called another day to talk about Dostoyevsky because did Reed know that when old Fyodor kicked off he left behind an outline for a sequel to *The Brothers Karamazov*? Did Reed know this? Just a little nugget of info I'm relating here. Reed had read *Karamazov*, right?

Reed was silent, alone in his room and nodding in that glazed way that indicated he hadn't but would never admit as much.

"Reed? You there? You've read it?"

"I'm f-f-familiar with it."

"Familiar with it. All right. Then you'll appreciate that in the sequel Alyosha—you remember Alyosha? Youngest son, would-be monk?"

"Of course."

"Well, he runs off to Moscow and becomes a Christian anarchist. A terrorist, I'm saying, Reed. A legitimate thrower of bombs. Boom,

boom, boom. Strange fact, right?" He laughed. "Just a little nugget is all. Something I thought you might appreciate."

Reed hung up, Googled "James Stone director," and read demented shit about torture and death, his connection to the billionaire Peter Keyes. When he searched for Keyes he found him everywhere, news about his wealth, about his murder. Profiles in *Wired* and the *New Yorker*. Someone had named a sandwich after him. Grilled tempeh on brioche. The kind of thing you'd eat in a Lucite chair while outside it rained.

And while those *meanwhiles* curled one inside the other—little seahorses fit fin to fin until one couldn't be discerned from the next—he decided to up his game, to make his overtures overt. Walk around Zuccotti Park talking shit, NYPD cameras everywhere. Buy a zero-degree sleeping bag and a SteriPEN water filter as if he was taking up permanent residence in the wild. Haunted army surplus stores and online anarchist message boards. Returned to the range alone to shoot exploding zombie targets because—he guessed— pumpkins were out of season.

James Stone drunk-dialed and cried, absolutely wept into the phone, but you couldn't say why, not that Reed would want to even if he could. The world is bricked out of sadness, a block-by-block construction, injustice on top of anger, as ugly as it is impervious— Is that not reason enough? *You aim with your dominant eye, but* do not *shut the other. That's the trick.*

When the zombies exploded they scattered a burst of pulpy gray matter. Like brains, obviously.

He bought something called a LifeStraw that could filter up to 10,000 gallons.

Read *Adbusters* on the 6 train.

His father was named CEO and transferred to Atlanta where he could occasionally be seen discoursing on the Eurozone crisis on CNN.

Meanwhile, a guy on the trading desk got hooked on hot chicken from a soul place in Dumbo but wanted his sour cream from some artisanal creamery in goddamn Fort Greene. It's Thorstein Veblen. It's conspicuous consumption if he wasn't confusing things, and he couldn't wait to blow it the hell up.

Meanwhile, meanwhile . . .

There were ads on Craigslist for assault rifles. Narco-traffickers laundered money through eBay. He read up, little nascent revolutionary in training. Tried to wrap his head around bitcoin. How it can be money but not money. It was baffling, but he knew that was just nineteen years of brainwashing speaking up like one of the yapping terriers tucked beneath another braceleted arm.

The girl holding the elevator had pale legs and a slide of gum between her upper lips and teeth and it was that pink he would think about later, that pink like the inside of a seashell. Whatever was precious tucked within the mother-of-pearl. He smelled her perfume, guessed her underwear to be lavender.

His mother called again: *Why don't you come to Atlanta, honey, why don't you come stay with us?* He said no, but secretly was already there, starting over at the whole starting-over thing.

Please, Reed?

When he said maybe she sent him a credit card which he promised himself he wouldn't use and didn't until one day on a whim he bought the elevator girl a $900 camel's hair coat he never had the balls to give her.

These were moral failings, chinks in his righteousness not even his puckered skin could redress. He drank from the bathroom tap which now and then went brown and he tasted the rust so thick he practically chewed the water. But even this wasn't enough. In this world how could it be?

There was a street off Houston that sold nothing but birds. Not just exotics, not just macaws and parakeets, but ordinary chickadees.

Wrens. Blue jays. Ornate cages. Mineral-enriched seed. Cracked corn. A block over people paid $300 a month for the privilege of swinging a sledgehammer at a tractor tire while a man with a shaved head screamed at them. *Faster. Harder. More.*

Excess.

Greed.

Ego.

He was almost certain his father belonged to three different racquet clubs in three different cities.

How do you live in the world a good man? was maybe the question.

Or maybe he was past questions. Maybe all he wanted was to be surprised by his life, to be overtaken by himself. Maybe all he wanted was to blow things apart so radically that what was left was unrecognizable because why the hell would he want to recognize the life he currently led? It was ridiculous; he knew it was ridiculous. He had things to offer, he had access. Why wasn't anyone else noticing this? He cared about the poor, about their suffering. He was on their side, goddamn it.

It was an argument he'd played out countless times with his father, the Great Professor who could do anything and everything except teach his son. Sitting together in some Chelsea brasserie, his father in town for a conference and having lunch on his expense account. *The white savior complex, son.* Reed's advocacy, Reed's interest, just another form of colonialism. *They're human beings, Dad.* And his father looking up from his *fritto misto.* *That's exactly what I'm saying. When you speak on their behalf you are taking away their personhood. You're acting as if they can't speak for themselves.*

But— But there were no buts, no responses. In the presence of his father Reed could never speak and soon enough that *impairment* (his mother's word) spread outward like ripples troubling a pond and he couldn't speak in the presence of anyone. *Tongue-tied* said his father. So he began seeing a speech therapist three days a week, and then a psychiatrist who wanted him to talk—*was she fucking serious?*—about his relationship with his parents, as if such a thing existed, as if such a thing was anything more than the leftover spillage of his well-appointed childhood.

Reed wasn't made out of his childhood, for God's sake.

Reed was constructed from the need to act.

Why wasn't anyone noticing this?

And then someone did. Someone made contact because at some point desperation begins to register. It moves outside the self to occupy actual physical space. Has to be addressed as much by the larger world as the sad sack son of a bitch sitting in his shirtsleeves, drinking instant coffee.

The summer groaning with heat and never-ending unrest and then the summons arriving with the swiftness of fall. Thanksgiving Day a message appeared in his inbox beckoning him to a theme restaurant in Times Square where they waited for him at a second-floor table, the place otherwise empty. A man and woman, early middle-aged, suburban, and safe. The decor was that of an Old West movie: a saloon with WANTED posters and potted cacti, a cardboard cutout of Clint Eastwood. The bar served sarsaparilla and the waitresses wore bonnets and gingham dresses. The waiters were in straw hats, twine strung through their belt loops. Reed paused for a moment at the head of the stairs, warm in a shaft of noon sun.

The man stood to shake hands.

The woman kept her eyes on the stairs.

"You've come to our attention," the man said. "There has been talk."

The woman wore a blue pantsuit. The man had a head of gelled hair and a mouth of tiny teeth that put Reed in mind of Indian corn, worn nubbins that belonged between the lips of a toddler. He put a manila envelope on the table, slid it past a smear of maple syrup.

"We are," he said, "in need of a courier."

"Who are you?"

"We represent a collective of sorts. But me personally, I'm the Voice of Reason."

Reed never opened the packages. A note would arrive in his box, a time, a place. There were flat DHL envelopes and larger boxes plastered with packing tape so that they appeared more as conceptual art than means of transference. They went to PO boxes or corner bodegas or, on one occasion, an apartment in the same Chelsea building where he had once lived with his parents. What effect these deliveries made he never fully knew. If something had happened—an attack, a bomb—he might have traced his movements, established some causal chain. But nothing ever happened. Yet, every week he felt a gathering rightness that bordered on religious ecstasy, every movement an act of devotion.

In February a package arrived from James Stone. The postmark *por avión*, stamped over the Arabic, stamped over the image of a dusty man in a djellaba. A copy of Fyodor Dostoyevsky's *Demons* and a book of Francisco Goya prints with a letter folded inside.

I want to thank you for your hospitality, Reed, and, particularly, for your quiet acceptance of my own uncertainty. My life as I know it has changed radically and already I know how ridiculous this all must sound, but if it isn't clear enough let me state it plainly: I've joined the group I've been filming. They—we—are committed to getting in the way, Reed, to sticking our puny twigs in the great big spokes, to throw our bodies into the gears of the machine. No matter what happens, Reed, I want you to know that I am trying (very inadequately most of the time) to stand in solidarity with the poor and oppressed. Thank you for understanding my choice of this path. I look forward to seeing you again with joy and hope and with the assurance that we will surely fuck them up.

I may call on your help in the future. In the meantime, abide in love,
James Stone

Reed put the letter in the trash, but couldn't quit thinking about it. Took it back out and put it in his pocket. He looked at the Goya. He tried for weeks to read the Dostoyevsky but it only made his head hurt, like some higher math understood by a grand total of no one. Suicide—that was the only thing he took from it. Suicide as the only act you could truly own. But the Goya, the Goya ignited something inside him. Some pure light that he felt scrape and gather until it shone so bright within him it began to shine *out* of him.

In March he could wait no longer and asked for another meeting with the Voice of Reason.

"This is uncommon," he told Reed, same upstairs table, same tourist trap. But no woman to study the stairs. "I trust you have a reason for such imprudence."

"I want to carry something of consequence."

"You have been."

"Come on."

"You continue to."

"Come on. I want something that really matters. I know you carry heavier things."

"You think we don't love this country, don't you? The crewcut cops. The amber waves of grain."

"I want to carry something with weight."

"Like a brick?"

"Like a gun."

"What do you know about guns?"

"Like a bomb."

"What the hell do you know about bombs?" He looked at Reed as if trying to untangle something, his hair, his motives, and Reed wondered at his own delivery. He had practiced before, alone at his mirror in Flatbush, because it was such a ridiculous thing to say. *A bomb.* So stagey. *A b-o-m-b.*

"Let me tell you how the world works," the Voice said, "the adult world, I'm talking about. You want to do serious work you immerse yourself in it, you disappear inside it. Most people don't have the focus for serious work, and those that do tend to have it only once in their entire lives. You look up and it's gone. It flutters away."

"I know you move bombs, bomb parts."

"Do you know what bombs do, Reed?"

"I've pretty much verified this is part of your operation."

"Do you *understand* what bombs do?"

But what was a bomb against the times? What was a bomb against the broken teeth he found swept to the gutter after the police attacked an otherwise peaceful march? You had to draw forth the blood, coax it out, to remind people they were alive, to break the sound of dull knocking—for some reason he heard this in the voice of James Stone, histrionic and flexed—to shatter the sound of the hollow men, dancing.

What was a bomb against global oppression?

What was a bomb against his father?

The package came three days later, a square of eight or ten inches wrapped in brown paper and packing tape, addressed to a man in University Heights. It felt heavier than it should, and riding north on the 4 train he thought it a sort of ballast, something to anchor his world as surely as it blew apart someone else's. He stared at the box from Thirty-Third Street to 125th where the train slowed to a crawl as it navigated past a baseball field and through the projects, a world of busted concrete stoops and yards crowded with lawn chairs on scabs of yellow grass. They were moving slowly enough so that on the buckled sidewalk he spotted a headless Barbie doll, a tricycle tipped onto one tasseled handlebar. Closer to the station, a man stood hosing down the sidewalk outside a Dunkin' Donuts while a boy sold copies of the *Militant*, body leaned against a NEIGHBORHOOD WATCH sign.

Near Yankee Stadium, he began rereading Stone's letter, eyes fixed until the train pulled into the Fordham Road station. *The poor and oppressed.* He knew the benighted poor, the favored children of God. *The poor will always be with you.* So said no less than Christ, and Reed told himself he believed it.

The train crept into light. He was doing this.

He was doing this, at least in part, because of his parents, because of the rich assholes back in Switzerland he couldn't bring himself to call classmates. He was doing it because of those fuckers on the seventh floor. But mostly it was about him, about Reed, about being in the world and reclaiming it in a way most could never understand. This wasn't about the poor and oppressed. It wasn't about the 1 percent he had chanted against either. This was a private conversation. The rich, like the poor, just happened to be in the way. So fuck the rich. But just the same: fuck the poor and oppressed. They were mostly poor and oppressed for very good reasons. The point was to shatter something.

He left the subway and walked among the iron grilles and fire escapes and Duane Reade pharmacies, passed beneath the green-and-red awnings of twenty-four-hour bodegas, the windows full of yellowing oranges and dusty cans of Sprite. Around him well-dressed men and women were speed-walking to work, dodging delivery trucks while staring down at cell phones. In front of a synagogue an idling H.T. Hackney truck waited for two transvestites in silver wigs to clear the intersection. One of them clutched a knockoff Vuitton handbag and flipped him off. The other sucked a ring pop while the driver laid on his air horn.

He kept going.

Brownstones lined University Avenue. It was spring and crocuses were newly planted, bright in the sections of dirt separating stairs. He passed a man sweeping his steps, watched him move in and out of a parallelogram of heatless light. Trees lined the walk, lacing intricate shadows, the leaves veined and almost phosphorescent with green light, and when the breeze gathered he watched petals fall, delicate as sails. The leaves alone, their drifting grace, were reason enough for the bomb. Discount the violence, the disparity of wealth, the displaced homeless carrying papier-mâché golden calves and living in packing crates in Central Park. Don't even consider the ornate indifference of his father. Throw it all to the side, forget every last bit of it.

Cupcakes in the spring sun, small dogs carried like handbags—that alone was reason enough. Disregard his father in his lavish Southern manse. Choose not to acknowledge the faithless pleading of his mother. Misremember the fascist police pepper-spraying the homeless. Rule out of bounds the greater Middle East, the drone strikes, the burning minarets, the million dead. Throw it all aside and right there, *right there!* standing on this quiet street with war no more than a rumor to be laughed at and still there was reason enough *as if I even need a goddamn reason.* Put the little brown-packaged square against the slaughter bench of history, against Goya, against *Saturn Devouring His Children*, against *The Madhouse*. Put the little square of paper and tape against the Holocaust, against the Middle Passage. It was laughable. He thought of Stone's sudden conversion and laughed at that as well. It was a crime not to deliver it, even if he was sweating, his ribs ratcheted around his lungs so that breathing was a conscious undertaking.

He stopped at the broad stone steps of an elegant nineteenth-century brownstone and double-checked the address, needlessly.

Here he was. What now?

Leave the package with the doorman and go. Leave the package and—

Except he couldn't. Its weight. All that impossible weight, that fierce density. As if what he held might form the earth, rather than blow it apart.

An elderly woman in pearls and a lacquered coif of dark hair came out the door, looked dismissively at Reed, passed on.

He had to do something.

But what to do?

Something of consequence, he thought, and it came to him what a fool he was, what a child. How right his father was, how right everyone was. *Do you know what bombs do, Reed?*

He stood on the sidewalk and held the box, sweating again, feeling the weight of the cardboard against his fingers, the glossy tape, feeling the sweat slide down the back of his neck.

He thought he might be dying, but realized what he felt was the toxicity he carried.

Not the box but his own soul.

His stomach forced him into the bodega, his sickness—tell yourself that, Reed, keep telling yourself that, brother, that it was sickness and not straight-up fear—past the wall cooler and beer and forgotten boxes of cereal—hep you, sir? hep you?—into the bathroom where he latched the wooden door and stood over the seatless toilet to take long, slow breaths. Still he couldn't breathe, and realized it was because he was laughing, laughing so hard he thought he might break a rib, doubled over, face shiny with snot and tears. How ridiculous, how utterly fucking ridiculous it all was. A bomb! Seriously, a fucking bomb? He had been right to practice saying it because it was ludicrous. He was laughing now, tearing at the packing tape, laughing, someone knocking at the door, laughing, ripping open the box to find—what? A bomb? Maybe, no, wait . . . no, not a bomb: a small laughing Buddha, cross-legged and cast in bronze. As solid as Reed was foolish. A laughing Buddha! Laughing at him!

All the while someone was knocking at the door and he unlatched it, pulled it open on a little Asian man who might have been the Buddha himself. A little bodhisattva selling two Red Bulls for $3. A little happy monk with his scratch-off Lotto and heads of wilting romaine. *Sir? Okay, sir? No mess. Go please, sorry, go.* Reed walked past him, the torn box on the floor, the Buddha held before him like a lamp unto his feet and a light into his heart.

The gears of the machine? Was it a punch line?

Probably, probably everything was, because Reed couldn't stop laughing, all the way home on the subway until folks had moved away from him and he was left alone in the car like a leper. Laughing, goddamnit, because it was a joke.

Okay, fine, then. A joke. I surrender. I give up. And that was exactly what he did.

Three weeks later, having said yes to his mother's repeated offer, he was on a plane to Hartsfield–Jackson and there she was, his mother, just beyond security. Little lost puppy come home. No more takeout coffee. No more elevator girl. Just Reed, stumbling out of his twenty-month joke. The longest setup you could imagine. But the punch line worth every second, worth every laugh. Even if it was the sort of laughter that never quite went away.

So maybe start there, start with the laughter.

Start with the way he couldn't get it out of his head.

Not that he didn't try. Wasn't everything he did an attempt to shake its echo? The way he took the MARTA to Midtown or to Decatur, the long solo walks into every corner of the city. The sports bars, the Coca-Cola, the Braves. There were black neighborhoods and white neighborhoods and poor neighborhoods where everyone was some indeterminate shade of sand. Rich neighborhoods—like the Druid Hills community where his parents lived with their travertine marble and Frontpoint security system. Poor neighborhoods with liquor stores and check-cashing outlets. The cookie-cutter suburbs that put him in mind of baking soda and guilty sex. Ethnic enclaves with souks and kebab shops and corner rugs spread on the pavement where men sold individual cigarettes out of the pack. Falafel joints. Roller rinks and corporate headquarters. It was mindless wandering and he disgusted himself, this was true. But whether he wanted to admit it or not he was an American, which meant he also loved himself. Above all, he pitied himself.

Mostly because nothing was different.

Atlanta was turning out like New York and it wasn't supposed to turn out like New York. The Voice of goddamn Reason. It wasn't supposed to happen like that ever again. The Goya prints and elevator girl. The way they had laughed at him.

What the hell do you know about bombs?

He felt his tongue push out against his teeth. It had started like this years ago, his inability to speak clearly the result of a nervous twitch. Conscious of the weight of his own tongue, feeling it in his mouth like a tiny whale, beached past hope. He would wake at night and feel it edged against his bottom teeth, trying to free itself, moving his incisors in the process. Mornings, he would study them in the mirror and find they had not moved. But he knew they had. He blamed his parents.

And then one day he wandered into a Muslim neighborhood in the corner of Kirkwood, a self-contained world of high-rises and satellite dishes, a cinder-block mosque with an actual minaret, and that day he felt something snap into place, he felt himself dissolve in a way he never had. What he liked was that they didn't stare at him there, or stared but only for a moment, saw him, measured him, and averted their eyes. It was because they were afraid of him—these green-carded politically asylumed refugees shoved into concrete towers—afraid of this grown child of Western wealth. Possibly they hated him. But he liked to imagine that it was because they saw in him nothing unusual, nothing worth staring at.

Which made them different from every other person he had ever encountered, every other person who reacted to him with pity or condescension or, most damning, plans for his psychic salvation. Eventually he learned to disguise himself, to dress in thrift store jeans and municipal work shirts grease-stained as rags. He loved it. Everything was real here, the moldering oranges, the smell of the hookahs. Here was traffic and smog. The girls in their headscarves walking to bus stops. Bored teenagers in keffiyehs posturing on motor scooters. Even the sky seemed different, the deep blues and stringy cirrus of the posh downtown giving way to reefs of gray cloud, the remnants of torn posters, the fresh graffiti over walls whitewashed to efface yesterday's graffiti.

The walks became his salvation.

He came early to watch the day brighten, the changing sun moving alley to alley like stage lights. Around the apartment buildings—massive, terraced monoliths, solemn as tombstones but for the blooms of satellite dishes and strings of laundry—stood aging shade trees pruned badly. Six A.M. and the streets already beginning to fill with domestic workers on their way to the homes of the wealthy. He would stop at a café, have a cup of tea, and just wait. There was a way the morning could touch binned fruit and he saw it for a moment from the corner of his eye, but then it was gone and there was no finding it and he'd probably just imagined it anyway. But he knew, too, that he hadn't. He smelled body odor and washing powder and the scald of the bleach used to scrub the walk, a few scattered pools bright as coins. It was a seductive smell, clean, but violently so.

His mother never knew where he went, and he could see how desperately she needed answers. But how afraid she was too. It was evident that she loved him, but her devotion seemed not unlike the devotion offered a small dog, the way you might wash it in the sink or carry it in your handbag. Brag to your friends about its open-mouthed loyalty. But there he was something else, and soon enough he was a part of it.

By the time he joined the fight gym he had been wandering into the neighborhood for almost a year, wandering around the edge of the Masjid of Al-Islam, hearing the amplified wail of the muezzin call the faithful to prayer. The day he found the flier marked KRAV MAGA AT ALTKOMBAT ATLANTA with its fringe of pull-tabs was around the time it had occurred to him that maybe what his parents had most thoroughly deprived him of was any sense of inheritance. That inheritance could be, he thought, either Islam or Catholicism. But given his location he made a snap decision that it was the teachings of Allah they had denied him, and he was pissed off about it. Without ever really deciding, he decided he was a devout man, a follower of the Prophet, or was meant to be.

He imagined his grandfather emigrating to the States to avoid religious persecution—which wasn't true.

He thought of childhood trips to a Baltimore mosque and how at home he had felt there, how serene—these never happened.

He remembered those rapturous days in Flatbush reading Malcolm X—which was true, the reading part. The rapture was bullshit, of course.

But he was inventing his past, not remembering it, and the invention was his, not his mother's or his grandfather's and surely not his father's.

That evening he looked at the gym website and when he was finished he watched several YouTube videos on Islam. The next day he checked out an English translation of the Koran from the local library and walked to the gym: $110 a month for unlimited classes. No contract, but there was a code of conduct, the idea of which appealed to him. He paid it on the spot, signed everything they put in front of him, and knew both decisions—the gym, Islam—were gifts.

He was a new man, or would be soon enough.

So maybe, for the sake of brevity, start there.

Start at the fight gym.

*

AltKombat was east of downtown in a converted hangar on the edge of a commercial airstrip. Concrete floor. Roll-up door. A giant attic fan that pulled air and dust toward the vaulted ceiling. Nearby was a parachute manufacturer and a broker in precious metals. Inside were blue wrestling mats patched with duct tape, gymnastic rings, heavy bags. A carton of various shin, head, and elbow guards. The class was around twenty-five people of all ages. A few teenage girls. Lots of ex-military twenty-somethings with keloid scars and American flag tats, T-shirts that read WOD KILLA and EAT THE WEAK and WOUNDED WARRIOR PROJECT. A scattering of older folks, white-collar professionals looking to get their asses kicked in a more authentic way. There were also three or four young men about Reed's age. But darker than Reed: dusky skin, midnight eyes. The instructor was a howling human bowling ball of neck, calves, and biceps. Six feet and maybe two-thirty. White hair flowing over his ears. A stone of Slavic extraction.

They started with warm-up drills—bear crawls, frog hops, burpees—and within seconds Reed was panting, fingers pressed into his sides as he gulped the thick air. There had been some fantasy about his level of fitness, all the walking he'd done, but it evaporated in seconds. Fifteen minutes in he was knocked to the floor by a focus mitt. He stood, wobbled, and just made it to the door before he puked.

Skinny fat, the instructor said and looked at him with what Reed could only interpret as disgust.

He drank from the fountain and a few minutes later was knocked down a second time.

But he got back up. That was the single right thing he did: he kept getting back up.

That night he lay in bed feeling as if he had been in a car wreck. His skin was prickled with mat burns, little heat rashes like shading on a map. But there was also the exhilaration of exhaustion. Packed away to the Collège Alpin International Beau Soleil in Switzerland, where despite, or maybe because of, a room that looked out over the Rhone Valley he had felt a sort of foggy desolation that he could no more pierce there than he could later in Flatbush. But that was gone now, wrung out in the tremors he felt waving up and down his body.

It was only when he got up to go to the bathroom—he expected to piss blood but all he managed were a few drops of flax-colored urine, too dehydrated for much else—only then that he remembered the copy of the Koran in his bag. How strange that was, how much like a sign. That he needed succor, but also felt himself a warrior. He was aware of the cliché of the pissed off, disenfranchised nonwhite immigrant. But he was none of those. Or maybe he was all of those.

Either way, that night he started to read.

The next day he returned to both the gym and the library. He picked out the shortest book on Islam he could find and read half of it in a beanbag chair in the kids' section. That was easy. The gym was harder. He was sore and tired, but managed to sleepwalk through the drills and sparring. Get knocked down and get back up, act like you don't mind, act like it was what you came for.

After class, he took the MARTA home and in his room used the GPS on his phone to point the way to Mecca which stood somewhere just to the right of his desktop.

But he didn't pray, not yet.

He did visit the mosque. The building sat across from an elementary school behind a wrought-iron fence and crowded by a parking lot of yellow buses. A few men slept on the vast open floor (only later would he realize he had visited during Ramadan), but no one saw him and he escaped unnoticed.

By the second week he felt better. His muscles ached less. His tiny contusions had blued. He went to four classes, Monday through Thursday, and on Saturday managed to jog seventeen minutes before slowing to a walk and he thought maybe that was the end of it, that he wouldn't return.

But by Monday night he was ready for class. He went back to the library and picked up two more books, read some shit online about Palestine, and it occurred to him that maybe that was the cause he'd been after the whole time he was in New York. It occurred to him that of course it was. He looked at the photos from Gaza and the West Bank, felt moved by it, felt grateful to have a mission so clear-cut.

He brought it up one evening with his mom, but all she wanted to talk about was what was the deal with the bruises?

"I want you to let a doctor look at those."

"M-m-m-om."

"That's a sign, honey. I think that's how leukemia starts."

"J-Jesus, Mom."

He could have told her about the gym. It would have pleased her, he thought. But he didn't want to please her. He said nothing.

He let her worry all week and that Friday he went to prayers. Not to pray so much as to simply bow, to be part of the mass of humanity, the bent knees, the outstretched hands. The imam spoke but in the wash of emotion Reed didn't hear him. He didn't need to, content to be a face in the faceless sea. But when he rose from his last prostration he found the imam staring directly into his eyes.

The following Monday at the gym one of the men—boys, whatever they were—spoke to him. It was a piece of practical advice, he needed to keep his arms closer to his body when he was on the ground, but it was the first time anyone beyond the instructor had spoken to him and he was grateful for it. The instructor seemed to hate Reed, stuttering and soft Reed. But then again he seemed to hate the other boys too. They were all skinny and underfed and wore what might generously be called starter beards. The ex-military guys seemed to take a particular pleasure in knocking them on their asses.

Reed went to talk to the guy again after class but the guy—the kid, whatever, Reed didn't know how to think of him—cut him off. He had to pray. They all had to pray. And in the burned grass beside the hangar the four boys kneeled on yoga mats and touched their foreheads to the dirt.

"I'm sorry," the boy said on rising. "What did you want to talk about?"

He walked with them west into the night, eventually to a tea shop in the immigrant corner of Kirkwood. Three were cousins born and raised in Atlanta though their parents were from Yemen. The fourth, the older one, the quiet one, had come from Iraq when he was thirteen and didn't talk about it. They lived together in a duplex near Bessie Branham Park. Did they like it? Of course not. The blacks were everywhere, the drugs, the noise. The women want only to distract you and there is the way to perdition. But their mosque was near and they could see the imam every day. They were in training. Soldiers in the service of Allah, blessed be his name.

Where was Reed's mosque?

He had no answer.

Why did he not wear a beard, did his father wear a beard?

He didn't say and the boy—Reed thought him no more than eighteen—didn't push.

"We are each of us fighting our own battles," the boy said, and if it sounded a little stupid to Reed, a little obvious, he couldn't exactly refute it either. He asked what battle, exactly?

"Against the state, against the nonbeliever. But also within the heart." He made a broad gesture that was perhaps encompassing, but might also have been dismissive. "We are the ones preparing against the onslaught of the West."

"And that's what the Krav Maga is for?"

He smiled here, the boy. He was an American teenager—they all were—but he was trying so hard not to be Reed couldn't help but appreciate the effort. "Partly yes," he said. "But that is only one small part. Do you know the history of Krav Maga, the logic behind it?"

"No."

"The logic is to kill Palestinians with your fingertips. Your thumbs. Eye, ear, instep. We study Krav Maga to get inside the fist of the Jew. But this is only one small part."

They drank their tea and Reed walked east. When they were out of sight Reed took a cab home.

That night he made his first attempt at prayer.

It was maybe a success, but he didn't really have the metrics to say.

The next Friday he met the boy—his name was Suleyman—outside the mosque. It was Suleyman who introduced Reed first to the imam, and, weeks later, to Professor Hadawi.

Eventually, Reed would meet Aida back at the duplex Suleyman shared with the others, but he was still months from that.

Reed's present tense was his training, his present tense was Suleyman and his cousins. Soon enough it became the imam. He was no more than thirty, Reed thought. Or perhaps he was forty, or fifty. He wore a full beard, but his face was brown and unlined and it was impossible to guess his age. He had come from Yemen to study engineering, staying on after completing his degree at Georgia Tech, as Allah willed it. The mosque was Salafist, a school of thought that believed Muslims had strayed from their roots. All must be rooted. All must flow from the holy Koran, the hadith, the Sunna. The imam explained it over a series of meetings, first with all of the brothers and then with Reed alone. He taught Reed to pray, gave him books and literature and hope.

Most importantly, he gave him something to fill his head.

Something besides, of course, the memory of laughter.

✳

One afternoon Reed and Suleyman took the bus out to a Dick's Sporting Goods so that Reed could buy his own equipment. He was sick of wearing the communal headgear of the gym with its flaking foam padding and greasy feel and had asked his father for money—so far as Reed could tell the single reason for his father's continued existence. They walked through aisles of indecency, the women made from molded plastic, headless and large breasted in their jog-bras and running tights. Yet no one was weeping, no one beat their chests in outrage. It was shameless, and it was their shame.

"It is an offense that we must enter such a den of iniquity to purchase that which Allah accords us." This was Suleyman talking, stilted and ridiculous, Reed thought. Refusing to use contractions as if English wasn't his first language. No doubt parroting what he had heard the imam say. But then again, could Reed refute it? Could he say that it wasn't an offense? Could he discount what Suleyman said simply because he was thumbing through his Facebook newsfeed as he said it?

He bought the headgear and a black mouth guard and they walked out into the bright sun. When they were in the car Suleyman told Reed how impressed the imam was with him.

"He thinks you might begin formal study in Arabic."

"He told you this?"

"The spoken Arabic of Yemen is said to most closely resemble that of the Koran. Most people do not know this."

"He really said he thought I should study?"

The next day Reed asked his mother for money: he wanted to enroll at Atlanta Metropolitan State College. She seemed thrilled and wrote out the check on the spot. It was only after she handed it over that she asked what he intended to study. Arabic, he said. And then she wasn't smiling anymore, and he wasn't enrolling at AMSC. Instead he drove to the World Language Study Center, an annex behind the mosque that had once been the basement fellowship hall of a Baptist church. The open space of block and tile had been divided into narrow classrooms and within one the imam taught classical Arabic to a few students, Reed and Suleyman among them.

The class began after morning prayers, two hours, and then exercises in a workbook. Reed did the work, a capable learner even if his script was sloppy and leaning, and then jogged to the gym where he got in a ninety-minute workout before he returned to pray. By now he was spending at least half his nights in the duplex, showing up with his mother's money. She gave it in spurts, swearing one day he would get no more until he devised some sort of plan—something, anything, my God, this is your future I'm talking about—but the next day passing over a wad of crumpled twenties and tens he would shove in his pocket before she could change her mind. Stuttering his fuck-you-moms as he eased out the door.

It was somewhere around this time that the imam introduced a guest instructor, Professor Edward Hadawi. Professor Hadawi wore an open-necked shirt, Italian loafers, his dark hair a wave of gel. As the imam introduced him, Reed watched his glasses clear. There was a name for it—transition lenses—but sitting there that day it seemed more like magic. After class, the imam asked Reed to stay a moment. When the others were gone the imam introduced him to the professor.

"So this is the one?" Hadawi spoke with a slight British accent. "I've heard good things about you," he told Reed, "such promise."

"Thank you, sir."

"Not that promise is always fulfilled. Promise is simply potential. This is my thinking," he said. "Promise is often an impediment. Do you believe that's true, Reed?"

"I don't k-know."

"There's no reason you should. But think on it."

A few weeks later Reed was hurrying from class to the gym when he was approached by a young white woman in a hijab who stuck a flier in his hand and said, *you should come.* The flier read SHARIANOW! and on it was a website, below that a place and time.

"What is this?" he asked her.

"A meeting."

"About what?"

"Come and find out."

"All right."

She smiled, flirting. "You will?"

"Yeah, I will. What's your name?"

"My name? Aida."

"All right. I'll see you there, Aida."

She laughed and said *maybe.*

It was only later that he realized he had spoken with perfect clarity.

*

He attended as much out of duty as curiosity. Except that wasn't true: he attended because of the girl, because of Aida. Aida before she was *his* Aida. It turned out to be more of a religious service than a political rally—but he was only then coming to learn that there was no true difference between the two. He entered through a shuttered convenience store beneath a banner marked SHARIANOW! Shelves dusty and mostly empty. Passed through a heavy security door into a crowded room of block walls and metal folding chairs. A fan that failed to oscillate. The squat heat thick with the smell of the thirty or forty young men packed into the airless space.

They watched a video of some distant imam, cross-legged on the floor, speaking flawless English as Arabic blocked across the bottom of the screen. The feed, the recording—Reed didn't know if this was some live event—but whatever it was, was shaky. The talk was of the rising caliphate. To replace what was democracy with shura councils. To expel nonbelievers. To execute homosexuals. Reed tried to listen but it was embarrassing, really, a cawing of anger and paranoia. Railing against Obama and the godless West while a bunch of teenagers sat in the boxed stink of poverty.

When the video ended a man stepped forward, the professor stepped forward—it took Reed a moment to place him—dressed again in the open-necked shirt, the black coif, the pointed loafers. He was smiling, the lenses of his glasses brightening, clarifying as he stood before the room.

"How many of you," he began, "know who that was?" He waited a moment, clapped his hands, paced. "No one? Or no one willing to speak. It's all right. A wrong answer and I'm not going to strike you down." He smiled again. "But that man was struck down. That man was Anwar al-Awlaki and he was born here in the United States of America, just like many of you. He was killed by that same country. A drone strike in Yemen. I suppose you might have heard something of these drones. I think now and then they might get mentioned on the Internet." Another smile here, a hint of laughter—nothing was more reviled on jihadi websites than the drones, even Reed knew this. "I suppose, too, that might have all sounded—I don't know. Perhaps a bit extreme. Perhaps a bit—how would you put it?—harsh?

"Well, my brothers—"

And now the smile was gone, and did Reed imagine it, or were his glasses, right there in the unfailing fluorescent light, were his glasses going dark? It didn't matter. Reed was trying to make his body as still as possible and as he did there emerged an invisible world of careful construction, a world that existed wholly in the fold of his unmoving. Everything shifted a half inch and through the crack centered in his vision he saw the world as it was, the angels and demons and the way this world is guy-lined to the next. The professor batted his eyes and around his head Reed saw a great mechanism of wheels and cranks, a system of pulleys making their intricate turns, and watching them he felt the darkness within him. He was uncertain if beneath it burned some buried light.

That was the moment Reed began to pray. Not to any god, but to himself. Which is to say he began to think, to attempt to convince himself that he had found his people, his cause. They were against his father, against his father's world, and whatever they asked, he would do. Wherever they led, he would follow.

"—my brothers, I am here to tell you that if what the martyred imam says sounds harsh, that doesn't make it any less true."

*

It was only after the service ended that he caught sight of Aida in the adjoining room—the women were kept separate—and only then he remembered she was the reason he had come. He stood to go to her and she caught his eye, turned into the crowd, and was gone. He couldn't find her in the street and walked home sweat soaked and heady with something he couldn't yet name. He collapsed in the foyer of his parents' home and woke in bed, his fever—103 his mother would later tell him—having finally broken.

When he woke in a hazy limbo he found his body emptied and waiting to be filled. His mother told him he had the flu, but what he came to possess—what came to possess him—was the disease of martyrdom. He lay in bed, attended by his mother, and dreamed the coming caliphate into being, drifting into long trancelike sleeps he understood not as fatigue but as a form of mysticism.

Three days later when he returned to the gym, Suleyman pulled him aside. Did Reed know, he asked him, that as the professor spoke Reed had floated on a cloud of air, suspended a full foot above the ground?

＊

He finally saw Aida again at the duplex. She and two other women were in the kitchen designing fliers on a laptop. Reed waited until they were finished and then followed her out into the street. Even in her hijab he could see she was as white as him, whiter, perhaps. Which meant she would get the usual questions, the ones he couldn't yet answer. *When did you convert? Why did you convert?* So he didn't ask, and neither did she. She asked his name as they walked together around the perimeter of the park. She was a student at Emory, or had been before dropping out of the religious studies program to immerse herself in Islam. Her parents lived in Virginia and wouldn't speak to her. He would later learn that her Arabic was excellent and that her understanding of theology extended far beyond that of Reed's.

"We shouldn't be out like this," she said finally.

They had completed a loop of the park and started on another.

"Like how?"

"Without a chaperone," she said, but kept walking.

He told her of his parents, of his father's disapproval, of his mother's quivering neediness, speaking all the time just as he had the day she had approached him: with perfect clarity.

Two days later he took her to the movies out at the Mall of Georgia, far enough out of the city that they wouldn't see anyone they knew. She wore her hijab, but it was a flouncy thing of lavender flowers and mourning doves and seemed to signal that while she was devout her piety had limits. Two days after that they drove to Lake Lanier and he put his fingers in her hair as they made out on one of the floating docks.

Meanwhile, he went to the mosque and the gym and studied his Arabic. In between it all, he saw Aida.

It was August when, with Suleyman and the cousins as his witnesses, Reed recited the shadada and officially converted to Islam. The imam gave him a Yemeni riyal as a gift. The professor sent a note with his congratulations.

*

One fall day the professor showed up at the duplex and took Reed, Suleyman, and the cousins to play putt-putt at a course in Druid Hills. It was October but no cooler for it, the day dry and still, the sun flashing off the conical mountain that rose from the shallow pond that marked the course's limit. The theme, it appeared, was Golden Age Hollywood. The lettered sign. *Godzilla vs. King Kong*. The professor walked Reed up above the course with lagoons and giant papier-mâché cameras on tripods, their feet just above the blanched face of Marilyn Monroe.

"All are Muslims, though some refuse Allah's will," Professor Hadawi said. "Do you believe this?"

Down below Suleyman putted toward the open mouth of Humphrey Bogart.

"I do," Reed said, and the professor patted his shoulder and then left his hand there as if he were a father showing a son what would someday be his.

"You are in a privileged situation, my son. You can have everything. Do you know this to be true?" He motioned at the sea of cars, the high-rises in the smoggy distance. "All this. Do you see how much could be yours, Reed? All of it. But the question is, do you want it?"

Reed felt something gather in him, almost anger, but not quite. Resolve, maybe.

"No," he said finally.

"What's that?"

"I said I don't want it."

"Do you not?" A squeeze of the shoulder. "Say it again then."

"I don't want it."

"A third time and it's true."

"I tell you"—and he was almost yelling now—"I don't want it."

And all the while the professor squeezing his shoulder, soothing him, saying *good, good, that's good, Reed. I'm so happy for you.*

＊

When they got back to the parking lot the professor gave him something, a gift, he said, a study aid. A thumb drive containing the teachings of Anwar al-Awlaki called "Constants on the Path to Jihad." Something to light your path. And something else, he said. It was a throwaway cell phone, a burner, they were sometimes called. Hadawi's number was preprogrammed. So we can stay in touch, the professor said.

That Friday after prayers he and Aida drove back to the lake and kissed for hours.

It went on like that until sparring one Monday evening just before the infidel holiday of Thanksgiving, Reed knocked the instructor on his ass and a look of wonderful surprise burst in the man's eyes. Behind that came a look of fear that said to Reed: now your real life has begun.

That night he thought for the first time in months of the way they had laughed at him in New York, the way they had mocked him. Stone, the Voice of Reason, all of them. He put that life against the now of his being and what he came out with was a sense of the great power residing within him. He thought: *now, now, your real life has started.*

And it had.

*

They screened the film in the abandoned convenience store. *Zeitgeist: The Movie.* You want a conspiracy theory, it had it. It had them all, from Jesus to the Federal Reserve Bank. *The Protocols of the Elders of Zion* to 9/11. Reed watched on the floor with the other men of ShariaNow! Watched the towers come down and thought of his childhood in Manhattan, walking to St. John the Divine. Just a boy alone in a church basement of old white ladies with costume jewelry and clouds of silver hair, a few younger dark-skinned mothers nursing babies papoosed in bright scarves.

They sat in metal folding chairs and spoke of the Bad Men who had crashed the planes. This was the time of the Bad Men, the time of the Towers. The Bad Men had been killed, but there were more bad men and they too must die. This was the imperative: to kill the Bad Men wherever they might be. His father said this. The Bad Men, everywhere the Bad Men. Over and over and about how there would be new dangers now, but new opportunities, too. They would kill the Bad Men and what else might manifest itself? The world had cracked open, the world was new.

Meanwhile, his mother sat at home watching the president speak. His father off to his office or taking the train to New Haven to teach. The Quiet Car down to DC to consult. When the boy got back his mother would be on her way out the door to somewhere, always his mother and the door.

He didn't know his father, not really, and sometimes imagined his father might also be one of the Bad Men. An unpleasant idea that seemed corked with the Chardonnay his mother drank in the evenings.

"What are you thinking, baby?" His mother's question.

And how he never responded, simply waited for her to leave him alone with the Filipino help so he could slip out and walk to the church, the days raw with wind and sleet and his mother, somewhere ahead. How she seemed to gather about her all the darkness of the broken city. Blue sawhorse barricades. Police in riot gear. It all came back. The signs in the subway: IF YOU SEE SOMETHING, SAY SOMETHING.

When they were finished they filed out onto the street so that the women could watch.

"Is this really true?" Suleyman quietly asked Reed once they were outside. "All that they have said?"

He was drinking a Coke, but had it in a plastic cup so no one would know.

Reed said nothing.

*

On New Year's Day he met the professor a few blocks from the duplex and rode with him out toward the airport. They parked by a fenced lot of paving stones and concrete angels. Fountains the size of satellite dishes. It was a cold, bright day, and airliners kept lifting in and out of the sky, close enough to see the landing gear as it tucked insect-like beneath the silvered wings.

They walked through the rubble piles and garden trolls and the professor asked about Reed's studies, about his Arabic. Finally, he asked about Reed's father.

"Soren Sharma."

"Yes."

"Or Dr. Sharma, as I knew him. Would it surprise you to know that I once took a course with your father?"

"He doesn't teach anymore."

"Of course not. He's on to other things. Do you know by chance the book he wrote?"

"He's written several."

"How about *Economic Stability in Unstable Times*?"

"No."

"He advocates—are you familiar with his positions, Reed?"

"Broadly."

"Broadly. I see. But you do know a man named James Stone. Your father certainly does."

It came out as a statement so Reed didn't bother replying. Not that he would have known what to say. Even with the professor he felt the need to keep something in reserve. Not that he could say why. Only that secrets are what we are made out of. He believed this. What we hold back is ultimately all we hold. The whole world spitting out their lives in 140-character bursts, but no, not Reed Sharma. You wouldn't catch him casting his pearls before swine. The professor let the question, the statement, whatever it was, go.

"Have you ever heard of something called Global Solutions?"

"Of course."

"Of course?"

"They're a consulting firm." He was relieved to finally say yes to something. "My father served on the board for years."

"Seven years. Do you know what Global Solutions does?" He looked at Reed. "Among other things—among many, many things—they broker arms deals. Patriot missiles for the Israelis. Aircraft for the House of Saud." The professor studied him. "Broadly," he repeated. "I suppose that's familiarity enough."

They walked on, the professor's hand on Reed's shoulder, guiding him.

"I want you to talk to me, Reed. I want us to be in dialogue. You still have the phone I gave you?"

"Yes."

"Memorize the number. Then throw the phone away and buy a new one, and then call me, all right? I want to hear everything."

He did everything he was told, memorized the number, threw away the phone, bought a new one. Told the professor everything except New York. That was his single lapse. Nothing about James Stone, nothing about the Voice of Reason, the elevator girl with her pale legs. The little gilded Buddha that churned in his stomach like a seed. He didn't mention Aida either.

One day he almost mentioned the book of Goya prints—it was in his room at that very moment—but in the end kept that to himself, too.

*

They all wanted to be in Raqqa, in Aleppo. This was what they said. Buy a ticket to Istanbul, cross the border at Antakya. Don't be surprised if you don't see me tomorrow, brother. Don't be surprised if I go. I might go. I shall go, *inshallah*. But there was no going. It was winter—January, February—and what could they do but dream of other places? They studied their Krav Maga to get inside the Jew fist. Do you know the history, brother, the logic behind it?

Ear, eye, instep.

Don't be surprised when you wake up and I'm gone.

They attended the same mosque, said the same prayers. There were others there, refugees from war-torn Iraq, from battle-ravaged Syria. You combine a descriptor with a geographical location. The violence of a place, a people, an entire way of being. *Whosoever shows enmity to a friend of Mine, then I have declared war against him.*

He went with them to the mosque, sat with them while they spoke with the imam, went with them to the gym, and then slipped away to be with Aida. Four, then five nights a week, arrived early, stayed late, and then slipped away to be with Aida. Attend class, struggle through the workbook. Pray to Mecca from the wrestling mats. Shrimp out of holds. Keep your chin to your chest. Protect your eyes. It was all drills—rolling, striking, bowing—and then they sparred in foam body armor. He could feel himself growing stronger, growing agile. There were two pit bulls so gray as to be almost silver, and they padded around the gym though not in any violent way. They were old and arthritic with the patchy skin on their joints beginning to open into sores. He watched them with gathering admiration, the muscled jaws, the thick haunches. They were made for a single thing. As was he.

His Arabic was improving and some days he felt like a sapling, growing but not yet grown, supple, able to bend and whip. He watched his brothers. They were all a little ashamed, Reed knew, these soldiers against the West, against the Jew, these soldiers not in the greater Levant but here, safe, eating Satan's food, masturbating to Satan's women. The only response was to develop a rhythm to life. The way was to bury the shame in the drills, the prayers, the repetition.

Reed worked on growing his beard. It seemed a task that required presence of mind, staring at his face, touching it. The hair came in black tufts and he knew people hated him for it, it's patchiness an affront to stability, to cleanliness. Something about good manners he never quite articulated. But Aida liked it, Aida touched it.

His mother hated it. He would catch her watching him from across the dinner table, gauging, he thought, the growth of her distaste.

"I'm going to the salon Tuesday, honey."

And he would look at her flatly, unamused.

"Want to go with me?"

"No."

"Please? I'd love the company."

"I don't think so."

"Oh, come on, Reed. We never do anything together. What do you say?"

"He said no, Sharon." This his father weighing in.

And if the look on Reed's face was the absence of amusement the look on his father's face was the presence of disgust. That thing you call a beard, it seemed to say. You think I don't know? Your bullshit trips to that bullshit mosque. Living on a nylon sleeping bag with a room full of acid-throwing, knuckle-dragging cavemen fully capable of joining the world and actually doing something useful. But too scared, too lazy. Too holy—until, of course, you wake up in the middle of the night and forget Allah just long enough to beat your dick to whatever Asian porn you've bothered to download. They were blowing up temples in Syria and you were supposed to cheer. They were cutting off heads and you were supposed to laugh. And he did, he cheered, he laughed.

You are becoming everything your grandfather fled.

You are becoming everything I have worked to deliver you from.

You have become the other.

These, Reed knew, were the complaints lodged against him. And if he was honest, *when* he was honest—because he was striving for honesty—he knew there was some truth to it.

"I want to tell you something, Reed," his father said on one of the rare occasions they were alone. "You think you're doing something incredible, this renunciation, and I will tell you, son, that on some level I admire it. But the vanity," he said, and at that moment he touched Reed's beard, more than touched it: he pulled it. "The vanity is adolescent. So too the ideology."

Aida touched it, too. But in a different, gentler way. Aida stroked it, smoothed it. He told her everything about his past, the boarding school, his time in New York. Jimmy Stone and the elevator girl. A few evenings they watched the sermons of al-Awlaki's the professor had given him on the thumb drive, and she wanted to know all about the professor, all about the imam and Suleyman and his cousins. Reed loved her curiosity, the way she listened. He was taking her to his parents' house three or four times a week, timing it so that mostly no one was home, but occasionally making sure someone was home, his mom especially, because he wanted her to know her little boy wasn't a little boy anymore.

They spent one languorous afternoon in his bed, kissing and touching atop the underwear Aida wouldn't remove—she had taken a vow of chastity until the caliphate was realized—then had come downstairs half-dressed to run into his suddenly blushing mother. But her embarrassment had quickly given way to interest, even enthusiasm. *A girlfriend!* Reed could see her thinking. *And they've been upstairs doing what?* He hoped his mother thought they had just made love, he hoped she realized how unafraid of her he had become, how unafraid of his father. But he couldn't quit reading the growing smile on her face: *does this mean my son is normal? A girlfriend! Does this mean everything is going to be okay after all?* Reed became drunk with her wondering, listening as Aida lied beautifully about her family and past, as Aida charmed his mother to such an extent he felt his own power wane and wilt.

They were still in the kitchen when his father came home, and his mother introduced Aida to her husband as if they were long-lost sisters. Reed's girlfriend, dear! He saw the surprise on his father's face, his father's quick appraisal of how attractive she was, how desirable, Aida standing in his expensive kitchen in shorts and tank top, bed-headed and—he badly wanted his father to believe—well-fucked. See what your boy has brought home, he wanted to say. You see, Daddy? See that I'm a man now?

But too soon his parents had glided back into the welter of their lives, and suddenly bold in a way he had never been Reed had led Aida back to his room where she had allowed him to dry-hump her until he came.

So here was this double life, or if not exactly a double life at least a new life growing within the husk of the old. He was his father's son, the stuttering, possibly stupid twenty-one-year old with no designs on a future that seemed to extend no further than the four walls of his bedroom. But he was also a key operative in the struggle. A trusted foot soldier, righteous and brave, who sat watching his beautiful girlfriend smile at him while she swabbed his cum from her stomach.

A part of him wanted to tell Suleyman.

A part of him wanted to tell the professor.

But to what extent was it real? A foolish question, and he had this sense that to speak of it would precipitate its evaporation. It would cease to exist.

Then in July he took Aida to his father's office Independence Day party, both glowing with purpose, Aida's hair blowing free and Aida not caring, Reed not caring because there were days he felt the righteousness of Allah in him like light and then there were days he just wanted to play *Madden NFL* on the Xbox.

That day the lounge was maybe two-thirds full of good-looking couples clustered around banquettes. He recognized them as the mindless drones of the great corptocracy, no different from the ones he'd known in New York. The men looking like they had stepped out of Calvin Klein ads, the expensive grooming, the bottle service and tax-deductible contributions to obscure ashrams. The women simultaneously thin and buxom. Ivy Leaguers. MBAs. Former interns with the World Bank. From across the room, an economist slathered over Aida, and Reed liked that, knowing that this powerful man wanted nothing more than to stand where Reed stood. He watched his father's secretary pose for a cell phone photo at a far table, fake smile, fake breasts, red heels, and black leggings.

Beside her, Aida appeared made from wire or string, a fragile construction that betrayed itself in every joint. Nothing at all like this woman who was all muscle and adipose, well-developed biceps and a spray-on tan. She came over and leaned against the bar beside them, drunk.

"You two," she said in her slurred voice, "you two are so cute. What's her name?" she asked him.

"A . . ."

"What? A?"

"Ah . . . Ad . . ."

It was the only time he had ever stuttered in front of Aida and he hated this woman for it, hated his father, hated himself for coming here. It was meant to be a joke—look at the worker bees!— but it was a mistake, a form of arrogance he had spent the previous months working to eliminate.

He felt the old anger rise up, the humiliation.

He felt something in him harden and set.

He doubled down on his training, on his life. Take off your shoes. Stay off the Internet. Despite the waning of Bashar al-Assad in Syria there was the possible sense not of the imminence of the caliphate but that history had already left them behind. They heard it on TV. Good Muslims one and all stood against jihad. They were relics. Their moment—Bush, Iraq, Bin Laden at Abbottabad—their moment was over. History would note a passing madness.

The smell of this was on their skin as surely as were the chemical astringents used to clean the mats at the gym. Reed came home exhausted, slept at the Kirkwood duplex on an inflatable mattress that kept deflating. Jew made, someone said. Jew this. Jew that. His skin was less prickled with mat burns, but still hurt. There remained nights he felt as if he lived in the tumbling of a clothes dryer. But he stayed with it. Studied. Learned. Prayed. Pushups and pull-ups. Ring dips. Long early morning runs along the Big Creek Greenway.

We are not relics.

We are not a madness that has passed.

There is no madness. There is no passing.

They were truth. He was truth, nearing fluency in Arabic, the best fighter in the gym. He was near it. He was making truth out of the everyday. He felt this in the numbing consistency of the hours, how truth came not from revelation but repetition, the ceremony of living, a contemplative strength found in readiness. When his brothers talked about capital markets or the godless drive of modernity he would cease to listen. All the talk—the endless abstraction of talk over the endless cups of tea—when it was something you could only know through the body, and what he was coming to understand was that the body was all. He kept this to himself—how could they fail but to misunderstand him?—but knew the Prophet had revealed such.

He didn't need the world. The kebab shops downtown. The agencies with red-haired secretaries who assist you in being a dog. Handouts. Pity. If the state didn't kill him soon he would kill the state. Bury it to its neck and then let the tide come in, just as he had seen done on YouTube to Ethiopian nonbelievers.

Do not doubt this book.

Do not doubt *me*, brother.

He was a soldier now, a follower of the Prophet drinking his Pu-erh tea and finding curling beard hairs in his mouth, his clothes, stuck to the Cloroxed wrestling mats. He called the professor on the burner phone to tell him he had renounced Aida.

Do not be hasty, the professor counseled.

Called the professor to tell him he wanted to go to Syria and fight.

Wait for the call, the professor told him. Wait for the summons. It may be that your work is here.

But he didn't want it to be here and he surely didn't want to wait. He was anxious. Nothing satisfied.

He started training mornings before prayer. Three sessions a day. He'd shower at the gym, shiny and wild-eyed, spend the day praying and studying and trying to stay away from Aida. Fish, vegetables, water, creatine—the Prophet had said nothing regarding supplements—whey protein. If he scared his brothers then that was all to the good. He saw now not just the impurities of their hearts, but their unwillingness to cleanse themselves. Amazing, Reed's deference, his actual fear when he had first arrived among them. He had thought them warriors, but saw now only he was pure of heart. He looked at Suleyman and saw weakness, not a human, not a brother, but an insect.

"They are calling you Yusef Islam," Suleyman told him. "The others."

Reed stared at him.

"Like Cat Stevens," Suleyman said. "The American singer."

"I know who he is."

"The great convert, holier than all others."

"I know who he is."

"They're making fun of you."

"I know who Cat Stevens is."

Then one day—thinking of Aida, but trying not to—he slept with a girl at the Boulevard Sit-n-Chat in Belvedere Park. Black girl, cornrows. Not something romantic or sexy but an animal slapping until he washed up panting on the shoals of her damp chest. Fire-engine red fingernails and the smell of cocoa butter. He paid $50 plus the cost of the room for the pleasure of smelling it.

That night he was determined to flay his dick with a kitchen knife, but wound up masturbating to a J.Crew catalog that had somehow found its way into their mail slot. Proof, he thought after, of the ingenuity of the Jew state, the insidious nature of the infidel. Like Aida. Like the pale elevator girl in New York. He sat there with his limp penis curled into his hand like a blind mole and thought of that time. The Voice of Reason. The laughing Buddha.

He knew then it was time to move forward, that this stage, whatever it was, was over. And how could it not be? He was hearing voices at night, long dreamless sleeps wherein he was visited by angels. Their lips by his ear—was this a dream? Sometimes they spoke in the voice of the professor, sometimes in the voice of Aida or his mother. Was this madness? Or was it the Word of God—some god, any god? He thought of the words of the prophet Jesus, peace be upon him: *I come not to bring peace but the sword. To set son against father.* Yes, his was a god of war and it was speaking.

It was possible, of course, that he was overtraining.

It was possible he was delusional, feverish, psychotic.

It was possible he was depressed and imagining everything.

It was also possible he was an instrument of History.

That he had not come to worship Allah, but to become Him.

And while the angel spoke—*if* the angel spoke—the world which had always felt so flimsy, something to be bent by his father's will, began to solidify, to stiffen. History. Blood—the ground was soaked with it. You would hear it pumping through the earth were it not for the mindlessness of living.

Their lips by his ear—how could it not be real?

A barely created place, a barely created life, had become actual. Meanwhile, he watched the Americans slaughter the innocent with their airstrikes and drones. He watched the Jew kill Palestinian children like stray dogs. He watched the world do nothing. He watched the world laugh. But he wasn't troubled. Once God became fact, there is no other. How could there be? When God manifests Godself, when God becomes *known*, what else can possibly exist in that blinding glare? The zealot isn't a fool or a fanatic. The zealot is a logician, a utilitarian squaring everything on truth. Was this what had happened to James Stone? The man had once sent him four bottles of pomegranate juice as if it were a warning, a portent of what was coming, and it occurred to Reed now that perhaps it had been.

For days at a time he refused to eat, but knew he was filling with something greater.

And then he was full.

He rose and showered. He was going to walk into the world, now, today. What he wasn't going to do was beg. What he wasn't going to do was be laughed at, ever again. An instrument of God instead of a punch line. A man who believes can drive a hole straight through the universe. You look at me with your disbelief, your doubt. You act like it's a joke only because you don't believe.

He got up, he believed.

He was no longer near; he had arrived.

He bought a new phone and called the professor and when he didn't answer left a message, something the professor had told him never to do.

I'm ready now, he said. I want to go to war.

*

The call came two days later. But instead of the professor it was James Stone. He gave Reed a location and time. *And one other thing, all right? Shave the beard.* Hadn't spoken to Stone in what, two years? And that's the shit he gets: shave the beard.

They met at the Ice Bar, a touristy place in Five Points that served overpriced vodka and handed out gloves and thermal suits. The booths inside a freezer. Five below Celsius. You could feel it in your sinuses.

"I've missed you, Reed. I ain't gonna lie."

They took five or six shots of Belvedere so cold you couldn't taste a thing and then went up to the terrace when some Emory kids wandered in.

"How's it in the Old South, young master? Sipping hot cocoa while mamma turns the eggs? Sometimes the zipper gets stuck and daddy helps out, am I right? You're tugging and spitting, pulling at the metal teeth. Fucking Chinese-made garbage, you're thinking." Jimmy's eyes spun inside his face. "Or I don't know. Maybe it's all prayers at the mosque. Some Yemeni princess for the formal gatherings. I hear you've converted. I hear you're a holy warrior now. Tell me how it is, Reed?"

"You s-set me up."

"This is me, legitimately asking."

"You s-s-set me up, Jimmy. In New York," Reed said. It sounded like a line from a Western, John Wayne sauntering into a bar, hitching his dungarees, but Stone seemed to give it due consideration. Dropped his voice several decibels as if this were some sort of concession.

"This is me inquiring," he almost whispered. "Because I have my reasons."

"The Voice of Reason. That was your joke. Hilarious."

"Maybe not ha-ha funny. I admit to this."

"You made a fool out of me."

"Maybe not laugh-out-loud," Jimmy said, "but humorous in its way."

"Fuck you."

"I'm not going to argue the point."

"F-f-fuck you, Jimmy. The idea of something real just kills you. You don't have to say it. I know it does. I know you understand me, too, so don't act like you don't." It was sounding more and more like bad John Wayne, but they were both drunk—Reed having not touched alcohol in months—and Reed figured this was the time to say such things.

Stone rubbed Reed's shoulder. "I have a feeling you're going to be hearing from the professor soon. I have a feeling you two are going to be taking a little ride together. If that happens, I want you to keep your mouth shut about seeing me. But you call me when you get back, all right? You call your old uncle Jimmy, you understand? Look at me, Reed. You understand?"

Reed was sliding out of his seat.

"Jimmy," he said.

"What?"

"Jimmy."

"What?"

The vending machines and kiosks. Nathan's Famous—you could buy it right off the street, take the train to Spanish Harlem. Do-rags. A purple Cutlass with hydraulics and spinning rims. Pants falling off the hips. Bustin a sag. He remembered the expression from childhood, *bustin a sag*. Jimmy drunk in a Williamsburg bar talking about Buddhist monks outside the U.S. embassy in Saigon.

Would you do that for me, Reed? Jimmy had asked. Give me that gift? Would you set me on fire?

You really want to burn?

I think I do. Sometimes I think I really do.

Reed tried to sit up, wedged one hand between his head and the wicker armrest for leverage, but it wasn't happening. *Jimmy*, he was saying, his head canted toward the concrete like a dead flower. Over and over: *Jimmy, Jimmy*. Because he wanted to tell him: No one will ever laugh at me again.

The next day the professor did indeed call and the following day they rode north to an out-of-season ski resort just below the Georgia-Tennessee state line. Professor Hadawi driving, both of them quiet as they wound past chalets of wood and glass and into a vast and otherwise abandoned parking lot. A glass cube held a blue-lit luxury sedan, the empty resort apparently brought to you by Lexus.

In the spare-tire well of the trunk the professor knocked aside the lug wrench and the bottle of antifreeze and the roadside flares, unzipped a duffel bag and removed a SIG 550, folded and wrapped in a quilt, and then a smaller pistol, a Beretta of some space-age composite. They hiked past the empty lodge uphill past sheds of machinery and beneath a chairlift. The hills were steep and green and looking back you could see the manicured ski lanes, broad carpets of a darker shade, as if someone had brushed the land against its grain.

Reed carried the SIG, two steps behind the professor who labored up the hill in silence. They were near the turn in the chairlift when they heard the first shots. The professor seemed unaware. When they crossed the peak they looked over at the back slope, an open valley where maybe a half-dozen men stood holding rifles. What appeared to be targets were pinned to hay bales along the tree line.

"Your brothers," Hadawi said. "These are your brothers, Reed."

✳

They drove back at dusk and when he was home Reed called Jimmy Stone.

They met at a McDonald's near the interstate.

"Little Reed Sharma," Stone said, "son of the most important man in Georgia." They were sitting on concrete picnic tables in the shadow of I-75, Stone licking his cone like a dog lapping at its own vomit. "I guess you understand at this point what you're being offered," he said.

"I'm going."

"Then go. By all means. No need to tell me anything."

"I'm only telling you because you were kind to me once. And I know you were a part of the struggle. Not my struggle, but still."

"Still, sure," Stone said. "So what's the plan? You tell your parents something. You got a job, maybe. You're going back to school. Make it plausible but vague. The professor tell you that?"

"I want to do something. If the professor won't let me take action, I'll need you. You knew people in New York."

"Who, me?"

"If the professor stops me I want you to put me in touch with them. But for real this time."

"So you don't trust the professor?"

"I trust him enough."

"First intelligent thing you've said all night."

"I trust him, but I have to be certain."

"Hedge your bets, absolutely."

"I have to do something. I can't wait any longer."

"I hope the professor gives good counsel. Keep your Facebook page up. But don't make any grand proclamations. Did he tell you this? Don't talk any Allah shit. Just quietly disappear into the hills."

"If he stops me or won't let me act I'll need to contact my brothers."

"Your brothers?" Stone said it all incredulous-like, but took it as his cue to take out the phone and place it on the concrete table. He licked his cone, a bit of cursory maintenance, keeping the ice cream in check. The phone—an iPhone 6—sat between them.

"What's this?" Reed said.

"This?" Jimmy gave it a little spin. "This is a gift. You know what telescope is?"

"I'm guessing not like at an observatory."

"No, Reed, not like at an observatory. Like the app."

"I know it."

"Well, it's on there. You see something, you get a look at anything at all, show me through the telescope. It's a private feed. Comes to no one but me. I want you to be my eyes. I mean," Jimmy said, "assuming you're ready."

"I'm ready."

"Assuming then," Stone said, "the world is ready."

✳

The camp was on the back side of the resort, abandoned for at least a generation. An old gem-mining operation but little left of it. A fire pit with log benches. A clapboard building with kitchen and rooms, all of it converted to a barracks for the six or seven men living there.

The professor picked Reed up and to Reed's surprise Suleyman was in the back seat, grim, but apparently relieved to see Reed. The professor smiled and drove through the Chick-fil-A drive-through. Peach milkshakes beneath a sky that seemed to have lowered itself, to have unbuttoned and dropped, and Reed wondered about that, the question of authority. Like who gave it permission?

Hadawi passed around straws.

"Now then," he said.

As subtly as possible Reed turned on his phone, tapped the telescope icon, and glossed the camera over the milkshake, a little something for Jimmy Stone, a little treat for him to unravel. Then he put the phone away and never took it back out.

A man in his early thirties met them on arrival and took Reed and Suleyman to the room they would share, two beds and a nightstand. A small arrow pointed the way to Mecca. In the morning they gathered to pray and then ran the abandoned ski trails. They were deep in the forest, at least four or five miles to the nearest town which was itself a pinprick in the vast north Georgia woods.

Reed didn't know the name of it, and after a week it came to seem more rumor than place. Red America. White-bread mountain folk. A world of Pixy Stix and video poker. Candy bars and condoms. The white-sided Pentecostal churches and Redbox dispensers paling with sun. (He'd seen it briefly riding up in the professor's car.) Mowing the grass with their iPods plugged into their ears. All the while not knowing, never knowing, that it is Allah who gives, and Allah who will take.

Do you know what the Koran says? the professor had once asked.

God is as close as the veins in your neck.

Their instructor was a man named Ahmad, besides Suleyman the only name Reed knew. Other men, experts on munitions or identity theft, came in and out of the camp, but Ahmad was the leader. At least so far as Reed could tell. Reed would see him at a meeting, standing silently at the back, and then he'd be gone for days. Returning with no word of where he had been or what he had done though the rumor was that he was organizing cells all over the Southeast.

He won't stop until the infidel kills him, the others said.

Reed reckoned it true. He was a dense, persistent man who gave the impression of unyielding if slow progress. The son of Iraqi refugees who had fled after the First Gulf War. There was talk that he had worked as a translator for the Americans and seen what the Americans intended for the umma. He had remained patient, parlayed his services into citizenship and then, inside the great gates of the infidel state, disappeared from the eye of the government. Thus he was underground, thus he was one of them. They said the Americans wanted him dead. As did the Israelis. As did the world for all Reed knew. But Ahmad was not afraid.

He knows what it is to hurt.

Reed was beginning to know the same.

They ran in the morning and in the afternoon he learned to fieldstrip a Bushmaster, to set explosive charges, to fire pistols and kill with pressure cookers and common household ingredients.

Give me an assortment of goods, a trip to RadioShack, a trip to Dollar General, and I will make you a bomb.

Detergent.

Batteries.

Christmas lights.

Roofing nails.

He didn't know their names, these other men, only Ahmad and Suleyman, and was careful to speak to Suleyman only in the privacy of their room. His friend was not well, worn down by the running, the bad food. Every morning they were given a single green pill for energy and one night Reed discovered Suleyman had a baggie of them, perhaps a dozen pills, concealed beneath his mattress.

"What are these?" Reed wanted to know when he came in.

"What are you doing? You're going through my shit."

"You took these, didn't you?"

"Why are you going through my shit?"

"At least hide them properly," Reed said.

"Give 'em to me."

"Does Ahmad know you took them?"

"Fuck you, Reed. I need them, all right?"

Worse than the pills was the way Suleyman spoke: he spoke like the American teenager he was, no longer avoiding contractions, no longer affecting the voice of one for whom English was a language learned late and with great care. He had become himself.

"I'm thinking of leaving," he told Reed a few days later.

"You can't do that."

"I'm thinking of going back to Atlanta. Look at my knee."

His knee was swollen, Reed acknowledged this. But what was a swollen knee against the dead in Gaza or Raqqa or Kabul? What was a swollen knee against the Jew fist?

Reed kept running.

He began to assist Ahmad with openhanded combat.

They had all cut off their beards and should they ever be approached they were capable of killing with their hands. But they would not do this, Ahmad told them. They would speak the language of yes, ma'am and no, sir and God Almighty and America first. If they were pressed they might talk about the gays. It was safe to talk about the gays and everything they were ruining. About the Mexican. Should you be approached you could lament the Mexican. But they were never approached.

They would run and fight until their bodies burned and they passed into fire, knowing that soon enough that same fire would pass into light. When they were light they would illuminate the illusion of power that was the Jew and the dollar and the fat ball-capped men he had seen outside the feed and seeds and First Baptists.

Now and then Reed took from his bag a print he had torn from the Goya book Stone had given him. *Saturn Devouring His Children.* He had the phone, too, the burner. He had the professor's number. He had James Stone's number. But he didn't call.

He ran. He fought.

He took his green pill and felt it within him, whatever it was.

He knew only that there was no more shame. They were doing what their brothers were doing in camps all over the world. ISIS. Al-Shabaab. Jabhat al-Nusra. Boko Haram. Jemaah Islamiyah. A roll call of martyrdom and faith, of bodies whispered into fire and then light.

In the meantime, so long as they were flesh, they were given antibiotics to fight the possibility of infection. The weakened immune system. The slightest cut. The mere trace of bacteria. Any of it might derail the coming of the caliphate. Not that they spoke of such things. Their concerns were practical. Each would leave here prepared to develop his own cell. Theory was left for others, the imam, the professor.

There was time for prayers, but he wasn't praying much. Maybe touch his head to the earth and wake ten minutes later with a kinked neck. Suleyman across the room eating green pills and staring blankly at the wall.

"Get down and pray with me, Suleyman." And Reed would wait, but there was no answer forthcoming. "Get down and pray, my brother."

And Reed would wait, but Suleyman would never move.

It didn't seem to matter. There was a time to cut off such, to do nothing but grow stronger. And he was growing stronger, a great carapace over his heart so that it was rare he thought of his mother or New York or Aida. The day he and Aida walked past MLK Jr. High to Coan Park. The old Victorian houses, the porches with sofas and wool-headed black men. Shopping carts in the meadow like grazing sheep, you saw them in pairs, two here, two there. Three together down near the trickle of stream. The spilling trashcans and yellow jackets. Glassine baggies like translucent petals, stepped on, flattened. Everything flattened. They had kissed just past the picnic tables but he didn't think of that, never did he think of that.

He watched Suleyman fall on a morning run and almost drown in a puddle.

His friend was weak, sick, thus he was no longer his friend.

The weather turned cold and they built fires in the pit. There were still no names, but some stories now. Time in camps in Afghanistan or fighting in Fallujah. Not the boys themselves—they were not old enough—but stories passed down reverently from fathers and uncles and older brothers martyred for the caliphate. He could sense Ahmad's disapproval. Now, he seemed to say, was not a time for talk. But outside of the pain, the talk was the only thing real. Perhaps the snow or the smell of cordite. The bright scent of Ahmad's winter-green Copenhagen, his one concession to his time with the American army.

One evening Jimmy Stone drove up after dark and sat around the fire pit with a metal canteen of J&B.

"Nine-fucking-eleven," he said. "Let me tell you about it." It was dark and outside the ring of light the night had grown cold. "Where were you when it went down, Ahmad?"

Ahmad was staring into the fire.

"At home," he said.

"But after, when you were over there." Stone looked at the circle of faces. "Ahmad here was in Iraq. A terp. He saw shit, did shit."

Ahmad did not look up when he spoke, his voice soft. "Mostly saw shit."

"What was it like, do you remember?"

"I remember the same as you."

"Yeah, but tell the boys."

"You go out, drive out, and then you see something."

"Like dead bodies," Stone said, "torture rooms."

"More like garbage. Dead animals, goats."

"You're disappointing me here."

"Sometimes bodies, I suppose."

"You're bringing me down, Ahmad. I thought we were going to tell these boys some stories."

His eyes were still on the fire.

"I found it to be a country very unclean," he said.

He took them on runs, homemade obstacle courses where they climbed trees and jumped streams. Drove to town and took them dumpster diving in the hours before dawn and they climbed out with sheet cakes and vegetables and loaves of bakery bread, declaring what American waste! What American arrogance! But it was a pose, a line, because with the exception of Ahmad they were Americans each and every one and it was their waste, their arrogance.

Meanwhile, it turned cold. October, Reed thought, though he had no way of knowing exactly. He judged he had been in the camp two months, eating oatmeal and amphetamines and losing weight. Though he slept beside Suleyman who snored and farted and slept, Reed felt loneliness float above him until one night it coalesced like a weather pattern, a storm against which his skin prickled.

He returned one day to find two of his brothers—if that was what they were—gone. Suleyman and another boy, the youngest in the camp. There was no talk of it, no explanation. They were simply no longer there. Still, the training went on, mindlessly, endlessly, and Reed worked hard thinking *Allah, Allah*, because sometimes he thought *God*. Not because he had ever given any thought to Him. It was just the language he'd heard as a boy, those twice-yearly masses with his mother. A linguistic tic he had to get past. But maybe—he might think this in the last miles of one of the trail runs—maybe it was only that: just a linguistic tic he had to get past.

Allah.

God.

The entire construct.

Some nights he would lie in bed and repent, tearing up with an overwhelming nostalgia for the person he had been. The absence of people—you could feel these things, come to know them as intimately as you knew presence. He missed the gym, the cousins. Didn't dare allow his mind to drift toward Aida or his mother, the elevator girl in New York. That deep focus the Voice of Reason had spoken of—Reed had that once. But no longer. Now he was only tired. He jogged the trails in a hoodie, face down, because the truth was, he had lost interest in jihad, and Allah had gone as missing as everyone else.

When they filmed his life this would be the moment of struggle, something to overcome, and he would overcome it. In the movie of his life this would be the moment the professor would return to send Reed into the world as an avenging angel. And not in the name of Allah or the umma. The professor would return and send Reed out to do damage to Reed's father's world because that, Reed had come to understand, was the world most in need of damage. The world without mercy, the world without forgiveness.

But instead of the professor it was Stone who returned, carrying a grocery bag of clothes, shampoo, Docksides. He even had a belt, a woven thing like you associated with afternoon sails on the harbor. *Been to the neighborhood T.J.Maxx, partner. Godless capitalism sends its regards, by the way.* Reed had run for hours that morning and felt hunger in him like a set of teeth. Natural then that he associated the moment not with a new stage of life but a possible meal.

"Get dressed. Put everything you have in the bag, all right?" Stone said. "And I mean everything. Have you written anything down here?"

"Have you seen the professor?"

"Anything at all. Notes, doodles. Scratched your initials into a tree? Try to focus, Reed."

"No, nothing."

"Get dressed then."

"You haven't seen the professor?"

"Use the cologne. Do you have any Spanish?"

"Not really."

"*Gracias. Sí, señor?* Nothing?"

"I think dog is *perro*."

"Forget it. Go on and change. But be thorough packing," Stone said. "And no, I haven't seen the good professor. No one has. That's the reason I'm here."

The clothes were too big, but he had nothing else and so he pulled them on, slipped out to the supply shed and took one of the target pistols, an antique Walther P5 he stuffed in his bag.

"Could we eat something?" he asked Stone when they were driving.

"You hungry?"

"I haven't eaten yet, no."

"What are you running on, pills?"

"One pill. Green."

"Allah's little helper."

They were in a knockoff Econoline van. The rear seats were torn out and the interior smelled of 3-in-One oil and body odor.

"How far did you run this morning?"

"I don't know."

"Ballpark it."

"Maybe ten or twelve."

"Miles for Muhammad."

"You aren't a believer."

"Neither are you."

"You say that at your peril."

"What's that?" Stone cupped an ear. "You sound like a dying robot over there."

They stopped at a Stuckey's an hour north of the camp and Reed ordered waffles and sausage and then a hamburger steak with gravy, hunched over his plate shoveling the food for a half-hour until the hunger was replaced by the sort of exhaustion you carried in the bones.

"I guess you know you aren't going back," Stone said when they were on the road. "You might remember two of your fellow campers walking off the reservation."

"Suleyman. I didn't know the other's name."

"Their names are Saddam and Osama for all it matters. They're now in the custody of the FBI."

Reed was silent.

"That would be the Federal Bureau of Investigation," Stone said.

"I know what it is."

"Just trying to judge your silence."

"They were captured?"

"Here's a scenario, all right?" They were in another small town, probably Tennessee by now. "Imagine this," Stone said, "the feds get word of a small training camp in the hills, put their eyes on it. Eventually send in a couple of agents, very deep cover. They collect info and disappear. At some later point as yet to be determined a SWAT team descends in helicopters. They do the raid at night. Fast-rope in. Bind 'em and gag 'em. You get a bag of peanuts and a complimentary promethazine suppository for the ride to Gitmo."

"They were spies? I don't believe you."

"Here's another one: the man you call Ahmad is actually an officer with U.S. Special Operations. Again, deepest, darkest cover. He runs you boys until total exhaustion, and then one quiet night strangles each and every one of you in your sleep. Piano wire 'cause those JSOC boys don't give a fuck."

"You're a liar."

"Or here's one more—last one I swear—for your due consideration. You want to hear it?" They were out of the town now and paralleling the shoreline of a lake. A Sea-Doo dealership. Real-estate offices. Ornate stone gates leading to whatever it was they led to. "Let's say there actually is a plan afoot for a major action. An attack let's say—speculatively—it's going to take place in Atlanta. But the heat's on, the feds, the Georgia Bureau of Investigation. So what do you do if you're the professor? You set up a little training camp in the hills. Send some boys up there. Upstanding brainless jihadis just dying to strap on a nylon suicide vest and blow up a few soccer moms, all to the glory of the Prophet. Velcro, Reed. You sew the vest right it fits perfectly under your jacket. Not so much as a panty line. Are you listening to me?"

"I'm listening."

"Good because I'm not shitting you now. You send these boys up to the hills and train them in a bunch of antiquated shit. You really think you need to run eighteen miles and make a bomb out of paper clips to praise Allah? This ain't the OSS, Reed. Nobody's going to parachute you into occupied France. It never occurred to you that maybe you were training for the sort of war they fought seventy years ago?"

Reed said nothing.

"You were swinging on goddamn monkey bars and you never thought: huh, this is oddly antiquated and why are my palms so goddamn blistered?"

Stone looked at him, back at the road, back at Reed.

"We're the most watched society in human history. Observed, intercepted, spied on. They got satellites and server farms and microwave arrays that do nothing but. I don't care how deep you get in the woods someone is watching or listening or something. You believe me?"

"What happened to Suleyman?"

"Do you believe me or not?"

"Yeah."

"What's that?"

"I said I do."

Stone nodded but it was a solemn act, as if in disappointment.

"I don't know where he is, but if he's not in federal custody already he will be soon enough. Sounds like he just flaked."

"His k-knee."

"What's that?"

"Something was wrong with his knee."

"Yeah, well, shit like that happens, don't it?"

They rode a few miles in silence before Reed asked then what?

"Then what?" Stone said. "Exactly. Get the boys in the hills, train 'em up big and strong, and then what? Simple. Keep 'em around until the feds catch wind of it. Bunch of ragheads ultra-marathoning their way through cracker America. How long you think it takes? Keep 'em around, Reed, and then the feds catch on and eventually they raid the place. Here again you get the helicopters. You get the night-vision goggles. Some Yemeni-American teenager dying in a stress position. And that whole Atlanta plot they kept hearing rumblings about? Well, shit, there it was. Busted. Beautiful work, gentlemen. Time to e-mail the good news to Director Comey. Time for a celebratory drink because it's a great day for truth, justice, and the American way. Back-slapping all around. Now wouldn't that take a lot of pressure off the real plot, the one that's actually going down?"

"Where's the professor in all this?"

"Things got too hot for the professor."

"He's gone?"

"He's cooling his prayer rug for a bit. Patient man, the professor."

"Where am I in all this?"

"Where are you?" Stone slapped the wheel with the heel of one hand. "Shit, son. You're in dead center. You're the *real* in the real plot."

∗

They stopped at a motel off I-24 just outside Chattanooga. A horseshoe of concrete and potted cacti. The pool long since filled, only a few deck chairs scattered as if misremembering their lives. Stone told him to sit in the car. He came back a few minutes later and slid back into the driver's seat.

"He's going to take a picture now. You don't say anything, all right?"

"What are we doing here?"

"He thinks you're an illegal. Up from Mexico or El Salvador or wherever they come from so don't open your mouth, you hear me?"

The man was grievously overweight, waddling around the motel room in athletic shorts and a T-shirt that read VOLUNTEER NATION. He took the photograph and told Stone and Reed to sit on the bed while he cut the light. The back of the room was set up as a makeshift darkroom, stop bath and hardening agent. A fishing line of prints. The chemicals smelled like his mother's nail polish remover. When it was dry he went to work with an X-Acto knife.

"Whatever happened to the film you were making?" Reed asked Stone.

"Shut up."

"Pacifism, right?"

"Anarchism."

The man heated a credit card, pressed the new name, cooled it.

"I have heart issues," Stone said. "I'm easily constipated."

"I'm the *r-r-real* in the real plot."

"I thought I asked you not to talk. I thought that was the single bit of instruction I gave you."

It took no more than an hour to establish Reed's new identity—credit card, driver's license—and then they were riding again.

"What now?" Reed asked.

"I'm taking you somewhere we can debate things," Stone said, though not with any enthusiasm. All at once he appeared tired, suddenly and irrevocably exhausted. "Sit on the back porch and count the angels on the head of a pin. Theological nuances the imam might have skipped right past."

"Where are you taking me?"

"Where do you want to go, Reed? Why don't you tell me that?"

"I want to go wherever I'm supposed to go."

"I think that might be a high-security U.S. detention center in a third-party state. A nice fenced enclosure with dogs and guards and a release rate of less than zero. They call that a black site. So how about try again?"

"I thought I was the chosen one."

Stone's face was pink and splotched, his breath catching in his nose. He appeared about to speak but then stopped himself. "There's a place I can take you for the time being," he said. "A little lake house up in the mountains. A safe house. Relatively safe, I think. When you get there I've got somebody for you to meet."

"Who?"

"Wait and see."

"The professor?"

"An old colleague of mine."

"This is part of the plan?"

Reed waited for some answer and finally it came in the form of Stone nodding his weary head.

"All right then," Reed said. "Take me there."

They drove another half-hour and then Stone turned onto a one-lane road.

"This is the place?" Reed asked. "This is the safe house?"

"Be patient."

"How did you know who Ahmad was? You worked with him?"

"Ahmad? Goodness, you're just full of questions, aren't you?" The road turned to gravel and here and there were signs for horse trails. "Difficult ones too. This question, this is more a metaphysical question, I think."

"You worked with him?"

"Are we talking vocation versus avocation here? 'Cause if so I'd like to quote the scriptures."

Ahead was a small house, shingled and quaint and completely empty. Beyond it the teardrop of a mountain lake. An old Toyota Camry sat beneath a shed.

"The Lord is a man of War," Stone said. "The Lord is his name."

He parked the van and they stepped out onto the gravel. The day was cold and gray, the sun risen, but without conviction.

"What I'm trying to say here, Reed, what we know, is that the known is never as powerful as the unknown. What *is* always bows to what isn't, to what could be."

"Who is *we?*"

"Secrets are power, sir. Do you believe me?"

"Why should I believe anything you say?"

Stone laughed. "You say that as if you don't already."

"Answer the question."

"The question?" Stone blew into his hands for warmth. "How 'bout the answer? The answer is that this whole little setup is nothing more than an excuse to get to you. First, the professor—"

"What do you know about the professor?"

Stone made the motion of zipping closed his lips and when he was finished Reed reached out slowly, almost gently, and put his fingers around Stone's throat. It seemed an exhausted gesture, but no less necessary.

"Give me one reason not to kill you," he said.

Stone unzipped his mouth. "You're letting your attachment to the professor cloud your judgment. Let me assure you that the professor is not suffering from the same blindness." He leaned toward Reed as best he could. "They even sent someone to watch you."

"Who did?"

"They did, Reed. The big *they*, the only *they* so far as you're concerned."

"Aida."

"You're not in love, are you?"

"The professor sent her?"

"They want your father, Reed. That's the one your so-called brothers are after."

"Who sent her?"

"Little shoulda-coulda straight from the American academy of undereating. How could you possibly imagine she's a convert? She's too gamine," Stone said. "That eating disorder of hers. In its infancy but you have to give it time, right, let it come into its own. I counsel patience."

"You stay away from her."

"They're going to get your father, Reed, and they're going to get him through you. That's the plan. Except they aren't. They're going to be locked in some basement cell and forgotten, which is exactly what the professor wants. But look at this." He held Reed's new identity. "You don't have to be a part of it. Right here, right now, you can walk away. Start a new life."

"Leave her out of this."

"Leave her out? She's a goddamn FBI agent."

"Don't say that."

"What do you think the professor is?"

"You shut your mouth."

"You think he's Captain Jihadi the Terrible or something? He's a Fed, and right now he's running the largest sting east of the Rio Grande."

"No."

"He's FBI and he doesn't love you, Reed. He's using you. They all are."

"No."

"Then take out that phone of yours and call him."

"You shut your mouth."

"Take out your phone and call him if you don't believe me. Ask the motherfucker yourself."

Reed was silent. His hand had loosened and fallen from Stone's throat without his realizing it.

"He's using you. But you can walk away."

"I'll kill you, Jimmy."

"Listen to me, Reed. You can walk."

"I kill you right here if you don't shut your mouth."

"Good, because the worst thing you could do would be to forgive me. The world needs confirmation: you're a monster. They couldn't bear your forgiveness."

"Shut your mouth."

"Forgiveness doesn't compute."

"Shut up."

"I wish I could," Stone said. "But like you, I answer to a higher power."

When he pointed one finger at the sky it was as much a gesture of defiance as obedience. It was a ballsy thing, and reluctantly Reed found he liked the man. So when he kicked the shit out of Jimmy Stone it wasn't personal. He kicked the shit out of Stone wholly as a matter of principle, knowing that when the man got up he would walk Reed into the safe house, and Reed, given enough time, would walk himself out. Reed would walk himself back into the war.

His war.

Because that's what it was now. It was his.

✳

A week later he was at the gym. It sat behind a strip mall on a four-lane highway, a three-story building of glass and brushed steel, a wall of lower windows beaded from the indoor pool. Reed sat in the car and waited. It was Jimmy Stone's car, the ancient Camry, but he hadn't seen Stone—he hadn't seen anyone—since Stone had shown up several days ago with John Maynard, the depressive counselor who was meant to convince Reed of something, even if Reed had no idea what.

Since then Reed's only communication with the outside world had been his call to the professor, but that, he knew, was enough. Sometimes life's purpose can be revealed in a single moment. Or two moments, in this case: Maynard's visit, and Reed's discovering the truth of Maynard's life. Which revealed the truth of Reed's too.

It had taken three days of calling, three days of the phone ringing and ringing, and then suddenly, on the third day, the professor picked up.

"Reed, what a pleasant surprise."

But Reed had no time for niceties. He told him what Stone had said, the accusations he made against Professor Hadawi, against Aida.

"The FBI? And you actually believed him? He's lying to you, Reed. He's the one with the government. Tell me where you are?"

But instead of telling him, Reed asked about the other man who had visited, John Maynard, the counselor with his tale of woe and regret. The dead wife, the lost daughter. The irrevocable nature of certain acts.

"He said he could help me."

"Help you, this Maynard? I know John Maynard. He told you about his wife, did he. Well, that's a true story, Reed. You should believe it. But did he tell you the rest?"

"What rest?"

"Tell me where you are, Reed. Let me help you."

He was alone in the lake house, but he didn't tell the professor that. He had found the money hidden in the kitchen ceiling, a dense shrink-wrapped brick. He had revived the engine of the Camry in the shed. The pistol he'd taken from the camp was still in his bag.

"Reed?"

"What rest?"

"Tell me where you are?"

"Tell me what you're talking about first. What rest?"

"I'm talking about what he did to our brothers. He's one of them, Reed. Listen to me. Do you have a computer, do have access to the Internet? I want you to look something up."

"Just tell me."

"I want you to know it for yourself, and after you know it you call me back and I'll come get you. I want you to write down these words."

"All right."

"Are you ready? Write these down, Reed."

"I'm ready."

"One: Global Solutions. Two: Peter Keyes. That's K-e-y-e-s. Are you writing this down? Three: black site. Write it down, Reed. Four: torture. Put them all in a search together. And then add John Maynard's name. And then add James Stone. Are you there, Reed? Reed?"

"I'm here."

"Write down the name Hassan Natashe and then go look for yourself. *Then* you call me back and tell me what you believe."

And he did, he looked it up, he read everything he could find. Articles about John Maynard's book and Keyes's death. Hassan Natashe and all the rumors of a place called Site Nine. But when he was finished he didn't call the professor, he kept searching, but searching for something different now.

It took only a moment to find Maynard's profile at Garrison College. Reed sized him as big but soft. It was good to know these things. Not that he thought it would come to that, but you needed that baseline knowledge. Maybe six-three and thick. All the weight in his chest. Heart-attack weight. A man who spent his days gliding around in an Aeron chair telling folks how to live. If he went down, if Reed had need to take him down, it would happen quickly and resolutely. Hook the lead leg and leverage your momentum, get a forearm across the carotid. There would be a single piggish squeal and then nothing. But it wasn't Maynard he was after.

He kept looking and found photographs of Maynard's new wife and family. He found a home address and mapped it. And then, without actually intending it, he found Maynard's daughter, he found Kayla, and knew instantly this was what he was after.

On the drive to Kayla Maynard's gym he stopped at a Hardee's drive-through and for the first time since the professor had driven him to the camp Reed had taken out the phone Jimmy Stone had given him and allowed the camera to glide over the menu, the window, an expanse of bill-boarded highway. A moment of geographical striptease for Jimmy, a moment of flirtation because where was Hardee's down here except everywhere? Let Jimmy wonder. Let Jimmy know that Reed was fucking with him. First one fast-food joint and now another.

He ate his burger while he waited for her.

Now and then, she wandered across the check-in counter and into his field of view, framed by fliers for Zumba and a Race for the Cure 5K. It was easy enough to recognize her; he'd already been through her Facebook page and those of several of her friends.

When she came back into view he got out of the car and crossed the parking lot. He was in sweats and had shaved the scruff of beard he had allowed to repopulate his face. He didn't need to hide. It wasn't at all like those early days at AltKombat. It wasn't like those days in New York, either. He was nothing but confidence, nothing but a wide smile and dark eyes. Everything else—the shame, the stuttering, the devotion to Aida and Allah—had dissolved somewhere between the moment he kicked the shit out of Jimmy Stone outside the lake house and found Kayla Maynard online.

He put his gym bag on the counter and smiled.

She was in yoga leggings and a hoodie, a small star tattooed on her right wrist, one ear pierced twice. Cute, very cute, the scar no more than a surgeon's blade.

"Hi, may I help you?"

"I hope so," he said. "I'd like to get a membership."

"Oh, wonderful. Have you been in before?"

"First time."

"Absolutely wonderful. Can I show you around?"

"Not even necessary."

"We have a pool, a spinning room. Weights, of course."

His smile was high-voltage—it would not wane—and she was smiling back. It amazed him, how happy she seemed. He took out the fake driver's license and a fold of Stone's cash.

"So maybe a tour?"

"Totally unnecessary," he said. "I've already checked everything out online and I know exactly what I want."

Part Four

He Who Made the Lamb

32.

Kayla sat in the parking lot of the Smoky Mountain Outlet Center beside the Ann Taylor Factory Store and waited. It was almost nine and the Black Friday crowds had just started to lessen, the four A.M.-ers beginning to wane and flag, trudging back to their cars with bags hooked over their forearms, throwing away their Starbucks, calling husbands to make sure the kids had breakfast. Flocks of mothers and sister and girlfriends, attractive women in their leggings and Pinterest-worthy boots. Kayla watched their solemn egress with some relief, a little less manic with every big SUV that pulled onto the highway.

The place was still crowded, the parking lot still near capacity, but it felt more manageable now and that was what she was waiting for. She'd been in the car since before eight, drinking coffee and trying to get control of herself. Somewhere here was Tess Maynard, her father's wife and Kayla's—could this actually be true?—maybe Kayla's stepmother, if that wasn't too weird a thing to imagine which, yeah, it pretty much was. Particularly since there was less than a decade between them in age.

They were planning to meet by the central fountain at nine.

Kayla was on Thanksgiving break from school, but had to trade shifts at the gym in order to make it happen. So she would work the desk from four to midnight tonight and then be back at work the following morning at six. It was worth it.

She knew about her father's family, had even met Tess and the two boys—Laurie wasn't yet born then—at Kayla's grandparents. That day had been a happy accident and it had thrilled everyone, she thought, but her dad. Her dad had hovered over everything, moving to some corner and then moving out again, hands floating but never actually touching. As if he were stranded halfway between the need to act and the need to disappear. Which, of course, he had been.

Kayla was sympathetic. She knew how awkward it was for him, how apologetic it made him, how that sense of lingering unrealized apology confused him.

She regretted that.

She regretted that because she loved him, and also because she held nothing against him. She was sure of that. Not even in some buried Freudian chamber was there any trace of resentment. That he had another life, that she had another life—she had long since accepted that, and was happy with it. She loved her life, loved her grandparents, loved her friends. In a way she wasn't sure she fully understood, she knew she loved her dad's new family, too. Loved them without necessarily needing to be a part of them. Still, it would be nice to be acknowledged as a daughter, and not some inconvenient reminder of tragedy.

She cranked the car and let the heat blow on her hands and feet. The window had iced again so when her hands were warm she let the defrost blow until the glass cleared and it no longer appeared as broken, because broken glass—the shattered windshield that holds, but only just—that wasn't exactly the place she wanted her thoughts to go this morning.

It was seven minutes till nine.

Time to get out, probably, but she didn't want to seem too eager. Her fear was that Tess had contacted her out of guilt and the entire day was an act of Christian mercy, a bit of charity that would only serve to embarrass them both. It was possible the day's theme was

Poor Kayla. She knew, too, that if it was she wouldn't say anything, just suck it up and smile and be polite. But God! What she was hoping for was friendship. It was a dangerous thing to hope, but why not? What did she have to lose really?

Their meeting, she told herself, meant nothing.

She wrote to her father and every third or so letter he sent a check. For over a year she waited for the accompanying letter and then for months she waited for the accompanying note, just a note. *Hope you can use this.* It could be as simple as that. It could be purely instructional: *Deposit to savings* or *use for school.* But all she had were the checks, the scrawl of his signature, the amount and date. Even the addresses on the envelopes were typed, as if the whole thing was done by a machine, some automated process about which her father had only a passing awareness.

Yet she kept writing him.

Not for the money. There had been a point when she realized that no message was forthcoming, only the checks, and she had paused then because she needed to be certain of her motives. Was she writing him for the money? She wasn't. It was another thing she was sure of. She was writing him because he was her father and to know he would touch and read the paper now in her hands was the only form of connection she could imagine. E-mails wouldn't do, and she could bear the thought of calling him no more than she knew he could bear the thought of answering.

Years ago he had asked if she would like to attend Garrison. She had declined, and not because of his presence. She simply hadn't cared to go. She'd been on campus once with a friend and while it was lovely, nestled—the absolute right word was *nestled*—in the mountains, she knew instantly she didn't belong. Everyone was tan. Everyone looked as if they played tennis and volunteered for obscure political campaigns, studied abroad in fascinating if insolvent nations.

Excepting the awkward day at her grandparents, that was their last real-life conversation, to the extent it could even be called such. So she wrote to him, and given his not writing back it became a sort of spiritual exercise. Writing to her father was like praying to Jehovah, some Old Testament God about whom there were legends and stories, but all the legends and stories were old. Nothing had been heard for generations.

Two minutes till nine.

Time to go.

She checked herself in the rear-view mirror, her hair, her makeup (she almost never wore makeup but wore it today).

She touched her scar.

At one point not touching her scar had been an act of discipline in her life. Not touching her scar meant not allowing the lightest brush of a fingertip to sink her into the past which inevitably propelled her into the future. Not this future, but a sort of what-if in which even the best parts of her life seemed a little less shiny than they might otherwise have been. But the truth was, she liked the way it felt. It was the thinnest of filaments, a spider's web tangling her lips, a soft parabola you had to be almost kissing to see. And because of that—its presence, but its nearly hidden presence, as she thought of it—because of that it was not just her, but a more intimate form of her. A glimmer of light—as it sometimes appeared in photographs—that was purest Kayla. Which was, she knew, ridiculous. But also, she knew this too, the sort of tortured logic necessary to any nine-year-old who goes mouth-first into the windshield while beside you your mother goes mouth-first *through* the windshield.

She fingered her hair back behind her ears, and in doing so let her hand glide across one cheek.

Nine-oh-one.

Past time to go.

She walked by the stores with their signs for DOORBUSTERS and BOGO, the crowds almost exclusively female, pack-like in their behavior. It was more a party than a seasonal duty: they were out with friends, the children were at home, there wasn't a man in sight. They were laughing and texting and tapping on Pandora's window jewelry display as if they might wake this ring or that tennis bracelet.

Kayla walked quickly, weaving through the clusters of women, past the opening doors of warm air and chai vanilla soy candles, the meadow of perfume counters, the leather of a shoe store. When she rounded the corner past Fossil and Dressbarn, she saw Tess almost immediately, standing by the empty fountain in a white toboggan and camel's hair coat. She had a tremendous mouth, the sort of wide-lipped look that you read about enviously in the sort of magazines that lined the grocery store checkout lane—HOW TO GET THAT SEXY ANGELINA POUT—and Kayla watched her tremendous mouth spread into a tremendous smile. She was prettier than Kayla remembered, and at the sight of her Kayla felt her heart both leap and sink, which was another piece of wisdom granted to the damaged preteen: how supple the human heart.

Kayla reminded herself it meant nothing, really, their meeting.

"Kayla?" She was coming toward her, arms out. "Oh my God."

"Hi."

"I'm so happy to see you. I am so, so happy."

They were hugging then, Tess's arms squeezing her harder than Kayla had ever thought possible. So tight Kayla had to remind herself their meeting meant nothing. And then she told herself that again: it means nothing, Kayla. Don't get your hopes up. But her hopes were up, and because of them, she was crying, very softly, onto the shoulder of Tess's coat.

33.

As soon as John stepped from the car into the frozen morning he knew he'd made a mistake. Driving from their condo in Pigeon Forge first into the national park and then down to Cades Cove he had watched the temperature fall steadily while the snow that lay in occasional drifts gradually came to overtake entire roadside banks. It was cold in town, but it was at least ten degrees colder here in the valley. The boys were in heavy ski coats and Laurie was zipped into some sort of nylon zero-degree spacesuit. But that didn't change the fact John had made a less than wise decision.

He stood by the picnic shelter and tried to clear his head, tried to recall what exactly Tess had said that morning when—

"Dad?" Wally's door hung open, his breath a silver fish. "Are you gonna let us out?"

"Sit still for one minute for me, all right?"

"We want to walk around."

"We will."

"Can we go down to that creek we drove past?"

"Just shut your door for one minute, all right? I don't want your sister to wake up."

"She's already awake." And then John heard her, the swish of her bundled self, and then the first itch of cry.

"I think she wants out," Wally said.

"Okay."

"She's crying, Dad."

"I hear her."

"She's crying."

"I got her. Thanks."

＊

He put Laurie in the BabyBjörn and made Wally and Daniel hold hands, an act that Wally was more and more finding not only unnecessary but insulting. He had a junior ranger badge and guidebook bought at the park store that listed the flora and fauna of the mountains, and while he knew the bears were hibernating he felt certain they could see a deer if only Daniel would be quiet. So that became the running theme of the morning, Daniel and his noise, Daniel and his coughing, his stepping on sticks or dragging his feet through the wet leaves. Wally shushing him until Daniel was in tears and John had to say something to Wally and then he was in tears, too. Laurie, for her part, was in some sort of body heat coma, tucked inside seven layers of synthetic North Face warmth.

They walked down to the river where beneath the skim ice the water ran shallow and clear over the bedded rocks. Snow lay on the mossy banks and hung in the forks of the poplar trees and gloved the pine boughs. Daniel found a twig encased in ice and this was much remarked on. Laurie babbled happily. John judged the hour-long hike a success, even if they were all frozen faces and runny noses by the time they reached the van.

It took twenty minutes for the children to thaw in front of the heater vents, slower, happily slower, than John might have thought. He took a Prilosec with his coffee, contented. But it was only eleven in the morning and he still had the rest of the day to fill.

Tess was shopping and he was glad for that, if a little puzzled. She had never been the shopping type, hated it, in fact. Claimed it made her skin dry and her bladder small. But she had been looking forward to having a day alone at the outlets since they had planned the trip, and John was glad to be able to give her this. So often he felt there was nothing he could give her, or nothing beyond a house and food and money and children, which were certainly something—from them you didn't so much cobble together a life as you lived one—but there always seemed to be some small, almost extraneous thing missing. Something you forgot because it wasn't immediately evident, then spent the rest of your days with it nagging at you, pulling at its insufferable absence. Except you could never say exactly what was missing.

What she gave him—besides the obvious—was a sort of human softening, a reminder of the necessity of kindness and consideration of which most people never lost sight. She had practically begged his parents to come with them, had even made certain to rent a place with an extra bedroom just in case they changed their mind at the last minute. They just smiled and refused, and John knew they were glad to see his family not in Florida with Tess's parents but doing something together, just the immediate family rather than the family as added onto—and thus diluted—by the presence of cousins and aunts and uncles.

"Y'all go on," his mother had said. "Just the family."

"You two *are* part of our family," Tess had replied.

And his parents had stood there smiling and shaking their heads.

"Y'all go on. You'll be glad you did."

And John was, he was glad.

They had spent the previous day at an indoor water park attached to the condo, John taking the boys down slide after swirling slide while Tess played with Laurie at the splash pad. They met for a lunch of pizza and Sprite and then another three hours of sliding while Tess and Laurie went back to the room and rested. Dinner was in the resort's faux-Italian restaurant and if the food wasn't particularly good—and it wasn't—the lighting was blessedly soft and the children happily exhausted and in the fuzzy good tidings of wine and candlelight he had looked out at all that spread before him and saw a family that loved him with the same intensity he loved them back. He had looked out at contentment, a life worthy of envy, and in that moment felt nothing but love for the entire world, and gratitude for his being in it.

The children fell asleep in the elevator and when they were tucked into bed he and Tess took a bath together in the giant Jacuzzi tub and then made a slow and dreamy sort of love, the kind of wordless act that dissolved so seamlessly into sleep he never once thought about Erin or Karla and Kayla, or Jimmy Stone and the troubled boy John had met at Stone's lake house hideaway.

But he thought of them now.

They were driving the eleven-mile loop past the barns and cabins, the valley and the surrounding slopes a delicate sculpture of ice and light, the sun an evident star as it rose brilliantly over the eastern mountains. Without meaning to he caught himself thinking of how much he would like to bring Erin here. He hated himself for that, but not as much as he did for thinking of Jimmy Stone. He had told the boy, Reed Sharma, about Karla's wreck, about losing touch with Kayla, or not *losing* touch, because it wasn't a thing he misplaced so much as threw away. He told him about throwing away his daughter. Stone wanted the boy to *look grief in the eye*— Jimmy's words—so that he understood the idea of consequences, and John could give him that.

They made their slow way through the valley.

It seemed the single thing John could give anyone.

34.

The parking loop at Garrison Montessori was full so Reed Sharma pulled into the gravel lot at the park beside it, sat for a moment to take in the situation, and then cut the engine. It was almost three in the afternoon, the first Monday after Thanksgiving, and all the moms in their yoga pants and Skechers and vintage eyewear were gathered in a disk of sunlight near the fence, baby strollers pushed against the gate. A few women were visibly pregnant though it appeared as no more than a series of precise knots each the exact size of a soccer ball. Reed figured they all smelled of Purell.

He recognized Tess Maynard from her photographs online. She was alone in running tights, staring down at the screen of her phone, a baby carrier strapped to her chest, a tissue crumpled in one hand.

He walked to the fence and drifted over to where she stood, oblivious to him.

"Hi, excuse me," he said. "This is where you pick up, right?"

She looked up from her phone, finger poised above the screen. Her nostrils appeared raw, pink and chapped, but it put a certain life in her face, an aliveness that felt mournfully rare.

"I'm sorry?"

"This is where you pick up children? Where they come out?" He smiled and did a sort of lazy shrug that fell apart before it ever really happened. "I'm supposed to pick up my brother's kid. First time."

"Oh, yeah. This is it."

"Thank you."

"Of course."

"And sorry," he said, and smiled at the white puff that was the baby's knitted cap. "I didn't mean to disturb her."

"Oh, no, not at all. She's . . . she's out."

"I just wasn't sure if . . ."

"No, right, this is the spot. They come out of the gate there."

"Perfect. Thank you."

He smiled again and when she turned back to her phone he made a point not to look at her, to appear nonthreatening and a little bored, the semi-responsible younger brother doing a favor though doing it inattentively. He put his hands on the top of the white pickets and looked over the schoolyard, the garden and swing set, the arbor tangled in dormant vines. He could feel her looking at him but didn't look back, kept his eyes forward, his lips nearly parting around a nascent smile. There were two picnic tables and a whiteboard around which were tiny handprints in bright colors and the words EDUCATION FOR PEACE. The sun shimmered, though it was a heatless light, a light without conviction.

"I just remembered," she said. "How old is he? Or she? Sorry."

He turned to Tess Maynard and cocked his head as if trying to comprehend.

"Your brother's child," she said. "Because I should have said before that the younger kids you have to go in and sign out."

"Oh, gotcha. She's three."

"Three, okay. Three is Maria's class at the end of the hall. You'll have to sign her out." She put her phone in her pocket and made a small adjustment to the baby carrier. "Do you know where?"

Again, he gave that shrug-thing out of which he was making high art.

"You know I've been here like once for a cookout," he said.

"It's okay. I can show you."

"If it's any trouble at all."

"It's no trouble."

He followed her through the gate—PLEASE KEEP SHUT! LITTLE ONES ON THE LOOSE!—and into the warm building where along the walls children were beginning to line up beneath a long coat rack, each peg adorned with a name and a wallet-sized photograph. They pulled on jackets and hats and picked up backpacks. Mothers kneeled in front of their boys and girls, met them at the level of crouch to zip zippers and tug at drawstrings. But it seemed more dutiful than loving. A few held their phones, the moment more about Instagram than affection.

Tess Maynard weaved through the crowd, body sideways, arms extended as if surfing, the baby carrier riding just above the heads until a voice called to her.

"Mom," a boy said, and from the side Reed watched her mouth widen into a smile.

She crouched onto her heels, the baby carrier like an anchor, and put both hands on the shoulders of a boy, the shoulders of her son, of John Maynard's son. He looked to be seven or eight, brown headed, shoes tied though not in anything resembling a bow. Reed took his phone, touched the telescope icon, and without ever looking at the screen began to film them.

"Hey, baby. How was your day?"

"You're supposed to wait outside, you know."

"I'm just helping this nice man back to Miss Maria's class."

The nice man filmed Tess Maynard with her wind-burned face, then the soft sleeping face of her daughter, the clasped eyes, the tracery of blue veins. He filmed her son, he filmed John Maynard's son, and then, with the same subtlety with which he had removed it, he put his phone back in his pocket. The image would go straight to Stone and Reed needed that, he needed Stone to see it. He needed Stone to know what he was capable of. See how long my reach, Jimmy.

"Can you find your brother and wait for me by the gate?" Tess Maynard asked her son.

"Sure."

"It was a good day?"

"Yeah."

"Be right out there, okay?"

She touched his face and stood, smiled at Reed.

"My son."

"Sounds like a good boy."

"Wally," she said. "He is. Now let me show you." She took a few steps, looked back and smiled patiently as another classroom emptied and the hall filled, separating Reed and Tess. "One sec," she said.

"You know if you can just point me in the right direction I can probably find it."

"Oh, okay. You sure?"

"Yeah, that was the tricky part, all the kids."

"Well, you just go to the end there, and then right."

"Thank you."

"Miss Maria's classroom. It's the only one down there."

"I really appreciate it."

He moved past them, pausing at the end of the hall to see the woman making her slow way through a sea of children back toward the door. When she passed through it he came back down the hall, back along the coat rack until he found WALLACE MAYNARD taped above an empty peg. The coat was gone, the child was gone, but on the shelf sat a plastic grocery bag full of what appeared to be his art projects, cuttings and pastings and jagged construction paper.

He took his phone back out and filmed it all—the wall hook and printed name, the drawings of birds and large cats. Let Jimmy see it all. Let Jimmy know.

When he was finished he quietly walked back to his car and dialed Kayla.

"Hey, girl," he said. "You still free tonight?"

35.

The first week of December it was like Tess couldn't not be happy. John was busy at work—it was the final week of classes and all the students who had spent the semester not doing what they were supposed to be doing were suddenly panicking, suddenly in need of counseling—but in another week exams would be over and campus would be empty and he would be home for winter break. Thanksgiving had been perfect. Christmas would be even better. There was a half marathon in Chattanooga in the spring and she was thinking of registering because looking at last year's times she felt certain she could win her age group.

One evening Daniel and Laurie both went down early and she sat for an hour with Wally and his *Minecraft* whales, these block creations that dived and hunted and spouted. He had posted a video on YouTube and they watched it together.

> Hey, guys, so I actually forgot the title of the mod but the download stuff is below if you look down there it should work but don't blame me if it doesn't, k?

"This is you?" she asked. "This is your voice?"

"Yeah."

If you look up, you see all the stuff. That up there . . . that's, yes, awesome, that's an angler fish up there with that angler thing and you can see how they look with those crazy teeth and all.

"What did you say, angel fish?"

"Angler fish."

"How do you know about angler fish? Honey, you sound so grown-up, so mature."

"Mom."

"You're going to be doing calculus and getting married, my grown boy."

"Come on, Mom."

The comments were funny and stupid and encouraging and she was proud of her son for his brilliance, his ingenuity.

StarShark123can u ride the whale?

haloboy17this is awesome. Can u ride the angler fish?

Leah_12whales don't eat fish

"Is that true?" she asked him.

He shook his head ruefully and they laughed.

StarShark123u know theres a mod where you can ride a turtle?

She was so happy she barely noticed the Middle Eastern men around her, the ones in the malls and convenience stores. She surely didn't allow herself to think about the man in the basement. She didn't dare approach the possibility that his death had somehow freed her, that his headless nonexistence had somehow pushed her back into the world. That she was alive precisely because he was not.

No, no, no, no—why would she even begin to imagine such?

She was so happy, her world felt so *balanced*, she called her dad and promised to spend better than a week in Florida, December 23 to January 2, does that work?

"Of course, it works, honey. Frankly, I wish you'd move back."

And was it crazy that not even *that* seemed crazy?

Ten days was nothing. And okay, maybe it was a rash thing to do—she hadn't bothered running it by John; they had never stayed more than four days—but if the giddy float of her life never ended—and how could it possibly ever end?—what did it matter? It would be ten or so days of carols and gifts and eggnog, and New Year's Eve she and John could leave the children with her parents and go out and have the sort of amazing night that seemed more and more possible lately.

Tess had returned from her day—her *secret* day—with Kayla late and a little tipsy, and with her fingernails colored the wildest of pinks, she and John had wound up back in the Jacuzzi tub, back in the bed, making the sort of tender love that felt like the lightest falling of rain. Since then, she wasn't thinking about the orange jumpsuit on the USB drive or why her husband kept disappearing every Saturday to Atlanta or Peach Creek or wherever it was. *Might want to check with your husband on that whole relicensure thing, honey.* She didn't care about the man in the basement, not anymore, and she hardly ever caught herself standing in the living room at two in the morning, clicking.

She was so happy she called her sister in Savannah and tried to convince her to stay the week, too.

"You've got to be insane, Tess. You honestly told dad the twenty-third to the second? You can't possibly make it that long."

"I will. I am."

"You've forgotten what it's like. You've got this idealized view."

"It's Christmas!"

"You've got this warped idealized view. Tell me you haven't?"

"It's going to be great. I'm thinking all the couples could go out on New Year's Eve to the Blue Coyote."

"Tess—"

"You know the place at the country club? You get drunk and drive the golf carts all over?"

"Mom was afraid you were depressed, but I just think you're crazy."

"I want the children to have memories."

"It's called Lexapro."

"Liz."

"It's called Wellbutrin."

"I want us all together. Think of all the fun."

"Think of all the crazy. Have you even called David yet?"

Her brother barely bothered to acknowledge the call. Crazy was too much trouble. He turned to practical affairs: his wife was shopping for Wally, Daniel, and Laurie. He had a bottle of Elijah Craig for John. Did she want a pair of those new Hoka running shoes, the giant orthopedic-looking things?

"I don't want anything except for you and Carol and the girls to stay the entire week."

"I'll see you Christmas Eve, Tess."

"At least through New Year's Eve, all right?"

"I have to be back in Charlotte on the twenty-seventh."

"David."

"I'll see you soon, Tess."

But not even her brother could burst the swelling bubble of her happiness. Part of it—a huge part of it—was her newfound friendship with Kayla. That they would hit it off hadn't been immediately evident. They had met at the fountain; they had hugged; Kayla had cried a little and then apologized for crying. From there they had walked to a coffee shop where they had sat making awkward small talk while time crawled toward whatever point at which they could both walk away without feeling like total fools.

Both were a little over-caffeinated. Both, Tess surmised, were a little regretful and embarrassed, as much for themselves as for the other. Kayla's hair was no longer streaked with pink but dyed black, and Tess wondered if that was some concession to maturity. She ran her tongue over her uneven bottom teeth and Tess wondered if that was some concession to fear. Either way, neither seemed to want to be there, and around ten Tess realized if she left right then she could drive to Cades Cove in time to eat lunch with John and the children.

She was on the verge of making her excuse when something else came to her.

"You know what," Tess said. "This is crazy and sort of out of nowhere, but would you want to get your nails done?"

"My nails?"

"I used to get them done when I was a girl. It was a thing I did with my mom and sister. But I haven't had them done since I was like fifteen."

"I don't think I've ever had mine done. I mean professionally."

"So maybe?"

"Sure."

"You don't mind?"

"No. I'd love to," Kayla said. "I mean why not, right?"

It was more of a spa than a nail salon and they wound up with matching mani-pedis.

"We should pick the same color," Tess said.

"I love it."

"Something totally crazy."

"I so completely love it."

Tess so completely loved this girl. She was happy. They both were. It was the Essie Raise Awareness Pink. It was the foot scrub. It was the mimosas the girl kept bringing and they both kept drinking, glass after glass.

"I have to work today," Kayla said.

"What time?"

"I have no idea. Now maybe?"

And they both burst into laughter because why shouldn't they? Tess felt like she had been denied laughter for she didn't know how long. But she didn't resent it. She just laughed. She had been denied the friendship of Kayla but she didn't resent that either.

They went for lunch at a cheesy hamburgers-and-margaritas place beneath a giant Ferris wheel. The place was packed with women, all happily exhausted, washed-out shoppers drinking early cocktails and recounting the morning's haul. The menu had a line of overpriced cocktails and they both ordered a Mountain Mist and then a Tennessee Sunrise.

"This is so breaking diet," Kayla said, "but I think I'm going to get a hamburger."

"What kind of diet?"

"A stupid one. I'm supposed to be in like a fitness contest in February and I should pretty much be living off greens and canned tuna at this point."

"But you don't need to lose weight."

"You always need to lose weight," Kayla said, and lifted her empty drink. "Should we?"

"Absolutely we should."

This time it was the Appalachian Apple Pie, which appeared to be apple juice and vodka and some sort of syrup, and then the Black Bear which was maybe chocolate and something that tasted faintly of lighter fluid.

People were laughing, music was playing—

"Do you know this song?" Kayla said, and Tess found her head cocked, listening not just to Kayla or the music, but to the whole earth, the way the floor shook, and then the ground beneath it, and the way it echoed out in perfect synchronicity. The entire planet one coordinated heart.

"It's 'Straight Tequila Night,'" Kayla said.

"John Anderson. I totally know it. I love this song."

"I am so, so glad you said that, because I love it, too, and I always feel a little embarrassed by it."

"Why embarrassed? It's a great song," Tess said. "You know who would hate it?"

"I know exactly what you're going to say."

"John would."

"He would, wouldn't he?"

"Actually, no, he wouldn't hate it. He would like it."

"I know exactly what you're going to say."

"He probably does like it. But it would be even worse."

"I know exactly," Kayla said. "He would analyze it!"

"Yes! Mansplain it!"

"John Anderson as cisgendered response to heartache."

"Normative emotional states in late-eighties ballads." Tess was nodding, smiling. "Analyze it, and never hear a thing."

"I know, right?"

She was so happy, Tess was. She was a little drunk, too. They both were. But it was the first time all day John had been mentioned and she was so glad it wasn't some taboo subject, some minefield through which she would have to step with blind precision. They kept talking about him, his habits, his past. Kayla talked about her mom and the time in Minnesota, then being sent back to Georgia while her dad was in California working for some mega-billionaire who wound up getting shot. Tess told Kayla about their new life, John's work, the children, her running. The sweetness of Kayla's grandparents.

It was so simply inexplicably uncontrollably fun.

It was fascinating too, to remember that Kayla knew John, knew him as only a child can, and for a moment Tess felt the briefest flare of jealousy—would her children ever know their father so well?

It was afternoon by the time lunch was over and they wandered for hours through the outlets and then it was off to another meal, no pretense of food at this point, just a carafe of house red and then, why not? Let's get one more.

"You have to work, right?"

"I think I missed work."

"Can you get home?"

"I'll maybe just sit in the car for a few minutes."

It was dusk by then and Tess was thinking: yeah, maybe I should sit in the car for a few minutes, too.

So now, a week later they were texting and keeping up with each other on Facebook and already planning to get together right before Tess and the family left for Florida.

Late one evening Tess's phone pinged and when she saw it was Kayla she put down her book and slipped out of bed. John looked up from his *New Yorker*.

"Who is that?"

"Wally's school."

"Pretty late for that. Everything okay?"

"Christmas party stuff."

She took the phone into the living room and looked at Kayla's message.

Met this guy.
Yeah?
Been coming to the gym and we sort of hit it off.
Yeah?

When her phone pinged again Tess was looking at a picture of Kayla and a boy with dark eyes and crinkly hair, their faces pressed together above the long extension of his arm.

Cute right?

Super cute. ☺

Kind of excited. About to go out. Third time!!!!

Have fun and let me know.

K

love you

love you back

So maybe it was all part of the happiness, the seemingly endless abundant nature of it that led her to forget to tell John about Christmas. Or maybe she just didn't want to tell John, knowing that the moment she did that clean laundry smell she seemed to find everywhere these days would begin to sour. So instead of hearing it from Tess, John heard of her plans for an extended stay from Tess's brother.

It was the afternoon of the last day of classes and they were calling for flurries. John came home in boots and scarf and hat and left everything by the door to dry.

"Is it snowing yet?"

"Blowing," he called from the kitchen, "not sticking."

"The boys are dying. They said maybe three inches on the news."

"I doubt it," John said, and if she hadn't detected something in the way his voice lumbered out she detected it in the darkening of his face as he came into the living room. "Your brother called today."

"David? What did he want?"

"He was asking about Florida. Wanted to know if you were serious about staying because he and Carol were maybe thinking about it, too."

"Oh."

"I told him of course you were serious. Why wouldn't you be?"

"I'm so sorry."

"It's all right."

"I meant to—"

"It's honestly fine."

It was honestly fine because he wasn't going. That was what he told her. Work, his parents. She should take the kids and he would see them all when they got back. They fought a little, but not really. His was an absurd overreaction—there was no reason she couldn't call her dad back and amend their plans—but she knew it wasn't a reaction at all. It was an excuse, an out. He didn't want to go and now he had his reason. Tess got to take the children to Florida while John got to take the high road.

She told herself it was actually better this way. That having him around—as much as a family should be together for the holidays—was simply too stressful. He got along well with her parents, too well actually, and what that did was remind Tess of their difference in age, which, naturally, reminded her of John's previous life. The dead wife. The kneeling man in his orange jumpsuit. And anything that took her thoughts there was to be avoided at all costs, including Christmas with him.

So, yeah, it's fine. No big deal. The children will be disappointed but they'll have their cousins and grandparents and so, yeah, whatever you want.

She was okay with it, she repeatedly told herself she was okay. Still, the joy was gone. It took her a few days to admit as much, but it was gone. It was Saturday, in fact, before Tess caught herself in the living room darkness.

John was gone again and it had just hit her what a mistake everything was, not just Christmas but tangling herself in Kayla's life, snooping through the closet at John's parents. For the first time in weeks she thought of the USB drive, she thought of the man no longer in the basement, but in some shallow unmarked grave. For the first time in weeks she found herself centered in a dark room, alone and clicking.

36.

Reed Sharma watched her go across the parking lot toward the stairwell and her apartment. Kayla Maynard stopped once to turn and wave, a little hopefully, he thought, and he waved back and after another moment she was gone. When the light came on in her second-floor room he pulled onto the highway and headed south.

It was something like their fourth or fifth date and they'd spent the last twenty minutes making out in the front seat of Jimmy Stone's Camry. Kiddie stuff, lips and slobber, pawing each other over their clothes. She wanted him to come up, but he said no, barely said no. He wanted to of course—it had been how many months since Aida or the debacle at the Sit-n-Chat?—but he had a larger plan and it called for patience.

Still, he thought about her the whole way south to Peach Creek. She was a beautifully needful thing, the back of her shoulders tattooed with tiny blue planets and stars, a celestial swirl that appeared to signal nothing so much as hope. Everything about her seemed to signal hope. Everything about her seemed to signal some radiant goodness. If he wasn't in love with her, he was at least charmed by her. They had met at the gym. He told her he'd been sick, had lost weight. He was a fighter, which was true enough, and with the flattened nose and early intimations of cauliflower ears it was easy to believe. Then he went into the other room and attacked the squat rack. He worked out like a pent animal suddenly freed, all the while watching her watch him, sauntering back to the reception desk between sets, smiling. He'd cut off his feelings of late—he didn't feel a thing beyond a cold mechanical indifference—but now there was the teasing sense that maybe he wasn't done with the whole being alive thing.

But that had to wait.

The previous Saturday he had sat by the entrance to John Maynard's gated neighborhood and then followed him an hour south to a house in Peach Creek. Maynard had spent the night there. Now it was Saturday again and Reed had the feeling Maynard wouldn't be hard to find.

And he was right.

Reed drove once through the neighborhood at dusk, an older part of town, split-levels on cleared lots, bungalows tucked back in the trees. Stoops and front porches with swings. Barbecue grills. A lone shopping cart pushed into a wall of kudzu. He parked in front of a fourplex with its dull primer coat, fleeces of insulation foaming through the plank siding as if spilling its own pink guts. He was three houses down from John Maynard's car, and sat in the failing light with the windows down, waiting. Kids came by on bikes, parting around his car, standing on their pedals, legs jack-hammering, four or five of them. Slapping their flat hands against the side panels so that it sounded personal, some coiled menace in the resonant thud. But then they were gone, gray shapes in the graying night.

He got out and popped the trunk, took the tire iron from the well and sat back in the driver's seat, the iron shaft balanced across his thighs because come on, motherfuckers, come slap the car again why don't you. But they weren't coming back. It was dark now. The lights were on in the house he was watching. He was too far away to see shapes, but he knew they were in there. John Maynard and whoever else, some woman. He touched the tire iron. It was very cold. He hadn't consciously thought about it driving down, but in some sense he had. In some sense it had occupied a central place in the life of Reed Sharma, whether he admitted it or not. But why not admit it? Why not own up to it?

It was something about the proximity to his parents, he thought. This inability to acknowledge his intentions. The weakening effect nearness to them had on him. He could be at their front door in an hour flat. In the house, in his old bedroom, in his old life. But he wasn't going to do that.

When his phone went off he saw he had a text from Kayla but didn't allow himself to read it. He needed to wait, he needed to focus. What exactly it was he was doing here wasn't completely clear to him. But Reed felt certain that if he was still enough and patient enough some larger purpose might emerge.

Then he gave in and looked.

Miss U!

He didn't reply, just put the phone face-down on the seat beside him. She'd had questions for him that first day at the gym. Where was he from? Atlanta. Did he do anything besides fight? Not at the moment. He told her he'd lost a fight, an undercard at the Georgia Dome, $10K it would have been and she just said *oh* because nobody asks about losing. Americans aren't made to lose. Then he went back to the bench press.

She came over later holding a weight belt.

"Have you ever used one of these?" she asked.

He had.

"How do you wear it? Like this?"

"Higher," he said.

"Here."

"Yeah. Sit it above your waist."

It was evident she knew exactly how to wear a weight belt. Not that he minded. He wound up asking her out and she gave this ridiculous pause as if such a thing had never occurred to her.

His phone went off again, screen-down on the seat so that the cheap upholstery glowed blue.

She had sent one of the selfies they had taken, one of about twenty they had made over the last few hours. Pouting, laughing, frowning. He cranked the car and felt the heat come on, warm and then warmer. There was one he particularly liked, their faces close, the long sweep of his arm reaching out.

He felt himself drifting toward it, that particular contentment, and knew he needed to move. He was freezing despite the heat and dropped the car into drive, eased forward so that he could see someone through the front blinds, the house bleeding light. Then he accelerated quicker than he'd intended.

It was definitely something about his intentions, about not knowing them but sensing something particularly dangerous there, something that once he started he might not be able to contain. The phone call he'd made to Professor Hadawi was part of it, so too the things Stone had said. The visit from Maynard. The sense in which they were all using him, that he was no more a person to them than he had been to his parents. The Voice of goddamn Reason, yo-yoing with his life.

Do you know what bombs do, Reed?

He drove to the Dunkin' Donuts out near I-75 and ate three glazed and drank two cups of coffee. An impossible indulgence, but why not? Let the caffeine and sugar carry him because what else would? Certainly not Kayla, at least not through this. His phone kept going off, pic after pic from her and he scrolled through them, but didn't answer, not yet.

When he felt calmer he drove back to the neighborhood and got out, the tire iron held against his thigh. The street was silent, a few windows squared in blue, otherwise shutters and darkness. Grandparents raising grandchildren in the nub of shadow, entire clans asleep behind bed sheets hung for curtains. A world of snapbacks and Timberland boots. In the storm drain were crushed forties and the nubs of cigarillos. He started walking, fully expecting to be stopped, some homeowner with a .410 and the ability to divine Reed's ill intent would step out and blow him into the outstretched arms of seventy-two virgins. The cops would arrive, sirens screaming, guns drawn. He'd be another dead kid with sixteen entry wounds and a hashtag attached to his name.

Yet somehow he made it to the house. Somehow he stood by John Maynard's car. Somehow he felt himself crossing the crinkly grass, brown and dormant. He stood on the porch waiting to be accosted, waiting to die, perhaps, and maybe it would be a welcome thing, an end to the confusion. But nothing happened.

The lights were off inside and the only sound was the quiver of breeze through the treetops. He held his hands out from his body. *Here I am. Here's your chance.* The tire iron there for the taking, his life there for the taking, and they should take it, they should come for him now if they knew what was good for them. He hadn't brought the Walther for this very purpose: to allow them to come for him.

But they didn't. So instead of dying he took out his phone and streamed it all to Jimmy Stone: the car, the house, the quiet street.

Let him see.

Let him know.

A moment later he stood outside the window where they slept, his feet sinking into the soft earth of the flower bed. Shrubs. Dead azaleas. The heater came on, the heat pump, whatever it was, sitting on its concrete hurricane pad, and when it went quiet it was like a stillness had descended, cosmic in its depths, some dispensation of suburban silence. Eventually, he heard them within. The clutch of their breathing. The window was cracked and through the slash he could hear them in bed, sleeping, waiting. They were no more than a few feet from him, less probably, separated by the double-paned glass and then, beneath that, separated by nothing at all. The human smell of bed sheets and quilts and some incense they must have burned.

Someone moved. He thought the man moved, turned over, adjusted the blanket.

The orange wires of a space heater pulsed and faded.

When the man was still, Reed moved out from beneath the azaleas, staying close to the house, staying in the darker pocket of shade past the spigot and past the coiled hose as he made his way back around to the porch. He went quietly up the three steps. The swing. The rocking chairs and a small table. The house was a Craftsman bungalow, assembled back beneath the live oaks, giant slouching trees deepening the night.

He felt around for a way in.

The door was deadbolted, but the window was unlocked. It was leaded glass, older than those along the bedroom, and he slid it up far enough to get his fingers in, slid it higher, and then moved through it—leg, arm, body—pulling himself behind himself as if this were his idea and not simply some surprising thing that was happening to him, something to which he was witness.

He was in the front room then. Couch, TV, end tables—all of it poorly articulated. He slid the window down when he felt the draft, moved along the bead-board walls until he stood between the front room and the kitchen. Boxes of cereal. A pot of coffee going cold on the dead burner. The tire iron was still in his hand, his fingers still wrapped around the shaft. He'd forgotten about it, its coldness, but knew, too, that he hadn't. He'd known all along it was there. That was the point, after all. It was what he was doing: entering a house to do violence.

He waited and gradually moved forward, listened. Moved again, waited, listened.

He was in the hall when the man yelled, when John Maynard yelled, and Reed felt his body constrict, his fingers a fist around the iron.

He called out again. But he was asleep, he was crying in his sleep.

The woman said something Reed couldn't understand.

The man was muttering and then speaking, his voice thick and frightened.

"What did I say?" he wanted to know.

And the softer voice of the woman: "You were just yelling."

"I didn't say a name or anything?"

"Drink some water."

They were just voices to Reed, sounds in another room.

"I didn't say a name?"

"Drink this. You were just yelling."

They were just voices. You couldn't exactly ascribe life. But then, without his intending it, he felt them change. He felt his fingers loosen around the shaft of the iron. His scalp was sweating, he felt the beads gather into an ill-worn halo, and standing there a small part of himself was afraid of the larger part, the part that was actually him. But something else, something deeper, believed what he was experiencing was the end of a long migration, that he was returning to himself, to both the person he had been and the person he might yet be. He had been a frightened child, an angry child, this was true. But he had also been kind.

He thought of what Stone had said just before Reed beat the shit out of him. The worst thing you could do would be to forgive me. The world needs confirmation: you're a monster. They couldn't bear your forgiveness. He wasn't sure that he could bear it either. Just the same, he backed out, climbed through the window, and left.

He used the pay phone outside the Dunkin' Donuts to call Hadawi.

I'm on my own now. I want you to know that.

But Reed—

You won't be hearing from me again.

Reed—

He hung up and drove north back to Jimmy Stone's lake house, stopping only once to buy two five-gallon containers he filled with gas to go with the container he'd found in the shed. There was so much he could have said, but also there was nothing really. Fuck you, he might have said. Except that wasn't exactly it, either. You couldn't tell them though, not in a way they would understand. But he intended to show them. He had in mind a gift for them, a play of sorts. One last thing for them all to watch.

37.

John's mistake was going.

But it wasn't that first trip to Poland that undid everything.

It was when he went back. It was that second trip to Site Nine.

John thought of that in Erin's bed, not that it was a new thought. But then again everything seemed new lately, or if not new, unexamined in a way he had never thought possible. It was talking to the boy, to Reed Sharma, as much as it was his sleeping with Erin. The woman beside him, Karla's old best friend. The skin he had touched. The lies he had told.

Out by the sidewalk the streetlight shone, hazy and opalescent.

The heat was off and the windows were cracked so that cool air moved through the gaps, just enough to make you want to bury yourself down beneath the comforter and the quilt. Which was exactly where Erin was, asleep on her side, withered arm cradled against her stomach, only the top of her head showing.

John was on top of the covers, sweating, and it was because of Poland.

It was because of that second trip.

He was married to Tess by then. She was happy and John was happy with her, happy so long as he could operate in the narrow constraints of justification, happy so long as he could imagine what he and Jimmy Stone and Ray Bageant had done not just as necessary, but as morally right.

Then they picked him up in Milan, a cleric. Hassan Natashe. Brown skinned and American-born, but traveling on a Canadian passport and the question was how?

The question was why?

The question was what's this jihadi shit doing on his phone?

Videos. Links to blogs and forums.

Numbers in Karachi and Jalalabad. Not the numbers of known terrorists but metadata indicated a sprawling web of implication. He was calling the numbers of folks who were calling the wrong fucking numbers, the ones keyed to, the ones being recorded.

So they plucked him off the street—what was John doing at the time? Probably having sex on the couch with his new wife—they plucked him off the street and put him in a Fiat van, drove him to the naval air station at Aviano and put him on a Gulfstream V to Katowice. The hood and hand restraints. The promethazine suppository.

Another van took him through the Polish night, past the chainlink and barking dogs and then he was in the room and John—summoned from Florida—was in the room with him. There was no separation this time, no watching through the distance of a screen: they sat face-to-face. John asked questions, made notes, and then prescribed the absence of sleep, or the standing, or the lifting by the same thin wrists the cleric one day tried to chew his way through. To chew his way to Allah. To chew his way out of the room in a zippered body bag.

It went on for weeks.

It amazed him.

John sat there through all of it, eighteen hours a day, wanting to know what it was the man knew. He didn't mean in any objective sense. The questions John posed were about networks and numbers. But what he wanted was internal. He wanted the locked secret of the man's being, for it was evident that he had one. It was evident that the man had discovered some inner resource, some truth only accessible to those who suffer. It was exactly what John had written about, exactly what he had pretended to know: that somewhere out past the torment was order. That past the storm of loss was a perfect calm of being.

One morning they hoisted him by his hands, allowing him to dangle for hours like a piece of meat, which was exactly what he became. It wasn't possible to survive it, yet that was what it reduced to: the inevitability of his survival. Later, they would beat him or scald him, but hanging there, his life no more than the roped pain in his wrists, John knew Hassan Natashe would live, and he would do it very precisely in his hands and arms and shoulders. And that was part of it; that, perhaps, was all of it. When they cut him down, life would come rushing back in. The questions. The soft-soled slippers, the bottled water. But in that moment it was suspended. What reigned was what was.

The next day John drowned him. Secured his wrists, the hood, poured the water over his mouth and nose and what followed was an awful wrenching of coughing and gagging and then, most frighteningly, what seemed a calm acceptance. John drowned him for hours. John drowned him for an entire day, and after that, he felt wedded to him. He needed what Hassan Natashe had.

Still, he wouldn't talk, or wouldn't talk right, because in some respects he never shut up. He confessed to everything, except everything was wrong. The man was a river of disinformation.

So John drowned him again.

And he spoke wrongly, falsely.

And John drowned him, and in between the gagging and vomiting he wept softly, stoically, and John drowned him as if these two men had been put on this earth for no greater purpose than to hurt, and to witness that hurt. He was breaking open, light—as much as intestinal fluid—was on the verge of spilling forth. Not intelligence but the secret he was after, the secret he had to have. So

John became Dr. Mengele. He drowned him. He strung him up and cut him down, scalded him and froze him, blasted him with noise and light and then took away all noise and light. Day after day, hour after hour, it went on without fail because John was close, John was so close to knowing. It was what Peter Keyes had promised him after all. *We're going to open up souls, John.* That was exactly what was happening, what was about to happen, then—

When word came that they had snatched the wrong man it was more the ruination of sound than sound itself, the abrupt dragging of the tune arm across the record.

How could this be?

But then again, more accurately, how could it not be?

It simply was. They had followed the right guy into the train station or the subway or whatever the hell it was, and then followed the wrong guy out. Brown guy, but the wrong brown. This from the directorate of operations, this colossal shoulder shrug.

What can we say? Mistakes were made. That kind of shit happens in the world.

As for the Canadian passport, he turned out to be a Canadian citizen. Born and raised in Toronto. An actual fucking Blue Jays fan.

The numbers in his phone, the videos?

Wasn't his phone, asshole. It got mixed up when the Evidence Team went to barcode it. This guy's phone came back clean. This guy's phone is loaded with pics of his kids, cute kids.

What can they do?

Well, first, they can drug him, they can fly him to Ljubljana and put him in another van. Stuff his pockets with travel papers and 500 euros in small bills, drive him south to just this side of the Italian border where they tell him to get out and walk, seriously. That way, motherfucker. Beat it.

A week later he's back home telling his tale of misery and grief to every major news outlet in the Western world. There's no proof, of course, but it's compelling shit, laced with details about stress positions and jargon that all checks out, right down to the nerve damage in his hands.

So when he files suit in U.S. District Court in Manhattan against Global Solutions, an otherwise unknown consulting firm, the ACLU offers representation and within twenty-four hours he's on both *Dateline* and *Charlie Rose*.

And then there are no more interviews and no trial because there is no more Hassan Natashe.

One starry night three weeks after his release he puts the kids to bed, kisses his wife goodnight, locks himself in the bathroom, and makes some serious progress on chewing through his wrists. Except this time the instrument of choice is not his teeth but a pink Bic Lady Shaver.

It's tragic, and the night John hears the news he stands outside his and Tess's condo and lets her see him. The idea is to go on as before, but as soon as she starts talking he realizes nothing is the same and never will be again.

"You've changed."

"Everybody changes."

"You've turned cruel."

"That was inevitable."

"Oh no, John, it doesn't have to be."

But actually, yeah, it does. He's cruel and she tells him as much, and he's glad for it, even if it isn't exactly true. The truth is, he's always been cruel. The truth is, he's wanted to hurt someone since Karla died. He's *needed* it. He's wanted some goddamn payback and now that he's got it he's happy, happy old Hassan is dead and his family's life is every bit as wrecked as John's.

And it's that happiness that breaks him.

It's that happiness that almost kills him.

It's—

*

"John?" Her hand on his shoulder. "Wake up, John."

"What?"

"It's all right. Wake up."

And then he was awake and still atop the covers and still sweating and Erin was telling him that he was crying out in his sleep, yelling.

"What did I say?"

"You were just yelling."

"I didn't say a name or anything?"

"Drink some water."

"I didn't say a name?"

"Drink this. You were just yelling."

He drank it while she stroked his hair, suddenly cold, suddenly shivering.

"I want you to go away with me," he said. "Next week. They'll all be in Florida. Go with me, all right?"

"Drink some water."

"Somewhere in the mountains," he said. "You'll go?"

"Yes," she said, "I'll go."

And he believed her, and then he was beneath the covers.

And then, finally, he was asleep.

38.

Tess thought she was done with it, with seeing them, or at least with being bothered by it. Even the crying had stopped. Then she took the children Christmas shopping at the city center mall in Dunwoody north of Atlanta and there they were. A Middle Eastern man, brown skin, loose white shirt—a blouse?—sitting at the food court and talking on his cell. Another outside the Limited, bored. Three women in chadors—the word just came to her, this entire new language she was learning—three women in chadors eating Auntie Ann's pretzels.

They walked through the shops, in and out of doors, Laurie strapped to her chest, Daniel holding her hand, Wally wandering somewhere behind, oblivious so that every few steps Tess had to stop and remind him to keep up. She felt so out of place. The shops were crowded with well-dressed people, women wandering in clouds of perfume and wearing either three-inch heels or sneakers from 1982. The leggings, the skin-tight jeans. You passed them and their scent was like a sonic boom, a delay, four, five steps before it hit you, a half second after you thought it wasn't coming. The men held bags or children, stopping to let them look at the window displays, the reindeer and sleigh.

"Come on, Wally. Keep up, honey."

They walked around the corner past the endless cafés with their craft beers and bamboo chairs, their heat lamps glowing like alien craft caught in the act of descent. She didn't know what exactly she was doing here. Shopping, yes, but for whom? For what? John had refused to come, or not exactly refused because she hadn't actually asked him because she was getting this vibe off him that was all *how many seconds till you and the children are out the door?* It was a frequent thing, this bad energy, and she was glad he hadn't come, even if she could use the help.

"Come on, Wally." Stopping again. "One more place and we'll get some lunch, okay, honey?"

What would John have said had he come? He would have made fun of them, all of them, himself included. Happiness seemed to invite his wrath. Happiness seemed to signal some moral failing. *Just look at them, Tess.* All the good Americans with their bathroom tiles and drone strikes. Driving too fast down highways lined with junk food and Chinese manufacturing. The entire world—could you say that he hated the world? That didn't seem exactly right. Maybe he was only sick of it. The abductions of African girls and the hashtag campaigns to get them back. Pull down the statue, chant outside the dictator's villa. Watch the revolution on YouTube, the refugees on the evening news, the life vests and drowned toddlers, the border fences in Hungary.

Maybe he was only sick of it and maybe that was fair, maybe that was a reasonable response.

But you know what, she thought, you know what, dear, guess what? Being sick of it is a luxury. You think you're the only one paying attention? The upcharge for sweet potato fries, the good heels and Coach bag. Everyone's profound sense of contented decency while *meanwhile in Syria* or *meanwhile in the Democratic Republic of Goddamn Congo* tickles like the sneeze that never quite arrives.

He had infected her, John had.

Those nights on St. Simons when he was failing to die with the same withering conviction with which he was failing to live. He had infected her, weakened her. She'd been strong and he had weakened her.

"Come on, Wally. Pay attention, honey."

She felt a swell of anger against her husband but also very much against the people around her. The pigtailed men in canvas sneakers, the women wandering in and out of Kohl's. Then ahead of her—*thank, God*—like some resplendent promised land thick with bourbon chicken and gluten-free wraps she saw the doors to the food court.

"Guys! Come on. Here we are!"

Thank God because her nerves were fissuring. Thank God because her legs and lower back were twitching with a consistency that promised imminent muscle cramps. That morning she'd gotten up at three to run fifteen miles along the over-lit streets of their neighborhood, mile after mile while the watch on her wrist logged steps, heart rate, cadence, stride length. But not exactly *gotten up* to run. She was already up when she decided that waiting for the sun was ridiculous—why not go now? Well, because it's night, Tess. But what was night, really? There was some celestial explanation, scientific and precise, but for Tess it was more and more becoming a social construction, and a very foreign one at that. Just when Laurie started sleeping through the night Tess found her body had lost interest in it. So why not be up? Why not burn off the exhaustion?

"Come on, Mom," Wally said, because now it was Tess who wasn't keeping up. "Come on, I'm starving."

They sat at a center table with their crunch-wrap tacos and slices of pepperoni, Laurie out of the BabyBjörn carrier and asleep on Tess's shoulder. Tess did not eat. Tess looked around. They were here, too. Brown skinned and young. Teenage boys but also girls, and she thought of the possibility of an attack, a suicide bomber weaving down between the Manchu Wok and the California Pizza Kitchen, stepping out from behind the potted palms to praise

Allah and self-destruct. A vest of ball bearings and ten-penny nails. This was always a possibility. There was a credible threat. She had heard this on the radio—a credible threat this holiday season, though Homeland Security reports no specific targets. But there was increased chatter. There were large gatherings in churches and malls. No specific targets, she thought, except Tess and her children and their collective life.

Something gurgled and beeped and she looked up to see Wally across the table with a phone in his hands. He held it horizontally and worked the screen with his thumbs.

"Where did you get that?" she asked.

"What?"

"That phone. Where did you get it?"

"I don't know."

"You don't know? How can you not know?"

"I just got it."

"It's a phone."

"Yeah."

"Did your father give it to you? Is that his old iPhone?"

He didn't bother to look up, just affected this monumental sigh that dismissed the matter as superfluous at best.

"*Minecraft?*" she asked.

"Let me see," said Daniel, and then he was hanging over his brother saying *touch that* and *go over there.*

"Please put that away," she said.

"One second."

"Wallace?"

"One second, all right?"

"Put that thing away this minute."

And he did, throwing back his head as if he might howl, as if he could barely contain the injustice. Yet he did, he did. All she got was the sigh.

"We're at the table," she said.

"We're at the mall, Mom."

"Still."

"I thought you liked it."

"I did. I do."

"Forget it."

"Honey, it's just."

"It's not even real."

"Please, Wally."

"Just forget it. It's not even real. None of it."

None of what? she was about to ask, but then she saw her, a woman, and Tess knew her, Tess knew her from her pictures. It was—my God—it was . . . She started strapping sleeping Laurie back into her carrier.

"Come on," she said. "Are you finished? Are you finished, Daniel? Put that away, Wally."

She was up, moving, winching down Laurie who was suddenly awake and whimpering, following the woman who was walking rapidly into the interior of the mall, into the crowds and escalators and glass elevators gliding up and gliding down between the plastic snowflakes.

"Mom?" Wally said.

"Come on."

"Mom, you have to bus your table?"

"Leave it."

"I don't want to—"

"Leave it."

She was getting away, the woman was escaping—could she say that, did that sound crazy, *escaping?* Tess didn't care. She felt her pulse in the too-tight straps of the carrier, she felt adrenaline flooding out into her muscles, loosening them. She was power-walking, speed-walking, half-dragging Wally and Daniel.

"Mom?" Wally said.

Laurie was crying. Daniel was muttering. She didn't even have his hand. She had his wrist, and maybe what he said was something like *stop* or *you're hurting me*, but she couldn't stop, she kept going. This woman—Tess had to find her, to catch her. She had to talk to her because if Tess could just have a word with her, just thirty seconds, she thought perhaps she could solve everything, or if not everything then so much. *Mom!* They passed the giant Christmas tree, the dangling ornaments, the shiny new cars from Fairway Ford and Al Beaver Kia. Old Navy, Sunglass Hut, GameStop. Was she crazy? *It's not even real,* he had said. What wasn't real? The little world inside his hand or the little world inside her head?

"Mom?"

She couldn't see her now. Oh my God, she had lost her. She couldn't see the woman.

"Mom?"

Laurie was still crying, louder now, and she had lost her, Tess had lost her. She realized then Wally had taken her wrist in his surprisingly strong hand. He was pulling her.

She said something, she said the woman's name.

"Who?" Wally asked.

It's not even real.

"Mom, stop. Who is it?"

She said it again, muttered it, and he bent closer, suddenly gentle with her, taking care of his mother, easing her back to what was or wasn't, but doing it so delicately that she felt a wave of gratitude so strong she whispered it so that only he could hear.

39.

Kayla woke beside him. Crazy, but also not. Completely sane, really, because that was how it felt: the most natural and most right thing she had done in she didn't know when. It was late morning—she could tell from the film of gray light filling the room—and somewhere down beneath the covers his hand slept on her inner thigh where it had come to rest after they had made love in the predawn darkness.

She wanted it to stay there and tried to stay as still as possible. He was breathing in a slow, deep rhythm and for a moment she studied his lashes, their delicate curling length below the thicker eyebrows—the only hint he wasn't as white-bread as Kayla. They'd talked a little that first day he came into the gym and then the next day when he had asked her out. That was a week ago, though it seemed like months. Owing, surely, to the fact that they had been virtually inseparable ever since. He would hang around the desk, disappear into the weights for twenty minutes and then return, smiling, always smiling. Clearly unable to leave her alone, clearly trying to impress her, and yeah, she was impressed.

That third night they went back to a place out on Highway 411 and the following night she had brought him back to her apartment. He'd more or less been there ever since, which was exactly what she wanted, exactly how it should be. Because being with him, the thing Kayla had come to realize wasn't that she actually did resent her father—she could no more conjure that emotion than she could call him—rather a part of her had always been grieving for what might have been. What might have been, it turned out, was a larger life, one beyond the rut of her classes and work and workouts, the expectations that were, if not low, wildly circumscribed. It was her new friendship with Tess Maynard—they were meeting that evening, and it was Reed. Mostly, it was Reed.

That larger life stirred now, moved his hand.

"Hey, there, sleepyhead," she said.

"Hey. Been watching me sleep?"

"All night. Creepy enough for you?"

He smiled and planted his palms over his eyes.

"My favorite kind of creepy. What time is it?"

"Time to get up," she said. "I want to take you to my gym today."

"I go to your gym every day."

"Not where I work. I mean where I actually work out."

"Is this like meeting the parents?"

"Except triple that. It's like the ultimate level of intimacy."

He reached out for her, her arm, her breast, her hair.

"Come here, first," he said.

"Time to get up."

"Come here for one second first."

"Later." She kissed the tip of his nose and slipped out of warm bed, feet on the cold floorboards. "Definitely later."

＊

East Tennessee Barbell shared space with a PT clinic in the front and a tanning salon in the back, the hall lined with glass-tubed coffins, housewives in robes ducking in and out of changing rooms. The lobby was full of old folks, a wheeled oxygen tank and the tube that forked up a man's nose. Aluminum walkers. Wheelchairs. One counter taking Medicare Part B and selling gel packs of Biofreeze. The other with a cooler of Ripped Fuel and Muscle Milk.

The weights were in the back. Bumper plates and a rack of giant dumbbells—110, 120—bent under their own weight so that they appeared as rusty frowns. There were three squat cages and a tub of chalk. Flags on the wall—she'd been coming here for two years and had the flags down—the American flag, the Army, the Navy, the Marines. A flag for the SEALs. An old Vietnam-era Green Berets with its empty-eyed skull, a knife through one hollowed socket.

Kayla scanned her key fob and paid his $5 day pass.

The place was crowded with the flat-topped, tank-topped powerlifters in Timberlands and knee wraps. Middle-aged and drinking out of shaker cups between sets. Some guy with a black widow tattooed on his neck dead-lifting ten plates. A couple of middle-aged guys in tracksuits. High-school footballers and guys who would never get over the fact they no longer were. An Island-looking dude, slick with coconut oil and cut crazily, wondering, she guessed, how the hell he wound up in this Ronald McDonald Reagan-ville.

All the while the stereo bounced Metallica off the block walls:

Exit: light.

Enter: night.

There was one other woman, maybe mid-forties, headphones on, eyes locked on the mirror in front of her. She was a bodybuilder, too. She wore sweats but it wasn't hard to tell, the flared lines and fake breasts, the spray-on tan that was almost orange. Hair dyed. Lips collagen-blown.

"I was going to squat," Kayla said. "And then do deads and calves and finish with some abs."

"You really come here?"

"You don't like it?"

"No," he said. "It's great. You just seem so."

"So what?"

"I don't know, just so."

"Well, I'm not."

His smile was cocked to one side, half-bewildered, half-knowing.

"Yeah, I'm starting to get that," he said. "I love it."

She got under the bar, that comforting sense of the cold metal pressed through the fabric of her shirt. The stereo was blaring and here amidst the noise was the thing about lifting: it was hers in a way no other part of her life could be. Take the past. Take a few expressions. Try: "standing water." Pair it with: "too fast for conditions." Consider: "facial reconstructive surgery," or "massive head trauma." Remember to include: "dead on arrival." Now shuffle them any way you like, mix them, toss them. But in the end you have to *use* them, you have to somehow form a life from them. But here's the joke: it's already been formed for you. You only thought you were in charge.

But under the bar, she was. It was the only place in the world where all the bullshit washed out clear. The only place where she pushed back against what was otherwise the total freaking acceptance of her fate.

They worked up in sets of three. He was wiry and stronger than you would think, had told her about fighting in Atlanta and you could see that bunched density in the muscle fibers of his chest and shoulders, could see how he had lost weight when he caught the flu.

She hit three reps of 185 and slid a ten on each end, paced to the water fountain and back and then slid beneath the bar. Three more reps. She was in yoga tights and a T-shirt that would have been loose had it not been sweat-stuck to her back.

He did a set of three at 275, as heavy as he would go, and they slid off the quarters so Kayla could do her last set at 225.

A couple of the powerlifters wandered over.

"You gonna squat that?"

"Three reps. Yeah."

"How much you walk around?"

"Like 117."

"Shit, girl."

Three reps. The exhaled breath, the spitting exhaustion. The sheer clarity of being.

It felt like magic.

It felt like love, and she knew that was exactly what it was.

✳

After they got back to her apartment, after they started kissing in the stairwell and barely made it through the door, she took a shower while he lay on the bed and flipped channels. Came out pink from the hot water, a towel around her like the sort of dress she could never afford.

"I have to go in like thirty minutes," she said.

"No problem."

"You want to just stay here or something?"

"I'll probably drive back to my place."

She had no idea where his place was, only that she didn't want him going there. She wanted him here when she came in to sleep, here when she woke the next morning.

"Just stay why don't you? I won't be that late."

He sort of shrugged and she pulled her panties on beneath the towel.

"Hey," she said, and let the towel fall. "Do me a favor."

He leaned forward and dropped the remote on the bed.

"You got it."

"Not that. Not right now. But look at me."

"Oh, I'm looking."

"Seriously." She turned and twisted toward him. "What about my abs?"

"Tight."

"What about my glutes?"

"Very tight."

"Be serious. I'm like weeks out from competing."

"I am being serious. Crazy tight." He took the remote back up and waved it at the tattoo on her thigh. "Tell me about the bird."

"I'll probably try to cover it with makeup for the contest."

"What is it?"

"It's a swallow-tailed kite. You ever seen one?"

"I don't know."

"It was my mom's favorite. She loved all sorts of birds, but the swallow-tail is maybe the most graceful flier. We don't get them up here, but when we went to the beach she would just watch them for hours."

"I think it's beautiful."

"I'll probably try to cover it."

"Come here."

"I don't want to be late."

"Come here first."

✳

She was late, but it didn't matter. Flushed with happiness as she drove south to a bistro in Chattanooga she and Tess had determined to be more or less halfway between them. She was late and it was starting to sleet, but she didn't care and knew Tess wouldn't care either. They had made love again and holding each other she had asked him to spend Christmas with her at her grandparents' and he had said yes. She wanted to take him to her special place, the original home place she had turned into a sort of shrine to her mother. Kind of embarrassing, but somehow it wouldn't be with him. She couldn't wait to tell Tess that. She couldn't wait to tell her she was in love.

40.

On the first day of exams John was back in his office. It was December and he had a full slate of counseling sessions, the end-of-semester panic that always ran thick with accusations and explanations. All of it followed by pleading and bargaining. He had spent the morning mediating a dispute between a sophomore and her U.S. lit professor whose use of *Lolita*, she claimed, was promoting a campus-wide rape culture.

It would have surprised John had another student not once claimed that the inclusion of Alice Walker in a course on Modern Christian Thought offended his evangelical beliefs thus violating the campus code on freedom of religious expression. The student asked the professor to allow him to read the Left Behind series instead. The professor refused. So he had his parents call and John wound up sitting down with all four, a fruitless discussion about which the best thing you could say was that they had all agreed to disagree.

He had twenty minutes between sessions and was eating a banana when Jimmy Stone pushed open his door and shut it behind him.

"There he is," Stone said.

"I've got a student walking through that door in about three minutes."

"Guess I'll need to hurry then."

Stone sat down and crossed his legs, pants riding up from one sockless boat shoe so that John was gifted a long expanse of hairless white shin. He put a piece of paper on John's desk and slapped it for emphasis.

"What is this?"

"Just read it."

It was an article from the *Atlanta Journal-Constitution* website. Two bodies had been found in a Kirkwood apartment. Both were shot in the living room, their throats slashed so deeply they were nearly decapitated. The bodies were covered with empty meth baggies and several hundred dollars in small bills, a ceremonial scattering it seemed. Stone had circled the name Suleyman Nawaf.

"You know the name?" he asked.

"Should I?"

"I want to assure you your colleague Professor Hadawi does."

"Sounds like drug crime, gang stuff." He slid the article away from him. "Sorry. I'm in the dark on this."

"Well, I want to assure you the good professor is not."

"Where is Hadawi?"

"Excellent question." Stone walked to the door. "Does this lock?"

"No."

He clicked the knob. "Yeah, it does."

"I have a student here any second. Don't lock it."

"Too late," Stone said.

When he turned he was holding a pistol.

"This is a Glock 23."

"Christ, Jimmy."

"See how small it is. Very easy to hide." He put it on John's desk. "But you need to be careful. It has a safety, but it's on the trigger, you understand?"

"There's a zero-tolerance policy for guns on campus."

"Be mindful of it. It's attention to detail. It's vigilance. You get what I mean when I say you cultivate it like a practice?"

"Absolutely no firearms on campus."

"Yeah, and naturally the folks who paid Suleyman Nawaf a visit are going to abide by that."

"Get it out of here."

"Let me tell you something first, all right, and then you get back to me on your zero-tolerance bullshit. Our little jihadi wonderboy, I can't find him. He's suddenly gone AWOL on us."

"I don't care.

"You don't care?"

"I don't care because I'm done with it."

"You're done with it? This is news to me."

"I never should have helped you."

"Helped me? Oh my fucking word. Well, let me be helpful for a change then. Let me ask a few helpful questions like what kind of security does your kid's school have? You considered that? How about your wife's level of exposure? You spent anytime considering that?"

"Jimmy—"

"Don't *Jimmy* me, all right? My Myers-Briggs tells me I have an aversion to this kind of bullshit." He heard Stone's voice go cold and automatic. "You have any clue how that supple leopard of a daughter is these days? Is that helpful? Dear wife keeping an eye on her diet, making sure it's all lean protein and amino acids?"

"What are you saying?"

"What am I saying? I'm saying touch the gun, John."

John looked down at the papers on his desk.

"Get it out of here," he said without looking up.

"Touch it first."

"Get it out of here."

"Touch it," Stone said. "Go on."

Finally, he did, but with just a fingertip, a single stroke, as if it might otherwise wake.

"Good. Good man. Now hold it in your hand. Be mindful that it's loaded."

John held it.

"Don't point it."

"What do you mean about Kayla and Tess?"

"Don't point."

"I'm not pointing.

"What did you mean—"

"Shh."

"Jimmy—"

"My father believed the blade of a knife reflected moral worth. My mother said the same thing about posture." He was whispering now. "Feels kind of nice, doesn't it?"

"I don't want it."

"Nobody ever does."

"I don't need it."

"Of course you don't. Except did you read that line about the throats cut so deeply they were effectively decapitated? Watch your family, all right? Know where they are, who they talk to. Download a good malware. Keep an eye on phone calls, your e-mails."

"What?"

"All the things they taught us."

"Nobody taught me anything. I'm a counselor."

"Sure you are, John. What else would you be? But the gun." Stone turned for the door. "Just be sure you keep it with you at all times. At all times in all situations."

41.

She was up late packing and just sort of got lost, Tess did. All the suitcases and duffels and rolling bags open in the living room, Tess with the laundry basket and the clean clothes.

Wally's sweater.

Daniel's corduroys for church.

Laurie's SleepSack and footed pajamas.

This here, that there, and so on until the day fell into dusk and dusk fell into darkness, a hushed slip like the exhale of breath, and Tess realized she was standing in the living room and had been for she didn't know how long. Just standing there with a—with a towel in one hand. The children asleep. John in Atlanta.

In the morning Tess would drink two cups of coffee, fill the sippy cups and the snack bag, and drive herself and the children the nine hours to her parents. *Would* if she could move out of the room, zip the luggage, go to bed. Yet she kept standing there, rooted, but so poorly she threatened not to move but to fall.

The first click she sent out was meant to ground her.

The second was meant to orient.

When it came back to her she knew she wasn't alone.

"Go back to bed, Wally."

He was in the corner, a gray shape in the grayer dark.

He clicked again, or something clicked, because she was no longer certain it was her son. Only that something was in the room with her. She felt the small hairs on her neck bristle and it came to her again:

Did he who made the Lamb make thee?

"Go back to bed, honey." She felt her voice break and realized she wouldn't go to him, she realized she was afraid. "You need your sleep."

And she did, too, Tess did. Wally did.

Whoever or whatever it was that stood in the corner, silently watching her—surely it was tired.

Yet they went on standing there, Tess and this other who may or may not have been her child, Tess and this other who may or may not have been what she had let in through the ISIS video, through the watching, through the knowing. Tess standing there, not quite seeing it, but almost feeling the space between them, and how that space seemed to be lessening, how it seemed to be coming closer.

The man in the basement.

She had gone to him so many times. Now he had come to her.

Then it occurred to her that perhaps it wasn't a man in the basement. It was a woman Tess had seen at the mall, the woman Tess had followed, and she was standing so close Tess could feel the heat off her body.

Tess spoke quietly, the merest whisper, and then louder, as if to assure the woman of her attention.

Tess said, "Karla?"

42.

The old Camry was missing from the shed—that was the first thing Jimmy saw when he pulled up at the lake house: the Camry as absent as the kid. The yard empty. The lights off inside. Dawn was gathering out over the water, all bugs and birds, but around the house there was no movement, no life.

It was confirmation of what Jimmy had suspected—that after days of stalking John Maynard's family Reed was gone. Still, something didn't feel right and for a few slow minutes he sat with it. Despite constipation and an impending myocardial infarction, Jimmy Stone sat and tried to think his way into the boy's brain.

Reed, Reed, Reed. What are you up to, Reed? Where have you gone, son?

For days there had been a stream of images: Maynard's daughter, his wife and boys and infant daughter. Jimmy had seen them at school and at what appeared to be a mall. He'd seen a dark house on a dark street. But nothing for the last few days. Nothing since Jimmy's visit to Maynard's office. Reed hadn't answered his phone and finally Jimmy had driven up from Atlanta. But having come so far he couldn't quite bring himself to take that last step, to get out of the van and walk inside.

There was a reason for this. The car's absence was comforting, but there was a part of him that still feared finding Reed's body. The kid's head disassembled only to reform itself inside Jimmy as unassailable guilt. It seemed more than a little possible. But he had to know, and finally he got out. Called for Reed from the yard, but not with any conviction. The place was abandoned and appeared to have been so for days.

He walked once around the house, past the dormant azaleas and the upturned canoe, beneath the river birch and finally up the front steps. He had the key but the door was unlocked. Before it was even open he could smell it—the eye-burning stink of gas. The place was soaked in gasoline. When he turned on the light he saw what it was Reed intended to burn. All over the paneled walls—it appeared as some roadside memorial wildly metastasized. First the photographs tacked to the paneling: eight-by-ten print-outs Reed must have had made at the FedEx two towns over. Maybe three dozen arranged like the sort of collage you might find in a college dorm. They were all of Kayla, all of the girl smiling her crooked grin, Reed beside her in a few. Then the Goya print, crumpled and smoothed. The thumb drive had been smashed with a hammer. The letter was on the table, a scrawl of hand-printed Arabic, the figures leaning and looped.

تالاقملا 1436 - لوألا - عيبر - 2

لدابت وأ فيلأ ناويحو أ لكأي نأ نكمي ائيش ائيش ديرن اعيمج مكل : ءيشلا انه

ءيشلا انه و . انا. انا نكلكو.ةيحلا ديق ىلع ائيش ديرت ال تنك . رانلا قالطالا

الآخر : انأ رفغأ كل.انأ رفغأ عيمجلا ىلع لك ىش ءيش.

It went on for three pages and he took out his phone and photographed each. He hadn't talked to Aida or whatever the hell she was calling herself since that summer day on the street in Atlanta, but he had her in his contacts and he sent her the pictures. No message. No explanation. Let her figure it for what she could. Let her make whatever goddamn call there was to make. Dial the professor if need be, let him translate, let him riddle out the tortured logic. Jimmy should have done it from the start, should have left the boy alone, should have let Agent Hadawi and the rest of the feds run their little sting. Reed Sharma would be in federal custody—or possibly as dead as his meth-head buddies—but at least Jimmy wouldn't be involved. He'd sworn to John he felt nothing about Site Nine except the grim satisfaction of having done a difficult job well. But that was a lie. He was as guilty as the rest, guilty enough to believe doing one right thing could undo many wrongs.

His eyes watered but still he stared at the graceful Arabic scrawl, looked again at the photos.

Reed and John's daughter Kayla.

A selfie of the two of them, face-to-face and happy.

The girl smiling so wide her face threatened to split.

He felt like a voyeur—but wasn't that exactly what he was, seeing things just before they disappeared? Reed was planning to burn down the lake house, to make ashes of it all, maybe even of his life. Coming was a mistake. Jimmy felt the wrongness on a cellular level, a life misdirected, mis-lived. What had Soren Sharma said? *Just another bug in counter terror* when he should have been a folk singer. The mistake was listening to his mother. *Everybody knows that the war is over. Everybody knows that the good guys lost.* Yeah, no shit, Leonard. As if the world taught any other lesson.

Too bad you're such a slow learner, Jimbo.

Too bad—

Then he remembered the day he had brought Reed here, stopping in the state park where Reed had systematically beat the shit out of him.

What was it he had said to the kid?

The worst thing you could do would be to forgive me.

Was that what he was looking at, some sort of forgiveness? The kid could have taken out Maynard's family ten times over. Yet he hadn't. At least not yet.

His nose was running.

He rubbed his eyes and looked down at his phone.

Sending . . .

Sending . . .

The signal was weak this deep in the National Forest, but finally gathered to four service bars and the *sending . . .* gave way to *delivered.* The time stamp there in the corner. Jimmy was looking at it onscreen and felt his thumb drift to the telescope icon in the lower right. A window opened—he was looking at it—and then he was looking at himself, the scratchy image of his own back, the rear of his thinning vulnerable head. There was a shudder of recognition and then confusion, but he wasn't confused. There was something inevitable in it, and he turned slowly to where Reed stood behind him, his phone in one hand, a pistol in the other. At his feet stood two five-gallon gas cans.

"I didn't hear you come in," Jimmy said.

"You weren't paying attention."

"What's going on, Reed? Are you planning on burning my house down?"

The boy was smiling, but it wasn't with anything approaching happiness. There was something arrogant to it. The mean tilt of his lips. The long lashes. The eyes like a wolf. He seemed to glow with a dredged-up purity, a malice so refined it became a form of saintliness.

"Where have you been?" Jimmy asked.

"You mean you don't know?" Reed seemed almost hurt by the question. "You should have been watching."

"I have been."

"Good."

"I've been watching," Jimmy said, and Reed nodded his head in appreciation.

"You know then," the boy said. "You understand."

"What do I know?"

"I was in their school. One day they went shopping. Another day, night actually, he was sleeping. I stood in the other room—maybe ten feet away, Jimmy—and listened to him breathe."

"What do I know, Reed?"

"He was talking in his sleep. He was scared."

"What do I understand?"

"Your eyes are red, Jimmy."

"What is it I should know?"

"You should know what I'm capable of doing. You should know what I could have done to them. What I *could have done.* But I didn't." He took a step forward. "Hey, guess what," he said, "I've always wanted to ask you. Do you know what was in the box?"

"What box?"

"The box I carried. Know what was in it?"

"What are you doing here?"

What he was doing was approaching, steadily narrowing the space between them. But that wasn't what Jimmy meant. The question wasn't physical so much as metaphysical. The question had something to do, perhaps, with God.

"It was a little statue."

"Reed."

"A little bronze Buddha. Did you know that? You were laughing at me."

"Reed, listen, the gun—"

"It's okay. I'm not going to hurt you. There's only one person left for me to hurt and it isn't you. I'm going to bless you. I forgive everyone for everything. Do you understand?"

"Put the gun down, all right?"

"You don't get what I'm saying. I forgive you. I want to bless you. I have a gift for you."

"Reed."

"It just came to me, Jimmy. Fire is the one thing I can give you. Do you remember you called it a gift? Well, I can give you that. You showing up here. It's so perfect."

"The gun—"

"It's so perfect. But first I want you to admit you were laughing at me."

He was closer now, and drawing closer still. Jimmy had his hands out, palms open in a way that was meant to signal not so much surrender as calm control of the situation, that he wasn't afraid. Even if he was. Because nothing could change the fact that the barrel was close enough to his face for the image to blur. Reed pressed it to his forehead and it was cold, as Jimmy had known it would be. But rough-grained in a way he hadn't. As if the world might surprise you right up until the moment it ceased to be, or you ceased to be, if there was any difference. Jimmy shut his wet eyes.

"Please," he said.

"Just say that you were laughing."

"Reed."

"Say it, Jimmy. Say I was laughing."

"I was laughing."

"Say my name. I was laughing at you, *Reed*."

"I was laughing at you, Reed."

"I was laughing but now I'm sorry."

"I am sorry," Jimmy said. "I truly am."

"I'm not going to hurt you. I *am* going to ask you to sit down. I'm going to tie you up. But I'm not going to hurt you. I'm going to bless you."

"Reed—"

"I'm going to bless you. Do you believe me?"

"Please just put the gun down."

"Tell me you believe me."

"I believe you."

"I hurt you before but I won't again. Even though I could, I won't. That's what you have to understand. It's what I've learned. It's what you've taught me. Sit down, Jimmy. Are you carrying anything?"

"No."

"Please don't lie to me."

"It's in the car."

"See, I believe you. I trust you. I won't even search you. Sit down and put your hands behind you."

He sat, put his hands behind him, and felt the zip ties bind his wrists to the chair legs.

"That isn't too tight?"

"You don't have to do this. You can walk away, disappear."

"But how would he see? How would I know he was watching?"

"Who was watching?" He felt the ties go around his ankles. "Who?"

"He has to see it."

"Who, Reed? Allah?"

Reed looked at him as if to determine whether or not he was serious.

"No," he said. "Not Allah."

"Who then?"

"People like you," he said. "People like my father. The professor. You all took something from me." He stood up, the ties in place. "But what amazes me is you don't even know it. The most basic simple human thing and you have zero awareness. But I've beat all of you. Because I've found a way to get it back. And I've found a way to make everyone see."

"Reed."

"So simple and you took it. But I know now what bombs do."

Jimmy's phone rang. Reed froze for a moment and then moved to it, held the screen so that Jimmy could see the name on the incoming call: JOHN MAYNARD.

"Leave his family alone," Jimmy said.

Reed shook his head.

"That isn't for you to say."

"His daughter."

"You need to be quiet."

"She's done nothing to you."

"You don't know anything."

"She's innocent."

"Jimmy"—it was the first note of strain in his voice—"honest to God, I'm speaking from my heart when I say it's best if you're quiet now."

"Don't hurt her, Reed."

"I'm going to let him watch, Jimmy. I'll let you watch, too." He took Jimmy's phone, tapped at the screen, and then held it where Jimmy could see: John Maynard's contact information, his number and e-mail. "I think you deserve that much."

"Reed."

"Sit still for a minute. You showed up before I could finish."

He took the two large red canisters and began to splash them in the back room. Jimmy could smell it, stronger now, and what it smelled like was pain, but only a moment's worth. After that would come the nothingness. And it was the nothingness he wanted.

"You used to talk about it all the time," Reed said. "You asked me once if I would be willing. You said heat and light."

"Please."

"You *asked* me, Jimmy, and now I'm blessing you. Isn't this what you wanted? You're going to be purified. You're forgiven. The way you showed up right now—how is that not a sign?"

He began to splash the gasoline around the legs of the chair and onto Jimmy's lap and down the sleeves of his bound arms. Even the scent burned, the fluid alone sharp enough to deposit you on the far shore. Jimmy's eyes watered and shut.

"What choice did I have?" he said.

"You had a choice."

"What fucking choice? You went after his family, his children."

He stopped and when Jimmy could look he thought the boy looked hurt, hurt and still very much a child.

"No, Jimmy. That's the point. I *didn't* go after his family. I *didn't* go after his children. I'm the one who hasn't hurt anyone." He went back to pouring and then stopped. "Except you," he said.

He emptied the first can and uncapped the second.

"Do you know what bombs do, Jimmy? That's what he asked me and I'll admit to you that I didn't."

"Nothing has to happen."

"But I do now."

"Nothing has to happen," Jimmy said. He could feel his voice getting away from him, beginning to scratch with altitude. His eyes were squeezed shut against the fumes.

"I had to learn, but I do now."

"This isn't Syria."

"You should have stuck with watching."

"This isn't Iraq."

"What's the difference, Jimmy? Once you get involved, I mean. You should have stuck with watching like all the other good citizens of the West."

"Reed—"

"The good citizens of these United States."

"You don't have to do this."

"I'm not doing anything. This is your choice."

"You can still just disappear."

"See, that's the part I'm afraid of." He had poured a long trail from the chair to the curtains. "I'm afraid of disappearing. Afraid no one will see, that no one will watch, and wasn't that the whole point? To see what happens to the soul under duress? I remember reading that in Maynard's book, I guess. That a pattern emerges. That a pattern asserts itself. So you had Hassan Natashe, and now you have me." He held the gas can in front of Jimmy. "Do you want it all? It's your choice, Jimmy."

Jimmy hesitated, eyes shut, tearing, and then he nodded his head. *Yes,* he said, or tried to say. If he was going to do it, he should do it right. If he was going to be purified, let him be purified.

"All of it?" Reed asked.

He nodded.

"Good," Reed said, and began to pour it over Jimmy's head where it soaked his hair and ran into his ears and clenched eyes. "You're a good man, Jimmy. You are. I believe that now."

Jimmy coughed and felt something being placed into his hands. It was a small lighter. He could feel the grating of the metal wheel.

"It's up to you, Jimmy. You get to decide."

"Reed—"

"You choose, Jimmy. The lighter's in your hand."

"Please, Reed."

"Do it or don't. But no more talking."

"I'm begging you. Leave her alone."

"Don't talk. The time to talk—well, no, Jimmy. That's over now. Use the lighter or don't. That's up to you. All that's left for me is to watch." He stood in the open door, one foot in, one foot on the way out. "Now," he said, "is the time for watching."

43.

Reed sat in the car and watched the flames go up the asbestos siding to shimmer and bend and lick at the asphalt shingles. He had left everything exactly as he wanted it be destroyed—the photographs, the letter, the crumpled Goya print and crushed thumb drive—still he was sorry to watch it burn, sorry to know it had come to that for Jimmy. He'd always known it was a possibility. Still, he had hoped it wouldn't end this way. But he needed them to know he wasn't like them, he needed them to understand how utterly and completely they had failed to understand him, how utterly and completely they had underestimated him. He didn't want Jimmy dead, but now that he was burning something was speaking to him.

It wasn't the money. He had left the money he had found hidden above ceiling tiles—there would be no need for the money. The money was useless. What he heard might have been coming from the gun. The Walther sat on the passenger seat, disassembled on a square of white chamois. He watched the house burn, felt the heat on his face, and for the third time took the pistol and reinserted the barrel into the slide. He flipped the slide-stop lever and when the slide snapped into place he popped in the magazine. The gun was loaded. He checked the safety and tucked it into his bag.

Then he took out his phone and texted Kayla.

See you tomorrow!

A moment later came her response.

Can't wait
luv U

Something was speaking to him, and maybe it came from the fire or maybe it came from the gun, but whatever its source it sounded not so much like the voice of Allah or God as the Voice of Reason.

Do you know what bombs do, Reed?

He thought he did, finally. He hadn't lied to Jimmy. Those days practicing in front of the mirror, mouthing *b-o-m-b*, as if he could conjure a violence apart from himself. How naive he had been. But not anymore.

The roof was beginning to collapse. It was time to go. But before he did he entered John Maynard's contact information and sent the telescope invitation to Maynard's e-mail account. The invitation was in Arabic, but he would know, and he would watch.

It was that time now. It was time for the watching.

Part Five

The Watching

44.

Two days before Christmas they drove north to Cherokee, John and Erin, and from there headed east on the Blue Ridge Parkway and into Pisgah National Forest, the highway a furrow plowed along the ridge tops and the slim edge of the viaduct. It was snowing, and he looked at the highway gates knowing they'd be closing them soon, closing the parkway to traffic. There would be no going back. So there was that sense of finality. But more than that, there was the sense of guilt. Guilt in not being with Kayla and his parents, and more guilt still in not being with Tess and Laurie and the boys. He felt its presence like something coming through the vents with the heat. But when he looked out at the fogged valley and bristled mountain slopes, the green quilt of fir and pine and snow it was there too, this guilt, and it wasn't just his.

"No one up here," Erin said.

"No."

"But the roads are fine. The roads aren't slick. They're all at home, I guess."

He twined his fingers with hers and thought of the fingers his father had exchanged for the chance to come home. Carrying his lunch in a plastic Ingles bag. Sending checks to Jimmy Bakker and *Praise the Lord*. Three fingers it had been. He knew his father would have exchanged even more to go back. And what was it they had gone back to? To the corn patch and fish fries. The fierce mountain streams and the good vine-ripe tomatoes. The church suppers and the baby showers. Easter Sunday. Hot days and cool nights when you can't help but make a fire just to smell the wood smoke.

"Hey," he said. "Do you remember Paul Harvey?"

"We went to school with him?"

"No, the radio guy. My dad used to listen. Is he dead now you think?"

Erin looked at him and then stared out the window.

"What's the name of this place?" she asked.

The name was Snow Tree, a cedar-shaked inn that overlooked the snowy valley.

The parking lot was plowed and empty. The room key hung from a plastic tree.

John passed over his credit card and carried in their bags while Erin shot up in the bathroom. The furnace was on high, the room stuffy and overheated, and he turned it off while she assumed that familiar pose, crouched on the lowered toilet seat, a lamp burning pewter light. The needle went into the crook of her smaller arm, as if she were vaccinating a small child against grief. He tried not to stare. She'd asked him not to be a prude. Aren't we all just doing the best we can? Aren't we all equipped differently? Isn't that what your job is about?

She came out in a slip, the bathroom light radiant beneath the door.

"Open the curtains, John."

"People can see."

"I don't care if people can see. Let 'em see. There's no one here but us anyway."

It was a heatless light that fell through the part in the curtains, a rind of yellow indifference, and they made love slowly, lingering in each other, as if knowing already that here in their beginnings their end was near. Outside, the flurries turned to sleet, not spun sugar but cracked ice. Inside, they lay in bed beneath the sheets. She touched the prayer rope that John had somehow failed to remove.

"What's this for?" She was on her stomach and had reached out so that one bead was pinched between thumb and forefinger. "You're not Orthodox."

"No."

"What are you then?"

"I don't know."

She pulled it toward her.

"Do you say the prayer that goes with it? Lord Jesus Christ, Son of God."

"Sometimes, yeah."

"You do?"

"No. Actually, I don't." He was looking out the window at a magnolia, its limbs weighed with snow. "I don't ever."

She idly touched the inside of his arm.

"What we need is a plan," she said, "that doesn't involve crazy."

Later, they drove down the mountain to eat. She wanted to cook for him—they had brought food—but somehow they ate nothing but strawberries, a pint of them in their plastic coffin while the Cure played on her iPad. John listened to her move about the suite, in the kitchenette with its mini-fridge and coffeemaker, in the bathroom. Twice he called Jimmy Stone but no one answered.

Down in the valley the sleet had turned to rain and they debated stopping. It was not even a town really, a strip of fast food and gas stations and, at the farthermost reaches of the halogen streetlights, a Chuck E. Cheese's with skinned carpet and laminated booths, a few families milling sadly around the skee-ball lanes. A ream of tickets hung brown and perforated beside the coin slot. They ate cheese pizza and stood outside to drink vodka and tomato juice on a wet putting green.

"I don't think this is it," Erin said.

"Don't think this is what?"

"What we need. This isn't what we need."

She kept moving, little involuntary fidgets that seemed to travel out along her wrists to compress as a twitch in the nail beds of her hands. Someone was singing in the car on the way back and it took him a moment to realize she had brought the iPad with her. The Cure. She was singing along with the Cure. Later, she dried in front of the heater vents and, still damp, passed out.

He carried her to bed and checked his e-mail. Happy students. Sad students. Nigerian princes. A message accosting him in Arabic.

He closed the screen and called his parents.

"Kayla will be here tomorrow," his mother said.

"I'm sorry to miss her."

"How is Florida?"

"Fine. Same as always."

He could hear his dad watching an old Detroit Pistons game, Isiah Thomas and Joe Dumars, big bad Bill Laimbeer with his acrylic facemask.

"Merry Christmas, Dad."

"Merry Christmas, John. Your mamma and I love you so much."

It was only at the very end that John had flown to Ukraine.

Hassan Natashe had been released and though Peter was sick he wanted to speak directly to John. So John drove from Site Nine to Krakow, flew to Kiev and eventually Simferopol where a car took him down a potted road to Yalta. It was August and the shingle of beach was covered with blistering Russians. Behind them palm trees and mountains that at dusk turned the color of wet gravel.

He waited to see Peter, walked the concrete promenade, bought a postcard—GREETINGS FROM SUNNY YALTA—thought about Tess back in St. Pete and the days they would swim off the point at St. Simons. He could have called her, but he didn't. He could have mailed the postcard—it seemed somehow more manageable—but he didn't do that either.

The next day he saw Peter. John had known he was sick but it always seemed more something passing than serious, a persistent cold, or the earliest incubation of flu. Something that would come and go. No need for alarm, just regular injections of B_{12} and an abundance of antioxidants. But that was no longer the case.

Peter owned a compound overlooking the Baltic and John found him in a corner of the main hall, an area crowded with tapestries and plush chairs gone ragged, over-upholstered as if for some impoverished lord. Above, a vault of glass and stone. Beneath, the dying billionaire. Even in the darkness John could see he had lost weight. Nothing but kale and edible flowers, Bageant had told him. He had quit his meds. No more combination therapy. No AZT, no prednisone. He was eating flowers when John arrived, purple ones, and even in the darkness John could see they were beautiful.

"God is a staircase that ascends to a place that isn't there," he said, "or isn't there yet. Do you know who said that?"

"No."

He exhaled. "Neither do I."

They sat like that for a while, long enough for John's eyes to adjust, long enough to discern the outline of his slippered feet, the robe that hung beneath the curve of his skull.

"Being," he said, "is not about persistence."

"Christ, Peter."

"Are you listening to me?"

"Tell me what we've done here."

"Tell you? You're supposed to tell me."

"Peter?"

"Life," he said, "is not opposed to death."

He had a thin smile on his face.

"Go home," he said, and a flower fell from his mouth. "Forget."
Or did he?

Without question he fell into a pit of coughing out of which he might rise, but only briefly. He was nearer to death than life. *Go home.* Did he say those words? *Forget.* Perhaps he didn't. Perhaps it was an aural hallucination, the thing John most needed to hear. He looked in Peter's eyes for an answer, but they were buried in the grave of his collapsing face.

Go home. Forget.

*

It was four in the morning on Christmas Eve when he woke with heartburn and went looking in his bag for his Prilosec. But what he found was the gun Stone had given him, and what he realized was that he had done exactly as Stone had told him: he had kept it with him. At all times in all situations.

45.

It wasn't like Tess remembered.

Or actually it was exactly like she remembered, only she had chosen to misremember.

The drive took longer, a front of rain that didn't break until they were in south Georgia and then it rained again on I-75, sideways, blowing east off the Gulf all the way to the causeway to Sanibel Island. She had burned off the fatigue with three espressos, but felt seared and jerky, twice thinking she saw someone in the front seat beside her—*it's not even real* Wally had said—her husband's first dead wife in her peripheral vision so clearly Tess had screamed inside the walls of her head. She knew then it was time to stop and pulled into a McDonald's where, standing in the bathroom stall, she refused to cry.

But by the time she got to her parents they were all four in tears, Tess and Laurie, Wally and Daniel, and she was exhausted. Pissed at John and pissed at herself. But then the rain blew over and it was a warm evening, Christmas Eve's Eve, and everyone was coming out to greet them, her parents, her sister, her brother and his wife and their three girls, and they were carrying up luggage and pouring Tess a glass of wine and already her mom was holding Laurie, and Wally and Daniel were playing Legos on the floor with her sister, and David's girls were dancing in front of the TV to Taylor Swift songs. The tree was all silver tinsel and silver star and off the back deck you looked out over the sawgrass marsh to the sea where a paring of bright moon hung like the sort of punctuation meant to signal contentment.

The wine flushed through her and she felt the tension in her shoulders release. She was here, she was happy. All of them piled into the living room and kitchen, happily disheveled. She hugged her parents and neither asked about John.

Her brother came out with a glass dish of raw steak and tin-foiled potatoes.

"Who wants to swim?" he asked, and of course they all did, the kids splashing in the heated pool, Liz wading in with Laurie. Night-swimming beneath the wire cage that encased everything.

Tess stood by the grill where her brother cooked dinner.

She motioned at his amber glass.

"Is that the bourbon you got for John?"

"Where is old John anyway?"

"Can I have a glass?"

"You can have three, but any more than that and you'll fall off these running shoes we got you."

"You shouldn't have done that."

"Maximalist. How could I not?"

"They are sort of orthopedic, aren't they?"

"You'll look like some speedy grandma."

They swam, ate, danced in front of the TV, and it was all exactly like she had hoped it would be, exactly as how she misremembered. But then exhaustion reasserted itself. The children got fussy. Her mother, pink with Cabernet, wanted to talk *really talk* about what was going on with her and John and talking, *really* or not, was the last thing on earth Tess wanted.

Then her father announced they were all walking down to the beach. Blue whales had been spotted close to shore. All Tess wanted to do was put the children to bed and sleep herself.

"Dad, it's after ten."

"But blue whales, honey. Your mother heard it on NPR."

So they did that, they trundled down the boardwalk over the dunes down to the sand, but Laurie was asleep and Daniel stepped on a sand spur and David's two oldest girls wanted to walk alone down to the pier where a reggae band was playing and—

She had to drag Wally back, pulling him from the surf a little rougher than she intended, and he kept fighting her, standing knee deep in the glossy water and clicking his tongue against the roof of his mouth.

"Please, Mom."

"Tomorrow, honey."

"Please, just five more minutes."

"I'll bring you back in the morning. I promise."

"But, Mom—"

"Wally, now."

Like the ride down it ended in tears, after eleven by the time she got everyone down and into the shower and then—*please just leave me alone for two minutes*—her mom was tapping against the bathroom door wanting to know if now was a good time to talk and no it wasn't, and no it never would be.

She wanted sleep and finally got it.

Alone in her childhood bed, Laurie in the Pack 'n Play, the boys on air mattresses in the playroom, and John, John far, far away.

And Tess realizing in that moment just before she collapsed into a dreamless sleep that maybe that was exactly how she wanted it.

46.

When his phone rang late the next morning John assumed it was either Stone or Tess. But when the screen read NUMBER UNAVAILABLE he wasn't exactly surprised. He thought he had heard it different, the ring, or maybe it was that he now occupied some different place, everything shifted a half inch off center, some ancient hairline crack in the world he only now detected. He took the phone out onto the deck and into the freezing morning. It was a woman's voice. She sounded young, but very level, and very much in control.

"You don't know me, but we had a mutual friend in James Stone. You tried to reach him a couple of times yesterday."

John felt the crack open. Coming through it was something more than the freezing air. He touched the railing and thought of those nights in Minnesota when there'd been something almost approaching friendship. *You think any society that sells life insurance could be anything other than damned?* Jimmy's question. A parable John no longer had any interest in considering.

"Mr. Maynard?"

"What happened?"

"A house fire. This was yesterday morning. A little lake house up in the mountains."

"It was set?"

"There was a good deal of accelerant involved, yes."

"Jesus."

"I'm going to send you something, Mr. Maynard."

"Who are you?"

"You can call me Aida. But listen. I'm going to send you an image. When I call you back I want to know what it means to you."

The text was a photograph of a letter, on it a blurry swim of Arabic.

أنا ارفع الجميع من كل شيءء.

His phone rang.

"What is this?"

"Stone sent it. Likely just before it happened. The line you're looking at translates as 'I forgive everyone for everything.'"

"'I forgive everyone for everything.' What the hell does that mean?" Then he thought of the message in Arabic.

"We aren't certain. What I need from you—"

But John had already hung up and opened his e-mail. The sender's name was in Arabic, unreadable, but below it he identified the same characters: I forgive everyone for everything. Beyond that, there was nothing except a green square that read: ACCEPT TELESCOPE INVITATION. He touched it and it pulsed for a moment before something began to download. A few seconds later a screen appeared, and in the center of that screen was his daughter, laughing. She wore a red coat and appeared to be riding in a car, filmed unsteadily by the driver. The image fizzed, came in and out, and was gone. When it wouldn't reopen he closed the window and put the phone in his pocket. Something inside him was dead, but something else was very much alive.

Erin was still in bed, propped on the pillow, when John came in and started going through his bag, both hands grabbing until he felt it.

"You want to shut that door?" she asked. "Chilly."

When he turned he had the gun in his hand.

"John?" and now the chill was in her voice, too.

"I have to go," he said. "I'm sorry, but this is an emergency."

She had her eyes on the gun.

"I guess it is," she said, and tried to laughed. "Let me go with you."

"I'm sorry. I can't."

"Why not?"

He put his wallet in his pocket.

"I just can't."

"So you're going to leave me here."

"I'm sorry."

"So am I."

He called Tess from the car—no answer, no answer, no answer, finally she picked up and before he knew what he was doing John was yelling at her and she was hanging up on him. He called her back but she didn't pick up and he knew she wouldn't. But he also knew Kayla was at his parents—that was where the car had been heading.

He called them, no answer. Called again.

He was straddling the centerline of the empty parkway, fifty, sixty in the straightaways, the window half-open and the sting in his face because without it there was some possibility of losing touch with his body, some possibility of allowing the car to go through the guardrail and into the snowy valley.

He called his parents—no answer.

Lost the signal. Called again when he had a single bar of service.

They were fixing lunch. They were blessing the meal. They were busy with their gratitude. He knew they wouldn't pick up.

The answer was to drive there. The answer was to hurry.

When the phone rang it was Erin.

She sounded as if she had only now woken to find the day not at all to her liking.

"Where are you?" she asked.

"I don't know exactly, driving. I might lose the signal in a minute."

"I'm waiting on a cab."

"I'm sorry. I would say I'll come back for you but I'm not sure I'll be able to."

"I'm sorry too. I'm—"

She stopped herself and with the phone against his cheek he pictured her as golden, all bronzed skin, her face flecked with pinpoints of mica, feet bright with granules of sand. Her arm restored. He was seeing her at twenty, except it wasn't her he was seeing. It was Karla that summer after freshman year, Karla down below the highway bridge, stepping barefoot into the current of Cane Creek. One ear made translucent with sun.

"I always knew this was coming," she said. "How could I not know this was coming? But it's harder than I thought. I feel like we've lost Karla all over again, we both have."

He said nothing. Stone's pistol was on the seat beside him and he wanted to touch it, badly he wanted the fit of it in his hand. He wanted it as an extension of himself, the trigger metalled to his finger, the one part of him that might actually matter.

"John?"

"You know you never told me about your dream."

"What dream?"

"That first night at church."

"No," she said. "I guess I didn't. I guess I won't."

He didn't speak again until he was sure his voice wouldn't break.

"If it's possible," he said finally, "I'll call back."

"She's dead, John."

"I might lose the signal up here."

"She's dead. We were stupid to think otherwise."

"I know that."

"But we're human beings too. We're lonely." She waited for him to speak, but there was nothing else to say. "I know you're married, John," she said finally.

"It's maybe not like you think."

"I hope that's where you're going. I hope you're going back to them."

"I might lose the signal."

"Please don't hang up."

But he had to, and he did.

He didn't bother calling his parents again.

He drove faster. He had to go faster. But something seemed to be containing him, holding him back. Then he knew what it was that was slowing him down, he saw it on his wrist. That old holdover, the vestige of his dead faith.

The prayer rope was half up the sleeve of his coat, half-fluttering in the onrush of air, and he slipped it off, slipped it right off and let it sail out the window where it fluttered once in the withered sunlight and was gone.

47.

Christmas Eve broke gray and overcast on the Gulf, and by the time Tess woke it was ten. The room was warm and behind the blinds was no more than the merest notion of light. Someone—her mom, she guessed—had taken Laurie from the crib.

She stretched her body beneath the sheets.

She had slept eleven hours and somewhere in the night seemed to have shaken loose from everything that had weighed not only last night but the last several months.

John and the USB drive.

The man in the basement.

John's man in the basement.

It occurred to her that what she had classified as some free-floating metaphysical dread might have been no more than exhaustion, sleep deprivation instead of existential angst.

She was in the bathroom when she remembered the whales, the blue whales her dad had mentioned, the blue whales that had caused all of them to clatter out to the beach. She would take Wally and Daniel on a long walk up the sand. It had rained during the night—she had some vague recollection of rain against the windows—and the beach would be littered with kelp and dead jellyfish. They might even see the whales. It might even be possible to take her father's boat out into the harbor. It might even be possible to spot them.

Then it occurred to her that of course it was possible.

Anything was possible in this new world she inhabited.

The boys were in front of the TV with her father and David and his three girls when she came down. Some teen movie entirely age-inappropriate.

"Sleepyhead," her dad called.

"Mom!" from first Wally and then Daniel.

They hugged her but somehow managed to keep their eyes on the screen.

"Who wants to go to the beach?" Tess called out.

"I do," Wally said. "We both do. But we want to watch this first."

"What is this?"

"*Diary of a Wimpy Kid*," Wally said. "Come watch it with us."

Tess switched her eyes between her father and her brother.

"Is this?"

"It's fine," David said.

"It doesn't seem fine."

"Doesn't matter now," her brother said. "There's like twenty minutes left."

She turned to her father.

"Where's Laurie?"

"Your mother has her out on the deck. Sit down with us, honey."

"Twenty minutes?"

"At most," David said.

"I'll be back."

She took her coffee onto the back deck where her mom, sister, and her sister-in-law sat looking at their phones and playing with Laurie.

"There's Mommy," her mother said, working Laurie's plump arms, "there's my mommy."

"She okay?"

"Happy as can be. I fed her out here with the pelicans."

"What time did she get up?"

"I don't know," her mom said. "What time, girls? Maybe eight? I didn't know if you were still nursing her or not so—"

"Not really. A little now and then, but—"

But she felt that warm tightness now and took her daughter and nuzzled her, pulled up the corner of her T-shirt and her jog-bra while everyone stared at their phones.

"Wally's dying to go down to the water," her mother said.

"I tried to get him to go."

"David tried to take him, but he said he was waiting on you."

"I tried just now but he's watching something."

"He said the two of you are the whale experts. That no one else quite understands them like you two."

"He's sweet."

"He's an angel. They all are. I want her back please when you're finished."

When she was finished Laurie was asleep and Tess passed her back to her mother. She went inside to refill her coffee and saw they were on to something else.

"What is this now?" she asked.

"Sit down," her dad said.

"I thought we were going to the beach? Wally?"

But he was ignoring her, or not ignoring her so much as completely oblivious to her presence.

She was in the kitchen when she heard her phone going off upstairs in the bedroom. She trotted up and saw she had three missed calls, all from John. She was about to dial him when it rang again.

"Hey," she said.

"I need Kayla's number."

"What?"

"I need Kayla's number right now, Tess. I know you have it."

"Merry Christmas to you, too," she said a little sadly, because although she still existed in the happy bubble of the morning, she knew in another second she would leave it, possibly forever.

"Tess."

"I don't have it."

"Don't lie to me."

"How would I know her number? Why do you need her number?"

"This is a goddamn emergency, all right? So—"

"I don't like you talking to me like this."

"I'm sorry," he said, "but listen, just give me her number."

"I'm telling you, I don't have it."

"Don't lie to me. I have to find her."

"Where are you? And did you give Wally your phone without so much as a word to me?"

"Tess, goddamn it."

"I'm hanging up now."

"I have to find her."

"I'm sure she's at your parents." Then she held the phone away from her ear so that she could scream properly into it. "Where are you?"

She hung up. It rang immediately but she cut it off.

And then everything rushed back in only it was closer now, so close she felt it cutting off her air. The days alone with the children while her husband was off doing whatever it was he did, and Tess, Tess never asking, Tess the good wife, the quiet acquiescent one whose husband was gone every weekend.

She thought of Pat Glenn in the grocery store.

She thought of the dark soles on the feet of the kneeling man in the photographs and she thought of the face of Jimmy Stone.

She thought of those weeks on St. Simons Island and how a part of her knew her survival was a one-time thing. She couldn't do it again, *wouldn't* do it again, but she sensed it, smelled it on the changing wind of the gray day.

She walked to the landing in the turn of the stairs and called to her brother.

"Hey, did you seriously get me a pair of Hoka Ones?"

"Seriously," he said without looking up from the screens.

"Could I have them?"

"They're yours."

"I mean now."

"Have at," he said, and made a broad gesture toward the tree. "They're wrapped."

She took the box to her bedroom, tore it open, cut the tags with nail clippers, and put the cushy shoes on her feet. All of it rushed, her fingers nearly useless but somehow working because she had to hurry. She couldn't breathe. She needed out.

Immediately.

She was coming down the stairs when Wally came running up toward her. He was still in his pajamas, his hair flattened with sleep.

"I'm ready, Mom."

"What?"

"To go to the beach."

"Now?"

"You said you would."

"Honey, I'm going running now. I waited for you."

"But you said."

"I waited for you, remember?"

"But I wanted to see the rest of the movie."

"And then another."

"It wasn't another movie. It was just a cartoon. Please, Mom."

"Give me one hour, all right?"

"Mom."

His voice broke and she could see he was on the verge of tears, but couldn't he see she was on the verge of suffocation? Couldn't he see she needed out, if only for a few minutes?

"Let your Uncle David take you."

"But it's supposed to be us."

"One hour, Wally. Be reasonable."

"Please, Mom."

She should have given in then, she knew she should have. But instead of giving in she squeezed past him, kissing the top of his head as she went.

"One hour."

"Fine," he yelled.

"One hour, honey."

"Fine."

She trotted down the boardwalk to the gray beach, the sky low-slung and hammered into a ceiling of clouds. There were people everywhere, walkers, families, people out shelling, but she hardly noticed them. Just started her watch and began to jog, steadily picking up the pace until she could breathe again, until her heart rate was no longer rising but settling.

Reasonable, she told herself. Be reasonable.

48.

John pulled into his parents' yard, his phone in one pocket, Stone's pistol in the other. It was snowing now, not much yet, but gathering, starting to stick on the banks and in the boughs of trees. Kayla's car—what John thought must be Kayla's car with its parking decal and IRON GIRL sticker on the back glass—sat in the yard. A line of smoke went up from the chimney.

He found his parents in the kitchen, cleaning up. His mother at the sink plunging dishes in the suds. His father clearing the table. A clear Tupperware container held what was left of a salad and he knew that was Kayla's.

"Where is she?" he said.

They both startled and then smiled. John! Merry Christmas! We didn't think you were coming. We didn't know if—

But John just repeating it: Where is she? Where is she?

Tearing through the house calling Kayla? Kayla?

He came back into the kitchen where his parents stood, their happiness giving way to confusion, their smiles just beginning to wilt. Their world of family reunions and Bible study, of vegetable gardens and green stamps, of things made right because things were *done* right—all of it just beginning to unwind in the face of their son's manic anger.

"Is he with her?"

"Who," his mother said, "Reed? John, we just love him."

"Where did they go?"

"Your father and I were just saying how much—"

"Where are they?"

"What's wrong, son?" It was his father now, stepping forward, sleeves rolled and forearms flecked with soap bubbles.

"I'm sorry. I don't want to scare either of you. I just need to know where they are."

His mother's lip gave the first tremor of fear.

"What's wrong? We like him so much. We were just saying—"

He had his phone out but there was no image, only a black square onto which he might project some future life he would prefer not to live.

"I have to know where they are."

"They went out walking," his father said.

"Where?"

"Just out. On the trails I guess. What's going on?"

"Is Kayla okay?" his mother said.

"If she comes back without me keep her here."

"John."

"Call the police, Dad."

"It's Christmas Eve. I can't get the law out here for no reason."

"Just call them."

It was at that moment he took out the pistol Stone had given him. In part it was to check it, but it wasn't that, not really. He wanted it to register on his parents' faces, he wanted them to see what their boy had become, what their boy had always been.

"John," his father said. "Stop for a minute. Look at me, son."

"Just call them."

"And tell 'em what?"

"Tell them your boy just shot a man."

49.

Tess ran as far as the pier, cut onto the road and followed Periwinkle for the length of its seven blocks. When she came to the end of it she zigzagged her way along the bike paths and back through the grid of streets, the houses tucked behind palm trees trunked with lights, plastic reindeer beside plastic mangers. A few driveways were crowded with cars because it was almost lunch now, people would be gathering.

She looped again and headed back toward the beach.

She liked the shoes. Fifty minutes and there was no rubbing, no slippage. The cushion was better than she thought.

At the pier she cut back down onto the sand and it was the same as before: a few couples hand in hand, metal detectors, surfcasters. All beneath a hem of gray clouds, the sun having made some agreement with itself: it would not shine.

She ran the sand, parallel to the ocean off to her left.

Sixty minutes. Sixty-one.

She wasn't far from her parents' house now and was glad for it. She felt calmer, and if her mind didn't hold the same clear light it held when she first woke it was at least empty of darkness.

She could see the boardwalk over the dunes and slowed to a jog and then a walk, stopped her watch at 1:03:24. She would run the half in March and thought she could win it. Laurie would be a year old and that would be something, some sort of milestone, maybe, like stepping into an early spring.

She took her socks and shoes off on the sandy stairs and let her vision drift out past the breakers to the flat silver of the Gulf.

She would take John with her to see Kayla compete in her fitness contest. She was mad at John, but not really. There was no anger in her, no real heat. They had maybe hit bottom and what was left was to climb out. They could do it. There was no reason they couldn't do it.

She watched the pelicans hitting the water and thought again of St. Simons. Except this time she was thinking not of their winter there, but of their honeymoon, that better time, that time that had come to seem less real but she knew wasn't. It was a good sign, maybe. This shift in her thinking.

The pelicans hit the water.

A swallow-tail was in the air.

Down in the surf a boy stood staring out to sea, out, maybe, toward the blue whales, navigating, finding their way. She would go in and apologize to Wally. Take the boys and spend the day walking the beach.

The boy was knee-deep in the water, intent.

She would take her father's boat.

That first trip just before Laurie was born, seeing the pod, it had been like a blessing and there was no reason to doubt it wouldn't be again.

The boy was out to his thighs and she thought of saying something then she saw a woman walking toward him, his mother, calling to him, and Tess turned up the boardwalk toward the house.

Everyone was inside, gathered as before around the television.

Her mother feeding Laurie in her highchair.

Her father in his recliner.

She wiped the sand from her feet and fixed a glass of water, took a banana and sat down on the floor to stretch. They were watching something they probably shouldn't be watching, but she wasn't going to say anything. It was fine, there were worse things.

Then she noticed Wally wasn't there.

"Where's Wally?" she asked the room, and no one answered.

"Mom, where's Wally at?"

"What?"

"Is Wally in there with you?"

"I don't know where he is, honey."

Neither did her father.

"He showed us the video he made, the whales. He's amazing, Tess."

She plucked Daniel off the couch.

"Honey, where's your brother? Where's Wally?"

"He went looking for you."

"Where, baby?"

"Looking for whales."

"Whales?" And it took her a moment and then she saw again the boy in the surf, his steady motion as he shuffled out to sea, and a light burst inside her and she was running, panicked, yelling to her mom to call John, to call him right now.

50.

John found their tracks along the shoulder of the road. The snow was coming harder now, but they were still visible, and he started jogging back toward the highway, hands in his pockets, phone and gun bouncing until he gripped each. A half mile down the gravel stood the marker for the trailhead where a laminated map was pinned beneath the shingled overhang.

They had stopped here. He could tell from the tracks.

He took out the gun and the phone and was trying to make sense of their direction when an image flashed onto the screen. Her red coat against a backdrop of white: she was somewhere up ahead of him in the woods.

He started up the trail and within a few steps couldn't hear a thing, not even his panting. Only the muffled silence, the whisper and tick of snowflakes that appeared incapable of settling. But they were settling: thirty or so meters up the trail there was no trace of anyone having passed. Just falling snow and swirling particulates of ice, his eyelashes and hair full of them. But no sign of Kayla's passage. The image was gone too. All that was left was the snow that heaved down through the sun-starved understory. The mountain laurel beginning to fold beneath the weight, the limbs of pine and fir betraying the first sign of slant.

"Kayla?" he called into the forest, and felt his voice go out from him, but out into nothing, out into the hush of the day. He started jogging up the left trail, the snow deepening. Called her name a second and then a third time and then thought better of it. Switched his way up to the ridge but all he could see here was the glare of sunlight, a bright luster that nearly blinded him, and for a moment he stood not in the National Forest but back at the small cemetery in Peach Creek, Kayla's plot in the back corner beneath the crows and mourning doves, and what he saw was not snow falling on the trees but dirt falling on an open grave, its length no longer abbreviated because she wasn't nine anymore.

"Please," he said out loud, and found his right hand going not to the gun but to the prayer rope around his wrist. But the prayer rope was gone. He had somehow lost it. Then he remembered that he hadn't lost it: he had thrown it away.

"Please," he said again, and felt his eyes blur with tears so that he almost missed the movement down in the far valley.

But it was there: the flash of a red coat, Kayla there and then not.

He started running, not down the trail but down the slope.

They were somewhere ahead of him. He couldn't see them, but he knew they were there.

He stumbled back into the tree line and there in front of him was the trail, there in front of him were boot prints, two pair pressed and scrubbing their way through the snowfall.

Then he was running again.

Ahead was a small rise and as he topped it he entered a clearing. A stream ribboned darkly along the edge and by it stood what was left of the old home place, the tarpaper roof just beginning to disappear beneath the snow. Through the open door he saw her red coat, still now, someone beside her. Then he looked at his phone and on the tiny screen he saw in great detail that she was kissing someone, she was kissing the boy from the lake house. He looked at the home place and then at the screen and neither felt more real than the other.

"Kayla?" he called. "Kayla?"

"Dad?"

He stumbled forward, no more than thirty feet away, and now his daughter came toward him, emerging from the house with her coat unzipped, shirt half-tucked. Her face was flushed and he stood there panting, his heart grinding.

"Dad," she said again, as if not quite believing in him.

Then movement. In the air he saw the boy behind her within the window. On the screen he saw the gun the boy held. He saw it rising.

"Dad?" When she smiled he saw the glimmer of her scar and then her smile was gone. "Are you all right?"

He didn't answer. He was looking down at the pixelated boy and the pixelated gun he held.

"Dad, are you okay?"

Her eyes had locked on what he held in his hand, which was the gun, except it wasn't—somehow he had put the gun away and all he held was his phone.

It was the boy who held the gun, the boy who brought the barrel up in a slow graceful arc, pointing. But not at John or his daughter. Framed on the screen John saw where it was going and then Kayla turned and opened her mouth to say his name—*Reed!*—but the report swallowed the sound. It swallowed everything. The birds flew—somehow he knew they flew. Even if all he heard was the blast of the gun. Even if all he saw was the bright flash contained within the window, the bright flash contained within the screen, and then the great slump of the body, collapsing as if in exhaustion, as if it knew no other way to be.

Then the screen was gone and the boy was dead and he realized his phone was ringing.

He realized it had been ringing the entire time.

51.

Tess sprinted down the boardwalk and the first thing she saw were the people on the beach, a knot of them, waving and calling. An elderly man in orange trunks was jogging into the water, hands cupped to his mouth as he yelled into the breeze, because out beyond him was her son, out beyond him was Wally.

She ran past the man into the waves, the water to her knees and then her thighs and then she was swimming. Behind her came the siren of the beach patrol, the flash of blue lights out over the gray gulf drawn like the skin of a drum, but she kept going because she knew it was Wally.

She knew it was Wally because the woman running beside her said it was.

The woman running beside her told her to go, to hurry.

Don't be afraid, Tess.

Only listen.

And she was. Tess was screaming his name, screaming and swimming, but she was listening too. Her son was clicking. The first wave went over his head and then the second, but the entire time—the third wave now, and then there was no fourth because she could no longer see him—the entire time, even as he disappeared beneath the surface, she could hear him.

The creaks, the slow clicks, the codas.

It had been her complaint from the very start, hadn't it, the noise?

But not this, not her son.

And she kept swimming and praying and calling his name because somehow he had gotten out ahead of her. But she wasn't afraid. She knew she would find him. The woman swimming beside her had taken hold of Tess's hand and was leading her to her son, leading her toward the clicking. And then they turned and the tide was with them. The woman swimming beside Tess had taken hold of her wrist and the wrist of her son, and was pulling them back toward shore. The tide was with them and the woman was pulling them.

Karla was pulling them and would not let them go.

52.

The phone was still ringing and Kayla was running toward the cabin and John's heart kept hammering not just in his chest but in his ears and eyes and out to the farther reaches of his body because he understood, he understood, *I forgive everyone for everything.* For Site Nine, for Hassan Natashe, for the senseless squandering of life. *I forgive everyone for everything.* It beat in him like the tiny muscled heart of one of Karla's fragile birds, like the giant-valved heart of one of Tess's lost whales. *I forgive everyone for everything.* He could barely breathe with it, it beat so strong and so right and he wanted to sit down, almost stumbled, but somehow remained standing, and he was looking at the screen and what he saw was not the dead boy but the white snow and the white sky and the scratch of darker trees that ran between. It was on the screen and all around him yet he was unable to tell where one ended and the other began and perhaps that was the point, he thought, that there was no line, no distinction, there was simply one, simply this.

So while his daughter was chanting the boy's name

Reed

Reed

Oh God, Reed

and the phone was ringing, John shut his eyes and squeezed them tight because it was a prayer he felt forming, and if it wasn't the right prayer, he knew too it was the only prayer he was capable of praying. And he did, he prayed it, he prayed *I forgive everyone for everything.*

Now forgive me.

Forgive me.

Acknowledgments

My love and gratitude to so many good people: Darnell Arnoult, Casey Clabough, Beverly Coyle, Michael Denner (and Sasha!), Pete Duval, Julia Elliott, Patricia Engel, the Goodworth family, Adam Griffey, Jonathan Haupt, David Joy, Adam Latham, Erik Reece, Ron Rash, Janisse Ray, James Scott, Jon Sealy, Bob Shacochis, Zuzka Tabackova, John Warley, the Weiss family, Charles and April White, Randall Wilhelm, and Terri Witek. Love and thanks to everyone at the Stetson Low-Residency MFA Program; all my colleagues at Appalachian State University; the U.S. and Slovak Fulbright Commission; the faculty at the University of Constantine the Philosopher in Nitra, Slovakia; and all my family, especially Denise, Silas, Mamma and Daddy, Dennis and Jane, Joy and Bryan, James and Stacie, Brooke, and Cliff.

I am fortunate to have a brilliant editor in Ben LeRoy, and an incomparable agent in Julia Kenny.

This book is dedicated to my daughter Merritt and her fierce spirit, and in memory of Pat Conroy, a writer whose honesty and talent was matched only by his kindness and generosity.